THE RIVAL QUEENS

ALSO BY FIDELIS MORGAN

Unnatural Fire

The Rival Queens

A Novel of Artifice, Gunpowder and
Murder in Eighteenth-Century London

FIDELIS MORGAN

WILLIAM MORROW
An Imprint of HarperCollins*Publishers*

First published in Great Britain in 2001 by Collins Crime, an imprint of HarperCollins Publishers, 77–85 Fulham Palace Road, Hammersmith, London, W6 8JB.

HarperCollins books may be purchased for educational, business, or sales promotional use. For information please write: Special Markets Department, HarperCollins Publishers Inc., 10 East 53rd Street, New York, NY 10022.

FIRST U.S. EDITION

Printed on acid-free paper

Library of Congress Cataloging-in-Publication Data has been applied for.

ISBN 0-688-17684-4

02 03 04 05 06 QW 10 9 8 7 6 5 4 3 2 1

Contents

Acknowledgements

Thanks to
Julia Wisdom and her magnificent team,
Clare Alexander and hers
And Doctor Wolfgang Wallat for advice on the symptoms of
tertiary syphilis and the 'sailors handsel'.

The Passions

To endeavour, is appetite.
To be remiss, is sensuality.
To consider them behind, is glory.
To consider them before, is humility.
To lose ground with looking back, vain glory.
To be holden, hatred.
To turn back, repentance.
To be in breath, hope.
To be weary, despair.
To endeavour to overtake the next, emulation.
To supplant or to overthrow, envy.
To resolve to break through a stop foreseen, courage.
To break through a sudden stop, anger.
To break through with ease, magnanimity.
To lose ground by little hindrances, pusillanimity.
To fall on the sudden, is diposition to weep.
To see another fall, is disposition to laugh.
To see one out-gone whom we would not is pity.
To see one out-go whom we would not is indignation.
To hold fast by another is love.
To carry him on that so holdeth is charity.
To hurt one's self for haste is shame.
Continually to be out-gone is misery.
Continually to out-go the next before is felicity.
And to forsake the course is to die.

Thomas Hobbes, *Human Nature.*

ONE

Terror

Fear without the apprehension of why.
Aroused by objects of aversion.

Eyebrow raised in the middle, nose and nostrils drawn up.
Everything strongly marked.
The face pale, eyes and mouth wide open,
the hair standing on end.

'If you don't reduce your pace, I shall have an attack of the spleen, madam,' shrieked the Countess at her maid, Alpiew, who was running a good twenty yards ahead.

'But the girl's heading for the Tower,' Alpiew called back to her panting mistress. 'If I slow down, we'll lose her.' Alpiew hitched up her skirts and prepared to speed up. 'You wait inside the gate, I'll give chase.'

Taking a great puff as Alpiew raced ahead, Anastasia, Lady Ashby de la Zouche, Countess of Clapham, Baroness Penge, reduced her stride to a very gentle trot. How had it come to this? At her age and station she should be sitting at home being served hot chocolate and biscuits while reading some juicy scandalous broadsheet. Instead she was near penury, forced into working for a living, chasing after scandal all over London to provide the tittle-tattle for *other* ladies to read while lounging in their cosy homes, gulping down buckets of best bohea tea.

With a sigh she trotted across the meadow of Tower Hill. High above her, on top of the slope, loomed the awful spectre of the scaffold and gallows. Luckily today was not an execution day, or she'd not be able to move for the crowds. The day before, however, had been one, so the place was still spattered with litter. The Countess side-stepped a pile of oyster shells crawling with maggots before joining the queue for the Tower of London.

This morning she and Alpiew were after a wayward girl. Miss Phoebe Gymcrack, only daughter of a City alderman, Sir John Gymcrack, fancied to raise herself out of the ranks of the City into the Court. The only trouble was, though she had told all and sundry of her plans to snare a rich lord, she had not bothered to drop his name into the conversation. This had to be wormed out or the story was *no* story at all.

The Countess pondered as she strolled along beside the wooden paling fence. Then she stepped briskly through the stone building known as the Lion Gate. With this story written up and waiting for delivery to Mr and Mrs Cue (printers of the *London Trumpet* and her employers), she and Alpiew could happily take the rest of the week off.

Miss Gymcrack had been dancing at a masquerade till midnight. The Countess knew this because she had also been there, watching to see if the potential lordly stepping stone discovered himself. But the girl had never danced twice with the same fellow, and from her demeanour it was clear that Mr, or rather, Lord Right was not even *at* the function.

When the girl rolled home in the early hours, Alpiew took over for the night-watch outside the alderman's City home. Mayhap the rake would come serenading at her window. But no. Alpiew had spent a fruitless and uncomfortable night curled up in a doorway for nothing.

At first light the Countess was preparing to leave her home in German Street, St James's, to bring Alpiew some food and to take over the watch. She had just popped upstairs to search out an old bag that she had left in one of the derelict upper rooms of her house when there was a thundering at the door. She peered down over the banister to see two bailiffs making their way through to the kitchen. One of them was waving a debt order in his hand.

The Countess had no interest is finding out how much the debt order was for, as she knew she didn't have any cash to spare at the moment. So she darted down the stairs and out into the street. Scurrying across the quiet road, she entered the church of St James's, exiting into Pickadilly, which (luckily) at this time of day was quite a commotion of wagons, as well as flocks of geese and sheep being driven to market. Thence she took a route involving as many bustling streets and markets as she could, making sure she blended into the crowd until she had lost the burly bailiffs.

At the very moment the Countess caught sight of Alpiew standing in the shop doorway, the Gymcrack girl appeared at her front door, wrapped in a great cloak and hood, and strode out. She had a furtive look on her face, and it was clear that the object of their interest would shortly be at hand.

Through the City they had given chase. The Gymcrack girl marched proudly along in front, with Alpiew loping behind and the Countess in her wake, rapidly getting left behind.

The Countess had expected her to roll up to some City mansion, but was surprised by this destination. The Tower of London! This turn-up presented only two possibilities: the favoured lord was using the place for an assignation among the crowd, or (and if this were true – what a story!) he was imprisoned within.

She marched on, passing a large wooden hoarding painted with a likeness of a lion, or rather a likeness of a man in a lion costume, which announced, 'Within: lions, a leopard, eagles, owls, a two-legged dog, a cat-a-mountain, and a hyena with the voice of a man.'

A Yeoman Warder stood just inside the gate, taking entrance fees. The Countess plunged her hand deep into her pocket, hoping she had the required pennies somewhere about her person. She paid and, looking over her shoulder to check that no bailiff was behind her, entered the Tower.

Shoving her way through the peering folk enjoying their morning excursion, the Countess stood on tiptoe, trying to locate Alpiew. She must already be across the moat. Gritting her teeth, the Countess trotted over the bridge. She crossed her fingers – Please let Miss Gymcrack come up trumps and provide them with a juicy story. She took a deep breath and instantly regretted it. In the April sunshine the moat-water lapped pleasingly against the grey stone of the outer wall, but it exuded a rank and stagnant stink.

At the Byward Tower a parcel of Warders stood chatting under a huge iron portcullis. The Countess suppressed a smile. For all their pomposity, in those silly blood red-costumes with ribbons and braids and fancy velvet hats they resembled nothing more than a group of Morris dancers up from the country for the May Fair.

'Whither goest thou?' A Gentleman Yeoman barred her way with a long halberd. The blade sparkled ominously in the sunlight.

'I would have thought that was rather obvious . . .' The Countess peered over his shoulder, still seeking a glimpse of Alpiew. For her smile he returned a dark scowl. Oh lord! Perhaps he would arrest her and drag her back to the bailiffs. She contemplated turning and running back the way she had come. Surely debt collectors didn't employ Yeomen of the Tower. Or did they?

'Madam,' huffed the man, looking her up and down, 'are you carrying any weapons – swords, daggers, muskets, etcetera, etcetera?'

'Do I look as though I am?' panted the Countess, still wondering whether this guard in pantomime costume was about to arrest her.

'Then you won't mind me checking.' The Yeoman started to frisk her, running his hands up and down her rotund form. The Countess formed the distinct impression that he did this rather more often to women than to men.

'Pshaw, sirrah! Could you hurry along. I have lost my maid. She has run on ahead.'

'Mmm,' sighed the Yeoman with a contented smile. 'Pert, pretty thing, golden hair?'

The Countess shook her head, then realised the man was talking about their quarry, Miss Gymcrack. 'Yes, that's her. Which way did she go?'

'As you can see, madam, at this point in the Tower there are only two ways to go: forward and backward. And as she did not pass you on your way in, we must presume she went forward.' His hands poked about in the folds of her skirts.

The Countess leapt back. 'Unhand me, sirrah! You are inches away from committing a rape upon my person.'

The Yeoman grunted. 'If you weren't wearing such volumni-ous skirts . . .'

'Is there a woman in the land who doesn't?' She adjusted her wig, which had slid back slightly, lending her an Eliza-bethan stretch of forehead. 'And the word you are searching for is voluminous.'

A dapper-looking man nearby in the queue was looking on, smiling.

'And at what' – the Countess frowned in his direction – 'are you smirking, sirrah?'

'If I am not mistaken . . .' The man stepped forward. 'You are Anastasia, Lady Ashby de la Zouche . . .'

'Baroness Penge, Countess of Clapham . . .' She automati-cally uttered the words, then her mouth ground to a halt. She'd been tricked. This grinning man was clearly a bailiff in disguise. He was everything one wouldn't expect in a bailiff – he was short, well shaved, clean, and elegantly dressed to the point of being foppish. And look how young he was! But that was what they always said – the forces of law were getting younger by the year. This fellow had the scrubbed pink look of a child.

The Yeoman gave her a shove. 'Pass!' he yelled, delighted to finish as a particularly attractive lady was stepping through the gate behind her. 'Yeoman Partridge!' he called to another beribboned redcoat. 'You can accompany this lady and gentleman.'

'It's all right,' simpered the Countess, nimbly stepping away from the gentleman in question. 'I do not need a guide. I am here upon business.'

But the Yeoman guide was already steering her further into the Tower.

'Step this way please-uh!' Yeoman Partridge had a pompous method of pronunciation that added a superfluous 'uh' to the end of every phrase. 'Members of the public-uh may not gratify their desires within-uh, without you must take a Gentleman Warder-uh.'

Whatever that meant. The Countess raised her eyebrows in the direction of the dapper gentleman. He raised his eyebrows back at her. If it was going to happen, if he was about to arrest her, she wished he would get it over with. The suspense was bringing on a sweat. Was he about to pounce with his wretched debt order, and have her thrown into the Fleet Prison? Or was he just another member of the paying public on an outing?

'This 'ere, upon our right-uh, is the infamous Traitors' Gate-uh.' The Yeoman pointed to a walled area of water with great iron wicket gates. 'Royal prisoners entered through these-uh said same gates. Most-uh never to see the outside world again-uh.' The Countess gulped as the waters roared through the gates like a cataract at full flood. She gave an involuntary shudder and, her eye sneaking a sideways glance at the dapper fellow beside her, followed the Warder up the hill to Tower Green.

Without any warning the young man took hold of the Countess's elbow. She jumped back, ready to make a run for it.

'You are a writer, milady, as I remember?' he said, hovering.

'I may be . . .' The Countess smiled wanly. 'Who says so?'

'May I introduce myself?' The man thrust his hand forward. 'Colley Cibber, esquire. Actor, writer and bon viveur.'

'Of course, of course . . .' The Countess smiled graciously with relief. She'd never heard of him, but at least he was not about to arrest her. 'I'm sorry if I appear distracted, sir, but I am on an assignment.'

'Me too!' Colley Cibber whispered in her ear. 'Who are you doing?'

The Countess inched away. She wasn't sharing her story with anyone.

'Anne Boleyn, perhaps?' Mr Cibber pulled a frivolous face. 'Or Sir Walter Raleigh?'

What was the man drivelling on about? They were both dead. How could you write a scandal story about someone who'd been a century dead?

'I understand.' Cibber tapped the side of his nose. 'Early days, early days. But I am quite willing to share with you the secret of *my* latest work.'

They had reached the top of the steep incline and the Yeoman Warder stopped and continued his well-rehearsed recitation. 'And before us-uh stands the impressive keep-uh, distinguished by the historical name of Julius Caesar's Tower-uh.'

'It must be very dark within,' said Cibber, peering up at the great white keep. 'For look, there's nary a window in the place. It is where they keep the gunpowder and weapons, I believe.'

'The Tower of London is one of the remaining Liberties-uh. Within its bounds any citizen is protected from arrest-uh.' He gave a little laugh. 'Which is paltry relief for those poor creatures the prisoners, whom we are employed to hold in captivity-uh.'

'I need to sit,' the Countess announced to the Yeoman, flooded with relief that the dapper man was only an actor, and that, anyhow, within these walls she was safe from arrest. She also had a distant hope of shaking the Warder off, along with this tiresome actor-writer. She flopped down on a great brass cannon and fanned herself. At last Alpiew was in view. She too had taken leave of her Warder by sitting and fanning. The Countess glanced over at Alpiew, who shrugged in return. The scheming minx, Miss Phoebe, was clearly cornered. Now as at last night's ball, all they could do was wait.

Cibber pointed to the building beside the hill they had just climbed. 'That's the place of interest to me.' He leaned down and whispered intimately: 'The Bloody Tower. Though it seems to me inconsistent to give the "Bloody" name to a Tower where two children were *smothered*.'

The Countess smiled vaguely. What was the man talking about?

'My project,' he said, as though he could read her thoughts. 'Richard and the princes!' hissed Colley Cibber. 'How about that? I'm going to write a play about Crookback Richard. There's a part to tear a cat in, eh?'

'Already been done,' said the Countess. 'By that Elizabethan hack, Shakespeare.'

'Ay, madam,' said Cibber with a smug smirk. 'But I hope to inject theatre with a new responsible morality.'

The Countess repressed a yawn. She could see that Alpiew had engaged her young Warder in conversation.

'Yeoman Partridge?' She rose. 'I have espied my maid, Alpiew. I shall no longer require your guided tour.'

'You may not be left to your own devices in this place, madam-uh. For although it is a place of recreation, I must remind you it also serves as His Majesty's prison-uh. And for all I know you are part of a plot-uh to secure the liberty of one of our ignoble inmates.'

'There is no problem in that, sir.' The Countess rose and waddled off. 'For I shall join the Warder yonder, who is speaking with my Alpiew, and leave you free to inform Mr Kipper of all he wishes to know about the Bloody Tower.'

'Cibber,' muttered the actor under his breath. 'But, milady, let me follow. I should prefer to assist you.'

Yeoman Partridge waved across to the Warder with Alpiew and signalled that he was relinquishing his two visitors, then set off down the hill to pick up his next tour.

'I met him, you know,' said Cibber, walking along in the Countess's wake.

'William Shakespeare?' snapped the Countess, giving him the up and down. 'You must be a lot older than you look.'

'No, no,' said Cibber with a gay laugh. 'The King.'

Clearly the man was demented. Richard III had been dead for centuries.

'I was only a child, but he cut quite a figure. He was in Saint James's Park, with his dogs, feeding the ducks.'

The Countess smiled wanly at the grinning fellow. His condition must be serious. She was in two minds whether to call for assistance.

'*You* were with him, actually.'

The Countess stopped in her tracks and turned on the young actor. 'I may look like a superannuated harridan, but I assure you my great, great, great grandfather had not been born in the time of Crookback Richard.'

'Oh, yes.' The actor rocked with laughter. 'They all said you were amusing. Now I see it for myself.'

The Countess gripped her fan, ready to give the young man a swipe.

'I spoke of *your* King, madam.' He held his hands up before him. 'Old Rowley.'

'Charles!' Instantly the Countess softened, her face took on a winsome expression and her body rearranged itself into a coy posture. 'The darling man. Everyone misses him so.'

'Indeed and indeed,' said Cibber with some enthusiasm. 'He had the peculiar possession of so many hearts. The common people adored him.'

'Those were the days, Mr Kipper . . .' The Countess took the young man's arm and strolled along in step with him. 'So you are an actor, you say, *and* a writer . . .'

It was with some difficulty that Alpiew had cornered her prey. Miss Gymcrack held a special pass that entitled her to be escorted immediately to her beau. The frisking Yeoman had taken particular delight in searching Alpiew, for she was exceptionally well endowed in the bodice area. He even had the nerve to ask whether he might search her cleavage in case she was hiding anything down there. It was all Alpiew could manage to prevent herself from giving the man a wherret in the chops. Instead she took a deep breath and peered ahead to see the Gymcrack girl trip past Traitors' Gate and turn into the main part of the Tower.

Once allocated, along with a party of enthusiastic foreigners, to her own Yeoman, Alpiew kept straying from the pack in order to peep through the gate and watch the pert miss skipping up the hill and turning to her right at the White Tower.

While the tiresome foreigners in her party were plying the Yeoman with their faltering questions about Queen Elizabeth entering the Tower as a prisoner, Alpiew marched on up the hill before them. Yeoman Jones, unable to decipher much of what was being asked, decided to take the tourists with him in pursuit of Alpiew. The party of exotically dressed Indian Musselmen, their silks, satins and feather headdresses rippling, raced up the hill after him.

Alpiew reached the Julius Caesar Tower just in time to see Miss Gymcrack disappear into a low door on the other side of the green to her left. 'What is that place?' Alpiew pointed after the girl.

'Beauchamp Tower' – Yeoman Jones was bent double, wheezing – 'prison quarters to errant members of the nobility. Lord Guildford Dudley, husband to Lady Jane Grey, was imprison–'

'Enough history,' snapped Alpiew, just as the bewildered foreigners trailed to the top of the hill. She marched off again, beckoning them all to follow. 'Who is locked up in there now?'

'Oh, only a young lord who has lived his whole life as a ne'er-do-well. Leader of the Tityre-tus gang, I believe . . .'

'The Tityre-tus!' Alpiew knew all about them. A gang of hell-raising rich boys who had great drunken sport each night in and around the taverns of the Covent Garden Piazza. Their delight was to upset chairs carrying elderly ladies, wrench knockers off doors, shout obscenities at pretty women and topple the boxes of the night-watchmen, preferably with the ancient Charlie asleep inside. It couldn't make a better story. 'Who is he? The name?'

'Rakewell,' muttered Yeoman Jones. 'Lord Giles Rakewell.'

'Where eez 'ed of Amber Lane?' One of the foreigners was pulling at the Yeoman's be-ribboned sleeve.

'Amber Lane?' The Yeoman scratched his head. 'Never heard of him.'

'No, Amber Lane is woman.' The visitors shrugged at each other in their very foreign way.

'Anne Boleyn!' The Countess was tottering towards the group. 'They are looking for the head of Anne Boleyn.' She pointed down the hill towards Yeoman Partridge and spoke clearly with dumbshow. 'He will show you head of Amber Lane . . .'

'Tourists!' She nodded politely to Yeoman Jones as the foreigners shuffled off, talking excitedly among themselves. 'Only ever after one thing – blood!' She rubbed her chubby hands together. 'So, Alpiew, the Yeoman seemed to be telling a very interesting tale before he was so rudely interrupted by our friends from the Indies.'

'He is guarding Lord Rakewell – leader of the Tityre-tus.'

'*Tityre tu patulae recubans sub tegmine fagi,*' said the Countess with a knowing nod. 'Virgil, first Eclogue. "Tityre-tus loved to lurk in the dark night looking for mischief."'

'Oh, bravo!' Cibber gave a little clap.

The Countess was so excited by their potential story she had almost forgotten the eager young fellow at her side.

'Oh yes, Alpiew, Yeoman Jones, allow me to introduce Mr . . . Haddock? Cod . . . ? What the deuce was your name again?'

'Cibber.' The actor made a slight bow towards Alpiew. 'I have been at the end of the jibes of the Tityre-tus,' said Cibber with a grimace. 'They climbed on to the stage once while I was mid-soliloquy, and tried to remove my breeches. It was very embarrassing.'

'Dissolute scapegraces, each and every one,' the Countess tutted. 'But their leader . . .' Her eyes scanned the bleak wall of the Beauchamp Tower. 'She has visited him often, the young Miss Gymcrack?'

'Two or three times only.' Jones followed her gaze. 'Brings him sweetmeats and suchlike. She is very pretty.'

'All you need is a title,' shrugged Alpiew, 'and the world's your oyster.'

'You don't have to tell me!' The Warder nodded. 'He lives a merry life in there. Gets all the best food sent up from his kitchens, has all sorts of luxury furniture. It's a better life than mine, and I didn't commit a murder.'

'Murder!' exclaimed the Countess, in a voice tinged with outrage.

'Oh yes,' said the Warder. 'Cut down a gentleman in an ambush back in January.'

'Disgusting, I call it.' Alpiew shook her head. 'A known criminal consorting with the daughter of a City alderman. What is the world coming to?'

'A murderer!' The Countess picked up the thread, still peering up at the gloomy grey walls of the Beauchamp Tower. 'How long has he got before . . . ?' She did a small mime of a noose being tightened round her neck.

'If it follows the same pattern as the last times, he'll be back on the streets in a couple of days, a free man, perpetrating his usual midnight brawls and atrocities.' The Yeoman gazed up at an arrow slit on the first floor. 'It's not the first time we've looked after Lord Rakewell here, nor the first time he was done for murder.'

'So . . . ?' said the Countess, following his gaze to the window beyond which she deduced the wild lord was held.

'His trial comes up the day after tomorrow. At Westminster Hall. But for some reason their lordships seem to like the fellow. They've already let him off twice for hacking men down in the street.'

The Countess beamed at Alpiew. This was an unbelievably juicy story for the paper. The eligible daughter of a prominent City alderman throwing herself at a known murderer. Mr and Mrs Cue would be very pleased with them. With a story as good as this, they might even ask for a little bonus to pay off the Countess's debts and get the bailiffs off her back.

'It makes one wish to have been born into that cosy club of port-swilling parasites, does it not?' Cibber looked ruefully at the Countess. 'To be born high gives you the right to comport oneself low.'

The Countess gave a little shudder at the dreadfully structured aphorism and smiled. 'Mr Kipper is a writer too, Alpiew.' The Countess took his hand and patted it. 'He writes for the playhouse. He is even this minute improving upon the work of a barbarous Elizabethan third-rater named Shakespeare, for the . . .' She looked back to Cibber. 'Which playhouse was it?'

'My last work, *Xerxes*' – Cibber shifted from foot to foot – 'was performed at Lincoln's Inn Theatre, but I am currently acting with the company at Drury Lane.'

The Countess gave him a sideways look. *Xerxes*! He'd written that overblown, mind-numbing rant. Perhaps it would be better to give the man a wide berth.

'I was just saying to your mistress how I once saw her walking in St James's with King Charles. How very lovely she was then – and of course she is so still . . .'

The Countess softened at once.

But Alpiew was not impressed. She did not care for the theatre, nor for actors and it come to that. She had worked backstage, and had seen what went on behind the scenes.

'Now, ladies.' Cibber clapped his hands together. 'I can see that you have had a prosperous day . . . So may I ask you to join me this evening. I am organising a lecture-evening. Tickets are as rare as hen's teeth, but I could get you in, gratis.'

'What kind of lecture?' said Alpiew, imagining two hours' purgatory while this little twirp prattled on about himself, as she knew from experience actors so often did.

'The Passions.'

'Oh, sirrah,' said the Countess, gently slapping Cibber's wrists with her fan. 'If I were younger, perhaps . . .'

'No, madam, not those sort of passions.' Alpiew looked to Cibber for confirmation. 'I believe the gentleman means the Passions as depicted in the philosophical writings of Mr Thomas Hobbes. Am I right?'

'I'm not altogether certain . . .' Cibber shifted uneasily. 'The lecture is to be given by Signior Ruggiero Lampone. I am told 'tis something to do with physiognomy and philosophy and painting and acting and so on.'

'Surely, Mr Cibber, the Passions is the system that will replace the Humours?' Alpiew was ready for discussion here and now. 'A codifying of the interior beginnings of voluntary motions.'

'My maid has some slight eccentricities.' The Countess was watching Alpiew with an open mouth. From whence had Alpiew picked up this useless information? 'She enjoys reading the many large works of philosophy littered around my house.'

When she said littered she meant it. For these books lived not on shelves but under table-legs and bedsteads, keeping an equilibrium. Alpiew, however, liked nothing better than to skim through these seemingly impenetrable tomes, leaving the furniture on a tilt.

'If it's philosophy you're after wanting, look no further!' Before them stood the rotund figure of a priest. 'Mr Cibber, your servant. And you two ladies must be playhouse creatures too, I take it?'

The Countess took this as a compliment. Alpiew did not.

'Allow me to introduce myself –' the priest spoke with a slight Irish brogue – 'Reverend Patrick Farquhar. Exile of Erin's emerald shore and the finest dancer of the Biscayan jig this side of the Irish Sea.' The priest held out his hand.

The Countess wasn't sure whether to shake it, kiss his ring, or start a foursome reel. She opted for a handshake. The priest grasped the Countess by the forearm and squeezed the inside of her elbow with his thumb. She felt as though he was performing the preliminaries for a wrestling match, but smiled wanly till he let her go and moved over to Alpiew.

'These two delightful ladies are new-found friends, Reverend Farquhar. The Reverend is chaplain of the Chapel Royal here in the Tower.'

'Yonder, yonder,' said the priest, pointing towards a building with a rugged brick exterior. 'I have in my charge,' he announced, 'the bones of three queens – Jane Grey, Katherine Howard and Anne Boleyn – and two heroes – Devereux, Earl of Essex, and Walter Raleigh. Though in the latter case it is only the bones of the torso. The skull is elsewhere.'

'How so?' The Countess shivered.

'His widow had a slight eccentricity. She kept her husband's head after it was removed from the trunk, and carried it about with her in a red leather bag.'

'The charming chaplain is going to show me into secret crannies of the Tower where even the Yeoman Warders dare not go, ladies.' Cibber rubbed his hands together. 'Would you care to join us?'

The Countess eagerly nodded, while Alpiew tugged at her arm.

'We have work to do, milady, remember? Much as we would love to join you,' Alpiew added.

'But you will come to the lecture?'

The Countess couldn't imagine a worse way to spend an evening. 'Will the chaplain be coming too?'

'Duty, madam. The Ceremony of the Keys.' The priest smiled brightly. 'But Colley will put on a good show, I am certain. I am full of envy.'

'The top players from both houses will be there,' Cibber coaxed. 'And the writers – Congreve, Vanbrugh, even Dryden, if his health permits . . .'

Alpiew wanted the philosophy, the Countess enjoyed encountering the famous. Both now accepted with alacrity.

'Then we must part till this evening, ladies. The talk starts at exactly eight of the clock, at the concert hall in York Buildings.'

The Yeoman was glad to escort them back to the exit. He had his well-rehearsed patter and preferred to stick to the run-of-the-mill stories of blood and guts that normal visitors craved. As the Countess and Alpiew swung ahead of him down the hill and through the gate that passed below the Bloody Tower, Alpiew obliged her mistress with the details of the murderous Lord Rakewell. 'Killed for the first time last year, when he was only fifteen.'

'Fifteen!' The Countess rubbed her chubby hands together. What a story! 'He is a mere boy.'

'Ay, milady, ran a man through outside a tavern in broad daylight. Gave him a wound twelve inches deep.' As they turned at Traitors' Gate, Alpiew glanced over her shoulder and watched Mr Cibber stroll off with the Irish priest. 'I didn't like to say in front of that foppish actor fellow, but my Lord Rakewell's first victim was a player.'

'A player? Was he well known?'

'No, a youngster. Non-liveried apprentice.'

The Countess remained silent till they parted company with the Yeoman at the portcullis.

'Hold, Alpiew.' From their position on the bridge over the moat, the Countess could clearly see the figure of this morning's bailiff standing in the meadow outside the main gate. 'This morning we had a visitor.' She indicated with her head. 'He must have followed me here.'

Alpiew recognised instantly the shape of a bailiff. After all, she too had spent most of her adult life avoiding them.

'On the green, madam! What are we to do?'

'That fellow in there told me we are safe from arrest while we remain inside the gates of this place. So there's nothing else for it,' said the Countess, sniffing at the frowzy air coming from the entrance to the Royal Menagerie. 'Phough, we can spend a happy, if smelly, time visiting the wild beasts . . .' She pointed up at the sign. 'I've always wanted to see a cat-a-mountain.'

'Me too.' Alpiew dug into her pocket for the entrance fee. 'I hear they're awful handsome fellows. And owls, I hear, have eyes as big as the glasses of a convex lamp.'

'I'm sorry, Alpiew.' The Countess took her arm. 'I hope we don't have to stay here very long.'

'I confess, madam, it smells foxy enough,' Alpiew laughed. 'But when we spot a large party exiting, we can leave among 'em. And you will wear my cloak. We will effect as good an escape from the Tower as many a noble prisoner before us.'

*　　*　　*

Later that evening carriages and chairs crammed the narrow north entrance into York Buildings from the Strand. More people were arriving from the south by river, and spilling up the York stairs from the shore.

Alpiew and her mistress stood across from the entrance to the concert hall, near the Watergate. Just as Alpiew had promised, they had escaped from the Tower amid a large party. Only when they were in the shadow of All Hallows Church did the bailiff espy the Countess and give chase. But there were enough alleys and twists and turns down behind Custom House Quay to shake him off.

They had retired to a little nine-penny ordinary full of sailors and spent the best part of their last shilling on a cheap but filling meal of oyster pie and syllabub. Doubly grateful now for Cibber's offer of the lecture – as it would provide somewhere warm to sit where they could delay their home-coming till well after the hours of darkness – they wandered along the riverside, passing the busy quays at Billingsgate, Fishmongers' Hall, and Queen's Hythe before attempting the city roads. Dusk was falling by the time they arrived at York Buildings and took up their position.

'Tell me if you spot anyone famous, Alpiew. My vision is not what it was in my youth.'

Although it was nearly eight o'clock at night the entrance was almost as bright as day, lit by scores of lanterns and links held aloft by servants, link-boys and postilions.

'I am so excited, Alpiew.' The Countess stood on tiptoe to see above the heads of the waiting crowd. 'To be among the beau monde once again!'

Alpiew didn't like to point out that the beau monde was wearing the latest fashion, while the Countess sported the latest fashion of a quarter-century past; or that the beau monde was being carried here, while they had footed it, evading the attentions of a particularly nasty-looking bum-bailiff.

'We must keep our eyes peeled, milady. Who knows, we may find next week's copy here tonight.' Alpiew crossed her fingers, inspired by the sudden idea that if they delivered two stories at once, perhaps Mrs Cue would pay them two weeks in advance and they could discharge the Countess's debt – however much it was. A sudden thought made her shuffle nervously. What if the dandified actor they had met that morning at the Tower didn't show up to honour his pledge of free tickets? What if he turned up with tickets and demanded two guineas apiece? It would be humiliating for her ladyship and infuriating for her. Now that she had had her appetite whetted for the lecture on the Passions she would be disappointed to miss it.

Only a few days ago, while the Countess was taking a nap by the kitchen fire, Alpiew had pulled Hobbes' *Leviathan* from a pile of books propping up the kitchen table. It was a fascinating read. Starting with Good and Evil, Hobbes had worked out a system to define the emotions, all of them from Hope and Despair through to Emulation and Envy. Love, he said, becomes jealousy when there is a fear that the love is not mutual. Appetite with an opinion of attaining is called Hope, while without such an opinion it becomes Despair. Alpiew's curiosity on the subject being so great, she had been particularly pleased when Hobbes pointed out that it was curiosity that distinguished man from beast.

'Duck!' hissed the Countess, turning and all but plunging her face into Alpiew's bosom.

'Where is he, madam?' Alpiew prepared to run. 'Which direction?'

'He?' The Countess shook her head. 'No, it's that ghastly old harridan, Honoria Bustle. I was at school with her, Alpiew. As you know I was given the Christian name Anastasia. Dear Honoria persuaded everyone to call me Nasty Ass. I abominate the woman. Come, Alpiew, let's go the other direction.'

The Countess turned her back on the milling crowd and trotted towards the shadows near the river.

'But the lecture, madam!' Alpiew chased after her. 'The lecture is that way.'

Torn, the Countess peered back at the glittering crowd. 'You are right. So tell me when she is safely inside the hall. I could not bear a confrontation with that grizzled old harpy.'

''Tis all hot! Nice smoking hot!' A man lit by the orange glow of his brazier stood down by the Watergate dishing out gingerbread. 'Hot gingerbread. Ha'penny a piece.'

'Why do you not wait here, milady, while I press ahead and find the Cibber fellow and his tickets?'

The Countess nodded and made much show of buying a halfpenny slab of hot gingerbread to explain why she was not jostling forward with the rest of the crowd.

Alpiew pushed through the throng. From the escutcheons emblazoned on the coach doors, she saw that there were members of the nobility here as well as notables from the theatrical world. She watched people effusively greeting each other. So much shrieking and laughter. How had Hobbes described it? The grimace of Sudden Glory.

Lady Bustle was in sight. With a physiognomy carved with disdain, she limped into the foyer of the concert hall where she was roundly greeted by a large fat man with the appearance of a gentleman farmer.

Alpiew pushed nearer. Milling around outside the doors was a group of poorly dressed people who reached out to touch the skirts or jackets of passing actors. Some of them held out posies and letters. One woman actually threw herself before an actor to plant a kiss upon his cheek. The actor merely smiled and, giving the crowd a little wave, strode inside, where, Alpiew noticed, he wiped his cheek dry with a handkerchief.

Alpiew marvelled at the enthralled faces around her. Some of these people looked as though they could not afford decent shoes, or food, and yet here they were prostrating themselves before these vain, conceited things called players.

With a surge she was jostled forward a few feet.

'I thought you'd let me down,' said a gentle voice behind her. Alpiew turned to meet the eyes of Cibber, who stood holding out the two tickets. 'Your writing partner is with you, I hope?'

'She was seduced by the aroma of the hot gingerbread.' Alpiew took the tickets. 'She will be here shortly.'

'Look!' screamed a nearby phanatique. 'It's Sir Novelty Fashion!'

The clamorous crowd swirled round Cibber. He plunged his hand into a deep pocket and pulled out a handful of sweetmeats, which he handed round to the enthusiastic mob.

One man took his sweetmeat and hurled it back at Cibber, hitting him hard in the face. 'For Anne,' cried the man. 'Merry Anne! My love.'

With a grin pasted across his face, Cibber steered Alpiew away from the rabble and up the steps into York Buildings.

'Who's Anne?'

'She is a fellow player.' Cibber thrust her into the foyer of the Music Room. 'Playing tonight, I hope.'

'And Sir Novelty Fashion?' Alpiew removed her arm from his grip.

'It's a role I played last season. Had quite a success with it. Wrote it myself, actually.'

'And the sweetmeats?' Alpiew was intrigued. It seemed that Mr Cibber had come prepared for the pestering of the playhouse phanatiques.

'It's the public who pays my wages. So I do my best to keep on their good side.' Cibber pushed against the crush of people. 'We must wait inside if we want to escape those desperate creatures.'

Alpiew gave a sly look round and saw the large backside of Lady Bustle push through the door into the concert hall. 'You go in.' She turned and waved from the step in the Countess's direction. 'I must wait for my lady.'

The Countess waddled along the street, ploughing through the crowd. 'Mr Salmon!' she called in Cibber's direction. 'What a delight to see you again!'

'Cibber!' He took the Countess's hand and kissed it. 'The delight is surely all mine. You are looking radiant this evening, my lady.'

Alpiew glanced at the Countess, her white Venetian ceruse make-up was not only riddled with cracks but now smeared with black specks from the gingerbread man's cinders. One of her painted-on eyebrows was smudged into a frown and her wig, tilted at a jaunty angle, hung low on her forehead.

Cibber was all smiles and grovelling. Alpiew wondered what he could be after.

'So did you find what you were looking for at the Tower, sir?' The Countess received a jolt from someone else trying to squeeze inside and stumbled into Cibber's arms.

'Yes, yes. I saw the very spot where the bones of the two boys were unearthed.' Cibber nodded keenly. 'It was not many years ago, you know, that they found them. I would have been three years old.' He pulled a large fob watch from his pocket and flipped open the cover. 'Only a few minutes to go. Come, milady, I shall show you to your seats, then I will see you again during the interval, when I have reserved a bottle of sherry for our personal consumption.'

'Do not bother yourself attending on us,' said the Countess, still eager to avoid a confrontation with the dreaded Lady Bustle. 'We'll wait till it is quieter.'

'Rebecca!' called Cibber to a woman standing in the corner with her maid. 'Are you coming in?'

The woman glared at Cibber. 'Anne Lucas was supposed to be doing this thing.' She flounced a little and unfurled her fan. 'But the wretched creature hasn't turned up! As a result, I have spent the last hour with that odious Frenchman learning all his ridiculous cant.'

'You are doing the demonstration?' Cibber exuded a strange mixture of concern and relief.

'His breath smells worse than asafoetida, and the grease he uses on his moustaches stinks like a civet cat on heat. And frankly, Colley, I have had enough.'

Alpiew felt a strange tugging at the hem of her skirts. A peculiar little dog had her skirts between his teeth and was pulling at them with all his might. She gave a surreptitious kick and the dog let out a high-pitched yelp.

Rebecca's face blackened, and she glared towards Alpiew. 'Have a care, miss.' She took the dog into her arms and cooed over him, while the animal licked at her neck. 'My dog is a precious pedigree of the papillon breed, favoured by royalty throughout the courts of Europe.'

'A papillon!' The Countess stretched out a plump finger and the little dog licked it. 'Louis XIV has them, or rather the ladies of his Court. How charming. See, Alpiew, the little fellow is named after a butterfly, because of the fall of his silky ears. Am I not right, Mrs Montagu?'

'I call him Red.' Rebecca smiled. 'An abbreviation, really – for Red Admiral.'

'Should we go into the hall, Mr Cibber?' inquired Alpiew, surveying the now empty foyer and keen to be out of range both of the actress and her canine companion. 'We don't want to miss the start.'

A muscle in Cibber's cheek was starting to twitch. 'Until either Rebecca or Anne is available the lecture won't start at all.' Cibber smiled grimly towards Rebecca. 'For one or other of them is the actress employed to demonstrate the expressions for Signior Lampone, who, for your information, Rebecca, is an Italian.'

'I am waiting to start, Mr Cibber.' A nearby door swung open and a large man with drooping black mustachios strode in, throwing his head back and twirling one end of the moustache between two artistically long fingers. But the most striking thing about his unusual face was that, perched in the centre, he had a silver nose. 'I must deliver my conference upon the expression of the Passions, while my juices are flowing.'

A commotion in the street pulled all eyes to the door. A chair had arrived and a flustered-looking woman fell out of it.

'Drunk, I suppose,' exclaimed Rebecca for all to hear. 'The trapes was always over-partial to cordial waters.' She tickled the dog under his chin. 'Isn't she, darling?'

'*Ridiculoso!*' The Italian threw his papers into the air. 'I am a grand maestro. I do not work with slatterns.'

Anne Lucas, dishevelled but sober, shoved through the crowd of phanatiques into the foyer. 'Signior Lampone, *mia apologia. O molti problemi in casa . . .*' She turned to Rebecca, and translated coldly: 'I have enormous troubles at home.' She greeted Cibber with a kiss on the cheek, then knelt on the floor before the artist. '*Perdona mia*, Signior Lampone. *Lavoriamo.* Come, let's work!'

'One moment, sir.' Rebecca handed the dog to her maid and stepped forward. 'I have just wasted a precious spring afternoon rehearsing your jigumbob. Does this mean I will not be remunerated for my efforts?'

The painter looked to Cibber, Cibber looked to the floor. 'I can give you a free seat . . . ?'

'A free seat! I assume you jest?' Rebecca put her hands on her hips, threw back her head and laughed. 'I have given up a full hour of my time in a professional pursuit, and for that I *will* be paid.' One eyebrow raised, nostrils flared, mouth drawn down at the corners, she stood tapping her foot and glaring at Cibber.

'You see!' screamed the Italian, pointing at Rebecca. 'The woman is *perfetto!* A great actress. She has demonstrated Wonder followed instantly by Scorn. *Magnificento!*'

Alpiew shot a sly look at the Countess. This bizarre episode would make excellent copy.

'So tell me, Colley. Do you want that second-rater to demonstrate the Passions?' Rebecca Montagu was clearly determined to milk the moment. 'Here: look at her face . . . Subtle, but you can already see Jealousy etched finely upon it.' With a sudden movement, Rebecca turned to Anne and gave her a hearty slap across the face. 'There we are . . . Physical Pain followed by Astonishment . . .' She took a step back. 'And what will come next? Either Weeping or Anger, I wager.'

Anne Lucas covered her face with her hands and ran into the auditorium.

'Now, sirrah –' Rebecca smiled at Signior Lampone – 'off you trot and give your tedious discourse.' She linked arms with Cibber. 'And I *will* take you up on that offer of a seat, Colley. I wouldn't miss this debacle for the world.' She turned to her maid, who had hovered inconspicuously behind her throughout the tirade. 'Sarah, you may go home and prepare my supper.'

The maid curtseyed and left at a brisk pace.

The Italian threw his arms into the air, uttered a few incomprehensible oaths and followed Anne Lucas down the aisle.

'Did I introduce you to my new friends, Rebecca?' said Cibber with a sly grin. 'This is Lady Anastasia Ashby de la Zouche . . .'

'Baroness Penge, Countess of . . .' muttered the Countess.

'And her . . .'

'Maid, yes.' Rebecca did not even look at them. 'Shall we go in?'

'No, Rebecca. I was going to say her writing partner, Alpiew.' Cibber smiled graciously. 'Lady Ashby de la Zouche and Mistress Alpiew write the society news for the *London Trumpet*.'

Alpiew was delighted to watch Rebecca's face struggle to suppress a rotation of the Passions, chiefly Horror and Rage, while demonstrating a frantic smile in her direction. She was clearly not used to displaying her passions in such close proximity to the press.

The candlelit auditorium was crammed full of chattering people. The only seats left were in the back row and had reserved signs upon them.

Cibber ushered the three women in as the pre-show music concluded and the musicians took a bow. Cibber stood by the door at the back of the aisle, prepared for all eventualities.

Signior Lampone and Anne Lucas climbed up on to the rostrum, and the applause swelled. Lampone raised his hands for silence.

'Ladies and gentlemen, I stand before you this evening to speak upon the subject of Expression. This chimerical science is a necessary study to all artists, whether painters like myself, or players, like my esteemed friend Anne Lucas, who has graciously agreed tonight to demonstrate the fundamentals of the theory.'

Another smattering of applause.

'You will also find my philosophy useful simply as a tool for living. So, ladies and gentlemen, first I will explain that a

Passion is a movement of the sensitive constituent of the soul. It consists of many parts – principally the internal movements, as when in Hatred the pulse races, or when in Desire the heart beats faster; and the external movements, as the clenched fist of Anger, or the running away induced by Fear.'

Rebecca shuffled in her seat and muttered under her breath. 'Or the yawning induced by abject boredom.'

The Countess smirked. She could not have put it better herself.

'But the part of the body most expressive of the Passions is, of course, the face. The face which receives quickest and most intensely the signals from the brain.'

The Countess suppressed a yawn. Over an hour of this claptrap? She glanced round the room for moral support, but she and Rebecca seemed to be the only ones who weren't enthralled.

'Now I will show you a simple exercise.' Lampone turned to face Anne Lucas. 'Please, Madam Lucas, empty the face of expression.'

Anne stood in the centre of the rostrum, Lampone moved behind her.

'Wrinkled brow, drawn down and frowning.'

Anne moved her eyebrows down.

'The eye sparkling, the pupil looking out at the corner, in constant fire.'

Anne Lucas moved her eyes into position.

'Nostrils open and drawn back, mouth shut, the corners pulled back and downwards, the teeth clenched.'

Anne flared her nostrils and set her mouth.

'Now, may I ask someone in the audience to tell me what they perceive?'

'A second-rate actress with constipation,' muttered Rebecca. The Countess restrained herself from laughing.

'Which of the Passions, ladies and gentlemen, do you see before you?' He pointed towards a gentleman in a shining brown peruke.

'Jealousy?' suggested the man.

Lampone gave a smug shrug and Anne relaxed her face. Applause.

'Now, Anne, eyebrows higher in the middle, down at the sides, eyelids lowered.'

Alpiew could see that many of the audience were also following Lampone's instructions.

'Mouth slightly open, corners drawn down. Head negligently leaning to one shoulder.'

He addressed the audience again.

'And this time? Madam?' He was pointing towards Rebecca.

'May I say, Signior Lampone, that I believe you are a genius . . .' A smattering of applause. Anne Lucas's facial muscles were starting to quiver. 'I would suggest that Mrs Lucas's expression indicates the sorrow she feels when she contemplates that I am the better player.'

Some of the audience laughed, others shifted uneasily in their seats.

Anne Lucas froze for a moment, then started sobbing as she ran from the podium through a small door at the back of the stage.

Lampone seemed unsure whether to follow the distraught actress backstage or continue his demonstration alone. He continued talking for some minutes, attempting to pull the appropriate faces as he spoke. At last he threw his arms up in the air. '*E un disastro! Un fiasco!*'

The audience shuffled uncomfortably.

'Ladies and gentlemen' – Cibber strode up the aisle and mounted the platform – 'may I suggest we take a short interlude. In ten minutes I am sure Signior Lampone will be delighted to continue his discourse.' He turned towards the backstage door, which was ajar. Two heads peered through the gap. 'Musicians? Please could you play again.'

Cibber looked up to where Rebecca Montagu sat smirking and gave her the signal to come to the stage and join him.

The Countess and Alpiew left with the other members of the audience, and decided to stroll along the terrace by the Watergate and compare notes.

'What a turn-up,' said the Countess, wrapping her cloak around her.

'I am heartily sorry she spoke,' said Alpiew. 'I was enjoying the lecture.'

'You jest?' The Countess looked at her in amazement. 'I'd be happier watching the waterworks in motion.'

A couple of row-boats bobbed gently a few yards away in mid-stream, although the river tide was low, and the black shadowy beach stretched along before them. One of the boatmen pointed to the terrace, noticing that there were people about – potential fares. He turned his oars and pulled in towards the shore.

'We have almost enough copy for a month,' said Alpiew, counting on her fingers. 'The Gymcrack girl and her murderous lover, the row between the actresses, this disastrous evening . . .'

Just then a shadow fell across the Countess's face.

'Nasty? I say, it's Nasty Ass!' Lady Bustle was upon them. 'Looking a bit worse for wear, dear. Where did you get that ancient dress? It should be in a museum by now, surely.'

The Countess flipped her jaw up and down, speechless. Bustle laughed.

'Well! There's a new Passion for Mr Lampone. What's it called, Nasty Ass? Moonstruck?'

'It is called,' Alpiew interceded, 'Dignity in the face of gross rudeness.'

It was Bustle's turn to be lost for words. 'Listen, wench, I will take no insolence from a mere menial. If I were you, I'd hold your clack.'

'If you were me, madam, you'd be a lot better looking and realise that wealth is no justification for discourtesy.'

A horse pulling a hackney coach gave a snort that seemed to punctuate Alpiew's retort with a raspberry as the carriage rolled away towards the Strand.

With a huff, Lady Bustle staggered through the Watergate and down the steps towards the water. 'Boatman!' she called. 'I am leaving. I have never been so insulted.'

Alpiew put her arm round the Countess, whose chin was set on a precarious wobble, and walked her to one of the stone seats within the Watergate.

'I might as well be back at school again. After all these years . . .'

'Watch this, madam.' They peered out to the row-boat; the shadowy outline of Lady Bustle sat facing the oarsman, jammed up against another passenger, presumably her farmer friend. The boatman, with the usual medley of curses, called Lady Bustle every name under the sun. 'I told you to step carefully, dowager. The excesses of your avoirdupois has got us stuck in the mud. I didn't know from your voice you were such a fat slubberdegullion, there's more blubber on you than on a whole school of whales.'

'Rivermen, madam –' Alpiew squeezed the Countess's arm – 'never let an insult go past!'

'The lecture will start again in a few minutes, ladies and gentlemen.' Cibber came out into the street behind them ringing a handbell. 'Please take your seats.'

The Countess gazed down at the river. With a plopping of oars the sculler finally drew away from the far end of the steps, taking Lady Bustle off into the darkness.

'Do you want to go home?' said Alpiew.

'With that awful bailiff waiting outside to apprehend me?' The Countess shook her head. 'I will join you inside the auditorium in a few minutes. Let them go in first.'

Alpiew looked around at the dark streets, the inky black river. This was not a safe place. 'I can't leave you here, milady.'

'Why not? You go on ahead. I'm not as interested in all that stuff as you are.'

'You are sure?'

The Countess shooed Alpiew away.

When the audience were all inside, the Countess walked back along Buckingham Street. It was very dark. Now that the famous faces were gone, the phanatiques had left their positions and had drifted away into the night. Nor was the gingerbread seller in sight. His brazier still burned fiercely, but the man was nowhere to be seen. The Countess sighed. She was hoping to get another slice. She walked round the side of the building and leaned against the balustrade.

Above her a sash window opened and an old bald head poked out. 'What's going on?'

The Countess pulled back into the shadows. She recognised the man, but couldn't think where they'd met. Wherever it was, it was many, many years ago.

'Mary?' The man turned back into his room. 'Did you hear it?' He leaned out again. Another window slid open on an upper floor and a female head popped out.

'You,' cried the man, pointing down towards the Countess. 'You in the shadow! Did you hear it? A call like an albatross, or shrieking of the wind through the sheets in a westerly gale.'

The Countess stepped forward, peering up at the bald head. It looked like the old navy man, who'd worked for King Charles. She remembered he had a silly name: Chirrup, or Toots, or something similar.

'There's been a bit of a stir at the concert hall, sir. That's all.'

'No no.' The man was banging the sill with his palm. 'I heard it distinctly. Wait a minute . . .' He leaned further out. 'Don't I know you? You used to work as an actress?'

'Take care, sir, or you'll fall out!' The woman in the upper window called down before disappearing back into the house.

'Ridiculous, building a concert hall on my doorstep! I retired here for a bit of peace and quiet. It's been worse than Bedlam ever since.'

'Come on, Mr Pepys.' The female head appeared alongside the old man. 'You'll catch a cold, and you know how you hate to be ill.'

Pepys! That was it. The Man from the Ministry himself. Samuel Pepys. Always trying to feel your legs under the table, and taking every opportunity God gave him to touch your breasts; with no conversation but the price of sailcloth and the number of barrels of tar required for a voyage to Flushing. Wherever that was.

'I know that woman.' Pepys shook the housekeeper off and pointed down at the Countess. 'Don't I? I know you. Would you like to come in for a plate of tripes?'

'Yes, Samuel.' A plate of tripes sounded like a better offer than having to sit through an hour of face-pulling. 'Of course you know me. It's Ashby de la Zouche – Charles' old friend.'

'See!' Pepys turned to his housekeeper. 'Told you I knew her. It's Lady Ashby de la Zouche.' He waved down. 'Come on up.'

'I must tell Alpiew where I am, Samuel. She is waiting inside the concert room for me. I'll be two minutes.'

Nodding happily, Pepys disappeared, aided by his housekeeper, and the window was shut.

The Countess started to cross the alley. At the same moment a great whoop came from behind her, accompanied by a stampede of feet. As the Countess turned to see what was going on, she stumbled into the wall. A pack of young men swept past her, hollering at the top of their voices. Two held links to light their way. As she pressed herself against the building to avoid them, a dark-haired beau caught hold of the Countess's wig and raced away with it. Slapping her hands up to her bald pate, the Countess reeled into a doorway, while the youth tossed the wig to a friend, and he to another, like a game of catch-ball. 'You niggardly sons of whores,' screamed the Countess. 'Give me back my top-knot.'

'Top-knot?' cried one. ''Tis no top-knot. Sure, 'tis a dead rat.'

At this, with a scream he threw it high against the wall and it smacked against Pepys' window and landed on the sill from which he had just been leaning.

Screeching with laughter, the boys tore off into the night, with the rhythmic chant:

> *'Don't sleep, don't snooze,*
> *Watch out for the Tityre-tus!'*

She waited for their voices to recede before she dared breathe. Then, sobbing with a blend of relief that they had not harmed her and embarrassment at the loss of her wig, she cowered in the doorway. She shut her eyes, slid down and sat huddled on the step.

A few moments later she heard footsteps, then a man's voice a few feet away.

'Hello? Are you all right?' Someone was walking slowly towards her. 'It's the gingerbread man. The swine upset my brazier. Did they hurt you?' His hands reached gently down. 'Boys these days!'

'They took my wig.' She pointed up to Pepys' window. 'It's up there.'

'I'll go find the watch,' said the gingerbread man. 'He can get it down for you with his long staff.'

The Countess looked up at the man's woollen hat. 'Could I . . . ?'

Without a word, the man took off his hat and handed it to the Countess, who pulled it tightly down over her ears. 'Thank you.' She was frightened that Pepys might start looking out for her. 'I can't stay here. They will think I am a vagrant and I'll be picked up by the constables.'

The gingerbread man helped her up. 'I won't be long.' He walked off into the dark.

'I'll wait over there,' she called after him. 'In the concert hall.'

The Countess walked briskly through the candlelit foyer, taking a smart glimpse of herself in a mirrored sconce. Then she pulled the auditorium door open a crack.

Alpiew was not sitting in the same place. But then, mercifully, neither was Cibber. From the stage, Lampone was talking intimately with his rapt audience.

'Rage, for instance, has the same basic movements as Despair, yet they seem somehow more violent. When Mistress Montagu has had time to prepare herself (I believe she is fetching a cup of water from the drinking fountain behind the building), she will show you the subtle difference between these related passions.'

The Countess at last spied Alpiew. The minx had managed

to get herself a seat in the front row. There was no question of her marching up the whole length of the aisle wearing a street vendor's woolly headgear. She took a quick scan of the room. Cibber too was seated near the front.

A heavy thudding was coming from behind the stage. Lampone smiled. 'Here comes the great actress, with a tread like a fairy!'

The back door flung open and Rebecca Montagu staggered on to the podium. Her hair was in disarray, her face contorted in a fixed expression.

'*Eccellente*...' said Lampone, resuming his talk. 'A little further into the programme than I was expecting, but see: the arms stretched stiffly forward, the legs in the act of fleeing, the whole body in disorder...'

Rebecca Montagu stood rooted to the spot, her expression frozen.

'You will note the eyebrows raised high in the middle, the muscles holding them swollen and taut, the nose and nostrils drawn up, the eyes wide, the pupils unsettled, the mouth wide open with corners drawn back, the veins and tendons very prominent, the hair seeming to stand up at its roots, the complexion pale. This is the epitome of...'

Lampone gave a smug smile: '... of Terror.'

Without altering her facial expression, Rebecca Montagu thrust her hands out for the audience to see and started to scream.

Her fingers were red. Dripping from her fingers and on to the floor was a scarlet liquid that was unmistakably blood.

TWO

Assurance

*An extreme version of hope – the expectation of
obtaining that which one wants.*

*The movements more internal than outward.
The eyebrows slightly raised. The corners of the
mouth curving upwards.*

In the pandemonium that followed Alpiew leapt up on to
the stage and led Rebecca Montagu to a chair. The audience rose, some screaming, others dashing for the doors.

The Countess raced out into the street. What was she to
do?

The artists had a back entrance, through which to cart their
harpsichords and suchlike. She would try to reach Alpiew that
way.

A group of link-boys, their links dead, loitered in the
shadows of the riverside walkway to the side of the entrance,
assembling to wait for the trade at the concert's end.

'You, child,' the Countess hollered. 'Light up and follow
me instantly.'

She scampered down towards the river and trotted gingerly
along the dark terrace at the side of the concert hall.

'Come, lad,' she called as the child's link threw long shadows
along the walkway. She pressed onwards, up a flight of stone
steps. The water fountain stood ahead in the street beside a huge
gate. The Countess looked around. The street was empty.

'Can you see anyone?' she asked the boy.

'No one here,' replied the boy, holding his link aloft. 'Why are you wearing that stupid hat?'

The Countess ignored his query. 'Did you see anyone earlier?'

'Only those rascally Tityre-tus,' said the child. 'But we run when we see them about for they catch us and hang us up from the signposts and leave us there, dangling.'

'Hold the link over the fountain.' The Countess watched closely. Even in the flickering light of the link it was clear that the liquid which spilled from the spout was red.

'Criminy, ma'am, what's that? Wine?' The boy leaned forward, anxious to try it. 'They have turned it to wine before – for the coronation, but I was only a baby then.'

The Countess held him by the shoulder. 'What is behind this gate, boy, do you know?'

'Why yes, ma'am. That's the entrance to the waterworks. Look there –' He held the link up and pointed to a dark tower on the other side of the wall. 'It's worked by a newfangled engine of sorts. Me an' the boys scaled the wall to take a look, but we got caught.'

Nothing stirred in the street.

'Do you use this fountain? You and the boys?'

'We play jokes on one another.' The boy laughed. 'My friend Dan washed his face in it t'other day, and Billy had got there first and put soot in it, so he came away with a dirtier face than when he started.' The boy held his sides and rocked with laughter. 'How we laughed.' The boy looked at the drinking fountain again. 'This'll be him again, ma'am, playing his tricks. Best leave it alone. It'll wash away.'

The Countess patted the child on the head, paid him a penny and, pulling the gingerbread man's woollen hat firmly down round her ears, entered the concert hall through the back door.

Alpiew sat backstage with Rebecca in the musicians' room. Cibber paced up and down, while Lampone sat alone, face in hands, muttering words like *fiasco* and *disastro*.

Rows of chairs and music stands surrounded them, and in the corner a pair of kettle-drums resonated every time someone raised their voice.

'I always wet my hands before I perform. It's a ritual. I go out, look at the sky, throw up my arms, and plunge my hands in water . . .' She collapsed into tears again. 'It was so horrible. It was all dark out there. Then, in the candlelight spilling from the stage, I looked down and saw my hands were red. I could smell it. I knew what it was.'

Alpiew looked up at Cibber, holding out the towel she had used to wipe Rebecca's hands clean. 'What's happened to the audience?'

'They're leaving.' He stood with his head in his hands. 'Slowly but surely.'

'And where is Anne Lucas?'

'She has gone home to the 'usband.' Lampone stopped his recitation of words ending in 'o'. 'I saw her giving orders to the coachman.'

Cibber looked to the corridor, footsteps were approaching. 'Someone is coming . . .'

The little dog leapt up on to Rebecca's lap and started licking furiously at her neck. She buried her face in his white and red fur.

The door creaked open.

'There you are, Mr Haddock.' It was the Countess. 'I believe the fountain episode must have been a prank. The link-boys admitted to me that they often tamper with the thing. Colouring the water with soot and ink and suchlike.'

'I can see what's happened.' Rebecca stopped looking sorry for herself and sat up. 'It wasn't them. Or if it was, *she* put them up to it. It must have been *her*. She knows my ritual; I leave the tiring room before each performance to do it. She must have followed me one day and watched. After all, performances usually take place in broad daylight, not at night like this ridiculous little farce.'

'I presume the "she" you refer to is Mrs Lucas?' said the Countess.

Flashing her dark eyes towards Lampone, Rebecca nodded.

'Well, that's the answer, then. The coloured water from the fountain was a revenge attack perpetrated by Mrs Lucas to startle Mrs Montagu.' The Countess rubbed her chubby hands together. 'So, to bed, to bed . . .'

'I could get you a chair, Countess. I'd pay the charge, of course . . .' Cibber fidgeted. 'Perhaps you would like to come back to my home for a drink . . . ?' He was clearly grasping at straws.

'No thank you, Mr Salmon.' The Countess beamed. 'Alpiew and I must get back. Thank you for your lovely evening's diversion.'

Grabbing Alpiew's hand, she exited quickly, before the subject got round to why she was wearing the gingerbread man's woollen hat.

'Bailiff called a few times. I hid outside in the privy.' Godfrey, the Countess's old retainer (once groom, but, now there was no horse any more, her general factotum), smiled his toothless smile as he poured the two women cups of hot sack posset. 'I 'eard him say to his friend he'd be back tomorrow.' He chortled and wiped a drip of drool from his stubbly chin. 'You gave him the right run-around today, he said.'

The gingerbread man, not having found the Countess and wanting to exploit the unexpected trade that was pouring from the concert hall, had left her wig sitting atop a bust of Purcell in the foyer. Alpiew had recovered it, put the woollen hat on an adjacent bust of Monteverdi, and they had walked briskly home in the dark, checking all the time for the footsteps of the bailiff.

Now, sipping at their drinks in the huge but cosy kitchen (which passed as bedchamber, dining room, living quarters and office, since the rest of the house was in very poor repair), Alpiew scratched out some preliminary copy for the Gymcrack story, while the two women talked about the strange events of the evening. The row between the actresses, the peculiar Italian with the silver nose, the drinking fountain episode.

'It's hard to know which story to submit first,' said Alpiew. 'The alderman's daughter and the murderer, or the philosophical demonstration wrecked by the rivalry of two actresses.'

The Countess took a long draught of sack posset while she thought. 'Maybe we should go to Rakewell's trial. See if the Gymcrack girl's there, and then fill in the story a little – outcome of trial, good description of the boy, etcetera, and submit that story this week.' She sighed and closed her eyes. With a jolt she sat up. 'Phough, those nasty boys, the Tityre-tus. We must collect many stories against them. See if we can't shame them into better behaviour.'

'Them stage plays, that's the cause of them Tityre-tus.' Godfrey, whose head had been lolling into his drink, sat up and scowled. 'In my day we had wars to keep boisterous boys in control. Put 'em in a suit of armour and let 'em sleep under the stars, with nothing to eat but rats . . .'

'Thank you, Godfrey.' The Countess raised a chubby hand. 'We are well versed in your opinions.'

'Coves like them, madam, would not be shamed by having their names in the paper.' Alpiew sucked on the end of her quill. 'Exactly the opposite. It would stuff 'em with pride.'

The Countess slumped back in her chair. What Alpiew said was true. Writing about their exploits would only spur the dreadful midnight boys on to worse things than stealing women's wigs. She groaned at the thought of her embarrassment. It was lucky the mob hadn't arrived a moment earlier and caused poor old Pepys to fall out of his window.

Pepys!

She leapt to her feet with a shriek. 'Pepys!' she cried.

'Toot, toot,' said Godfrey.

'No, Pepys, Pepys. Pepys and his tripes.'

Alpiew looked at the Countess in astonishment, wondering if the shock of her encounter with the unruly gang and the temporary loss of her wig had put her mind into some strange delusion that would land her in Bedlam.

'He'll still be waiting for me.' She sat and took another quaff of possett. 'Poor old fellow. Never had much to say about anything. Poor Pepys. Poor Pepys! Ah well, I shall have to call round tomorrow and make my apologies.'

They were all rudely awoken in the morning by someone hammering at the front door. Terrified it was the bailiff back, Alpiew dashed up the stairs to look down at the doorstep and find out who it was, while the Countess threw on her mantua and made ready to run.

To Alpiew's infinite surprise their visitor was Rebecca Montagu in a beautiful satin gown. Lurking a few paces behind her was her mousy maid, Sarah.

Alpiew showed the actress into the front room, and offered her an easy chair.

'It is early, Mrs Montagu, the fires have not yet been lit.'

In fact the fire in here was only ever lit when an important visitor was expected. Alpiew turned and yelped. Something had nipped her ankle. She looked down to find Red, Rebecca's dog, snarling at her feet. She tried to control her anger.

The Countess bustled in. She had a very good idea why the actress was here. The woman would be frightened about the bad publicity last night's events could bring her and wanted to make amends. She stooped to stroke the dog and smiled.

'Ladies,' said Rebecca, 'I come here with a proposal for you both. A proposal that could earn you some money.'

The Countess's ears pricked up.

'Of course I admire your column very much. As you know, since the two theatrical companies split four years ago, there has been a popular misconception that all the good players and writers are at the Lincoln's Inn Theatre . . .'

'Bracegirdle, Betterton, Congreve, yes.' The Countess lowered herself into a chair.

'And younger players and writers like myself cannot attract the attention we deserve. After all, the Lincoln's Inn players are all twenty years too old for the roles they play. I mean, look at Mrs Barry. She is at least forty, yet she still plays young wives, virgins and coquettes, while younger players like myself have no chance . . .'

Alpiew and the Countess nodded, waiting for the woman to get to the point.

'We could never advance while they were still in the company, so we *elected* to stay when they marched off. But I believe that the general impression the public has is that we were left behind.'

'I see, Mrs Montagu.' The Countess tilted her head to one side. 'But what do you think Mrs Alpiew and I can do about it?'

'Well, I would pay you, of course,' said Rebecca, glancing at each in turn. 'And in return . . .' she assumed a very serious expression, '. . . you would puff for me.'

The Countess and Alpiew exchanged a look.

'Puff?' said the Countess.

'Puff,' said Rebecca.

'Like this?' said the Countess, blowing out her cheeks and exhaling.

Rebecca threw back her head and roared with laughter. The Countess and Alpiew tittered, trying to be polite.

'Is that a yes?' asked Rebecca.

'We'll have to think about it.' The Countess hadn't a notion what the woman was talking about and was not going to be put on the spot.

Alpiew gave a sage little nod. She was equally in the dark, but money was money.

'I could offer you a guinea a mention. And I really don't mind if occasionally you say something bad – like writing about my being taken ill at the performance last night. In my opinion, all publicity is good publicity.' She rose, and her maid moved silently to open the door.

'So should I call to hear your decision, or would you like to visit me at the theatre? I am rehearsing all day today. We are bringing back *The Rival Queens*.'

'Mr Nathaniel Lee's greatest work!' smiled the Countess. She had seen the play frequently over the last twenty years.

'I'm playing Roxana, of course. And Lucas is Statira. That is if she can take enough time off from her domestic life to attend rehearsals.'

'We'll come to the playhouse,' said Alpiew with a weak smile. She loathed everything to do with the theatre, but going there was one way of avoiding the bailiffs. The dog sniffed at Alpiew's hem and emitted a low growl.

'There is only one condition.' Rebecca gathered up her skirts, in preparation for her exit line. 'No one must know of our arrangement. It will be our little secret.'

The Countess gave her an inscrutable look. 'That goes without saying.'

With a final smile the actress swished out to the street, where a hackney carriage waited, Red ambling happily behind her, sniffing the furniture disdainfully as he went.

'Covent Garden punk.' Godfrey was standing, hands on hips, snarling at the kitchen end of the hall. 'Overdressed trull.'

'Thank you, Godfrey,' said the Countess, sliding past him into the kitchen.

'So what did she mean, do you think?' Alpiew hung a pot of milk over the fire and flopped down on a bench by the fireplace. 'We mention her name wherever possible and she pays us each time?'

Another violent thudding erupted from the front door. Alpiew and the Countess exchanged a worried look.

'She must have changed her mind,' said the Countess as Alpiew hovered by the hall door, peering through the keyhole. All she could see was a bouquet of flowers. An unlikely possession for a bailiff. She opened up.

On the step stood Colley Cibber.

'I brought you both a present.' He shifted from foot to foot. 'A peace offering.'

'You'd better come in.' Alpiew took the flowers and ushered him into the front room.

The Countess was already waiting. 'Mr Herring, how lovely to see you.'

'Cibber,' muttered the actor-writer.

'So what can we do for you so bright and early on a spring morning?' asked Alpiew.

'I have a proposition to put to you.' Cibber took in the elegant room, and smiled.

'Mmm . . . ?' The Countess signalled him to sit.

'I would pay you of course . . .' He settled in an easy chair and took a deep breath. 'Since the companies split four years ago, you may have noticed that the public perception of our rivals at Lincoln's Inn Fields is that they are the superior company? Now, I have observed that the private character of an actor will always affect his public performance, and likewise the public perception of his character will affect his fame.'

'You want us to puff?' asked the Countess with a nonchalant air.

'How amazing. Can you read the internal humours of the mind?' Colley Cibber nodded meekly. 'But it must be our little secret.'

The Countess tapped the side of her nose with her forefinger, leaving a round smudge in her white make-up.

'And what kind of things would this puffing entail?' asked Alpiew, staring intently into the flowers and doing sums in her head.

'The usual thing,' said Cibber. 'The odd favourable mention now and then.' He looked up and added: 'And, of course, to make it seem natural, the occasional criticism.'

'We do not write theatrical reviews, sirrah, or accounts of plays.' The Countess was a frequent gambler at the basset table and knew a lack of keenness could up the price.

'No, no.' Cibber grinned. 'You need only say you saw me at Lord Such-and-Such's dining, or I was seen out walking with Lady So-and-So.'

'And what will your wife make of it, sir, if we say that you were seen in a carriage at Rosamund's Pond on a Sunday afternoon with a ravishing actress?'

'My wife would understand. She has given up acting. She is with child.' Cibber blushed. 'Actually, I'd prefer her to live in the country. Hillingdon, or Uxbridge. Then she could devote all her time to breeding successors for me, surrounded by nothing but ducks and geese and fields. Women suit nature best.'

'I must put these in water.' Alpiew hugged the flowers and took the opportunity to leave the room to commune with the blossoms before she hit him.

'How much?' asked the Countess is an easy manner.

'Pound a mention?'

The Countess grimaced. She hoped her face was expressing the Passion 'Fiddlesticks'.

'I'm just a poor actor . . . I have a young family . . .' Cibber shuffled uneasily. 'Well, all right. A guinea, it is.'

'Thank you for your visit.' The Countess thrust out her hand. 'My partner and I must think on this and we will see you at the playhouse later today. You are rehearsing *The Rival Queens*, I presume?'

'I take the pivotal role of Polyperchon, Commander of the Phalanx.'

The Countess had frequently noted that actors never admitted to taking a minor role. In the players' lexicon the word 'unimportant' became the word 'pivotal'. With a brisk bow, he was gone.

'Who'd have thought players rose so early,' said the Countess, holding a chunk of bread to the fire.

'Fiddle players,' snarled Godfrey. 'Housekeeping money's gone. You want any more bread today, you'll have to top me up.'

'Ah well,' the Countess sighed. 'At least *that* can be dealt with.' She turned to Alpiew. 'So we will take up these two thespians on their proposition of puffing?'

'Both of them?' Alpiew was doing sums in her head. 'Well, why not?'

> *'Is then Roxana's love and life so poor*
> *That for another you can choose to die,*
> *Rather than live for her?'*

Rebecca flared her nostrils and gazed across the stage at George Powell, whose face was hidden behind his script. 'George, I know you are not on top of your lines, but might I have some eye-contact, please?'

George obliged by lowering the script.

The Countess and Alpiew had hot-footed it to the playhouse to see if they could rustle up some advance on the puff money, keeping a watch against bailiffs all the way. Luckily this early in the morning it wasn't hard as their route took them through the bustling St James's Market, the noisy Hay Market and the Covent Garden Piazza, which was always busy, all day and all night. Now they sat huddled at the back of the pit, waiting for a break in rehearsal. Alpiew was sorry she had not brought a book.

> '*I am now grown so indifferent,*
> *I could behold you kiss without a pang,*
> *Nay, take a torch and light you to your bed.*'

Rebecca threw back her head and gave a great stamp. Colley Cibber, who was snoozing in the pit, woke with a start.

'George! Will you react or are you just foxed with drink as usual?' George let out a hiccup. Rebecca stamped again, and flung down her book. 'This is absurd. Why must we start on Act Five? I am not prepared.' She clasped at her neck. 'My voice is not warmed up sufficiently to demonstrate such height-ened passion so early in the day. Particularly when I have to play opposite an elderly drunken sot.'

'She is upset.' Cibber had clambered over the benches to sit near the Countess. He turned and hissed an explanation. 'Lucas is late again.'

Alpiew and the Countess grimaced back, but they were secretly delighted; it would make their job easier if there were more dramatic scenes to witness.

'My dear Rebecca,' said a man from one of the stage boxes, 'you are a sublime actress. Your professionalism shall not go unrecorded.'

'He's one of the patentees,' hissed Cibber. 'Mr Rich. Our paymaster.'

'Count yourself lucky that you are doing *The Rival Queens*. I could have got a troupe of rope-dancers this week on the cheap. They would have filled the house and you would have earned nothing.'

Rebecca mumbled something under her breath.

'Perhaps you'd prefer to fill the time showing off your skill at juggling, Mrs Montagu?' Rich threw her a patronising smile. 'And naturally Mrs Lucas will be *fined* for her lateness.'

Rebecca gave a satisfied smirk and picked up her book again.

> *'But do not trust me, no, for if you do,*
> *By all the furies, and the flames of love,*
> *By love, which is the hottest burning hell,*
> *I'll set you both on fire to blaze forever.'*

One of the auditorium doors swung open with a loud jolt. All heads turned to the entrance.

In the windswept doorway stood a constable.

He surveyed the auditorium. 'Are you missing a Mrs Anne Lucas?' he growled.

Everyone nodded, except Rebecca. 'We most certainly are,' she snarled. 'This morning we are rehearsing an unusual play called *The Rival Queen*. Not "Queens". Only the one, you understand. The other queen apparently has another engagement.'

'Well, I believe I can provide the explanation.' The constable stepped forward. 'For we have just found her body.'

'Body?' Cibber rose, gasping.

'Yes, sir, her *dead* body,' said the constable, dropping his constabulary manner the moment he caught eyes with Cibber. 'I say, aren't you Sir Novelty Fashion? My wife loves you especially, sir. Seen all your plays.'

'Yes, yes, certainly,' said Cibber. 'But what of Mrs Lucas?'

Rebecca jumped down from the stage, her hands covering her mouth, her eyes startled. George let out another hiccup, and Mr Rich leaned forward over the box edge. 'Well, man – tell us. What has happened to her?'

'I am sorry to have to tell you' – the constable pulled his

gaze from Cibber and took off his hat – 'that your colleague, Mrs Anne Lucas, has been murdered.'

It was a gruesome sight. The headless body of Anne Lucas lay in a small water butt in the York Buildings Waterworks, neck down. The head was nowhere to be seen.

Workmen at the waterworks had found the torso a short time ago. The butt in which it was crammed fed the street fountain in which Rebecca had washed her hands the night before. The force of the landing body had bent the input pipe so that it was spewing water all over the courtyard, and the only liquid at the bottom of the butt was now blood.

The Countess gazed at the mangled torso laid out on the cobbles of the courtyard, then looked up at the beadle. 'So how do you know it is her?'

The beadle bent down and opened a great leather bag at his feet. 'She's famous, milady. We'd all recognise this face.' He held the severed head of Anne Lucas aloft. 'But it's me asking the questions here. We've sent for Justice Moore. He should be here shortly.' He turned to one of his cronies. 'Where are the upholders? Is there a new plague broke out that keeps them so long from coming to fetch away the body?'

The Countess looked around her. Cibber was sitting with his arm round Rebecca. Mr Rich was deep in conversation with George, who was looking rather green. Alpiew was prowling round the gates, looking intently at the ground.

'Where was the bag found?'

'What is it to you?' The beadle gave the Countess a penetrating look. 'Did you know the deceased?'

'I did not.' The Countess couldn't take her eyes off the grisly contorted face, the severed neck. 'Although, like you, I'd seen her in plays, of course.'

'But you work for the theatre?'

'Absolutely not.'

'So why, may I ask, were you at a rehearsal this morning?'

'I am a writer, sirrah. The social whirl of London is my

subject.' She pointed towards the head, still hanging, dripping, from the beadle's hand. 'Do you mind putting the poor woman back into the bag?'

The beadle shrugged and strolled over towards the theatre gang, Anne Lucas's head still held dangling from his mighty fist. Rebecca thrust her face into her hands, while Cibber jumped furiously to his feet. 'For God's sake, man. She was our friend. Please have some respect.'

'It seems to me' – the beadle now placed the head beneath his arm –'that you have all got some questions to answer. Some one of you, I suspect, took this head from the body where it belonged, and left it in a bag under the bench in the York Watergate.'

'Let's get away from here as soon as we can,' Alpiew whispered. 'This business has nothing to do with us. Let them find some other hacks to puff for them.'

'I agree,' said the Countess. 'It might win us two guineas a week, but I have a nasty feeling about this set-up. The debt is probably some trifle I overlooked. We can certainly pay it off slowly out of our weekly income.'

'You're right, milady. What is money when set against integrity?'

'It wouldn't be worth the trouble.'

'Or the risk.' Alpiew surveyed the row of theatricals leaning against the riverside balustrade and shivered. 'Do you think one of them did it?'

'Do you know, Alpiew' – the Countess too glanced in the direction of the players – 'I confess I don't care to think about it at all.'

Alpiew bent down to tighten her boot-lace and looked at the cobbles. 'It didn't rain last night, did it? The cobbles are clean.'

'No blood anywhere . . .' The Countess knelt down, and ran her fingers across the ground. 'Hey day! What is this?' She picked up a button and handed it to Alpiew.

'It's certainly an expensive one,' said Alpiew, slipping it into her pocket.

The Countess peered up at the tall fence, then thought better of it. 'What am I doing? We don't want to know anything about it, do we, Alpiew? It is none of our business.'

'I wish he would let us go.' Alpiew met the gaze of the beadle then briskly turned to look at the water fountain. 'While we're here, it's hard not to think about it. I washed Anne Lucas's blood from Rebecca Montagu's hands.'

'And I must have been yards away from her when she –'

A hand fell upon the Countess's shoulder, making her jump. It was Mr Rich. He spoke in a deep and warm voice. 'May I have a private word?' He inclined his head, indicating that Alpiew should back away.

When she was out of earshot, he made his proposition. 'This episode could be tricky for the theatre. Our finances are on a knife-edge at the moment. I was wondering whether you would . . .'

'Puff?' snapped the Countess. 'I'm afraid not. We are both very busy.'

'I could guarantee you two guineas a mention . . .' He glanced back over his shoulder. 'But obviously not a word to them. It would be our secret.'

'You want us to write about this murder?'

'Oh yes. Takings will shoot up.' Rich nodded enthusiastically. 'No more dancing dogs and squeaking eunuchs, it'll be house-full every show. And no novelties required. Let's see how Lincoln's Inn handles this one!'

A few feet away, Alpiew let out a squawk. The Countess turned to watch her bend down and scrape some dog dirt from her boot.

Before Rich could restart his tirade a carriage rumbled into view and the Justice alighted.

When they had been released from the scene, in a daze the Countess and Alpiew made their way home to German Street. Evening was upon them, and although the sun was struggling to shine, it was cold. They stood looking up and down the street for a minute or two before approaching their front door.

They had barely entered when there was a hammering behind them.

'We've got eighteen shillings, milady. He can take that. You go into the kitchen. I'll handle him.' Alpiew doubled back and opened the door. As she feared, it was the bum-bailiff. 'Countess Delta Louche?'

'No,' replied Alpiew.

'She owes us for the Poor Rate.'

'How much?'

'Nine pounds.'

'Nine pounds?' Alpiew tried to suppress a gasp. Nine pounds was more than some folk could earn in a year. How could they lay their hands on nine pounds? 'She's moved. She doesn't live here any more.' Alpiew felt as though she should sit down. 'Nine pounds, you say. Well, you'd best look for her in . . .' She couldn't think of anywhere. 'York Buildings.'

'Which?' grunted the bailiff. 'George Street? Duke Street? Buckingham Street?'

'One of them,' said Alpiew. 'I can't remember which.'

A crash of crockery came from the kitchen. The bailiff shoved past Alpiew. 'York Buildings, indeed!' He strode into the kitchen. Alpiew heard the conversation clear as a bell.

'Countess Ashby de la Zouche, I am here to collect the sum of nine pounds. If you cannot produce this sum here and now, then you are compelled to place yourself in my custody until such a time . . .' He was already marching her out towards the front door. 'She'll be in the Charing Cross sponging house if you need her.'

The Countess, mouth wide, eyes staring in horror, just had the chance to utter the words, 'Puff, Alpiew! Puff for anyone, everyone!' before she disappeared out of the door into the bailiff's cart.

Alpiew sank down in the hall and wept. Nine pounds! How had it come to this? Where could she get hold of nine pounds?

A clack on the door made her jump to her feet. Perhaps there had been a mistake and the bailiff was bringing her lady back.

But it was Rebecca Montagu again. Alone this time.

Alpiew tried to look composed. 'Do come through.'

Rebecca sat down and arranged her skirts for maximum effect. 'I need your services.'

Alpiew nodded. 'It is under control.'

'Control. What do you know about anything?' Rebecca leapt to her feet, moved across to the window and looked out. A carriage passed, with two link-boys running ahead. 'Where is her ladyship?'

'Her ladyship cannot be contacted at the present time. But I can tell you that you are already mentioned in the copy we are writing for the *Trumpet* this very week.'

Rebecca seemed not to be listening. 'You solved that murder, didn't you, the pair of you?' She picked at the lace on her skirt. 'The Male/Female Slasher? You discovered him?'

The actress was referring to their recent success in uncovering a dreadful plot in which a man dressed as a woman had killed two people.

'You must help me.' Rebecca turned and faced Alpiew. 'I need you to find Anne Lucas's killer.' She spoke with a desperate earnestness.

'You?' Alpiew studied Rebecca's face. She seemed to be sincere. But wasn't that the whole point of last night's lecture? A player was trained to control the passions, and express them clearly, even when they did not feel them within. 'Why? Do they suspect you?'

'How dare you!' Rebecca reeled back a few steps, then stepped up to Alpiew and hissed, slapping Alpiew's face. 'No, of course they don't suspect *me*. She was my dearest friend, everybody knows that.'

'Are you all right?' Alpiew noticed that the actress's hands were shaking. 'Would you like a hot drink?'

'Yes, please.' Rebecca sank down into a chair and put her head in her hands. 'A cup of tea would be lovely.'

'Tea!' howled Alpiew. 'Fie, madam, do you think we're made of money?'

'I'm sorry,' the actress blushed. 'I wasn't thinking. Some hot sack posset?'

'Godfrey brews up a fine posset.' Alpiew called out to Godfrey to bring the drink in. 'Pleasantly heavy on the sherry.'

'I'll pay you in advance.' Rebecca was fiddling with her purse. 'How much do you want? I'd like to take the services of the pair of you, and that old boy who waits on you, if necessary.'

'I don't work for people who feel they have the right to strike me,' said Alpiew.

'It was wrong of me.' Rebecca's lips were quivering, and her eyes brimmed with tears. 'But I am so shaken by the horror of what I have seen, the quarrel we had before she died, the thought of her blood on my hands . . .'

Alpiew kept her eyes on Rebecca's face. 'Do you have any idea who it could be?' she asked.

'Would I be here if I did?' The actress flashed her eyes again.

Alpiew had never been partial to players, after her experience helping out in the tiring room. And for Rebecca she felt not only that instinctive dislike, but realised she was rather afraid of her.

'I would that I knew.' Rebecca slumped down in her chair. 'They would surely die at my hands if I could worm them out. But . . .' She looked up at Alpiew. 'You see the miserable types who sit ogling us every day, and those moonstruck fools who follow us about, giving us presents, wanting to touch us. As though we were something divine, not just whores and strumpets hoofing about on a wooden stage, speaking someone else's words as though we were making them up ourselves! They think they know us. But they haven't a notion.' Rebecca sat forward again. 'Have you ever thought what a ridiculous method it is of making a living?'

'As a matter of fact, I have,' Alpiew sighed. 'Frequently.'

'But it's hard work, don't get me wrong. It's emotionally draining, and you have to give all of yourself, all of the time. The hours are long, the pay is poor, you can't go out in the street unless you look your best . . .'

Alpiew nodded. She'd heard actors doing this recital before

and knew it was best to sympathise, and on no account to mention the hard work of, say, coal-men, or the night-soil men, who disposed of the excrement from the privies and middens of London in the dark of night.

'Then there are the Antis,' said Rebecca. 'It could be any of *them*. And the groups are proliferating by the day.'

'The Antis?'

'Anti-theatre. Society for the Reformation of Manners, People for Purity, Londoners Against Lewdness. They have the odd idea that there never was a murder before, nor unruly behaviour. Every one of society's ills they lay at the playhouse's door. Every immoral act, in their opinion, is the result of watching stage plays.'

Alpiew crossed her fingers and hoped that Godfrey wouldn't return with the posset until Rebecca had got off this subject.

'They are, in the main, quite mad,' said Rebecca, recovering herself. 'Spurned men and jealous spinsters, most of them. They'd do anything to get us closed down.'

'But surely they wouldn't kill?'

Rebecca shrugged. 'They are lunatic enough. Most of them can't see the difference between acting and reality. Look at Cibber: the whole world thinks of him as Sir Novelty Fashion. I frequently play a wicked murdering queen, therefore they imagine that I am a wicked murdering actress.' Rebecca stopped short and let out a sob. 'I know everyone thinks I did it. After all, I had her blood on my hands.' Rebecca reached out and grabbed Alpiew by the wrist. 'You must protect me. I am so frighted.'

'Protect you?' Alpiew had the uncomfortable suspicion Rebecca was trying to bribe her to create a cover-up. 'What type of protection do you mean?'

'I need a bodyguard. Like the King has. I will pay you.' Rebecca leaped to her feet. 'I need someone to be with me at all times. In case . . .'

'I would be your guard, you mean?' Alpiew considered. That wouldn't be too awful a way of earning some extra cash. 'Protect you from the Antis?'

'The Antis, the phanatiques, the players themselves.' Rebecca clapped her hands in the air. 'That's it! You're good-looking enough to take a minor role. You've got a decent cleavage and speak clearly. Bit long in the tooth, but look at Mrs Barry! You will join the acting company.'

Alpiew gaped in horror. 'But I . . .'

'Player's pay. You'll be on the basic, having had no training. A hireling. You'll not get the full company livery, etcetera.'

'Listen to me. I will puff, I will investigate the murder. I will even guard you. But I am absolutely *not* going to be a player. No. No. No.'

'You will change your mind.' Rebecca gave Alpiew a withering look. 'Secretly everyone wants a chance to be famous.' She strode to the door. 'You can get me at the playhouse, and on off-days you will find me in my lodgings in Little Hart Street. At the sign of the Brazen Serpent.'

Alpiew raised her eyebrows. The brazen serpent usually indicated a bookseller specialising in medical and surgical pamphlets frequently entitled *The Secret Disease Unmasked*, or *The Tomb of Venus – symptoms of the Pox and the Clap uncovered*.

'It's a proper bookshop.' Rebecca had caught Alpiew's look. 'It *used* to house a quack, but the new owners are stuck with the sign, I'm afraid.' She pulled open the front door, and looked right and left. 'It's not too far from here. I have to go back home to learn my lines now. I will see you soon.'

And with a dramatic swirl of skirt she was gone.

THREE

Disdain

*When the object of our wonder has nothing which
merits our esteem.*

*The eyebrow frowning, the inner ends drawn
down, the outer very raised. The nostrils flared.
The mouth drawn downwards and shut, the
under lip thrust out.*

The sponging house where the Countess was held was in a filthy narrow street behind Charing Cross, up a flight of stairs above a truss-makers.

After a night spent staring at the ceiling, watching the shadows cast by the fire against the sconces while Godfrey's snores echoed round the strangely empty kitchen, Alpiew had come here to tell the Countess about Rebecca's wild proposal. Life in German Street was not the same without her ladyship.

She was left waiting in the dingy front room while the woman in charge of the place went to fetch her prisoner. Compared to some of the places Alpiew had been held, this looked quite comfortable. Better than prison, any day. Sometimes, once you got to know them, the bailiffs and their wives were really quite nice. Almost like normal people.

The Countess was led in, her hands chained.

The wardress, the bailiff's wife, stood a few feet away watching. Alpiew noticed how well-dressed she was. No doubt she or her husband had a neat little sideline in bribery or extortion.

'So you have had a visit from Mrs Montagu?' The Countess perched on an oak bench. 'You said you'd puff, I hope?'

'All those players are suffering from over-heating of the brain, madam,' Alpiew whispered. 'She wants us to investigate the Lucas affair.'

'I've been having some thoughts about the murder.' The Countess leaned forward eagerly. 'I think we could get to the bottom of it.'

'Not from in here, we won't. I wish I could find an easy way to get you out.' Alpiew looked down at her lap and bit her lip. 'I should have let them take me instead.'

'Alpiew!' The Countess reached out and stroked Alpiew's hair. 'How noble you are. Did you deliver the Rakewell and Gymcrack story to the *Trumpet*?'

'Godfrey took it in this morning.' Alpiew gripped the table edge. 'I wish I was in here in your place. It's too terrible to contemplate.'

'What's that?'

'She wants me to be an actress. I told her to go to the devil.'

'You! A player?' The Countess suddenly looked rather pinched. 'But you don't have the feel for the drama, Alpiew. It's me she should have asked.' The Countess rose and assumed a noble posture. 'Ah!' Her eyes flashed and she shot out a pudgy hand. As it was chained to the other, they both flew up together. '"Ah, poor Castalio!" I could do it better, of course, without these impediments to my art.' She rattled her chains, then putting on a coquettish smile she minced forward. '"I have been toiling and moiling for the prettiest piece of china, my dear . . ." – You see, I know all the fashionable plays.'

'But Countess, I hate the playhouse, and you know I do. I don't want to do it. I don't like players, madam. I don't trust 'em.'

'You turned down an opportunity to earn the money for my release simply because the playhouse is your aversion?' The Countess turned on Alpiew with a dramatic flounce. 'Very nice.' She gulped and glanced back to the bailiff's wife. 'The girl is as good as my own daughter, and yet she is prepared to let me languish in perpetual imprisonment, rather than go to work at the playhouse!' She assumed another posture. 'And half of London would claw her eyes out if they could have her chance. Take me back to my cell, please, Mrs Turnkey. Oh that ever I was born to see such ingratitude.'

'Dear madam . . .' Alpiew reached out, but the Countess turned and flung her hand away.

'Don't you "Dear madam" me, you thankless child. Go, Alpiew! Go! Thou serpent nurtured at my own bosom.'

Alpiew turned to leave.

'And why are you here, anyway? You should be at Westminster Hall this morning, minx.'

Utterly bewildered, Alpiew left the sponging house, marched past the entrance to the Royal Mews and down towards Westminster.

How had she forgotten about Rakewell's trial? She realised she was failing the Countess in every way. What a dreadful day. How she wished it was over.

As usual the traffic in Whitehall was at a standstill. Postilions stood on top of their coaches screaming at each other to make way, while hay carts and private chairs trying to overtake the larger vehicles had blocked the pedestrians' way. Scores of workmen lounged around the Banqueting House, the only surviving building of Whitehall Palace since it burned down. Most of them lay basking in the sun, like lazy swine upon a warm dunghill, thought Alpiew. Somehow one never saw most of them do a jot of work. But the more industrious workers stood in the road, stirring pots of boiling pitch and carrying planks and wheelbarrows back and forth across the ruins, only adding to the chaos.

Everyone was stuck. Alpiew squeezed herself between the wall and the side of a stagecoach to get through Holbein Gate and joined a stream of walkers climbing up and over various stationary carts and carriages. All around her men were whistling and catcalling as she leapt down and her skirts caught in the wind. She made a rude gesture back and shoved into an alley where she knew that after manoeuvring through a busy market she would emerge at New Palace Yard, and the front entrance to Westminster Hall.

It had never occurred to Alpiew that the Countess would be so upset by her decision not to act. Or was it because she had been *asked* to act and not the Countess? Alpiew was at her wits' end.

Lawyers and parliamentarians stood in intense huddles, plotting their business, and the usual crush of street pedlars and pick-pockets swirled around them. Alpiew pushed through and entered the lofty hall. Did the Countess seriously want to go upon the stage? More to the point, would she be jealous if Alpiew now went ahead and accepted Rebecca's proposal? She was perplexed beyond thought. She loathed the frenzied state of Westminster: the noise of the tradesmen echoed in the vaulted ceiling.

'The royal unparalleled wash-ball,' screamed a stallholder with a voice like a corncrake. 'With admirable virtue for cleansing the skin from all discolour, such as sunburn, freckles, swarthy, yellow, or tawny colour.' The woman's own complexion wasn't much of an advertisement, thought Alpiew as she strode past.

'The excellent and by other nations called Tay,' yelled a man holding tiny packets. 'Alias Tea. The sovereign drink of pleasure and health. Infinitely more good than any other, for by its peculiar operation and effects it cures the most stubborn and dangerous distempers of the head, such as apoplexies, epilepsies, lethargies, vishegoes, megrims, pains in the head . . .' Alpiew paused at the man's stall. Perhaps the Countess would be placated with a present of some tea. '. . . Humours in the eyes, giddiness, vapours, loss of memory, deafness, worms in the teeth, etcetera. Two papers at most times making a perfect cure. Only four shilling the pack, with directions.'

'Talking of directions,' Alpiew panted, 'which way to Rakewell's trial?'

'Buy a pack and I'll tell you,' said the man with a wink.

'Four shillings!' said Alpiew. 'How much tea is in each pack?'

'Excellent value,' said the man. 'At one shilling an ounce, you won't find as fine a tea cheaper, without you go to China for it.'

Alpiew gave the man a withering look.

'It's not my fault tea's this price. Blame the government. Ninety per cent is tax.'

Alpiew marched away, passing book and print sellers howling out their wares. 'All the latest scandal in the Indies.' 'Murder most foul!' 'A paper by the eminent oculist, chirugeon to King William.' 'The worst maladies revealed, altogether without mercury.'

Alpiew jostled past. Why were there no sign-posts in this wretched place? Where was the court? '. . . Wherein both sexes may, without being exposed to quacks, cure themselves of that distemper which is dangerous and ignominious. Only a shilling.'

'The past misdemeanours of Lord Rakewell. Read the lives of those cut down by the rebellious young lord, on trial this very afternoon.' Alpiew jumped into action. She ran to the pamphlet-pusher and asked him in which chamber Rakewell's trial was taking place, purchasing a copy of *The Misdemeanours of Lord Rakewell* for good measure.

By the time Alpiew took her seat in the gallery of the House of Lords, Rakewell was in the dock.

From her seat at the back she could only see his face when she leaned forward and peered round a post, but she could hear his testimony clear as a bell.

'And after the unfortunate death of Tobias Flynn, esquire, you were picked up by some chairmen, one of whom testifies that you were carrying a drawn sword. Was the blade bloody?'

'It was a steel sword, my lord,' replied Rakewell with a dignified smile, his smooth pink cheeks emphasising his youth.

'And while the man lay dying in Leicester Fields . . .'

What kind of answer was that? Alpiew couldn't believe that the judge had not pressed Rakewell further on the bloody sword. 'It was a steel sword', indeed. She felt like yelling out: 'Steel, yes, but was it bloody?'

'You refused to let the chairmen lift their chair over the railings to retrieve Mr Flynn and carry him off to the chirugeon who might have saved his life?'

'It was not so much that I refused, my lord. But I could see that, if they were having so much difficulty raising a chair over the railings, with the extra weight of a man within it, the same chair would be *impossible* to retrieve across the same railings. It was simple deduction. I applied my intelligence, my lord, as anyone would have done. My purpose was to save time, in order to save the life of Mr Flynn.'

Alpiew surveyed the Bench made up of more than eighty lords, slumped in their leather seats, dressed in all their ermine and red velvet finery with glittering coronets perched on their periwigs, and shuddered. What a doddering crew! Old enough to be Rakewell's grandfather, the lot of them.

'Now, Lord Rakewell, these wounds, fatal to Flynn, were two: one down from the collarbone, five inches deep, the other six inches under the left ribs, and perforating the diaphragm. You are an excellent swordsman, my lord, am I right?'

'Not really.' Rakewell gave a modest little bob towards the Lord Chancellor. 'I am average. But on that evening, you may recall I told you that earlier, in a silly brawl in the tavern I had hurt my finger. And as a result my swordsmanship that particular night would have been no good. No good at all. A drawer from the Rummer Tavern can speak for me on that point.' He flashed a deferential smile at the judges. 'For the drawer wrapped the injured finger with a napkin soaked in Rhenish wine.'

'And where were the watchmen throughout all this kerfuffle? Surely the sound of a pitched fight in the quiet of Leicester Fields would have attracted their attention?'

'They did come, my lord,' said Rakewell, affecting a serious tone. 'But when I pointed out to them that a crime might have taken place, they simply told me they could do nothing about it, Leicester Fields not being within their ward.'

'So why had they come to Leicester Fields?'

'I believe the boundary of their ward takes in the southern-most side of Leicester Fields, but Flynn was lying on the other side of the railings, and was therefore outside it.'

Alpiew sighed. The case was over. With that last statement the boy had practically admitted his guilt! He had evaded the truth on every point, except for the ones when he supplied it, only to condemn himself further. Without a qualm he had just announced that it was he himself who ensured that the dying man was left on the wrong side of the fence, outside the jurisdiction or assistance of the watch! Alpiew looked around the gallery. Miss Gymcrack sat not far from her. She was holding a dainty handkerchief up to her face, revealing only red eyes. Small wonder, thought Alpiew. Her wedding would have to take place on a gibbet.

'And why did you keep changing cloaks that night, Lord Rakewell?'

'Did I?' Rakewell cocked his head and affected a puzzled expression.

'The drawer describes you wearing a black cloak, while your friend Simpson was in a blue cloak. Yet the chairmen say *you* were in the blue cloak, and the watchmen have you back in a black cloak?'

'Perhaps they confused me and my friend, for we stayed in the same cloaks all evening.' He gave a little laugh. 'And, my lords, I should remind you that it was midnight on a moonless night. Don't they say "At night all cats are grey"? I should like to submit to you that at midnight all cloaks are black. Unless of course they are blue.'

The lords chuckled. A bell was ringing outside the court. The lords started to rustle in their seats, some even took out watches and checked them. It was time for lunch.

'So my lords, I think we can say that the inquiry has heard enough evidence.' The Lord Chancellor looked about him. 'I need not remind you that Lord Rakewell represents the budding flower and tender leaf of the nobility. Let us take a vote. Is my Lord Rakewell guilty or not guilty of the wilful murder of Tobias Flynn, esquire?'

'Lord Peebles?'

'Not guilty.'

Alpiew strained forward to hear better, sure the echo in the hall must be distorting the sound, for she could swear the noble lord had said 'Not' before the 'guilty'.

'Lord Solihull?'

'Not guilty.'

Alpiew stared down into the hall, trying to look at the lords' lips.

'Lord Wilton?'

'Not guilty.'

'Not', 'not', 'not' . . . and so it went on. Before Alpiew's very eyes, and against all the evidence, all eighty-seven elderly lords voted the young Lord Rakewell a free man.

'I am not cut out for the life of a player, Mrs Montagu,' Alpiew pleaded. 'Could I not assist you by holding your properties, or cleaning your place in the tiring room? There must be a thousand things I could do in order to undertake the role of a bodyguard, and to help find the murderer of your colleague, Mrs Lucas?'

Rebecca stamped her foot. Alpiew had seen this gesture quite a few times by now, and gathered it was quite one of Mrs Montagu's trademarks.

'Repeat: "*No boding crows nor ravens come*
To warn her of approaching doom . . ."'

'If you go on any longer, I will have forgotten the start,' Alpiew interrupted. 'And why teach me the words of a role I will not play?'

'It is to sharpen your understanding, miss.'

Alpiew shot her a surly look. She didn't like that use of the word 'miss', an appellation used only for children and saucy harlots. 'How did it go again?'

'Forget the speech.' Rebecca flung herself into a chair and flicked her hair from her face. This training session was not going as smoothly as she had hoped. 'Let us start on Action. Action is motion, and motion is the support of Nature, which 'without it would sink again into the sluggish mass of Chaos . . .'

'Excuse me, Mrs Montagu, but what are you talking about . . . ?'

A sharp rap on the front door interrupted the actress before she could reply. 'Get that. Sarah is out on an errand.'

Alpiew bit her tongue and headed for the door. Signior Lampone was standing on the steps, his silver nose shining brightly in the reflected light of the hall mirrors. 'I am come for my session with Mrs Montagu,' he announced, pulling off his hat and striding in.

Alpiew showed him into the living room.

'Signior Lampone!' cried Rebecca, as though surprised to see him. 'How lovely.'

'I need to . . . You know what . . .' He whipped a tape-measure from his pocket and turned to Alpiew. 'If I may have a few moments with Mrs Montagu, please.'

Delighted for a minute's peace, Alpiew slouched out.

On her way from Westminster Hall she had stopped to purchase a small booklet on the expression of the Passions. She could use the time trying some of them out in front of one of the looking glasses in the hall.

Eyebrows pressed forward over eyes. Alpiew frowned. Eyes more than usually open. Alpiew alternated between the book and the mirror. She started to smile at the sight of herself and had to start again. What a business! Eyebrows, eyes, nostrils pinched and drawn up towards eyes. Mouth slightly open. Corners slightly back. Tongue on edge of lips. Right. She inspected herself in the glass. This was supposed to look like Desire. She thought she looked half-baked, a potential candidate for Bedlam. She threw the book down. She would never make a player.

She could hear the dark murmur of voices from Rebecca's living room.

She tiptoed up to the door and applied her ear to the thin wooden panels.

'Such a pretty neck,' murmured Lampone. 'It is sad we must separate it from the body.'

'But the head,' muttered Rebecca, 'is ofttimes more

strangely beautiful without the hindrance of a body supporting it, don't you think?'

Alpiew gasped, then crammed her hand across her mouth. Barely breathing, she tried to listen again, but her heart seemed to be beating too loudly, and the rushing in her ears was deafening.

''Tis a pity you didn't attempt another,' whispered Rebecca. 'Anne Lucas deserved to . . .'

The mumbling grew darker, it was hard to pick up phrases, just the odd word. 'Money' recurred a few times, and 'Head . . . Murderers . . .'

Alpiew jumped and caught her breath as the dog appeared at her feet, giving her the usual disdainful look.

She re-applied her ear to the door. Silence, and footsteps approaching.

Alpiew dived up the corridor and started pulling faces into the looking glass.

With a doleful expression, Signior Lampone was taking his leave. Rebecca summoned Alpiew back into her master class, as Lampone descended the stairs to the street.

'Have you got that line mastered?'

Alpiew looked at her suspiciously. What was she talking about?

'"*No boding crows nor ravens come*
To warn her of approaching doom . . ."?'

'Mrs Montagu,' said Alpiew with determination, 'I will never make a player. But, as agreed, I would like to assist you in the search for Mrs Lucas's killer.' Alpiew grabbed the moment. 'I wonder if perhaps you don't know more than you are telling me?'

Rebecca flinched. She was gripping on to the back of a chair until her knuckles showed white, and she clearly chose her words carefully. 'Of the murder of my colleague, I know nothing. That is why I came to you.' With a sudden toss of the head she turned on Alpiew. 'Are you going to help me, or am I wasting my time?'

'Perhaps it would serve more purpose if I spent some time asking you more questions on that score?'

'What questions?' Rebecca was jumpy. 'I know nothing. She was murdered, that's all I know. You were there. What more can I tell you?'

'You can tell me about Anne Lucas, for a start. The woman. Why would anyone have cause to kill her?'

Alpiew noticed the slight pause before she started. 'She was a bore,' said Rebecca with a sigh. 'Always going on about her home life, as though it made her better than the rest of us.'

'And what of her home life?'

'Who knows? Who cares?' Rebecca twirled a ring on her smallest finger. 'I never listened. If it wasn't her gorgeous husband, or her sweet child, it was how an ounce of cheese was cheaper at this stall than that, or how you could get a penny off a loaf in a certain market at a certain time of day.' She let out a huge groan. 'She was just *so* domestic. She simply didn't have the soul of an artist.'

'But she was successful, I believe?'

'Men!' Rebecca snorted. 'They like small women. They think that because they're the same height as children they'll be as pliable.'

'She flirted a lot?'

'Not at all. But that's a charm too, isn't it? She was too, too modest and retiring for words. Not quite the professional virgin, but maybe the professional Madonna. Homely and inaccessible.'

'Did she have many admirers?'

'Real admirers or the rabble?'

'Either.' Alpiew wondered what the difference might be.

'One presumes her husband was a real admirer. As for the others, we all have them. Even the men, and the fat wrinkled old women who specialise in the roles of duennas, harridans and maids.'

'Could one of those phanatiques be spinning out of control, perhaps?'

Rebecca let out a huge laugh and leaped to her feet. 'Are

any of them *in* control?' She opened a drawer in a large carved oak chest. 'Here are some of my trophies.' She pulled out piles of letters, home-knitted gloves, scarves, pieces of perfumed silk, small dolls, boxes of sweetmeats, trinkets. 'And I may point out, these are only *this* season's spoils. Since September. Six months' worth of unsolicited presents from theatre fanatics. At the end of each year I get rid of them all.'

Alpiew sifted through the drawer in amazement. It was like a stall at a market. 'What do these people want in return?'

Rebecca picked up a particularly revolting knitted doll. 'To touch me as I pass, hoping I might notice them and bestow a smile upon them. It's as though since King William stopped touching people for the King's Evil, players are expected to do that service instead. The only difference being that the phanatiques are not afflicted with the scrofula, only with lunacy.'

Alpiew cast her mind back to the crowds outside the concert hall, how demanding they seemed. And how intense.

'The highest accolade is to mention them by name. I make sure *never* to do that. But Anne Lucas, she remembered each and every one.' Rebecca went into a little performance. '"Good afternoon, Martin. Why are you here again? Sure, you have seen this piece three times now." "John, how lovely, thank you so much for the 'kerchief." "Sam, you are SOOO kind, the sweetmeats were delicious." It was a repulsive sight.'

'Mr Cibber gives out sweetmeats to the phanatiques.'

'Cibber is a creeping, crawling, oozing sycophant. He flirts with the actors, the audience, the managers, the phanatiques. In short, he woos *everyone*, with one exception.'

'And who is that?'

'His wife, of course.'

'Why not her?'

'Because he has won her already. And now she is nobody. She used to be an actress. He thought it important that one of them should give up to look after the other. He keeps her at home and treats her like a breed mare crossed with a slave from the sugar plantations.'

'You don't like Cibber?'

'No one likes him. His own father-in-law wouldn't even come to the wedding. Just to be sure Mr Cibber didn't get his hands on any of it, the old man spent all his money – and it was a very great fortune – building that floating pleasure palace on the Thames.'

'The *Folly*?' Alpiew knew the place.

'Not that it mattered really. Cibber's a wily fellow. He must already possess a fortune, if his gambling is anything to judge by.'

'He's rich? From what?'

'Acting, writing, creeping, crawling . . .'

Alpiew was forming an idea regarding Cibber. If he had money to spare, she would ask him to lend her some, then she could get the Countess instantly released.

'How did Cibber get on with Mrs Lucas?'

'It depended on what he wanted. I know he chased her around a bit.'

'Chased?'

'Oh, you know, tried to feel her bubbies, stood too close in the wings, the usual things. At least I can deal with that sort of thing.' She sighed. 'When you care not what people think about you, you can tell them where to go. Anne Lucas wanted everyone to like her, so she said nothing, and therefore it got worse. Then she'd rush into the tiring room in floods of tears because he'd snatched a kiss. If she'd simply slapped his smirking chops at the start it never would have gone that far.'

'What about Anne's husband, Mr Lucas?'

'I can certainly imagine him wanting to kill her. All that relentless niceness would drive anyone to murder.'

The mantel clock chimed the hour.

'We'll be late.' Rebecca rushed round collecting things and throwing them into a leather bag. 'I need you to understand, Alpiew, you have to be out there with me on stage. You, or someone I can trust.'

'But why on stage? Surely no one can kill you there.'

'Oh, the public!' Rebecca laughed. 'You all see the stage as another world.' She leaned across the table and spoke seriously. 'We are feet away from the audience. If someone chooses to leap upon the stage and slash my throat with his sword, it would happen in the flash of an eye . . . I wouldn't be at all prepared, I'd be too busy concentrating on what I was doing.'

'So I would need to keep watching the audience . . .' Alpiew could see an escape route. 'And if I had lines to speak, you must see, Mrs Montagu, that I could not do that.'

'Perhaps the threat wouldn't come from the audience. Perhaps it was a player who killed Lucas, and that player could stab me on stage. For all the audience knew, it would be part of the show. People are always getting stabbed in plays, and sometimes the player claims to have got a little carried away with his role. What if someone substitutes a real dagger for the blunt stage prop? It could easily happen.'

'It seems to me,' said Alpiew firmly, 'I could never remember lines and actions and gestures *and* concentrate on guarding you at the same time. It would be better if I found a pivotal point in the theatre where I could keep an eye on the other players and the audience at all times during your performances.'

'Come along' – Rebecca glanced at the mantel clock – 'or I'll be fined.' She grabbed Alpiew's wrist. 'You win. You will hold my train. That's easy enough to do. No lines.'

She was already out of the room and half-way down the stairs, Alpiew stumbling behind her.

'But . . . Mrs Montagu, I cannot . . . I must visit my lady.'

'Visit?' Rebecca turned on the step. 'What do you mean "visit"?'

Alpiew bit her lip. 'To let her know what I am doing.'

Rebecca gave her a penetrating look. 'We're going to be late, and if we're late we get fined.' Then, grabbing her hand, she dragged Alpiew along Little Hart Street.

The Countess had not enjoyed her lunch: a dry piece of bread, which she was sure was all chalk, and some kind of stew. She had no idea what. It could as easily have been haddock as rabbit. She slid her plate away. Suddenly even Godfrey's cooking seemed something to look forward to. And infinitely cheaper.

Her debt now had already gone up ten shillings. For the lodging, the gaol fee, the bed fee, the overnight fee, the food fee. It was never ending.

She stood up and took a few steps round the room. Lord, but these chains weighed a ton. Rattle, rattle, clink, clink, every time she scratched an eyebrow. She was glad there wasn't a glass in the room. She dreaded to think what she must look like. There were more chunks of make-up perched in her cleavage and sprinkled round the floor than there could possibly be left on her face.

She wondered what Alpiew was doing. The thought of that pert little miss as a player! She imagined Alpiew would be rather good. The Countess remembered that player friend of Charles's, Nell Gwyn. She was a pert little miss, too. The woman might have been a perfect ignoramus, but no one could deny she was a fine player, and had the figure for it.

Downstairs she heard a door bang. Then footsteps. Perhaps she had a visitor. Or maybe it was another prisoner, come to break the monotony. She applied her ear to the door and listened.

'I spoke to the Justice,' said a gruff male voice. It was not the bailiff, the Countess was sure. 'About the Anne Lucas business . . .' The Countess tried to hold her breath to hear better.

'And?' That was her gaoler, the bailiff's wife.

'I was worried at first. There's no creature so obstinate as a godly man.'

'You didn't take it to Justice Moore?'

'Justice Moore!' The man laughed. 'What kind of fopdoodle do you take me for? I went to Ingram.'

'And you reminded him of his . . . interests?'

'He understood your problem. He could see that having a crime like that committed upon your very doorstep – for to

tell true, 'tis only a spit away from here – would be a worry
to you.'

So the bailiff's wife was worried by the proximity of the
killing!

'So what's he going to do?'

'He said he would look into it.'

'Look into it!' spat the bailiff's wife. 'Phough, what good is
that? 'Twould only make matters worse. Too many other
people will get hurt.'

'Calm yourself.' The gruff man pitched his voice even lower.
'He will get the matter wrapped up, finished, closed.'

'That sounds easier than it is.' The bailiff's wife now took
to whispering: '. . . Too many interested parties. Where will
he lay the blame?'

'There are many choices,' said the man. 'Another player,
perhaps, a vagrant . . . anyone.'

'Best find some itinerant.' The woman seemed calmed. 'No
one would care if they saw one of those swindling fellows
dancing on the end of a rope. Jack and I can get that sorted.
The watch pick them up by the hour.' She started to walk
downstairs again, the man following. 'Tell one of your fellows
to get me a weapon to lay upon the fellow, to prove his guilt
for all the world to see.'

Then the front door slammed, and the Countess could hear
the bailiff's wife start singing to herself as she flicked a duster
round the house.

When Alpiew and Rebecca arrived at the theatre quite a few
people were gathered, but the rehearsal had not begun.
Rebecca went to the tiring room to prepare herself.

Mr Rich was sitting in a box smoking a pipe. Alpiew
approached him.

'Mr Rich, sir?'

Rich peered at her. 'Yes?'

Alpiew lowered her voice: 'I wondered whether you could
give me an advance against the puffs?'

Rich let out a snort. 'You jest, I presume?'

'Nine guineas?' Alpiew looked eagerly at him. 'Or a loan, perhaps, which I could also set against the puffs?'

'No.' He slammed his fist down on the ledge and growled. 'You deliver – then I pay, and not a penny more than our agreement. Understood?' He shouted the last word.

On stage a boy balanced on a rickety step-ladder was slowly lighting the candles on two huge wooden chandeliers over the stage. He let out a squeal as the ladder toppled precariously. Alpiew ran to steady it, glad to have an easy exit from the awful Mr Rich. Once the boy was stable again, Alpiew looked down from the stage into the pit.

Mr Cibber, already in his costume and make-up, was sitting on a bench preening himself, silently mouthing his words. Alpiew jumped down and slid along the bench beside him.

'Mr Cibber,' she began.

'Mrs Alpiew' – he smiled his famous smile, and flicked at his lace cuffs – 'what can I do to assist you?'

'It's a difficult matter, Mr Cibber.'

'I know.' He nodded sympathetically. 'Nerves are bad enough when you are a trained professional . . .'

'No, it's not nerves.' Alpiew got in quickly before he started a lecture on how he'd spent so many months preparing himself for his role. 'I will only be holding Mrs Montagu's train. But you are a very successful actor, and a writer too . . .'

'Modesty,' Cibber beamed, 'prevents me from denying it.'

'I hear that your last benefit brought in a tidy sum . . .'

'Oh yes. The house was packed. Must have got eighty guineas.'

'So could you oblige me, sir, by lending me nine guineas? I can repay you within a month.'

'When I admitted to being successful . . .' He fiddled with his cravat. 'I don't mean I have any ready money . . . Overheads, you know. I have a wife to support, and children.'

'I don't ask for a gift, Mr Cibber, merely a loan. Might we say against the puffs . . . ?'

'Oh, look at the time!' He pulled out his pocket watch. 'I

must learn these lines.' His face was still fixed in his professional smile as he sidled out of the auditorium.

'How did you do that?' Rebecca was staring down at her from the stage. She was in thick stage make-up, sardonic expression drawn upon her visage. 'He never leaves the pit during rehearsal.'

'I don't know.' Alpiew shrugged. 'I only asked him for a loan.'

'A loan from that hunks!' Rebecca exploded with laughter. 'He is as tight as a nun's fundament, my dear. Wouldn't lend you the rag he'd wiped his arse with.' She sat down, swinging her legs from the side of the forestage. 'How much do you need?'

'My mistress has overlooked the Poor Rate for a few years . . .' Alpiew gulped. 'Nine guineas.'

'Oh. Now I understand. The visit!' Rebecca put her hand into her pocket. 'I take it the bailiffs have got her?'

Alpiew nodded.

'Then run along. Get her out and both of you come back here as quickly as you can. Which lock-up?'

'A sponging house at Charing Cross.'

'Free her and be back here within an hour.' She handed Alpiew the cash and climbed back up on to the stage. Alpiew gazed with awe at the money in her hand. Rebecca had given her ten pounds. The actress clearly understood the rising predicament of a debtor.

'Hurry along.' Rebecca was standing again, flouncing out her skirts for maximum effect. 'I want you back here without delay.'

'To rehearse carrying your dress?'

'I'm sure you will be able to manage that without much practice. But this afternoon rehearsals are to be cut short.' Rebecca stooped and spoke in a low voice. 'Mrs Lucas is being buried this evening at St Giles in the Fields. I know you wouldn't want to miss the funeral.'

After Alpiew had paid off the debt and garnishes as well as the fee and the Countess was released from her chains, she started to talk at once.

'So Rebecca told me . . .'

The Countess shook her head and rolled her eyes.

The bailiff's wife was in the corner of the room writing out a release note.

Alpiew started again. 'I am going to go on but not in a speaking role . . .'

The Countess had a wild coughing fit, still shaking her head, her eyes glaring wildly.

'What's the matter, madam? Are you unwell?'

'Ah, Alpiew, I cannot wait to get out in the open air. To go to my dear home and lay my head down peacefully, away from all talk . . .'

'Ah,' said Alpiew. 'That will be impossible, for a few hours at least, because Mrs Lucas is –'

The Countess lurched across the room and almost knocked Alpiew to the floor. 'Oh, poor Alpiew, have you stumbled? Dear me. Let me help you to your feet.' She started talking in a weirdly deliberate fashion. 'Then – you – and – I – can – go – home – quietly – *together*.' The Countess flicked her eyes in the direction of the bailiff's wife.

Alpiew put her finger to her lips, finally understanding. 'Yes – madam – you – are – right.'

'Here you are –' the bailiff's wife turned to face them. She held the vital piece of paper aloft, waving it in the air to help the ink dry. 'You are free to go, Countess.'

By the time they arrived at the theatre, the rehearsal had come to an end. Rich stood on the stage in the midst of the actors, their make-up gleaming with sweat in the heat of the many candles illuminating the stage.

'*You* wish to go on doing these long-winded plays.' Rich clapped his hands together. 'But I tell you the public don't want it. We won't make a profit with this bombast.'

'It keeps them going well enough at the other house . . .' George was raising his voice, slurred with the leery tone of a couple of brimmers of sherry already downed.

The Countess, delighted to be free, slid along a baize-covered bench at the back of the pit with Alpiew. On the walk from the sponging house they had told each other all developments, and were now separately lost in thought, while the actors had some sort of policy discussion with their manager.

'I only tell you,' said Rich, in the kind of voice normally saved for addressing children, 'that the addition of a rope-dance between the scenes and a short dance by a troupe of performing dogs in the last act will better attract the crowds.'

'You cannot seriously' – Cibber was looking tight-lipped – 'put a dancing dog into the last act of Nat Lee's famous verse tragedy.'

'Why, pray? It would stand in place of the dance by Indians.'

The players stood gaping in disbelief.

'Why such astonishment?' Rich flicked a stray thread from the front of his jacket. 'William Shakespeare employed just such tricks and diversions in all his plays.'

'Precisely why no one does them any more,' said Cibber, 'and why I am having to rewrite *Richard III* to suit more modern tastes.'

'I tell you, Mr Rich, if a dancing dog makes an appearance either before or after my great speech' – Rebecca stepped forward, a black scowl on her face – 'I will walk from the stage and home to my lodgings, and will never appear here more.'

'Maybe that would be for the best.' Rich picked at a fingernail. 'I seem to remember that Mrs Lucas once made such a threat – and look what became of *her*.'

The assembled company fell silent for a moment, then Rebecca lurched forward and fell upon Rich, battering his chest with both fists. 'Vile villain! Foul, filthy, murdering toad.'

'Mrs Montagu –' Rich threw her to the floor. 'Might I remind you that women players are two a penny. Look how little time it took me to fill Lucas's role.' He pointed to an artless blonde standing simpering near Cibber. 'Women of a certain type want to get on the stage. Some of them would gladly pay *me* for the opportunity. They see it as a shop-window for their . . . shall we say, their "charms".'

Cibber took a step away from the buxom wench.

'You yourself, Mrs Montagu, have made a tidy profit advertising yourself on these boards . . .' Rich pouted and imitated Rebecca's famous stamp.

'How can you talk like this?' Rebecca started battering him again. 'You are talking about a woman who has only a few days past been robbed of her life, and to whose funeral we will shortly repair.'

'Rebecca is right,' said Cibber. 'I think you should make an apology.'

George entered the fray. 'Calm yourself, madam.' He pulled Rebecca from Rich. 'Ladies should not kill but with their eyes.'

'Stand off, you drivelling drunkard,' snarled Rebecca. 'Or I'll scratch *your* eyes out.'

Cibber had drifted upstage, off the playing apron and past the proscenium arch. He wandered in and out of the painted scenery flats. 'Let us continue with the business at hand, Mr Rich.' Standing at the far end of a long faux perspective of a castle hall, he looked like a giant. 'Might I suggest that, since you have already removed yards from the front of the stage so as to cram more of the paying public in the pit, you will certainly make more of a profit without the deployment of the prancing canine comedians.'

'This once, perhaps.' Rich continued to brush down his expensive velvet jacket. 'No doubt the tragic loss of Mrs Lucas will drag the curious to our theatre anyhow.' He smirked, then turned and looked down at the Countess and Alpiew. 'Whenever our two friends from the *Trumpet* get around to mentioning it in their column, the public will be queuing round the block.'

Alpiew flushed. Nothing inclined her less to puff than this hideous display of avarice and self-interest.

'Perhaps, Mr Rich, you should put it in your playbills, and plaster it over every post in Town.' The Countess rose and surveyed the assembly. '"Drury Lane Theatre – hotbed of greed, corruption and murder!" Listen. The bells are ringing six. Alpiew and I intend to attend Anne Lucas's funeral, and to be there on time. I expect neither the priest nor the upholders will wait for you. So if you wish to pay your respects to a poor dead woman who was only yesterday your friend and colleague, I suggest you leave with us now.'

The entire company turned and looked down at the Countess. 'I might note that not one of you seems the least upset. Where are the tears that brim so artfully at each tragedy's denouement? Where are the breast-thumpings and the heart-rending cries you are so famed for? None of you cares a damn. Poor little Anne Lucas has been brutally murdered and still you squabble over trifles.' She grabbed Alpiew's hand. 'Or are you saving up your emotions for public display in the graveyard?'

Rich jumped down into the pit. 'Not so fast, ladies.' He leapt over the green benches and stood blocking their exit. 'You have an agreement with me . . .'

'Hold your clack, you maw-wallop,' said Alpiew, taking the Countess's elbow and marching onwards. 'We have no agreement with anybody. Prithee let us pass, or we will call a constable and have you charged with false imprisonment.'

Rich did not move.

'You heard her, you uncivil toad. Make way.' The Countess shoved him aside.

Alpiew tugged the door open.

A muscle was twitching in Rich's cheek as he took a sideways step and allowed them through the door.

Rebecca swung out behind them. 'I will share a hackney coach with you, ladies, if I may?' She smiled, and pointed down the road. 'The nearest stand is that way. Walk on. I will catch you.'

As Alpiew and the Countess descended the steps to the street, Rebecca turned and faced the other actors now emerging behind her.

'She wants to get rid of us for the moment, I think,' said the Countess, glancing back over her shoulder. 'What's happening now?' The Countess faced the other way, and whispered, 'Watch and note everything. I will pretend not to see while I look for a hackney cab.'

Alpiew also feigned looking up the street while whispering a commentary. 'Rebecca whispers to Rich. Rich shakes his head in reply. Rebecca gestures exasperation and moves on to Cibber, who gives a shrug and pulls his pockets inside out. Ouch! Rebecca has slapped him roundly across the chops.' She turned back to face the Countess. 'Lord, milady, she seems to wallop anyone who comes in her sphere.' She slyly sneaked another look back. 'Rebecca moves on to George, who holds out his hand to her. She takes something, then, inspecting it, laughs and throws . . . some coins to the floor. He seems to be giving her money . . .'

'Perhaps she can't afford a hackney coach any more than we can.' The Countess chortled. 'Madam Hoity-Toit.'

'Oops!' Alpiew grabbed the Countess by the arm and steered her briskly down Drury Lane. 'She's heading our way.'

'There's one,' Rebecca called in her throaty voice, hailing a hackney and holding a hand out for the driver to stop. She held the carriage door open for the Countess then moved to speak to the driver. 'St Giles, please, by way of Little Hart Street.'

'I have forgot my mourning ring,' she explained, climbing in, then the horse trotted off into Covent Garden. 'I cannot be seen at Anne Lucas's funeral without a mourning ring.'

The Countess pressed Alpiew's foot with her own.

Outside her home, Rebecca jumped out and slapped the side of the coach. Before the Countess and Alpiew knew it, the cab moved off, without waiting. Alpiew stuck her head out of the window and screamed up at the coachman to halt.

'She said not to wait,' he yelled back.

'Oh lord, Alpiew!' The Countess clutched her pocket. 'Have we money enough?'

The driver turned round and peered into the cab. 'That's that actress, ain't it? Tell you who I drove once . . . What's his name? The Italian singer with no nuts . . .'

'Signior Fideli?' suggested the Countess, referring to a celebrated castrati who had recently taken the town by storm.

'That's the fellah. Nice chap. Big tipper.'

'Really!' The Countess watched Alpiew count out the pence on her lap.

When they arrived at the church the Countess peered out. Despite the drizzle the public were already pressing round the lych gate. Alpiew clambered out and looked up at the driver. 'How much?'

'Nah,' he smirked. 'Roxana already paid me.'

'Who?'

'Rebecca Montagu – she that plays Roxana so famously.'

Trying not to look surprised, the two women walked towards the churchyard as the hackney rattled away towards Seven Dials. 'What's she after?' hissed Alpiew.

'Don't ask me,' said the Countess as they pushed through the crowd, heading for the gate. 'It seems to me that everyone even vaguely related to this business has something to hide.'

'Who're they?' One of the phanatiques was leaning over the wall to get a better view of the mourners.

'Nobody,' replied his friend, looking back to see if any real celebrities were following them.

'I never thought I would be so content to be described as a nobody.' The Countess hoiked up her skirts and strode into the churchyard of St Giles in the Fields. It was bleak. Despite being on the edge of Town and with fields only yards away, it seemed greyer and more depressing than any other graveyard that Alpiew had ever seen. 'What's wrong with this place?' said Alpiew. 'Why is it so sad?'

The Countess looked around at the gravestones, stacked so closely, like dominoes.

'The plague started round here. Hundreds were buried in the first week. No one knew what it was then. Just some mystery disease. Puritans said it was because we were all so promiscuous, and enjoyed ourselves frequenting theatres and taverns.' She reached out a hand and took Alpiew's. 'Poor little Alpiew. It took your parents, of course, but for me that was a blessing because then you were brought to me.'

Alpiew shuddered. She didn't even know her parents' names.

For all she knew they lay here under her feet, represented by any of this myriad of slabs.

'It was before anyone realised they were going to need great open pits for the thousands who were to die each week.'

The Countess stared across at the upholders, who had dug a hole for Anne Lucas's coffin, and were now cleaning up the edges, ready for the funeral. 'How do they know where there's a space between all the bodies?'

A sudden surge from the crowd outside the gate alerted them to the arrival of the players.

Alpiew noted that Cibber was wearing his fixed public smile but had added an element of tragic sadness to it. The eyebrows up in the middle and drawn down at the sides. The eyes downcast. He'd obviously studied it well in the glass before coming out today.

'No sign of Madam Roxana,' hissed the Countess.

Another hackney drew up and a small apprentice boy jumped out carrying what looked like a large jewel case. He pushed into the graveyard and leaned against a gravestone near the gate while unlocking his box. He pulled a list from the box and skimmed it as though trying to memorise what was upon it, then gathered a handful of rings from the box.

He looked round the churchyard. Discreetly he stepped towards the players, who were standing in a gang by the church door with the officiating priest. 'Mr Rich?' As Rich nodded the boy discreetly handed him a ring. 'Mourning rings, sir. Sorry they are late. There was a mix-up at the goldsmith, sir. Mrs Lucas left notice in her will for mourning rings to be provided for you all.' The boy moved along the line, handing out rings, and uttering the names of the recipients. 'Mr Cibber, Mr Powell . . .' The Countess noticed that Cibber shot George a questioning look.

There was another commotion outside and the crowd pressed forward. The coach carrying the coffin had arrived. The priest gave a signal and strode down the path to start the ceremony. 'I am the resurrection and the life, saith the Lord: he that believeth in me, though he were dead, yet shall he live:

and whosoever liveth and believeth in me shall never die.'

'Still no Mrs Montagu,' whispered the Countess into Alpiew's ear, while the pall-bearers trundled the coffin into the church. 'And, more to the point: no Mr Lucas.'

'Thou hast set our misdeeds before thee: and our secret sins in the light of thy countenance . . .'

Alpiew and the Countess knelt in pews at the back of the church and watched the others as the priest droned on.

'. . . For when thou art angry all our days are gone: we bring our years to an end, as it were a tale that is told.'

The door pushed open, and Signior Lampone sidled in. He made a genuflection and moved into the pew opposite, silver nose a-glimmer in the light of the tall windows.

'Papist!' Alpiew elbowed the Countess. 'Did you note?'

'All Italians are, I believe.'

'Look at that,' said Alpiew, indicating a nasty crack in the floor.

'The dead rising up!' The Countess gave Alpiew a wink. 'As they putrefy. I told you they buried too many people here.'

The coffin was trundled out into the drizzle again, for the burial.

Alpiew glanced at the crowd of theatre phanatiques pressing against the iron railings, jostling to get a sight of the actors as though this was just another show.

'Madam?' She touched the Countess's elbow. At the roadside was a large black coach. A man in a long dark wig leaned out. He was grinning a demonic grin.

'Who is that?' the Countess whispered to Alpiew.

'Looks a mighty strange cove to me, madam.'

'Her husband has turned up.' Rich whispered loud enough for them both to hear. All the players turned momentarily towards the coach and back again to the grave.

'Anne's husband?' said Alpiew to Cibber.

He nodded and stooped to gather a handful of earth, while the Countess turned to give the coach closer attention.

'He's not alone,' she murmured. 'Look, Alpiew, he has a woman with him.'

'The last enemy that shall be destroyed is death. For he hath put all things under his feet.'

Each player tossed his handful of earth on to the coffin and turned away.

'And she has her arms around him,' added Alpiew.

'O death, where is thy sting? O grave, where is thy victory?'

Just then a small gig arrived with Rebecca on board. She jumped off. She was looking furious.

The crowd turned away from the churchyard to watch her.

'The sting of death is sin, and the strength of sin is the law.'

'Poor Anne Lucas,' said the Countess, tossing her handful of earth on to the coffin. 'Not even allowed the leading role at her own funeral.'

Rebecca stopped at Mr Lucas's coach. As she put her face to the open window, Lucas could be seen to grab her face and kiss her on the lips.

'Before everyone!' the Countess shrieked. 'The little madam.'

Rebecca took hold of Mr Lucas's hand, patted it, then, looking intently across the wall first at the grave and then at the players around it, walked quickly away.

FOUR

Wonder

The first and most temperate of the Passions.

If there is any facial change, it is the mere raising of one eyebrow. The eye fixed upon the object which causes the wonder.

When the service was over, the Countess and Alpiew walked briskly down through Seven Dials, watching out for the notorious Irish pick-pockets who worked the area. It was now dark, and the roads they had to take had scant lighting.

They only slowed down as they crossed the Covent Garden Piazza. The square glowed with a hundred links. Taverns spilled their customers out of doors. Under the portico of the church, prostitutes with vizard masks were doing a brisk trade.

'Almost home.' Alpiew rattled the coins in her pocket and gave the Countess a sly look. 'Shall we use up the last few pennies on a small supper hereabouts?'

'Rather than face one of Godfrey's ox-cheek broths?' A twinkle came into the Countess's eye. 'Have at you for a mischievous wench! Let's do it.'

They took a table in a small room at the Blackamoor's Head, and ordered a nine-penny special. Alpiew went for the oyster pie, the Countess chose hogs' light pudding with stewed salads.

They sat chewing in silence, both turning over the events of the last few days.

'Milady?' Alpiew gulped down a spoonful of oyster. 'Do you not think we are in a strange position?'

'Why so?'

'We are in the employ of a person who wishes us to find a murderer, and that person . . .'

'Most probably committed the murder. Yes, I was pondering that. Mark you, they all had a grudge against Anne Lucas.' The Countess screwed up her face, causing a chunk of white make-up to fall into the gravy in her spoon. 'Rebecca may make it clearer at every turn that she despised the woman; but look at the others. Mr Mackerel . . .'

'Do you really forget his name, each time you call him a different fish?' Alpiew toyed with a sop of bread.

'I think he's full of himself.' The Countess gave her a coy smile. 'I enjoy watching him panic each time I get it wrong.'

'A perfect torture for a player as conceited as he.'

'Yes, yes, I know. So what have we, Alpiew? Note it down.'

Alpiew took out a pencil and paper from her pocket.

'We know from my stay in the sponging house that shortly someone will be apprehended for this crime, regardless of their guilt. Though why so is a perfect mystery. For if I lived a street or so from the scene of a brutal murder I would be happier if they picked up the right person, not a scapegoat.'

'Perhaps it gets the bailiff and the watch some extra reward, for clearing up the crime in their area?'

'So our real suspects are: Mr Kipper . . .'

Alpiew put down the name Cibber. 'He had a grudge against Anne Lucas because she had ruined his attempt at entrepreneur-ship by spoiling his lecture. And he appears to have made some unwanted romantic advances upon her.'

'Mr Rich.'

'Yes, Rich seemed to dislike her because she was always putting in for pay-rises, and now hopes to make a profit from her death with increased takings due to the public's morbid fascination.'

'The husband.' She put the spoon into her mouth and chewed.

'Certainly.' Alpiew took another swig of ale. 'He seemed positively overjoyed to witness his late wife's interment. Grinning like a fool. Already in the arms of some other woman in the coach, and kissing Rebecca for all the world to see.'

'What a disgusting place.' With a grimace the Countess pulled the lump of make-up out of her mouth and held it between her fingers. 'Look, Alpiew, there's a piece of wall in my gravy.' She pushed the plate aside. 'Yes, the husband is a suspicious character, but he only makes me believe Rebecca to be even more so.'

'Lampone is a shady fellow, too.' Alpiew jotted down the name. 'I overheard some things when I was at Mrs Montagu's this afternoon,' said Alpiew.

She told the Countess of the snatches of Rebecca's conversation with Lampone, which she had heard through the door. 'All severing and head and neck . . . horrible, it was.'

'I don't doubt but they are in the thing together. Look at this!' The Countess fished a coiled piece of gristle from her plate. 'Yes, yes, Alpiew. Rebecca is the obvious one. She had the poor woman's blood on her hands, after all.' The Countess waved in the air to summon the serving wench for the bill. 'We must keep her sweet until we have the money to repay her, then we must distance ourselves from her.' She shuddered. 'The woman is a termagant, by any account. We've both witnessed her fiery passion.'

The slatternly waitress slouched up to the table and Alpiew gave her the two shillings due.

'It is ironic, madam, that we are dependent upon the cash paid us by three of our four suspects.'

'Scandal!' The Countess stood up, scraping her chair back. 'The Goddess of Fortune will have to work wonders and land us a juicy one, very soon. In the meanwhile I suggest we clink cups to keeping on the right side of Rebecca Montagu's temper. For it is to her we owe the biggest debt.'

They walked home in silence.

'It's good for a change not to be ever looking over our

shoulder for the bum-bailiff,' said the Countess, pushing open the front door.

As they entered the hall they heard Godfrey calling from the kitchen. He lurched into view, nodding frantically towards the front room, and mouthing the word 'visitor'. The Countess glanced at a stack of boxes and trunks propped against the wainscoting and at once became disconsolate. She crossed her fingers and prayed it was not her husband back for another attempt at grabbing whatever valuables were not nailed down.

Alpiew gently eased open the door to the front room. The fire was lit, and beside it sat Rebecca. Her maid, Sarah, stood behind her brushing out her long black hair.

Hearing the creak of a floorboard, Rebecca turned.

'At last, you're safely back.' She gave them a gracious smile. 'I was worried you might have been lynched by the Tityre-tus.'

'What . . . ?' The Countess staggered forward, astonished at the casual domestic scene before her. 'Why . . . ?'

'I think you'll agree with me, Countess.' Rebecca rose and turned. She was in dishabillé, the ruffles of her night-gown showing beneath her light oriental silk wrapper, her feet encased in pretty pink satin slippers. 'I believe it would be safer if I stayed here with you. More convenient for you two to protect me as well.'

Alpiew and the Countess stood by the door, mouths agape, and said nothing. The little dog, curled up in front of the fire, cocked his head, looked at Alpiew, bared his teeth and growled.

'Sarah will prepare a candle to light me to bed when you have decided which room is to be mine.' Rebecca bent down and picked up the pages of script that she had been studying. 'I'll pay, of course. Usual rates for an inn round here, which I imagine would be pretty high, with a little on top.'

The Countess and Alpiew did not move. Rebecca laughed.

'You two look as though you have been petrified and become caryatids.' Still they did not move. 'I shall have to install you on a plinth in New Palace Yard.'

There was a movement in the hall behind them and

Godfrey's head bobbed up. 'There's a caudle cup on the fire, if anyone would like to partake.'

'How lovely, Godfrey.' Rebecca beamed at him. 'Aren't you a sweet boy.'

'I'm not carrying it all through here,' he snarled. 'You'll have to come through to the kitchen.'

Rebecca nudged Sarah forward. The girl bobbed and stumbled into the hall.

For the first time Alpiew noticed that the maid wore a patch on her upper lip. She realised that she always had done, but now, at night, and with her mistress in dishabillé it seemed incongruous.

As Rebecca reached the Countess and Alpiew she linked arms with them both. 'Come on, girls. Let's partake of Godfrey's drink.'

The dog scampered along at his mistress's heels.

'Mrs Montagu . . .' At the kitchen door the Countess stopped. 'Before you enter my kitchen it is with great reluctance I have to confess something.' She pushed open the door revealing the eccentric kitchen furnished not only with the usual culinary paraphernalia, but also with its three beds, writing table, piles of books and papers, and a washing line hung with linen. 'There are no bedchambers in this house. The rooms upstairs are dilapidated beyond habitation, and totally without furniture.'

Rebecca surveyed the cluttered white room before her, and lifted an eyebrow. She had never seen anything like it in her life.

'The only inhabitants of the first and second storeys are pigeons,' the Countess pressed on. 'But do feel free to join them if you so desire.'

Rebecca glanced up at the shadowy staircase.

'Alpiew will light you the way.' The Countess grabbed the candlestick from Sarah and passed it to Alpiew. 'I feel sure that once you see the accommodations you will decide to go back to your comfortable home in Little Hart Street.' She shooed the actress and her maid up the stairs, Alpiew leading with the light.

'I ain't having no glamorous actresses sharing my bed . . .'
Godfrey was mumbling to no one in particular as he twiddled
a hunk of bread on a fork in front of the fire. 'Whores of the
devil! You know what Prynne says about female players, don't
you, milady?'

'Yes, yes, Godfrey.' The Countess rolled her eyes and
flopped into an easy chair. 'You tell us often enough. I believe
I know the whole book by heart.' She too spiked a piece of
bread on to a fork and held it to the glowing coals.

'It's a well-known fact' – Godfrey gave his groin a hearty
scratch with his black fingernails – 'that actresses lead a man
to adultery, self-pollution and sodomy.'

'I wouldn't worry, Godfrey –' The Countess paused, con-
templating Godfrey's claim. 'Mrs Montagu won't be staying.
I assure you, there'll be no sodomy in my kitchen.'

Rebecca was back at the kitchen door within minutes.

The Countess rose, toasting fork in hand. 'I knew you'd
change your mind, once you saw the state of things.'

'I haven't changed my mind at all.' The actress's face was
strangely tense. 'You owe me a lot of money, Countess. I will
give you a choice. You let me stay, and for every day I remain
your debt to me will go down proportionately. If you do not
let me stay I will start to charge you interest. What's more, I
will expect you to pay me in immediate instalments or I will
set the bailiffs on you again. And maybe this time they will
drop you in the Marshalsea or Newgate, without recourse to
a sponging house.'

'But there are no chambers, no beds . . .'

'That is my concern. But, Countess, I tell you, I *will* stay
here, beds or no.'

Next morning, after a night spent on the floor in the front
room, Rebecca rose at dawn and sent for carriers to fetch
luxuries like a huge feather bed and an easy chair, which were
hauled upstairs to one of the peeling rooms. At the sight of
the invasion, Godfrey threw on his greatcoat and marched out
of the house with a great harrumph.

While Rebecca and Sarah arranged the furniture, the

Countess and Alpiew crept out to the privy in the yard and bolted themselves inside. 'She had me over a barrel,' hissed the Countess. 'Thanks to you borrowing that money.'

Alpiew felt the rest of her day was already looking bad enough without recrimination from the Countess. This afternoon she was to appear on stage, dressed in her best gown topped with a great feathered headdress, to play Rebecca's train-bearer in *The Rival Queens*.

'What if she did murder Anne Lucas? What if she comes and knifes us in our beds?' said the Countess, grasping her neck. 'We'll have to agree with everything she says, or risk waking up headless.'

'Don't you trust her?' Alpiew asked, knowing the answer already.

'She's as cunning as a dead pig, but not half so honest.'

'Ay, sharp's the word with her.' Alpiew put her finger to her forehead. 'But diamonds cut diamonds. I think there is a simple solution.'

The Countess pursed her lips and waited.

'We must solve this wretched mystery, and find the perpetrator and get them locked behind bars. Only then can we be free of this anxiety.'

'Of course, Alpiew, it's as clear as the meridian light!' the Countess snorted. 'I'll pop out this morning, and have the killer apprehended by luncheon.'

'I know it is not simple. But I feel sure we can unlock the puzzle, as we did before. I can continue to ferret out the secrets of the playhouse, and while I am there, you can find out about *her*.'

'Who? Madam Stamp-a-foot?'

'No. The murdered woman, Anne Lucas. Find out where she lived, discover the secrets of her precious domestic life, find out why anyone would have wanted to kill her.'

'We certainly know one person who did.' The Countess cocked her head back towards the house. 'The famed Roxana herself, with her celebrated stamp.' The Countess thumped her foot down on the ground inside the privy and a spray of foul-smelling mud and sewage splattered her skirt. 'Euugh! We must get the night-soil men in to clean this out before her majesty complains.' The Countess flung open the privy door, revealing Sarah scurrying away towards the kitchen.

The Countess primly lifted her skirts and followed her.

'Madam Montagu,' she spoke as she marched into the kitchen, thereby interrupting Sarah who was busily whispering her tittle-tattle into Rebecca's ear. 'We need some details from you.' She shot a look towards the maid. 'And we need to speak to you alone.'

'You're the one who's done all this before.' Rebecca leapt to her feet. 'I'm just an actress. What do I know of murder and mayhem?'

'Mrs Montagu, I only wish to ask if you have any idea where we should investigate first.' Alpiew tried to remain calm. 'You know of no background, no previous threats against Mrs Lucas?'

Rebecca flipped a hand and dismissed her maid: 'Prepare the bedchamber, Sarah.' She flopped down on a wooden kitchen chair. 'I hear you suspect *me*?' She shot a surly look in Alpiew's direction.

'Tell us about Mrs Lucas.'

'She was a sycophantic . . .'

'No!' The Countess clapped her hands. 'Facts. Where did she live? Where is her husband? Who was her banker? Did she have children, lovers?'

'One child, one husband, no lovers.'

'So where would we find this husband?'

'At their home.'

Alpiew was making notes. Rebecca strode over and snatched the pencil from her hand.

'But you must not go there, you understand me . . .' She towered over the Countess. 'I order you to leave Mr Lucas out of this.'

'He seems to be the most obvious suspect . . .'

'He has nothing to do with it, and I would appreciate it if

you would obey my wishes on this matter. You are *not* to talk to Mr Lucas.'

'Whatever you say.' The Countess gave her an inscrutable smile, and cocked her head. 'What time did you say your performance was today? I am sure I heard the bells of St James's ringing one o'clock. Won't you both need to go in to apply your addition and tire yourself in your oriental dress?'

The performance! Alpiew's stomach lurched.

'I will come with you.' The Countess busied herself getting her things together ready to leave. 'I cannot miss Alpiew making her stage debut.'

In silence the four walked to the theatre. It was not too cold, but a steady drizzle soaked them.

Despite the damp, Covent Garden Piazza was the usual crush of stalls, carts, chairs, and pedestrians. The Countess and Rebecca, with Alpiew and Sarah stringing along in tow shoved past the row of stalls selling trinkets and vegetables. Between the market and northern posts a Punch and Judy show was in full swing.

> *'Who'd be plagued with a wife*
> *That could set himself free*
> *With a rope or a knife,*
> *Or a good stick, like me?'*

The grotesque little puppet bashed his puppet wife until the poor little figure lay cowed in a corner.

'There, get up, Judy dear, I won't hit you any more. Get up, I say.' The puppeteer removed his hand from Judy, leaving her limp and lifeless.

'Well then, get you down.' Punch picked up Judy and tossed her away.

Very apropos! thought the Countess. The husband does away with the wife.

'Hee, hee, hee! To lose a wife is to get a fortune.' A pretty female puppet appeared in the tiny open square of a stage and Mr Punch clapped his hands. 'What a beauty! What a pretty creature! I'd like to jig it with her.'

There he has hit it! thought the Countess. Mr Lucas disposes of the wife because he is tempted by other women. One of whom was her rival in more ways than one: the stamping player, Rebecca Montagu.

'I hate that thing,' said Rebecca. 'All that hitting and killing while he sings away in a voice like a raven. Still, it rakes in the money.'

As they neared the playhouse the crowds seemed to get denser where usually they thinned.

'It seems that Mr Rich's hoped-for audience has materialised,' said Rebecca. 'They're crushing to get into the playhouse.'

'Alack, no,' said Alpiew, standing on tiptoe, peering ahead. 'I believe they might be those you called the Antis.'

Alpiew was right. The street before them was packed with a crowd of placard-waving demonstrators surrounding the theatre entrance.

'What do the signs say?' The Countess looked ahead, screwing up her eyes, which together with the damp smeared her black eye make-up from her eyebrows to her cheeks, giving her the look of someone who had walked into a door.

Alpiew recited: '"Theatre the devil's playground"; "Eleventh Commandment: Thou Shalt not go to the playhouse"; "God Says Close All Theatres" . . .'

'Who did he say that to?' said the Countess, hitching up her skirts and striding into the throng. 'I don't remember any declaration at all about the theatre in the Bible.'

'Whore!' screamed a woman into the Countess's face. 'Painted trapes!'

Rebecca leapt between them. 'Rather a painted trapes, madam, than a sour-faced, foul-mouthed bitch!'

The woman gasped and stepped back, leaving room for the Countess to squeeze towards the door.

'Smut, Scum and Sex! Bring back decency,' shouted a pimple-faced man with a squint. 'It's all Smut, Scum and Sex with you people.'

As they reached the entrance Rebecca turned and addressed

the crowd: 'Shouldn't you be at home sewing or cooking, ladies, rather than disturbing a quartet of lewd women going about their heathenish business?'

'Pox-ridden harlot, stop your mouth –'

'I am no harlot, you flea-bitten streak of vinegar, and were I pox-ridden, would not my skin be less smooth? See! I am wearing no addition. And mayhap if that spotty fellow over there let out the impurities of his body with a little more smut, scum and sex his complexion might improve. Sarah, the door.'

Once inside, the Countess turned to Alpiew and wished her good luck. 'And now I shall venture out again and find a nearby stall and take a cup of chocolate while I wait.'

'But the protest?'

'Despite being a painted trapes, Mrs Montagu, I too have a sharp tongue and can deal with the Antis as well as you.' The Countess stood by the exit. 'I shall see you both in an hour. On stage.'

Ten minutes later, having got the home address of Mr Lucas from the burial register at St Giles, the Countess was on the road north. The Lucas family seemed to live outside town. The Countess couldn't understand it. Everyone in London, particularly theatre folk, lived in walking distance from their place of work. Why had Mrs Lucas chosen an out of the way place to live? Or perhaps it was Mr Lucas's decision. She recalled that nasty little Kipper fellow saying he wanted his own wife to live in some far-flung godforsaken village.

While she had been in the church the spring sun had burned away the drizzle, and now it was rather warm. Trotting briskly up St Giles High Street she hoped the Lucas's place wasn't going to be too far out. The verger had assured her it was walking distance, but as priests weren't reputed for their frequency of taking hackney carriages, she started to panic.

She wished the Lucas family only lived in nearby Soho, where she could find some nice little French cake shop. But no, she had to head north. She surveyed the fields on the other side of the Tyburn Road. Some idiot wanted to call it Oxford Street! The Countess couldn't see the point; after all, it was clearly the road to Tyburn, not Oxford. It might eventually reach Oxford, in the way that they say 'All roads lead to Rome', it doesn't mean you have to call them all Rome Street.

With an indignant puff she launched herself forward. On the other side of the Tyburn Road, fields stretched far into the distance. And in those fields, apart from the dangerous-looking wildlife – cows, pigs and sheep running seemingly wild – there were nasty-looking hovels and tents crawling with all sorts of unscrubbed humanity. The Countess made up her mind not to venture the cross-country route, but instead to take the Tottenham Court Road.

Most London highways were bad. But the Tottenham Court Road was hell on earth. There was not much traffic, only the occasional stagecoach rattling north carrying passengers through tiny hamlets like Hampstead (where they could take the spring waters) and beyond the woods of Edmonton Chase (where the highway robbers would probably take all they were carrying) to Hendon (and why *anyone* wanted to go there was a mystery indeed). It was quiet. But worse than the quietness were the rubbish tips. Both sides of the road were piled high, and now that the sun had come out they were steaming, venting their pent-up odours of refuse and waste. And even worse than this abominable barren landscape was the company it provided. For all along the roadside the rubbish tips were crawling with people: the cinder-sifters, a kind of human vermin.

Alpiew gazed into the cheval glass in the tiring room. Her face was plastered with paint, and on her head was a great turban with a spray of multicoloured feathers.

The music had finished and she could clearly hear the hum of the audience chatting. Suddenly she was gripped by a fear that made her gasp. She grabbed the back of a chair and took a deep breath. How many years had she mocked the players for their self-importance? Now that she was due to walk out on to the stage herself she became overawed with admiration. How did they do it? *Why* did they do it?

Rebecca swept into the room shaking her hands, which were dripping with water. Alpiew suddenly remembered the strange pre-performance ritual. 'Come. Our cue is coming.' The actress looked herself up and down in the glass and moved swiftly towards the door leading to the scenery wings.

In the eerie light of the stage chandeliers, which filtered through the slats of scenery, they walked sedately to the side doors, which opened out on to the playing forestage. Rebecca raised a hand and shot Alpiew a look. The time was coming for Alpiew to hold her train.

A voice came from the stage:

'See where the jealous, proud Roxana comes;
A haughty vengeance gathers up her brow.'

As the next line was spoken, Rebecca shook her head, loosening her hair. The transformation was total. Her face assumed a furious glare and, taking a deep breath through flared nostrils, she stormed on to the stage.

Shaking from head to foot, Alpiew tripped on behind her.

Steam rose from the heaps of rubbish all along the desolate Tottenham Court Road where the poorest of the London poor spent their days sorting through the city's waste. Tattered clothing was mixed in with the foul dumpings of the night-soil workers, the ordure of animals, broken furniture, rotting food, and all other types of detritus from London's teeming city.

The Countess shuddered as she marched along. Watching these poor creatures she felt so lucky. After all, she had a lovely house, and an excellent companion in Alpiew. As for Godfrey, he was a miserable, grumbling wreck, but he had been faithful to her, no one could deny that. So, the bad side was that she was now indebted to a mad actress who had quite possibly murdered a rival and who was presently living under the same roof!

The Countess turned. Behind her came a thundering of hooves. All she could see was a cloud of dust rising atop the highway. The clatter grew louder and as the horses came into view she drew back off the road, stumbling into the heaps of rubbish.

The horses were sublime. The most expensive of race horses, probably belonging to some duke or earl. As they drew near, the Countess took a closer look at the riders. But they were not gentlemen, just boys wearing the unmistakable pink ribbons of the Tityre-tus. They ground in their spurs, whipping the horses on, racing each other.

As they swept past the Countess fell back into a mound of rotting vegetable matter. An old cinder-sifter nearby leapt forward and helped get her back on her feet.

'Here, mistress, take a grip.' He wiped his hands down his grimy clothing and stared after the horses. 'Tityre-tus. They race horses up here all the time. Spoilt little tykes.'

'Strange place to race. Why not take them to Newmarket?'

'Ah, you didn't understand me, then, lady. More likely than not, those are not their own horses. They will have stolen them from some City tethering post. The poor owner won't know they're missing till it's too late. These kids choose only the best, fastest horses, and ride them carelessly. Run people over. Even ride horses into trees. Occasionally kill themselves into the bargain. Or those young 'uns they sometimes carry pillion fall off and smash their brains out.'

'Why do they do it?' The Countess stared after the riders at the ever-diminishing cloud of dust. 'Why would they want to do such a thing?'

'No reason.' The man wiped his hands down his filthy britches. 'They do it for the joy.'

'Joy riding!' said the Countess. 'Sure, young people today have too much time on their hands. When I was their age we were at war.'

'Ay,' said the man. 'And look at me now! Crawling around the tips trying to get wood for my fire.'

The Countess felt desperately sorry for the old man and pulled out a shilling. 'Take this. And tell me: am I far from a place called Paradise Row?'

*　　*　　*

'O, you have ruined me. I shall be mad.'

Rebecca gave the famous stamp to drag every eye in the audience towards her.

'Said you so passionate, is't possible?
So kind to her, and so unkind to me?'

While Rebecca ranted, Alpiew tried her best to look serene while keeping a look-out, both at the other actors (Cibber looked particularly threatening and was carrying a huge shiny scimitar) and the audience. Unfortunately the moment she looked towards the pit her stomach did another wild somersault and her knees started shaking so wildly she could see her skirts quivering. All those people staring up. Why did players put themselves through this?

Without any warning, Rebecca lurched forward. Caught unprepared, Alpiew pitched after her in the most ungainly fashion, and the crowd in the pit let out an almighty yelp. When Alpiew regained her equilibrium she realised that the actors had stopped speaking and were staring at her. A strange whistling was coming from the audience now, and some were clapping.

Cibber moved forward, shuffled past her and whispered in her ear as he went: 'Tuck it back in, dear.'

She didn't know what he was talking about. She looked to Rebecca, who was glowering.

'Away, begone!' she cried, turning on Alpiew.
'And give a whirlwind room,
Or I shall blow you up like dust. Avaunt!'

Rebecca was so realistic, Alpiew felt that she was shouting at her personally. Alpiew hung her head to avoid the tirade. Then she saw what was causing the stir. Her right bosom had escaped from her corset as she tripped and was displayed for all the world to see. Appalled, she turned upstage and pushed it back into the confines of her dress.

'Wake then, bright planet that should rule the world . . .' declaimed Cibber.

The audience sniggered.

'Wake, like the moon, from your too long eclipse . . .'

The audience hooted and screamed with laughter, and Alpiew felt she might die of shame.

The tiny cottage stood up a path lined with pretty flowers. The Countess opened the gate and felt relieved to be at her journey's end. She couldn't believe that an actress as successful as Anne Lucas lived so far out of town and along such a dreadful route. She dreaded the walk back, and wondered whether there was a nearby tavern that had a cart upon which she might get a ride back into the city.

She rapped on the cottage door and it was opened promptly.

A young boy stood before her. He was about twelve years old, with freckles and tousled hair. The son of Anne Lucas, she presumed, as he wore a black arm-band.

'Is Mr Lucas in?'

'Who is asking?' said the boy, effectively blocking the entrance.

'Lady Anastasia Ashby de la Zouche, Countess of Clapham, Baroness . . .'

'We need no more charity, thank you.' The boy tried to shut the door in her face, but she had already placed her foot across the threshold.

'I am not charity. But I must speak with your father.'

'Who is it, Jack?' A woman appeared, wiping her hands, which were covered in flour.

It was the woman who had had her arms around Mr Lucas in the coach. Fast work, thought the Countess. So much for the valued domestic life. His wife barely in her grave and here he had another woman already settled in.

'Are you from the theatre?' said the woman.

Hoping this might be a good way in, the Countess nodded. 'I have come to speak privately with Mr Lucas.'

'Not possible,' snapped the woman.

'He is away?' The Countess took a step into the hall.

'In a sense.' The woman gave a sideways glance which told

the Countess that the man was in the front room. 'Run along, Jack. Go play in the sunshine.'

As the child ran off, the Countess took a step forward and grabbed the door handle. The woman let fly, pulling her away from the door. They wrestled for a moment, but the woman was large and strong and the Countess grew frightened. What if this woman and the husband had conspired together to get Mrs Lucas out of the way? And here she was at their mercy, all alone, and no one, not even Alpiew, knew she was here. She let go the handle.

'Madam, I am afraid I must have words with Mr Lucas regarding the playhouse. It is proposed to play a benefit in his wife's memory to provide funds for her poor child. But first I need his permission . . .'

The woman looked her up and down.

'You're not from the theatre,' snarled the woman. 'If you were really from the theatre you wouldn't be here. Who are you?'

'I am Lady Anastasia Ashby de la Zouche, Countes of . . .'

'Mmm,' the woman was growing more surly by the second. 'And I'm the Queen of Sicily. What do you want here?'

'I need to speak to Mr Lucas.' The Countess hoped that if she said it firmly enough the woman might give in.

'You're from some rag, aren't you? Some smutty journal.' From the back of the house came the sound of a dog yelping. Momentarily the woman turned her head.

The Countess lunged forward and thrust open the door that hid Mr Lucas. But what met her eyes was not at all what she had expected.

The floor of the room was covered in canvas, and there was no furniture at all. Blinds were pulled down across the windows, giving the room an eerie white light. In the centre of the room, sitting cross-legged on the floor, was Mr Lucas. Apart from a thick loincloth like a baby's napkin he was naked. He was flicking at his pale skin with long fingernails.

'Too hot. Too hot.' He rose. 'I must apologise. Flies, flies, flies. It always happens when it gets too hot, you understand.' He winced. 'Not my fault. God chose me, that's all.'

The Countess glanced back at the woman, who shrugged, as though to say – you wanted to see him!

'Flies! Flies! Shut the door!' exclaimed the man. 'If I let them out, the sky will go black. It's a well-known fact.'

The woman closed the door and stood just inside, beside the Countess.

'It's the sweat, you see. It makes flies come out of me. The sweat turns all to flies.' Mr Lucas looked up at the low grey ceiling. 'I so wish it wouldn't get hot. If it didn't I wouldn't sweat and there would be no flies. It's all my fault. Too many flies.'

The Countess could see that the man was void and discomposed of his senses.

'So you've found what you wanted to see.' The woman whispered into the Countess's ear. 'Like to ask your questions now?'

'Is it the result of losing his wife?'

'Oh no.' The woman let out a grim little laugh. 'He's been like this for years.'

The Countess suddenly wondered if she had the wrong house.

'This was the home of Anne Lucas, the celebrated player?'

'Oh, bonny Anne, I'm your man.' The man rose and slowly started a strange dance. 'Bonny Anne, quick as you can.' He looked to the Countess and gave a winsome smile. 'She died, you know, Anne Lucas. Not long ago. She was famed throughout the Town, I am told, but she ate too many strawberries. Strawberries in April! Whoever heard of such a thing?' He started his rustic jig again. 'That'll teach her. Poor Anne, catch her if you can, hit her with your fan, Anne, Anne, Anne!' He started swatting wildly at the air. The woman moved forward and with well-practised dexterity sat him down again.

'I'm sorry.' The Countess touched the woman gently on the arm. 'I didn't know.'

'So you're certainly *not* from the playhouse then?' The woman marched them both out of the room and along towards the garden. 'They all know about it there. She lived out here to keep it quiet from the public.'

'They all know at the theatre?' The Countess was mystified. As far as she was concerned, the picture that had been drawn of Anne Lucas was that she lived in cosy domestic harmony. 'You are telling me the players know that Mr Lucas has lost his senses?'

They walked out into the garden, where Jack was throwing sticks, playing with a large dog. The woman pointed the Countess to a bench.

'Some of them.' The woman nodded as she sat. 'There's that smug Cibber fellow. He took advantage of the situation a year or two back. Thought Anne needed a bit of "affection", he called it.'

'And that termagant, Rebecca Montagu. She knew, all right. Came out here a couple of times. Always left Anne in tears, every time. I didn't take to her at all.'

'Anyone else?'

'The manager knew too. He had to, being her employer.'

The Countess tried to remember everything she had witnessed. Not one of the playhouse people had painted a picture of anything but domestic bliss.

'Don't look so surprised. Mrs Lucas was a wise little thing. Had her head on her shoulders . . .' The woman put her hand to her mouth and gasped. 'Forgive the expression. But she was coping. In her way. She earned money enough to keep them all, and pay for me.'

'You are his nurse?'

'The child's nurse only. Mrs Lucas insisted on nursing the poor deluded man herself.'

They both looked toward the shuttered window behind which the lunatic was gently crooning his song about flies. 'He's quiet now. But he can get violent. Accidentally so when he is stampeding after the flies.'

'You don't think he could have . . .'

'Killed his wife?' The woman gave a wry shrug. 'He could have, if the deed had been done here. But he never leaves this house, that room. And when she wasn't here to keep an eye on him, I was. And that dreadful night he was definitely here with me and Jack. His madness that night was at boiling point. It was as though he knew before we did, poor soul. He wept and wept.'

'What will happen to him now?'

'He is to be removed to Bethlehem Hospital.'

'And the child?'

'Unless some funds turn up, the parish will take him.'

'And you? Mrs . . . ?'

'Mrs Leigh.'

'Where will you live?'

'I have relatives in Newgate Market. And I will be looking for employment thereabouts.'

> *'And when she sees*
> *That to my arm her ruin she must owe,*
> *Her thankful head will straight be bended low,*
> *Her heart shall leap half way to meet the blow.'*

The Empress Roxana swept from the stage. In the scenery wings she transformed back into Rebecca and at once cuffed Alpiew across the ear. 'I am trying to give a performance here, woman.' She snatched her skirt from Alpiew's grip. 'With you traipsing around behind me like a petrified looby, I suspect they took me for a Bedlamite, or worse.' She took a step, then turned. 'And you will remember from what I told you of the play that I do not become distracted until the next scene.'

She stomped off towards the tiring room. As she reached the door she gave a little gasp, and Alpiew raced after her to see what was wrong.

A shabbily dressed man stood before them. 'Oh, Mrs Montagu! I am lost for words.'

'I am not,' said Alpiew, striding in and gripping the man by the elbow. 'This is the ladies' tiring room. You should not be in here.'

'Let me be. 'Tis Mrs Montagu I came to see.' The man

shook Alpiew off. He held his hat in his hands, and looked up coyly. 'I wondered if you would consent to be my wife.'

Alpiew looked at Rebecca. Her face revealed no recognition, rather a gruesome horror.

Holding firmly to the architrave of the door, Rebecca spoke quietly and firmly: 'I do not know you, sir.'

'Yes you do, Becky.' He smiled and shuffled on the spot. 'It's me. You know me. I always sit on the front bench in the pit. Every play you are in. You often shoot me a smile.'

Alpiew stared. This fellow was a queer cove and no mistaking. He thought that because he recognised Rebecca, Rebecca should recognise him. Alpiew changed her tactic.

'Jeremy, isn't it?' Any name would do, if it would prompt him.

'No.' The man shook his head angrily. 'Nickum.'

'Of course. Now, Nickum, you won't want to miss the end of the play. Mrs Montagu goes back on for the big scene in the last act. You should be out in the pit, sir, or you will miss her. She will be winking especially for you.'

'Really?' He smiled. 'It's not a trick?'

'Why would I trick you?' Alpiew laughed. 'You are Mrs Montagu's very special friend in the audience.'

Nickum gave Rebecca a penetrating look. Rebecca returned it with a little bob of the head.

'Come along, Nickum,' said Alpiew. 'You know she must prepare for her next scene. Her cue is almost upon us. I'll escort you to the door and you can make your own way round. I will be looking out for you.'

After he had gone Alpiew tried to calm Rebecca. 'You yourself told me all sorts of people came backstage, invited or no.'

'See, my face is falling off! This is dreadful cheap addition.' Rebecca stood before the glass, dabbing at her make-up with a damp sponge. She took a brush and re-applied white to her forehead, then drew the eyebrows on again. 'I *have* seen him before. I recognised him instantly.'

'From the pit?'

'No, not here.' Rebecca applied a brush dipped into the red

pot of addition to her lips. 'But he was there outside York Buildings, on the night. When I was quarrelling with Anne, I remember seeing him, face squeezed against the glass of the window into the foyer . . .'

Alpiew thought back. She too felt she had seen him. He was the man who had jostled Cibber when they were waiting to go in.

The two women stood in the tiring room silently searching their memories for moments of that terrible night. The silence was resounding.

'You have missed your cue, Mrs Montagu.' A scenery man dashed into the tiring room. 'Mr Cibber is giving a piece of his well-rehearsed extemporanea.'

Pulling at her hair and dress to resemble a woman who had lost her senses, Rebecca Montagu snatched up her skirts and dashed for the stage.

'The dagger?' She turned in a frenzy. 'Where is the dagger?'

Alpiew grabbed it from the properties bench and ran after her.

'Alpiew, you were diabolical!' The Countess shook her head. 'I have seen bad players in my time, but you! I'd as soon see a monkey holding Rebecca Montagu's skirts as you.'

The Countess made it back to Drury Lane Playhouse for the final moments of the last act. She saw Alpiew's last scene. To her astonishment she observed that Alpiew seemed to spend much of the time glancing down at her own cleavage. The Countess marvelled at her. Here she had an opportunity to shine on stage in the famous King's Company and all she did was admire her own figure!

They had both walked Rebecca and Sarah home to German Street, then made their excuses. The Countess told Rebecca she had to pop in and visit the Duchesse de Pigalle, her best friend, who lived a few streets away and who was suffering from a quinsy.

In fact she had no intention of visiting Pigalle, and couldn't even if she wanted to as the Duchesse was in France for a month overseeing her vineyards. Instead, leaving Rebecca in Godfrey's care, the Countess needed to talk to Alpiew alone. The two women now sat on a bench in St James's Square. Dusk was falling, and boys came to light the newly contrived street lights that hung around this grand square.

'What do we do about finding Anne Lucas's murderer?' asked Alpiew, anxious to change the subject from her own performance that afternoon.

'While you were cavorting about on stage, I took the opportunity to visit Mr Lucas.'

Alpiew's eyes opened wide. 'And . . . ?'

'He is stark mad. And in my opinion would have been incapable of perpetrating an act of murder upon his wife. But seeing him made me understand that in the players we have a bunch of lying, dissimulating toads who are incapable of telling the truth. They conspired to spin us a web of deceit regarding the domestic bliss of Mr and Mrs Lucas.'

'So we have not really narrowed down our search.'

'Far from it, Alpiew dear. As they say at Newmarket on race day: the field is open. Have you paper and pencil?'

Alpiew pulled these implements from her pocket.

'Let us sketch out the order of events that fateful night.'

'First Anne Lucas arrives late.'

'"*O molti problemi in casa . . .*" Well, we understand what she meant by that now. The lunatic husband.'

'Then Rebecca and Anne Lucas quarrelled, with Lampone between. Rebecca threatened to leave, but as Anne made her way to the stage, Rebecca took a seat in the audience.'

'Why?' The Countess clapped her hands together. 'Why did she stay to watch? It doesn't make sense.'

'The performance starts and is brought to an abrupt and deliberate end by Rebecca.'

'An interval is called, and from now our paths diverge: I sit by the river for a while. Then the contemptible Tityre-tus sweep by and remove my wig and the gingerbread man comes to my assistance. I peek into the auditorium just in time to see Rebecca Montagu's bloody entrance. You?'

'I returned to the auditorium,' said Alpiew. 'Seeing that, like you, many of the spectators had vacated their seats, I moved forward to get a better view. After a short pause, Lampone came back on to the stage, and talked in detail about the theory of the Passions.'

'Where did Anne go?'

'She was seen getting into a coach . . .'

'Seen by whom?'

'The Italian.'

'So in fact we cannot know if it was the truth,' said the Countess. 'If he had killed Mrs Lucas he could fudge it by saying that. Where was Cibber all the while?'

'Everywhere. Onstage, offstage, mingling with the audience . . .'

'So if Mrs Lucas was killed between us being dismissed from the auditorium and Rebecca's re-entrance with the bloody hands, it could have been . . .'

'Any of them!' Alpiew picked them off on her fingers: 'Lampone, Cibber, Rebecca . . .'

'The gingerbread man, the Tityre-tus . . .'

'The mad phanatique, Nickum. In fact, any member of the audience.' Alpiew let out a long sigh. 'Or the coachman, and it come to that.'

'How about all three of them, together? Rebecca, Lampone and Cibber.'

'But they seem to hate one another.'

'And Rebecca of all of them seemed to hate Anne the most.' The Countess shuddered. 'And where is she now? In my house in German Street. Probably plotting how she can murder us all in our beds. At least Godfrey has the right idea. He simply won't acknowledge her presence, hoping to freeze her out.'

'Perhaps we should do the same.'

'And risk her throwing me into Newgate?'

'Or worse,' Alpiew shook her head, 'her wrath. She likes to strike when she is roused.'

'I have another story about that bunch of unruly renegadoes the Tityre-tus. A couple of those ungodly boys passed me today, riding horses that they had obviously stolen. I was told by the kind farrier who gave me a ride back into town that one of them rode the horse he had stolen smack into a tree just past the Tottenham Court turnpike. Killed the horse on impact, and the boy himself was carted off to St Bartholomew's Hospital.'

'I hate the Tityre-tus!' exclaimed Alpiew. 'Lord Rakewell is lucky enough to have a solid alibi. Being prisoner in the Tower I think gets him off the hook.'

'They managed to throw my wig right up to the window sill of . . .' The Countess put her hand to her mouth and let out a little shriek. 'Pepys! The man will take me for an ill-mannerly brute. I never returned for my plate of tripes, nor to apologise.'

'Who is this Pepys, whose name you keep exclaiming?'

'Oh, Samuel Pepys. He's someone I knew from years ago. He lives beside the Music Room at York Buildings. He's an old navy man. A quill-pusher, not even an actual sailor.'

'Maybe he saw something that night?'

'He's practically blind.' The Countess cocked her head. 'But he did talk of hearing a noise.'

'Shall we go and talk to him?'

'Tomorrow.'

'Nine of the clock on a fair cold evening.' A night-watchman had come into the Square. He ambled round looking up at the well-lit windows. 'And all is well.'

'Nine o'clock!' The Countess jumped up. 'We'd better get home.'

As they pushed through the German Street front door, the first thing that hit them was the smell.

'I'm afeared, Alpiew,' said the Countess, creeping forward towards the kitchen. 'What can have happened?'

'I cannot imagine, milady.' Alpiew slid in front of her. 'It smells like the inside of an expensive ordinary.'

'I know. It is the most delicious aroma,' said the Countess. 'But we both know that Godfrey cannot cook.'

Alpiew edged the kitchen door open. Both women gasped

at the picture of domestic harmony before them. Godfrey, washed and brushed, sat upright at the table, which had been cleared of papers and was nicely laid. Sarah was up at the window re-hanging the previously yellowish curtains, which were now an astonishing shade of white, and Rebecca was crouched over a set of pots that swung over the fire.

The steam that wafted from those pots was more aromatic than those exuding from Locket's diner.

'I have had Sarah go out and buy half a dozen different bottles from Widow Pickering's as I was not sure of your taste,' said Rebecca, indicating a row of bottles on the sideboard. 'There's Barbados Water, Black curaçao, Hungary water, Persicot, some Rhenish, and for afterwards some spirit of Clary.'

The Countess and Alpiew were rooted to the spot. Their heads turned and they stared at the row of alcoholic beverages.

'As for dinner: to start,' said Rebecca, removing her apron, 'I have prepared Kink.'

'Kink?' said Godfrey with a hopeful sparkle in his eye, as Sarah bent down to pick up another curtain, thereby exposing inches of cleavage at his eye level. He let out a contented grunt.

'It's a French broth with garlic, saffron and leeks, garnished with oranges and lemons.'

The Countess had made up her mind that this was all a dream and that any moment she would wake up. She gave Rebecca a benign smile.

'Then, beef à la mode.'

'À la mode?' Alpiew spoke if only to get her jaw to move out of its gaping position.

'Cooked with bacon, claret, cloves, mace, pepper, cinnamon and served on French bread sippets.' She lifted the lid from a pot and another waft of the heavenly scent of exquisite cooking swirled round the room. 'That will be served with boiled salads of carrot and beet.'

Godfrey took a slurp of best Rhenish wine. Alpiew and the Countess stared down at him as Rebecca pressed on.

'And, finally, snow cream – that's cream and egg beaten with rose-water and rosemary, also a little furmity and almonds, to mop up the drink.' She pulled open a package. 'I almost forgot. I bought you a present for letting me stay.' She took out a white linen square. 'It's a set of napkins from that smart new shop D'Oylys in Henrietta Street.'

The Countess and Alpiew still stood frozen at the door.

'D'Oylys!' said the Countess.

'Sit down, sit down.' Rebecca waved them to chairs, laying a napkin at each place on the table. 'The food will get cold.'

Still the Countess and Alpiew were transfixed.

'Oh, no,' cried Rebecca. 'You are not vegetarians, are you?'

'Certainly not,' said Alpiew, moving forward to hold out a chair for the Countess. 'We're Church of England.'

When the meal was over, while Sarah was washing the dishes in a bucket out in the yard and Godfrey was snoozing in his usual easy chair by the fire, Rebecca poured out another glass of Barbados water, finishing the bottle.

'To more sombre subjects . . .' The Countess stared Rebecca in the eye. 'Why did you lie to us?'

Rebecca did not reply.

'I repeat, Mrs Montagu, you lied to us. You knew a lot more about Mrs Lucas than you let on.'

'Like what?'

'Mr Lucas . . .'

'The theatre is different from real life,' said Rebecca. 'There are different priorities.'

'Don't give me that stuff,' snapped the Countess. 'I didn't come up the Thames in a Newcastle coal barge. You can tell the difference between make-believe and reality, between truth and falsehood.'

'You don't understand . . .'

'I do understand that you think you can wheedle us by making a lovely supper . . .'

'No!' Rebecca pounded the table, making the glasses shake.

'I love cooking. I love food. It's easier to cook for five than for two. I thought you'd like it.'

'We do like it,' said Alpiew. 'But we cannot work together unless you tell us the real truth. About you, about Anne Lucas, about everything.'

'There is nothing to tell.'

'There is plenty to tell, Mrs Montagu. For instance, you can tell us what went on when you visited Mrs Lucas at home, when her child's nanny tells us you always left her crying?'

'I don't know about that. I never ever wanted to hurt her.'

'We saw how you treated her,' Alpiew snorted. 'We were there in the concert hall on the night, remember, and you made her cry in front of us all.'

Rebecca fell silent. The door opened and Sarah bustled in with the clean dishes. The only sounds were the cracking of the fire and the clanking of cutlery being put into drawers. Rebecca never took her eye from her wine glass.

'Take a warming pan up to our beds, please, Sarah.' She downed the brimmer as the girl lifted hot coals from the fire and tossed them into the copper pan. 'Then you may go to bed.'

When the girl had gone, Rebecca bent forward to check whether Godfrey was asleep, but the rattle of his snores was proof enough. She poured out a shot of spirit of Clary and took a quaff before speaking. 'Anne Lucas and me . . . it was an act.'

The Countess tossed her head back and snorted.

'I swear to you it was. And that night we laid it on thick.'

'And why would you want to do that?' said Alpiew. 'You insulted each other openly.'

'Yes, we did. We had rehearsed it during the afternoon, when Cibber told us he had snared you.'

'Snared?'

'The little sharper couldn't believe his luck when he bumped into you that afternoon at the Tower. He thought you would write some piece on him. Make him famous. And when we heard, we decided to upstage him.' Rebecca topped up her glass. 'We planned it all. Anne was to be deliberately late. I was to learn all the claptrap from Lampone, and then she would turn up and we would stage a fight about who was to perform.'

'I don't understand. You mean you knew she would be late?'

'Yes, of course. I went with her myself to the Maypole in the Strand to order the hackney coach to bring her to York Buildings.'

'But why would you get together to make her late for rehearsal?'

'For you. So you would write about *us* and not Cibber, and he would look like the little grabbing jack-ass that he is. We did it all for your benefit.'

Alpiew interjected, 'But since the death you have continued to talk about her in an unfavourable way. Why keep up such a pretence?'

'We've been doing it so long, making up this antagonism. The public love it, you see. They don't want to know *us*. They don't want the real person. They want the person they see on stage. In my case a termagant. And Anne was always the victim. Sadly for her, in reality she suffered even more than all the poor miserable wretches she portrayed on stage.'

'Whose coach was she seen getting into after she left the theatre? Do you know that?'

'She didn't get into a coach at all.' Rebecca placed her glass on the table. 'She was paying off the same hackney man, who we had hired to hang around by the back of the building, to whisk us both off, if necessary.'

'And you would know this coachman again?'

'Of course. I know him well. He is my . . .' the pause was almost imperceptible '. . . cousin.'

'And you could take us to him?'

'Yes.' Rebecca emptied the bottle. 'I am fuddled with drink now. But I do not care. I know I am among friends.' Tears were welling in her eyes. 'The whole thing was supposed to be a frolic.' She started rubbing her hands together, as though trying to wash away the blood that had been on them. 'What we didn't plan for was her . . .' She started to sob uncontrollably. 'I can't abide it. We were quarrelling in her last moments on earth.'

'You said it was an act.'

'It was. Nonetheless, the last words I said to her were cruel.' She gulped and then pulled herself together. 'But she knew the truth. She knew that I would have done anything for her. Poor little Anne. You see, the truth is, I simply adored her.'

FIVE

Simple Love

*Pleasant delight, with reference to the object, is
called Simple Love.*

*The eyebrows raised to the side on which the
eyes are turned, the head inclined towards the
object which causes love. The eyes moderately
open, white and shining. The rest of the face
filled with warm spirits. The mouth merely open,
the lips moistened by the vapours which rise
from the heart.*

Next morning Rebecca gave her maid Sarah the day
off to visit her family in Tower Hamlets. In her place,
Alpiew agreed to accompany the actress to her rooms
in Little Hart Street to collect some things. But as Alpiew
rounded the corner into Covent Garden Piazza she tried to
turn back, for a terrible fight was taking place. A sudden surge
of people behind shoved them forward into the melee whether
they wanted to or no. Rebecca lunged to the ground and
scooped her precious dog into her arms.

A gang of young men were scaling the piazza's central column and someone's wig was perched on the globe on top.
The slashing of sword play filled the square, and stallholders
retaliated by throwing their produce at the rioters. The air
was thick with cabbages, carrots, rolls of lace and books of
pornographic prints.

'If we edge along the other side we should get through,'

said Rebecca, pushing Alpiew in front of her like a shield as they shoved through the grand portico of St Paul's Church. Ducking in and out of the pillars, they finally reached the north side and dived for shelter in a shop doorway. An upturned stall lay broken on the paving stones before them and its owner sat sobbing on it while she lobbed random objects back into the fray.

Rebecca gritted her teeth. ''Tis nothing but anarchy.'

The dog started yapping. Rebecca cooed into his ear as a surge of chanting boys dashed past.

> 'You *can't win*
> We *can't lose,*
> *We are the Tityre-tus.'*

Alpiew was smacked across the head by a flying sausage. She grabbed it and hurled it back into the melee. It hit one of the marauding boys, knocking his beaver hat to the ground. He bent down, swiped up the hat, dusted it, and tossed it on to his head, before turning and walking slowly but purposefully towards her, a scowl forming under his lowering brow.

'Did you throw this?' The sausage dangled from his gloved hand. Alpiew recognised the boy's face instantly. It was Lord Rakewell, celebrating his new-found freedom in his usual method. She backed away.

'Did you throw this?' he repeated, still marching forward, as though addressing an imbecile. 'You don't throw sausages at me!'

'I could say, also, sirrah, that you don't throw sausages at *me,*' cried Alpiew, with a lot more bravado than she felt.

'Why make such a fuss, Lord Rakewell?' said Rebecca, stepping forward. 'It is a sausage, not a hand granado.'

'Mrs Montagu?' Rakewell spun round to face Rebecca. 'Becky Montagu, is it not – the player with the fiery temperament?'

'It is no fitting accomplishment in an English gentleman to have the manners of a savage, sir.' Rebecca hoiked up her skirt. 'Now make way and let us pass.'

The dog in her arms growled and yapped, baring gums and yellow teeth in Rakewell's direction. The young lord glowered, then with a twist of the mouth he let out a little sigh and licked his lips. 'I will have you, Rebecca Montagu. I will have you even yet!' He took a step back. 'Never forget, Becky, I know your little secret.'

Rebecca froze for a moment, then grasped Alpiew by the hand and ran off, ducking as an airborne cabbage whirled past.

'Have a care, Mrs Montagu.' Alpiew pulled the actress into a doorway. 'Look yonder.' Before them a stream of men were pouring into the square from Bow Street, lining up, priming their muskets. 'The train-bands.'

'Oh lord, Alpiew! Which is worse, to die at the hands of a bunch of homicidal maniacs or in a riot by the random fire of the forces of law?'

'For myself,' said Alpiew, pushing open the door behind them, 'I intend to live.' She heaved Rebecca after her into the darkened house.

'What is this place?' Rebecca wrinkled her nose as they stumbled into the dark hallway. 'It smells worse than the King's menagerie.'

'It's a Mollies' house, madam.'

'Mollies!' Rebecca did a sharp about-turn. 'Perhaps it would be better to face the train-bands and the Tityre-tus.'

'No, madam. Truly. Molly men will be much too busy playing with each other to bother with us.' Alpiew gave a laugh and plunged down the long dark corridor. 'We're women, remember. The creatures in here may dress in our clothes, and imitate our little vanities, but they're far too busy aiming their weapons at each other to worry about real women...' There was another door ahead. 'If I remember correctly, this abuts a small courtyard that leads into Madame Choler's House of Correction.'

'Alpiew!' shrieked Rebecca. 'I have a reputation to think about. I cannot be seen in a whorehouse. What if someone sells the story to the scandal sheets?'

Alpiew realised what an ironic position she was in. 'I *am* one of the scandal sheets, and I shan't tell.'

They stood in the small courtyard, panting.

Rebecca looked towards the two doors, one leading to the House of Sodom, the other to the Land of the Whip.

'We will race through the place at the speed of light, which Mr Newton is so proud of, and no one will notice. Come along. Head down, Mrs Montagu, and run. Beyond lies the peace and quiet, we hope, of Little Hart Street.'

Samuel Pepys was peering from his window with a brass telescope when the Countess was ushered in by his housekeeper.

'Blast London Bridge!' he cried, not removing his eye from the scope. 'Upstream of it there's nary a decent boat, let alone a ship. Lighters, barges and the odd custom-house cutter, no barquentines, brigantines or schooners. Not even a decent yaugh!'

Having barely understood a word of the preceding sentence, the Countess turned the subject to something more familiar. 'But it *is* a lovely house . . . What a view!' She took in the wide swathe of river, with the York Watergate below to her left, and the octagonal tower of the waterworks to her right.

''Twill serve.' Pepys looked about the room. 'But it's not mine. I just live here. Owned by my old clerk; Will Hewer by name. Mediated for me when my late wife, may God rest her poor soul, discovered me in flagrante delicto with a delicious little girl called Deb. Governor of the East India Company, now. (Hewer, I mean, not Deb.) You know, The John Company. Import–export. Abundant tonnage of ships under his control, enormous first-raters down to the lowliest cutter. Best ships on the high seas today, in my opinion, the East Indiamen; awkward to windward, but still finer in construction than the ones I looked after when running His Majesty's Navy.'

The Countess was beginning to despair. Why had she come here? She knew the man had only two subjects of conversation: sex and ships. He was a terrible bore.

'I was wondering, Samuel, whether you remember seeing anything that night when you thought you heard a cry. The night the actress was killed.'

'Little Anne Lucas!' Pepys sighed. 'I saw her dance a pretty jig once in some silly Shakespeare thing. What was it called . . . ?' He scratched his periwig with a pencil end.

The Countess scraped her memory for a list of Shakespeare's plays. '*A Midsummer Night's Dream*?'

'Lord, no,' Pepys tutted. 'Saw that back in '68 and 'twas the most insipid, ridiculous play that ever I saw.'

'*Romeo and Juliet*?'

'Nor that neither, which was I confess the worst play that ever I saw in my life.'

'*Twelfth Night*?'

'Lord, madam, you vex me. I wouldn't venture myself twice to see that weak thing. No, no.' Pepys perched on the window sill near her and gazed out upon the river. 'This one, as I recall, with much music, some excellent scenes and machines, a handful of comical sailors and a mighty good monster, was about the sea and ships.'

'Ah, you must mean *The Enchanted Island*.'

'That's the one.' Pepys leapt up and clapped his hands together. 'So full of good variety.'

'Only after Mr Dryden and Mr Purcell improved it, I think. Shakespeare's original play is pure pish.'

'And dear little Lucas danced the part of Dorinda, Prospero's younger daughter, to perfection.' Pepys nodded vigorously as though reliving the experience, then his smile faded and he glanced towards the waterworks tower. 'Poor lady, to come to such a violent end.' He sat again. 'I wish I could say I witnessed anything important on the night of her murder, but I did not. My eyesight is poor, and at night my telescope is good for nothing but searching out the mysteries of the Moon. Yes, Lucas was very good in that, but my lord, the sailors were the best, most comical creatures, their hornpipe . . .'

'So, Samuel' – the Countess cut him short before he

launched into another nautical paean – 'you remember nothing more of events the night Mrs Lucas died?'

'I remember I saw you and offered you a plate of tripes, and you did not come.' He scratched at his periwig again.

The Countess slid back in her chair to get out of range lest it was infested with lice. 'Now I think on't, I do remember a mob of mad, silly people romping in the street and behaving themselves like most insolent and ill-mannered men.'

'The Tityre-tus.' The Countess shuddered at the thought of her wig landing on the sill where her elbow now rested. 'Nothing else?'

'Why do you ask so many questions? Are you employed by the Justice of the Peace?'

'No, no, Samuel. I am a writer.'

'Oh, really.' Pepys beamed. 'I also. Allow me to present you a copy of my only published work.'

He scuttled off into the next room, and came back holding a leather-bound book which he was wrapping up in an old newspaper.

'Excuse the packaging!' Pepys grinned in the Countess's direction. 'It's that scurrilous rag, the *London Trumpet*. My housekeeper gets it. Personally, I wouldn't have it in the house.'

Blushing, and pleased she hadn't exposed herself by admitting to her job with the *Trumpet*, the Countess rose. 'I look forward to reading your book, Samuel. Are you writing anything else?'

'No. I think I'll leave it at that. The eyes aren't what they were, you know.' He squinted down at the newsprint. 'It's all just a grey blur to me.' He glanced out of the window. The river was crowded with small craft plying up and down stream. His eyes followed the wake of a nifty customs cutter in silence. 'My long-sight is better, but . . .' He shrugged his shoulders and held out the wrapped book. 'I may not be an author of the first water, like the present Poet Laureate, Nahum Tate, or even his predecessor, the great Thomas Shadwell, both of whose names will surely echo throughout posterity, but, cross-fingers, this little volume may favour me with a small place in the annals of English history.'

The Countess had crossed the room. Pepys was holding the door open for her to leave. She was aware that, as she passed him, he stood a little too near, so she was forced to rub her body against his. After all these years, the old fellow hadn't changed a bit.

'If you want a nice cosy evening, settle yourself down with a cup of chocolate by the fire to read it.' He gave her a kiss on the cheek and leaned over the banister, watching her descend to the ground floor. 'I think I can still maintain my modesty while assuring you that you will not be disappointed.'

Once safely outside, sitting on the stone seat within the Watergate the Countess tore open the wrapper. She was anxious to see what on earth it could be that Pepys had written that would give him a claim on posterity.

Eagerly she opened the cover and stared at the title page: *Memoirs Relating to the State of the Royal Navy of England.* She flicked gingerly through a few pages. Lists and descriptions of ships and victualling. Who'd read this drivel? With a yawn she thrust the book into her bag. It would do to prop up the wobbly kitchen table. But as for a place in posterity . . . Pshaw! Samuel Pepys had as much chance of achieving *that* as men had of landing on the Moon.

Alpiew went first up the stairs to Rebecca's lodgings. Cautiously she pushed open the door and poked her head inside. Something before her moved slightly and she jumped. But it was only her own reflection in a couple of looking glasses that lined the hall. She stooped to pick up a handful of letters that had been shoved under the door, and handed them to Rebecca as she moved stealthily ahead into the actress's living room.

'I won't be long.' Rebecca put Red down and he scampered happily along the hall. 'I need to fetch some more addition, bodkins, and a spare whalebone for my stays. You know, the usual woman's stuff.'

Alpiew nodded and wandered to the front window.

The view was quite pleasant: a row of shops, their signs swaying in the breeze. She could hear the distant sound of musket fire from the piazza, and Rebecca singing in the bedchamber.

What had Rakewell meant by Rebecca's 'little secret'? She glanced round, noticing how well appointed the place was. Did all players live in such luxury? The walls were lined with silk brocade, the looking glasses on the wall looked suspiciously like best Venetian, as did the sparkling sconces. The furniture was elegantly carved and upholstered.

But hold! Perhaps it was all a front, like the Countess's house. Maybe all the other rooms in the house were in hideous disrepair. Tiptoeing, Alpiew wandered across the hall and through a door that lay ajar. Another very well-furnished room lay before her, full of expensive furniture: a handsome dining table and chairs, a large oak chest on a sideboard near the door. She could not resist peeking. She tried the lid. It was not locked. The chest was filled to the brim with dried leaves. Alpiew ran her hands through them. Tea! Alpiew gasped. Best bohea! The woman must be rich as Croesus! Everyone knew what a luxury tea was, and how much it cost. And from the aroma and size of the leaves Alpiew knew this was the very finest bohea. Most India-shops in town sold tea that resembled nothing more than dust.

Gingerly she lowered the lid, and peered into a cupboard. Where she expected linen or china she found bottle after bottle of brandy. Why, the woman must be richer than the Scotsman who owned Coutts, the new banking company at the sign of the Three Crowns in the Strand.

'Had a good poke about in my private things?' Rebecca stood at the door, arms folded, tapping her feet.

Alpiew leapt back and slammed the cupboard door, causing the contents to rattle.

She was sure her face was displaying a pretty good rendition of Terror.

'You are right to be frightened, Mistress Alpiew.' Rebecca

gave a black scowl. 'Sure, if you could display such pure emotion at will, you'd be the best player in the universe.'

'I'm sorry.' Alpiew sidled away from the cupboard.

'And before you ask: Yes, I have a bit of money. I was left it by my father. He was a barrister. You know how lawyers seem to earn a hundred times more than anybody else.' Rebecca left the room, and Alpiew followed her into the front where she had filled a box with things. 'Is this too heavy for you?'

While Alpiew tried it, Rebecca flicked through her letters. She looked quizzically at one, then flipped open the seal. Blanching, she dropped the note to the table and staggered to sit in a nearby chair.

'Are you all right?' Alpiew peered at the note. Rebecca plunged her head into her hands and let forth a great sob. The note was prepared from cut-out words from newspapers, roughly glued to the paper. And the words read: 'It should have been YOU.'

The Countess had walked from the concert room's back entrance in Villiers Street to the waterworks, and along the waterside walkway to the front of the concert room in Buckingham Street and back four times. It was less than a minute's walk from the back entrance, where Anne Lucas had last been seen alive, to the waterworks, where her body had been found. Carts rolled in and out of the waterworks, but apart from that the streets were quiet. And at night, once the audience was inside for the concerts, they were still and dark, as she herself had witnessed.

She strolled past the Watergate and peered up at Pepys' window.

'Thanks for leaving my hat.' The voice came from behind her. She spun round to face the gingerbread man unloading his brazier and boxes of gingerbread from a small handcart. 'I love Monteverdi.'

'And thank you for saving my blushes,' said the Countess, 'on that tragic night.'

'Poor lady.' The gingerbread man poured a sackful of coals into the brazier. 'To think that I was only a few yards away, and yet saw nothing.'

'Nothing at all? Are you sure?' The Countess watched as he struck his tinderbox and applied the flame to the kindling twigs. 'Recount to me the whole evening. As you remember it.'

'The usual crowd pouring in, attended by the usual hangers-on: the link-boys, carmen, valets, maids. And of course the phanatiques.' The gingerbread man blew on the flame, and sparks rose into the air. 'Then as the audience disappeared into the hall, the crowd of followers dwindled and evaporated into the night . . .'

'Leaving?'

'Me. One phanatique, a handful of link-boys. Then the audience poured out again for ten minutes and when they went back inside, there was you, still the link-boys and a whirlwind visitation of Tityre-tus.'

'What had happened to the phanatique?'

'He was gone.' The gingerbread man shook his head. 'I know not where.'

'What did he look like?'

'Ordinary. Speckled grey hair, brown clothes, thin face, beady black eyes, with a squinting look.'

'Did you ever leave your post?' The Countess looked up and down the street. From this position, even in broad daylight it was impossible to see the entrance to the waterworks. 'For a call of nature . . . ?'

'I did nip down on to the beach to relieve myself. I went down just before the interval. And again after the interval, as the Tityre-tus passed.' The coals were starting to glow orange. The man put a metal grille over them and placed a few gingerbread pieces on top to warm. 'Good old Father Thames is an excellent jakes. When I came back up, I found you.'

'And you didn't see *her* that night?'

'Anne Lucas?' He took a knife from his belt and flipped the gingerbread. 'Yes, I did. Just before I went down to the sand for the first time, before the surprise interval, she walked along here. She was wrapped in a cloak, the hood pulled up. But I recognised her ... Well, she's famous. She smiled at me, and winked. Then turned and went back the way she came.'

The Countess followed his gaze. 'So she came here, and then went back along the walkway, past the waterworks.'

'Yes. Then a few minutes later the audience started coming out.' He flicked up a piece of hot gingerbread with his knife, wrapped it in paper and handed it to the Countess. 'Gratis, madam.' He picked up a piece for himself.

'Did you see anyone particular leaving or ... ?'

'A row-boat pulled out towards the end of the break, carrying some fat woman they were abusing to the sky.'

'Bustle! You saw her?'

'No, I did not, but you know watermen. I could hear the jibes from the shore.' He pulled his hat down over his ears. 'Then the Tityre-tus came screaming along the walkway, leaving you in its wake.'

The Countess looked over to Pepys' doorway, where she had cowered in the dark.

'Did Anne Lucas not seem upset?'

The gingerbread man cocked his head. 'Should she have?'

'There had been a scene inside the Music Room. I thought she would have been upset.'

'Oh, really.' The man shuffled a little. 'I wouldn't know anything about that.'

'Did you see a big hackney coach go off up towards the Strand?'

'Coaches came and went all the evening.'

'No one came past you after the Tityre-tus passed?'

'No. I fetched the watchman from the box in the Strand, retrieved your hairpiece, then packed up. Out of gingerbread, by then. Tossed the hot coals over into the river, and dragged my cart back up to the Strand and home. Whoever killed that actress must have gone back up Villiers Street.'

'Or blended with the audience.' The Countess swallowed a

delicious chunk and looked at the Watergate. 'Or perhaps they hid in the dark till we had all gone.'

The Strand was blocked by a flock of sheep heading for London Bridge. As coachmen around her cursed, the Countess strolled along, looking into hackney carriages and smiling serenely at the furious faces of passengers who were paying for the pleasure of sitting in the same place. One man hastily pulled up the tin-sash to obscure himself. She could see Alpiew and Rebecca waiting for her on the green at the Maypole hackney stand. Rebecca gave a wave as the Countess crossed the road at Somerset House.

The actress was leaning against a carriage; at her feet sat Red, one leg in the air licking his backside. As the Countess and Alpiew darted out of the path of a rumbling stagecoach heading out to Kent, Rebecca introduced a tall dark-haired man in coachman's attire. 'This is my kinsman, Jemmy, Countess.'

'Countess.' The man held out his hand. 'Good day to you.'

To the Countess's surprise, he spoke with a thick West Country drawl. She shook his hand.

'I was there that night to pick up Mrs Lucas, but she said she'd decided to wait for Rebecca, she was going to tarry in the Watergate till it was over.' He lowered his face into his gloved hands. 'If only she had got in with me, she would still be alive.' He gave a few dry sobs then sniffed and straightened up again. 'I'm sorry.'

'Was she alone when she spoke to you?' The Countess was inspecting his face for signs of artifice.

'Yes.'

'Did she seem upset?'

'On the contrary, madam. She was all upon the grin. She spoke to me, then pulled up her hood and walked down towards the river. I turned my coach about and returned to the Strand. The last sight I got, as I leaned out to check the carriage would not bump the tethering posts, was of her green cloak disappearing round the corner into the dark of the riverside terrace.'

* * *

'I need to get some shopping.' Rebecca swung into the New Exchange, Red waddling cheerfully at her side. 'And within this gay quarter are the best shops in London.'

The Countess looked around her. This overwhelming palace of shopping covered the ground where she had once lived, when Alpiew was a child, King Charles was very much the Merry Monarch and she was in the money.

A covered walk lined with fancy mercers' shops, India houses and jewellers now spread across the ground floor, with many staircases leading to the upper shopping galleries. Rebecca strode up the stairs. 'Come along, ladies. Tonight is the wake for poor Anne. We must all look our best.'

The Countess hovered at the foot of the steps. 'These shops, they look awfully . . .'

'Expensive.' Alpiew finished the sentence, grabbing the Countess's elbow and pushing her on. Having seen the pricey items Rebecca kept at her lodgings, she was interested to see how heartily the actress spent her cash.

They passed windows displaying lace and linen, gloves, ribbons, rich fans painted in India ink, hoods, scarves and silk stockings. Rebecca entered a shop that displayed combs, scissors, tweezers and all aids to the face and hair.

'What is that music?' asked the Countess, as a stately chaconne swirled up from ground level.

'The shopkeepers pay the Society of Fiddlers to play relaxing music,' explained Rebecca. 'It elevates the tone of the place. And with the lack of interference from the elements, thanks to all the shops and walkways being within doors, like a sort of weatherproof mall, 'tis hoped will prove a most successful enterprise.'

The Countess picked up a small box of six silk patches and inspected the price. She let out a squawk. 'With prices like this, I feel sure the place will make a profit. But I doubt the idea will catch with the common people.'

Rebecca pulled a crumpled list from her pocket.

'Pearl plumpers are what I've always taken a fancy to,' said the Countess, peering into a looking glass and puffing out her cheeks a little.

Alpiew glanced round at the shelves lined with rows of jars, the cabinets, the mysterious drawers. 'What on earth is this?' she said, picking up an odd-looking stick with a vertical brush at one end.

Rebecca looked to the assistant.

'That, madam, is the latest novelty from the Continent. We call it the tooth-brush.'

'And for what is it used?' Alpiew marvelled.

'For applying salt or vitriol to remove the scales, or scurf, for making clean of the teeth.' The assistant snatched the brush and put it back on the display. 'Personally, I still think a finger does the job better. However, I *can* recommend these.' She picked up two floppy grey objects that looked like hairy caterpillars. 'They are improving eyebrows.' She held one up to her forehead. 'A lady glues them upon the ceruse base, to achieve a full eyebrow, where perhaps the hairs are too thin, through excessive shaping or age, but when a pencil line looks unnatural.'

Transfixed, the Countess strolled over and fingered one. 'They certainly have a good texture. What are they made of?'

'Mouse-skin, madam.' The assistant swiped them back and turned to face Rebecca. 'Mrs Montagu? With what pretty things can I please you?'

'Mere workaday trifles.' Rebecca squinted up at a row of large white jars behind the assistant. 'What have you in way of addition?'

'There's Venetian ceruse ...'

'No –' Rebecca shook her head – 'I don't like the way it cracks if you need to smile or wrinkle up your face in any way. Awful for a player, unless you wish to undertake the role of Galatea and never move your face from prologue to epilogue.'

The Countess looked down at her own bosom, which was sprinkled with a fine white powder, the results of a day's smiles and frowns, and winced, causing another little white shower to drift down. She looked keenly at the assistant.

'We have an alabaster-and-oil-based addition.' The assistant presented a large bottle. 'It is more expensive, but more pliable.

See, I am wearing it myself.' She swooped the back of her hand in a circle round her face.

Rebecca slid the bottle along to start her order.

'What about Spanish papers?' The Countess was eagerly fingering all variety of packets and pots.

'For cheek-rouge these days, ladies prefer Spanish wool. It gives a more subtle effect.'

'The less red the better.' Rebecca laughed. 'I knew a tire-woman once who wore Spanish red so thick she resembled a talking Holland cheese.' She consulted her list again. 'Crayons: red, blue and brown.' Rebecca held the Countess by the chin and scrutinised her face. 'You are very pretty, milady, behind that cheap addition. You must let me give you a painting session. I assure you I can transform anyone, in complexion and expression, so that even their own parents would not recognise them.'

The Countess blushed, and another chunk of paint landed in her cleavage.

As the assistant placed three crayons on the counter, Rebecca glanced again at her list. The assistant lowered her voice. 'Any depilatory cream?'

'Frankly, I'd prefer a beard.' Rebecca turned to the Countess and Alpiew. 'It's made of vinegar and cat-dung. A box of patches.'

'But you don't patch,' said Alpiew.

'No, I do not.' Rebecca lowered her voice. 'But Sarah needs must patch. She has a problem with her skin, and I aid her.'

'And more belladonna drops, Mrs Montagu?' The assistant placed a small bottle upon the counter top. 'You bought some last time.'

'Marvellous effect, lovely black sparkling eyes.' Rebecca shook her head and pushed the bottle back at the assistant. 'But when I tried it I couldn't see four inches beyond my nose. So, no thank you.' She turned to the Countess. 'I gave my last bottle to Anne. She used it on stage.'

As the Countess and Alpiew exchanged a look, Rebecca fiddled with a little wooden box on the counter. 'Oh, Countess!' She looked up with a start. 'Would you mind if I bought a present for little Scrinkle-shanks?'

'Who?'

'It's only a trifle.' Rebecca gave a dreamy smile. 'He's such a sweetheart.'

The Countess and Alpiew looked blank.

'Scrinkle-shanks?' repeated the Countess.

'Are you sure we know him?' said Alpiew.

'Of course, you do.' Rebecca took out two guineas and handed them to the assistant. 'It's gorgeous Godfrey.'

Godfrey was waiting in the hall, shoes polished, to hold open the door as they entered. His lace cravat, which had always seemed tan in colour with a multicolour pattern of stains, was stiff, white and fluffy.

'Milady, Mrs Montagu . . .' He inclined his head. Alpiew scowled at him and he let the door slam in her face, before skipping round in front of the two women to hold the kitchen door ahead of them.

'Milady, Mrs Montagu . . .'

'Are you feeling quite well, Godfrey?' asked the Countess as she passed him for the second time in one corridor.

He leapt ahead again and held out a chair for Rebecca. 'Mrs Montagu . . .'

'Thank you, Godfrey.' She piled her parcels high on the table and sat.

'Would you like me to put these away for you, madam?'

The Countess and Alpiew could but marvel at the transformation.

'Now, Godfrey, you've been so good, and so sweet, that I have bought you a little something.'

Godfrey's jaw hung loose, and he stared at Rebecca with glistening eyes.

'Come along, you big looby,' said the Countess, shoving past him to get to a chair before the dog leapt up and claimed it.

'Tonight, Godfrey, there is a party, in celebration of the

life of my great friend, Anne Lucas. We are going to her favourite place for a bit of dancing. And I would like you to come with us.'

Godfrey let out a great moony sigh, and a glob of spittle poised itself upon his lower lip.

'And I want you, Godfrey, to be my private guard. To keep watch over me, so that I can be as calm and comfortable as I will need to be at such a time.'

Godfrey drew himself up to his full height and saluted. Both Alpiew and the Countess were amazed to see that he stood a good foot taller than they'd ever seen him.

'Now I am going to assist the Countess, and you must run along, Godfrey, and get ready. I would like you to sit up with the coachman, and when we arrive at the wake you must look after Red for me, and make sure he is in no danger of falling overboard.' Rebecca handed him a small box. 'And here is your present.'

'Overboard,' howled the Countess. 'Oh lord, we don't have to go by ship, do we?'

'Yes, milady,' said Rebecca. 'The wake is to be held on the *Folly*.'

'The *Folly*!' screeched Alpiew. 'That nocturnal haunt of whores and strumpets.'

The *Folly*, a great timber pleasure boat, sat on the Thames at Somerset Stairs just south of the Savoy. A moveable mansion with four corner towers like minarets, the place had been very fashionable once, but now the whimsical floating summer house had fallen into disrepair and attracted a clientele suitable to its name.

'I assure you it has been hired solely for our private use, Countess.'

'Why the *Folly*, pray?'

'Anne booked it herself, weeks ago.'

The Countess thought she must have mishcard and looked up at Rebecca.

'Anne Lucas booked her own wake?'

'Not exactly. Today would have been her birthday. If she

had lived she would have had a party there tonight.' She gripped the table and squeezed her lips together. 'She was looking forward to it so much.' She started ripping open the packages on the table. 'Come, Countess, or we will be late. I am going to apply addition and when I am finished you will not recognise yourself in the glass.' She looked down at the Countess's threadbare clothing. 'It must have been a beautiful gown, Countess, but today the line is quite wrong.'

The Countess followed her gaze down at the maroon mantua, its lace torn, the edges frayed, and realised that Rebecca had actually been rather polite in her criticism. 'As good out of the world as out of the fashion, eh?' She closed her eyes and presented her face to the actress. 'Do your worst.'

'So, Rebecca . . .' Alpiew watched from the fireplace as Rebecca carefully washed away the flaking white ceruse from the Countess's skin before applying the more expensive alabaster base. 'What do you think happened to Anne?'

'I think she ran from the stage, as we had planned, then went out into Villiers Street and straight into her killer.'

'What of Jemmy?'

Alpiew noticed Rebecca's body brace.

'What of him?' Rebecca bent in to concentrate on the detail of the Countess's addition. 'According to him, he came to pick up Anne, and she sent him on his way.' Alpiew pressed on. 'But is Jemmy telling the truth?'

'I'm sure he is.' Rebecca spun round, a red crayon in her hand. 'He is my relation and I paid him to take care of Anne. Why would he do otherwise?'

Alpiew made a mental note that she would seek out this Jemmy and ask him a few more questions.

'What is this for?' The Countess was holding a blue crayon.

'To apply the faintest outline of the veins to the hands and breast.' Rebecca leaned back and squinted at the Countess. 'As to your hair – shall I style it in the French manner?' Rebecca fingered the lace headdress which sat tilted and limp on top of the Countess's matted wig. 'I shall have Sarah neaten up your commode with a little fresh Flanders lace.' She deftly unpinned the wire commode and placed it on the table, then turned to deal with the hair beneath. 'A couple of crèves-coeurs at the back . . .'

'What are they when they're at home?' said Alpiew.

'Heartbreakers. Little curls at the nape of the neck.' Rebecca twisted the hair round her finger and left two dainty curls lolling upon the Countess's neck. 'And now for the coup de grace –' she gathered up the loose strands of hair, twisting them into a bunch of curls. 'I will give you a meurtrière.'

'Indeed!' The Countess gasped and leapt up from her seat, causing her wig to slide forward giving her a narrow simian forehead.

'What is wrong, my lady?' Alpiew leapt to her side. 'What has she done to you?'

'She has offered me a murderer!'

They both rounded on Rebecca for an explanation.

'It's the new name for a top-knot of curls. I meant nothing by it.' Tears brimmed in Rebecca's eyes. 'Believe me, Countess, if I could present you with the murderer of my friend I would do so now. For I have told you, of all the things in the world, I cared for her the most.'

The turreted wooden decks were lit by little turbaned link-boys. The darting flames of their links reflecting in long orange lines upon the black water of the Thames.

Music from the ballroom floated out into the night air.

The Countess, resplendent in her newly fashioned clothing, leaned on the outer-deck handrails and gazed down into the murky waters of the Thames. She ran a hand down her dress. It was only one of her old mantuas, but Rebecca had worked wonders to alter it. The over-skirts were pinned back in the latest style and held in place with new silk ribbons; French lace was piled high on her head and tumbled about her ears to form lappets, and her bodice was lined with yet more lace to give it an à la mode square neckline.

Rebecca with her entourage of Jemmy, Godfrey and Sarah had gone straight inside to the party.

The Countess turned back and joined Alpiew, looking up at the four corner turrets of the floating pleasure palace. 'It resembles the Tower, does it not?' she whispered.

'But the only strange beast aboard is that yapping little creature, Red.'

They strolled around to the dark shore side and watched as the last guests came aboard, the gangplank was pulled up, and the crew cast off.

'Madam!' Alpiew touched the Countess's arm.

'Not Mr Mackerel,' she whispered.

However it was not Cibber approaching them in the flickering darkness, but the saturnine figure of Lord Rakewell. His sparkling smile caught the light, and he cocked his head. 'Don't allow me to interrupt your conversation,' he said, pulling his cloak and gloves off. 'I am here, like you, to celebrate the life of Mrs Lucas, and drown my sorrows in Rhenish. I am Giles Rakewell. We met before, over a sausage, as I recall.'

Alpiew remained silent. Rakewell clicked his fingers and a serving wench lurched forward to fill his glass. 'Allow me to introduce my good friend Dickie Alnwick.' A man in a crimson suit strode across the deck and bowed to them.

Alpiew was tempted to ask after the health of Phoebe Gymcrack.

'We were saying how the design of this place is not unlike the Tower,' said the Countess, turning to face him.

Rakewell raised an eyebrow and gave half a smile. Which Passion was that, wondered Alpiew? Probably Utter Smugness. Alpiew glanced at the Countess. She seemed transfixed by Rakewell's face – or was it the new face-paint, which Rebecca had applied so skilfully that the Countess didn't look at all like herself? Perhaps it had set stiff and she could not change her expression from Bemused Wonder if she wanted to or no.

'Lord Rakewell, you said?' asked the Countess, stooping forward to peer even closer, and waving her hands around her. 'The rushing water, the sailors' shouts . . . I didn't quite hear. I am Lady Anastasia Ashby de la Zouche.'

'Milady,' Rakewell smiled and bowed. 'Rakewell, at your service.'

'Hey day!' said the Countess, turning and looking into one of the many windows on to the inner deck. 'The dancing has begun. They're all eating their pleasure, my belly thinks my throat's cut and to top it all it's cold out here.' The Countess grabbed Alpiew's arm and tugged her inside. 'We will surely see you later, sirrah.'

Within, the large cabin was divided into curtained compartments around a central dance-floor. A small ensemble played boisterous jigs from a dais. The Countess dived for an empty cubicle, drew the curtain and pulled Alpiew into a huddle.

'That can't be Rakewell. The boy is an impostor.'

'But, my lady –'

'No, Alpiew, listen to me.' She lowered her voice until she was simply mouthing the words. 'On the night of the murder that boy was not imprisoned in the Tower. He swept past me, with a gang of Tityre-tus, laughing in the dark as he whipped off my wig.'

'But that is the self same cove who was tried at the House of Lords, milady. That is most surely Rakewell. The ruddy cheeks, the black brow . . .'

'Indeed and indeed. Then I tell you that Lord Rakewell was there howling around York Buildings on the night of the murder. I saw him with my own eyes. I heard that sneering laugh. It was him.'

The curtain swept back and Alpiew and the Countess jolted up into a casual pose to face Rebecca.

'My stays had come loose,' the Countess gave a smile. 'Alpiew had to tighten them for me.'

'I did not know you were acquainted with Rakewell, milady?' Rebecca sat and furled open her fan.

'I am not.' The Countess kicked Alpiew under the table.

'Why is he here?' Alpiew asked.

''Tis that I would like to know, madam,' replied Rebecca, never taking her eyes from the young lord as he stood sombrely in the doorway chatting with his friend Dickie.

Some of the actors and musicians from the Drury Lane company were slouching past, demonstrating a desultory horn-pipe, but their hearts were heavy and their feet plodded through the steps.

'The girls should get more drink into everyone's glasses.' Rebecca rose with a start. 'Everyone is too gloomy.'

A row of serving wenches stood by the entrance to the inner dining room clutching large jugs of ale and wine, keeping the glasses topped. Rebecca signalled over to them.

'Where is Godfrey?'

'Attiring himself,' snapped Rebecca.

The Countess did not like to ask what exactly Rebecca meant, and before she could formulate words polite enough, Rebecca was speaking again.

'I have told him to remain in the inner room with Sarah. They are quite happy. I am treating them to a meal.'

'Mistress Alpiew! Have you left your lady ashore tonight?' Cibber had been hovering on the edge of the dance-floor, beaming his oily smile. Alpiew looked to the Countess, then realised that in her new-fixed apparel and paint he had not recognised her.

'Are you in need of spectacles, Mr Halibut?'

'Cibber.' Cibber jumped, not happy at having been fooled. 'You are looking radiant tonight, madam.' He raised his glass and affected a tragic expression. 'To poor Anne Lucas.'

They all drank the toast, then Rebecca moved abruptly away.

'Anne would have wanted this to be a joyous occasion, I know. She was always full of fun and pranks.' Cibber gestured to the dance-floor. 'I keep reminding myself how she would have behaved had she been here. She'd have kicked up her heels, cut a caper.'

'If that is how you feel, Mr Pilchard, then let us dance . . .' The Countess grabbed Cibber by the hand and steered him on to the floor just as George lurched into the room, tankard in hand. George managed to weave his way through the dancers without spilling a drop. With a grunt, he flopped down beside Alpiew, lay his head on the table and passed out.

Alpiew looked about her. The Countess was leading Cibber a merry dance. She recognised some of the tiring-women and orange girls spilling out of a cubicle on the far side of the room and waved. Rebecca had had a word with the serving wenches and now walked purposefully through the door, but Alpiew noticed that as she passed Jemmy she gave him a furious look, and saw him reciprocate. Jemmy glanced around the room and then surreptitiously followed Rebecca out. Alpiew extricated herself from George's arms and, shooting a look at the Countess, followed them.

She saw Jemmy slide into an alcove and hide himself.

Rebecca was ahead. In the shadowy light of the outer deck she could see her, standing up by the prow, arguing in a most animated fashion with Lord Rakewell.

Alpiew pressed herself into a cubbyhole used for stowing coils of ropes. She lowered her head as Rebecca slapped Rakewell's face, then strode away from him in her direction. Before Rebecca walked past Alpiew she stopped and turned, calling back at Rakewell.

'You are uninvited at this wake, sir. So I would be thankful if you would do as you are told.'

Rakewell inclined his head and trotted along behind her like an obedient puppy.

Only when both had gone inside did Jemmy come out of hiding. He strode briskly to the prow, took a reflecting tele-scope from his pocket and looked through it. He then slammed the 'scope shut and marched back inside.

Alpiew decided to leave a few minutes before following them all in. The last thing she wanted was for them to know she had been watching. She took refuge in her sheltered cubbyhole and watched London go past: the row-boats huddled for the night in the mouth of Puddle Dock, the wharves behind Thames Street, piled high with crates and boxes waiting to be carted in or barged out. She gazed for a moment at the stone tower of Baynard's Castle, all that had survived the Great Fire, and behind it the huge, new shadow of St Paul's, topped with a skeleton frame-work which she supposed would form the base of the spire.

It was only when she could see the masts of ships filling Queen's Hythe Dock that she decided it would be safe to go back inside. But as she stepped out of her hiding place, two cloaked figures in soft silent shoes slid past her in the dark.

'Will it work?'

'Of course it will . . . Have faith.'

The two men moved to the prow and started unfolding a huge piece of tarpaulin.

Sailors, thought Alpiew, tiptoeing along the deck in the other direction and re-entering the main salon.

Rakewell was seated in a booth surrounded with orange girls. His friend Dickie perched uncomfortably on the edge of the bench.

Alpiew noticed that the Countess had moved from Cibber to Rich and the couple was leading a courant. She approached Dickie Alnwick, grabbed him by the hand and dragged him to the floor.

'I don't know the steps,' she said, pointing a toe and marching forward, 'but if we follow the ones in front, I reckon we can't go wrong.'

'You've picked the wrong partner,' Alnwick laughed. 'I'm no dancer.'

'Good.' Alpiew copied the Countess and gave a little hop and a bob, then took three steps forward, gripping Alnwick by the hand. 'Do you know Rebecca Montagu well?'

'Who?' Alnwick tripped and steadied himself. 'Which one is she?'

'Everyone in London knows who she is.' Alpiew gave a little forward jump and took three steps backwards. 'The famed player.'

'I am from my lord's estates in the north. I know nothing of London society.' He was gripping Alpiew's hand tightly, as though frightened he would fall over if he let go. 'I am a person sans consequence, I'm afraid.'

'You are not a lord then?'

'Oh lord, no!' Alnwick giggled and stumbled forward. 'A childhood companion from his father's seat.'

'So you know Lord Rakewell well?'

'Not well . . . I . . .' Alnwick hesitated then smiled. 'My Lord Rakewell always was an obliging spark, full of merry jest and capers.'

That's one way of putting it, thought Alpiew, as the band played the closing chords of the dance, and with some relief Alnwick extricated himself and returned to his perch on the edge of Rakewell's compartment.

'So YOU invited him here this evening,' said the Countess to Rich. 'I was wondering what connection Lord Rakewell had with the late Mrs Lucas.'

'I don't think he knew her at all. He is simply an aficionado of the King's company,' Rich smirked. 'I want him to invest in the playhouse – perhaps, buy a share of the patent. To alleviate my financial burden.'

'An aficionado or a phanatique?'

'He sees that the theatre needs patrons now that the royal family have lost their passion for it, and has offered his services to me. He was also very keen to pay his respects to Mrs Lucas.'

Rich led the Countess back to her seat, and en route Rebecca whispered into his ear. He winced, deposited the Countess, and made his way across to the band's dais.

The drummer performed a roll and Rich clapped his hands. 'Ladies and gentlemen, at the particular request of many of the company who remember Anne for her love of games, I propose that we have a round or two of Clapperdepouch.'

The whole company groaned. 'Too much kissing involved, thank you,' a young orange wench yelled out.

'Romps?'

'Anne liked Questions and Commands,' said Rich from the dance-floor. 'There never was a decent party carried on without it.'

The assembled company clapped and smiled, as Rich started the game.

'George – What is the name of Princess Anne's husband?'

'Oh lord.' George blinked his eyes a few times then leered and waved. 'He's Danish, isn't he?' He looked round for a hint. 'Someone help me.'

A compartment full of women shrilled with giggles as the count-down began. 'Five, four, three, two . . .'

'Prince Hamlet?'

The company roared.

'Well, it's a Danish name!'

'Everybody . . . what's the Princess's husband called?' said Rich to the company.

'George!' they yelled.

'Trick question.' George winced and took another gulp of wine. 'Who'd think a Dane had the same sort of Englishy name as me.'

'I command George to walk a straight line.'

'Easy!' George grabbed the table and hauled himself up. 'Where's the line?'

'Here,' cried a tiring-woman, pulling out a long roll of tape. 'We can use this.'

She held one end and tossed the other to Cibber. They pulled it into a tight white line across the room.

'I'm not drunk.' George stood at Cibber's end, swaying. 'It's this bloody floating thing. Are we quite out to sea? I fancy we are half-way to France it's rocking so . . .' He looked slowly round the room. 'Count me in . . .'

The Countess was aware of the craft softly lurching as though passing into the wake of another boat.

The crowd started to count. 'One, two, three . . . Go.'

George tripped along the tape like a peewit, never straying from the white. 'You should see me perform on the slack wire,' he said, throwing his hands up. 'I win, and I question whomsoever I next touch . . .'

He spun round on his heels and lurched across the room, tripping over someone and landing at Rebecca's feet.

'Rebecca Montagu,' he said from the floor. 'How many pints in a peck?'

'Sixteen.' Rebecca replied without apparent consideration.

She glared across the room. 'I question my lord King of the Tityre-tus.'

Rakewell shot her a surly look.

'How many pints in a firkin?'

'Are you toying with me, mistress?'

'Then how many pints are left when a hogshead is divided by two?'

'Seventy-two pints in a firkin,' Rakewell lowered. 'And no hogshead of mine *ever* gets divided.' Slowly a smile crept over his face. He spun round, pointing his finger. 'Dickie! I choose you.'

Alpiew noticed Alnwick shudder.

'Name me the author of *The Rival Queens*.'

Dickie looked blank.

'Everyone . . .'

The company yelled: 'Nathaniel Lee.'

'So, Dickie, I command you to recite from memory . . . the service of a wedding. For every paragraph you remember, I will give a guinea, and the whole may be shared around the room.' He placed his hat at his feet. 'Dickie, we await you . . .'

Everyone started scraping round their memory to help Dickie.

'I shall be the groom.' Rakewell surveyed the room. 'Who will be the bridesmaids?'

A gang of giggling tire-women leapt to the floor. 'And who the bride?'

'Becky,' called Cibber. 'She's the only one who's never done it!'

'Not me,' said Rebecca. 'The groom is too young for me.'

The boat gave another gentle lurch, and some thudding sounds came from the deck.

'What is going on?' hissed an orange girl. 'Are we about to sink?'

'No, madam,' Rakewell laughed. 'We must be at London Bridge and the crew are rearranging the oars so we can get back upstream. Let us go out on deck and watch them manoeuvre this unwieldy vessel through the eddies and currents of Old Father Thames.'

'All right then!' Rebecca leapt forward. 'Let's get on with the game, my lord.' She stood before Dickie Alnwick. 'Come along, sirrah, the company is anxious to get a full hat.'

'I can't do this,' said Dickie Alnwick. 'You're all professionals. You can act!'

'Come on, away with you!' Catcalls echoed round the room. 'A guinea a part.'

Dickie scratched his head. 'Someone help me – what comes first?'

'Dearly beloved,' whispered a bridesmaid, while Dickie recited after her in a priestly voice: 'We are gathered together here in the sight of God, and in the face of this congregation, to join together this Man and this Woman in holy Matrimony.'

Cheers around the room.

'One guinea.' Rakewell dug in his pocket and dropped a coin into his hat.

'If any man can show just cause, why they may not lawfully be joined together, let him now speak, or else hereafter for ever hold his peace.' Dickie laughed and clapped his hands. 'I remembered that bit myself! Well?' He surveyed the room as another coin went into the hat. 'Any protestations?'

'Ay,' said George. 'She's too pretty to marry!'

'What about Phoebe Gymcrack instead?' suggested Rebecca. 'At least she's only a *couple* of years older than you.'

'This is a mere game,' said Rakewell, turning away from her. 'Come, Dickie. We are letting you off the hook. A guinea a part.'

Dickie looked at Rakewell. 'Wilt thou, Giles Rakewell, have this woman to thy wedded wife, to live together after God's ordinance in the holy estate of Matrimony? Wilt thou . . .'

'Love her . . .' An orange woman spouted up. 'Everyone knows that bit, dear: love her, comfort her, honour, and keep her.'

Dickie repeated as a tire-woman strolled across the dance-floor towards the door to the deck.

'No one to go outside or they forfeit their share,' called Rebecca.

The woman turned about.

'I will,' said Rakewell, lobbing another guinea into the pot.

The boat shuddered.

'. . . and, forsaking all other, keep thee only unto him, so long as ye both shall live?'

Another coin tinkled into the hat.

'Give me a large glass of claret . . .' Rebecca turned to her 'bridesmaid'. 'And I will.'

'Where in heaven's name is Godfrey?' The Countess wiped a piece of bread across a nearby plate, mopping up the gravy. 'Isn't he meant to be her guard of honour?'

'I think he's taken with Sarah, madam. I saw them in a tight huddle whispering away to each other when I fetched our food.'

'. . . and thereto I plight thee my troth.'

Rakewell lobbed a handful more coins into the bag.

'Go fetch Godfrey,' the Countess nudged Alpiew. 'If he sits with us we will have three shares in the pot.'

The boat thudded again. Rakewell looked Rebecca in the eye. 'It's your turn . . .'

Rebecca let out a gay laugh. 'And five guineas into the hat if I do?'

Rakewell lifted an eyebrow.

'I, virtuous Rebecca Montagu, take thee, notorious Giles Rakewell, midnight boy and stealer of dreams, to my wedded husband, to have and to hold from this day forward . . .' She looked round the room for help. A bridesmaid was muttering the words at her. 'For better for worse, for richer for poorer, in sickness and in health, to love, cherish, and to obey, till death us do part, according to God's holy ordinance; and thereto I give thee my troth.' Rebecca looked round the room. 'Should I stamp now?' A ripple of laughter and she slammed her foot down on the wooden deck.

'The ring,' said Dickie. 'We have no ring.'

One of the serving wenches pulled off her own and handed it across the room. 'No need, mistress,' said Rakewell, sliding one from his little finger and putting it on Rebecca's wedding finger.

'It's a pretty one.' Rebecca surveyed the ring. 'Can I keep it?'

But Rakewell was already speaking. 'With this ring I thee wed, with my body I thee worship, and with all my worldly goods I thee endow.'

Rebecca waved the ring above her head. 'I have gained a gold ring out of a frolic.'

She gave a sideways glance. Alpiew followed her line of vision. Nobody there, just the open windows. The boat was now moving again, slowly plying upstream.

'In the name of the Father, and of the Son, and of the Holy Ghost,' said Dickie. 'Amen.'

'I've had enough of this game now.' Rebecca pulled away. 'Let the band play again.'

'Those whom God hath joined together,' said Dickie, looking to the ground as though desperately searching for the words. 'Let no man put asunder.'

Rebecca drifted away from the game, grabbed a brimmer of wine and downed it.

'You have forgot something,' said Cibber, with an eye on the pot. 'Witnesses.'

'Is the game still on, my lord?' asked a serving wench. Rakewell peered down into the bag. 'I hope 'twill end shortly or I shall be destitute. Countess?' He held out his hand to her. 'Will you be witness? For another five in the pot.'

Alpiew noticed Rebecca's cousin Jemmy come to the doorway, give Rebecca a look and go back out. Rebecca did nothing in return, but as soon as he was gone, she took another swig of wine and sank down on to a chair, relaxed.

'And Alpiew will second,' said the Countess.

'. . . I pronounce that they be Man and Wife together, in the name of the Father, and of the Son, and of the Holy Ghost. Amen.' Dickie threw up his hands and fell to his knees. A crowd of girls surrounded him, throwing their arms about him and kissing him.

'Toss the stocking, Becky, do!' called an orange woman.

'Enough!' Rebecca waved her away with a tired nod. 'The jest is out-played.'

Rakewell picked up the hat and started counting heads. 'By my estimation there should be ten shillings apiece.'

'Lady Rakewell,' Rakewell called to Rebecca, holding up some coins. 'Your share.'

'Keep them, husband. You have more need of them than I.'

'Get our shares would you?' The Countess pushed Alpiew forward. 'There's a gentleman just come in giving me the eye.'

A man leaned in the doorway to the dining room, flashing a sparkling white smile, the curls of his red periwig flopping down over his broad shoulders. The Countess gave the man a coy smile and tottered over to him.

Silently the man held out his hand.

The Countess shook it and was surprised to find it was rough and gnarled. 'Good evening, I am Countess Ashby de la Zouche . . .'

But before the Countess could continue the man yelped and stumbled away back into the dining room holding his mouth.

At that moment Alpiew arrived with a pound in coins.

'That man. The one with the sparkling smile . . .' The Countess pointed into the dining room. 'What is his name?'

Alpiew peered into the dark room. 'Madam?' There was only one man in there.

'Him. The red peruke?' snapped the Countess. 'He looks as though he could eat me without salt.'

'I beg your pardon, madam?'

'I think he's got a month's mind for me, Alpiew. He's been smiling at me all night.'

'But, madam!' Alpiew grabbed the Countess before she went marching into the dining room after him. 'He was painted by Rebecca too.'

'So? A player. How lovely.'

'No, madam. He is wearing a stage wig and addition, like

yourself, and a gift from the New Exchange – a set of wooden teeth, painted white.' Alpiew stared across at the apparition grinning to show his snow-white smile. 'That man, madam, is none other than your own steward, Godfrey.'

Jemmy's carriage was waiting at the top of the steps. The cabin was loaded with boxes. 'Sorry about this, milady, but I have a living to earn. I'm dropping these off after I've taken you ladies home.'

Rebecca declined to sit inside, choosing to sit up with God-frey and Jemmy. Sarah sat in with the Countess and Alpiew.

'So you are close to my man, Godfrey?' The Countess patted Sarah's hand.

'Oh, no, madam.' Sarah whipped her hand away. 'I have a beau of my own. My mistress told me I was to look after Godfrey tonight.'

'I did not recognise him.'

'My mistress is a virtuoso of the toilette.'

'Have you worked for Mrs Montagu long?'

Sarah nodded.

'It must be very interesting working for a famous actress . . .'

Sarah nodded again.

'Did you see a lot of Mrs Lucas?'

Sarah shook her head.

The Countess took a deep breath. It was not going to be easy getting anything out of this tiresome girl.

'Did Mrs Lucas like Mrs Montagu?'

Sarah nodded.

'Did Mrs Montagu like Mrs Lucas?'

The girl nodded again. 'Countess, I am tired and would rather sit in silence, if you don't mind. I fear I have a quinsy coming on.' She gripped her neck and gazed out of the window.

The Countess shifted up the seat towards Alpiew. The last thing she wanted was to come down with a sore throat.

'What do you think these are?' Alpiew kicked at one of the boxes.

'They are boxes for the gentry, madam.' Sarah swung round, her throat suddenly improved. 'There is not much passenger trade at night, so Jemmy delivers parcels.'

They rode on in silence.

When they alighted at German Street, Rebecca swept past them. 'I have drunk too much. I swear I am half-seas over.' She ran straight up the stairs. 'I need my bed. Goodnight.'

Silently Sarah scampered up after her.

Alpiew and the Countess went straight through into the kitchen. A few minutes later Godfrey joined them.

He fished his fingers into his mouth, pulled out the snow-white teeth and flung them on to the table. 'Odd-so! They may look fine, but a fellow can't talk with all that hardware in his mouth. Not to mention I couldn't eat a morsel o' that tasty-looking food. God's truth, now I could eat a dead horse, fur and hooves and all.' He whipped off his wig and slung it over a bedpost, then gave his scalp a good scratch. 'Don't know as how folk wear those itchy things. I hope it ain't given me a fit o' the nits.'

The Countess shuddered. There was no mistaking Godfrey now.

SIX

Horror

The eyebrows more frowning than in scorn, the mouth partly open, more so at the sides than the middle. The nostrils raised and drawn up. The lips and eyes somewhat livid. The body drawn violently back from the object which causes the passion.

Next morning the entire household was woken by violent knocking.

It was Rakewell. Alpiew showed him into the front room and went up to fetch Rebecca.

The Countess hovered in the hall as Rebecca, still in a silk wrapper, went in alone.

'What does he want with her?' hissed the Countess.

'Search me.' Alpiew stooped and listened at the door.

They heard low murmuring, then the famous stamp.

'Fetch Godfrey.' The Countess dispatched Alpiew and applied an ear to the thinnest part of the wood panelled door.

The voices grew louder and more intense, until Rebecca let out a piercing scream. The Countess threw open the door and burst in.

Rakewell had hold of Rebecca, who was struggling hard to free herself.

'Unhand her, sirrah, or my man Godfrey shall fly about your ears!'

'That superannuated booby!' Rakewell laughed. 'He has

trouble enough standing on his own legs, let alone knocking me off mine.'

Godfrey took one look inside the room and headed rapidly back towards the kitchen.

'Oh vile perfidious villain!' Sobbing, Rebecca slid to the floor, repeating over and over to herself. 'No, no, no.'

Rakewell bent down and snatched hold of Rebecca, trying to haul her to her feet.

'Let go my hand, detestable malicious toad.'

Rakewell snarled and pulled all the harder.

'This is my lady's house' – Alpiew strode into the room – 'and while you are here you will behave like the gentleman you are supposed to be.'

'Unhand Mrs Montagu, Lord Rakewell, or we shall raise the hue and cry and have you apprehended for molesting her person.'

'Unhand my own wife?'

'Pish!' the Countess snorted. 'Last night's ceremony was a frolic, my lord, and you know it.'

'No, madam.' Rakewell let go of Rebecca's hands and walked slowly towards the Countess. 'That was no game we played last night. I failed to tell you all that, unlike me, Dickie is no rake nor ne'er-do-well. He is the chaplain from my north-country estate. He is a priest, madam, an ordained clergyman, whom I introduced to the wake in lay-habit for that purpose. Every word he uttered was from the official ceremony of marriage as found in the Book of Common Prayer.'

'But the banns,' cried Alpiew. 'What about banns?'

'I applied for those some days ago. There is nothing in law that says I must tell Mrs Montagu of my plans.'

'How could you plan to be where she was?'

'I knew Anne Lucas had booked a party on the *Folly* that night; I knew therefore that the players would all be there . . .' He glanced at Rebecca. 'And there is another reason, which I am sure Mrs Montagu will tell you about.'

Rebecca's lips tightened.

'But . . .'

'No "buts", Countess. Rebecca Montagu is my legal wedded wife, and all her worldly goods are mine for the taking.'

'Canonicals! The wedding took place outside canonical hours.' The Countess rubbed her hands together. 'Therefore it is not valid.'

'We were on board a ship, madam, and therefore under its special rules. Have you forgot?'

Rebecca was back on her feet, beating Rakewell with both hands.

'So, wife, if you would care to dress yourself, you can take me to your goldsmith and start off-loading that famous fortune of yours.' Rakewell cuffed her with the back of his glove and Rebecca reeled away.

'You cannot marry a lady without her consent, you ruffian.' The Countess thrust herself forward. 'This is a match of the devil's making.'

'Out of my way, hag.' Rakewell gave the Countess a look full of contempt. 'If you want to bring in the forces of law, do so. For you are my guarantee. An elderly titled lady for the witness. Who will contradict *your* word that the wedding took place? I may be young, but you are far from it.' He spun round and sneered at Rebecca. 'As for you, you are no saint, madam. And, apart from your money, no man in his senses would want to touch you. You are too much the termagant.'

Rebecca tried to slap him but he caught her hand.

'Listen, Actress! I know all about you. Do you want me to tell these two, so they can paste it across their paper?' Rakewell pulled her close to him.

'I am not frightened of you, Lord Rakewell,' Rebecca sneered. 'All of London knows you for a wild reprobate.'

'If I told about Rosamund?' Rakewell lowered Rebecca's hand. 'If I told John.'

She hung her head, and took a sharp breath. 'So?'

'You crossed me, and I will be avenged.' He flung her away. 'Get dressed. I will await you in my carriage.' Rakewell turned to Alpiew on his way out. 'If you are lucky, my bride will toss her stocking as she leaves your house, and you may try to catch it. Unless, that is, you wish to lead apes in hell, and die an old maid.'

He slammed the door behind him.

Alpiew and the Countess dashed upstairs after Rebecca. The actress was yelling 'Fidelia' at the top of her voice. Sarah crossed them coming down.

The Countess and Alpiew stood on the threshold of the room and watched as Rebecca Montagu hacked off her long hair and hastily smeared her face in swarthy brown addition.

A few minutes later, Sarah came in carrying Godfrey's rakish suit from the night before.

'Help me into these,' she cried. 'Then I can make my escape.'

Rebecca threw on the clothes. 'What is over the back wall here, Countess?'

'If you run through the gardens you come out at Blackamoor's Lane, then down into St James's Square.'

'Thank you, Countess, for your kindness.' Rebecca took a glance in the cheval glass. 'I will reward you one day, I promise.' She left the room and leapt down the stairs, the others in pursuit. Red, who had till the downstairs stampede been asleep on the bed, woke and started yapping.

When Alpiew reached the yard Rebecca was already scaling the privy.

'I will call or contact you as soon as I can.' Rebecca teetered along the top of the dividing wall. 'I could make a career on the slack wire!'

As the Countess and Sarah came out, Godfrey, who was inside the privy, started to shout, 'Murder ho! Murder ho!' He battered at the door, to the accompaniment of a strange tinny rattle. 'Rape and ravishment, ho!'

'Run to the playhouse, Sarah.' Rebecca lowered herself, ready to jump. 'Tell Rich what has happened to me.' She blew a kiss to the dog who was leaping eagerly at the foot of the wall. 'Bye, bye, Red, my angel. Look after him for me. I will return.'

As she vanished over the top of the wall, the privy door flew open and Godfrey burst out wearing full armour, cap à pied.

'Let me at the scoundrel,' he cried, clanking across the yard, and throwing open his visor. 'I shall curry his jacket for him.'

Red yelped around his feet, intermittently leaping forward and trying to bite his metal-clad boots.

Sarah had run on ahead and darted out of the front door. Alpiew reached the street and watched Sarah as she gripped her skirts and ran.

Waiting in his coach with a gang of his pink-ribboned boys, Rakewell threw open the carriage door. 'I venture something is afoot,' he cried, leaping out into the street and watching Sarah disappear into the distance. 'I fear the bird is flown.'

The gang of Tityre-tus shoved past the Countess, who stood in the doorway, and spread out to search the house. In less than a minute they all piled back into the coach. Godfrey teetered out on to the street behind them, growling through his white grinning teeth.

Rakewell leaned out of the coach and laughed. 'Stand off, thou drivelling drunkard!'

Godfrey slammed down his visor and strode forward. Rakewell put out his arm and gave Godfrey a gentle push.

The coachman cracked his whip and the coach sped along German Street after Sarah.

Godfrey raised an arm, teetered and fell backwards with a metallic crash.

'Godfrey?' Alpiew stepped over his sprawling figure. 'Should we help you up?'

A small crowd had gathered to witness the spectacle. Godfrey groaned, rolled over on to his front, then crawled back into the house on his hands and knees.

'Excuse my man Godfrey,' said the Countess to the onlookers. 'He has spent too many days up at the menagerie studying the great tortoise.' She slammed the front door in their gaping faces.

'So?' said Alpiew from the front room. 'What now?'

The Countess came in and flopped down on to an elbow chair. 'First we write up this episode for the *Trumpet*.'

'I'll see whether I can squeeze the names of Rich and Cibber in too, so we can pick up the puff money,' said Alpiew and ran out to fetch paper and pencil.

Helmet under his arm, Godfrey stood in the doorway, grinning his white smile.

'Godfrey, please remove those dreadful teeth, unless you can find a way to stop smiling with them in. I shall go blind from the glare.'

He slipped them into his hand and his face fell into the usual sullen scowl.

'Why did she scream "Fidelia"?' asked Alpiew, resuming her seat.

'Don't you know?' grunted Godfrey. 'It's a role she played. Fidelia is a breeches part.'

'Of course, she dresses up as a man.' The Countess leaned forward and thrust a poker into the fire. '*The Plain Dealer*. She follows her lover – a sailor. How on earth do you know that, Godfrey? Does Mr Collier give the plots of all the plays he wants banned in that vile diatribe you are always reading?'

Godfrey was too busy trying to lower himself into a chair to make a reply, as the relevant joints of his ancient suit of armour, not worn since the Civil War, had rusted up.

'Godfrey, you are squeaking like a hinge that wants oiling.' The Countess sank back in her chair. 'If you can't control that hideous noise I shall have a megrim.'

'At least while *she* was here I was treated with a bit of civility . . .' He lurched up again and clanked off, muttering under his breath.

'Countess . . .' Alpiew scribbled a few words down then toyed with her pencil. 'I believe we have just effected the escape of a killer.'

'Rebecca! Indeed and indeed.' The Countess slid down her chair. 'Everything points to it. And Rakewell's accusation adds to the conundrum.'

'Exactly. Who is Rosamund?'

'Perhaps a former love of Rakewell?'

'But what interest does Rebecca have in her? And who is John, that he can threaten her with him?'

Alpiew read out the copy she had written: 'The Wake at the *Folly*, together with the bizarre Nuptials of the leader of the Tityre-tus and the famed Rebecca Montagu.'

'It's a wonderful story.' The Countess glanced down at the paper. 'But it leaves me feeling strangely sad.'

'Why did Rebecca join in with the wedding game?' Alpiew scribbled on, then her pencil paused. 'It is not the usual way with her.'

'Perhaps she wanted the party to go well? She wanted to help the tire-women earn their money from Rakewell? And Questions and Commands is a more dignified game than Clap-perdepouch. Who would think it could go so badly for her?'

'But she pulled out before 'twas all over. She went hot and cold with it.'

They went over everything yet again. How the evening of Anne Lucas's murder had unfurled, the order of events, the behaviour of those at the concert hall, Mr Lucas's insanity and the family home, the gingerbread man's version of events, the Tityre-tus and the possibility of Lord Rakewell's being in two places at once – the Tower and York Buildings, then the events at Anne's wake, and Rakewell's snaring of Rebecca.

'Why would he want to marry her so much?' the Countess mused. 'Surely he was after Phoebe Gymcrack.'

'For her money only. Now he has Rebecca's more consider-able fortune instead.'

'But Phoebe Gymcrack was worth two thousand a year. Even the great Mrs Barry couldn't amass that from acting.'

'Her father was a barrister. He left her a lot . . . She told me.' Alpiew took the page from the Countess, dipped her quill in ink and started to copy it out for the printers. 'But really, Countess, all of this matters not a whit. We have no idea who killed Anne Lucas. And even if we discover her killer, what will we get out of it? Nothing!' She threw up her hands in a dramatic gesture, and a fine spray of black ink drifted across the Countess's forehead.

'We have a button, Alpiew.'

'Of course! A button. Very good and very well . . .' Alpiew

threw down her quill and pulled the button from her pocket. 'And it might belong to anyone who walked along the river terrace past the waterworks that night.'

'Nonetheless we have a button.' The Countess took it and peered at it. 'It is a wooden button, covered in passementerie of brown silk cords and silver frisé thread. An elegant button. What's more, it was torn from the fabric upon which it was attached; there are still threads. I would say cashmere, or some other fine wool. Green.'

'And Jemmy told us he saw Anne Lucas disappearing round the corner in a green cloak.' Alpiew took it back. 'So we are possibly in possession of the button from Anne Lucas's cloak.'

'Of course, Alpiew, you are right.' The Countess stretched her arms out and yawned. 'However, now I think on't, when we saw Anne Lucas's body, she was not wearing a green cloak, was she?' Alpiew was dusting the inky copy with sand against blots. 'She was simply in the mantua she had worn for the demonstration of the Passions.

'There!' The Countess clapped her hands. 'You see, the button does mean something. Now we needs must find the cloak. I presume it will be in the possession of her murderer.' She rose and ambled over to the pantry. 'I think I'll make myself a little snack. Do you feel partial to a caraway jumbal?'

'I will miss Rebecca's cooking, it has to be said.' Alpiew smiled and blew the sand into the fireplace. 'But at least we have the house back to ourselves.'

The Countess pulled open the pantry door, and jumped back in surprise as Red waddled out, licking his lips. On the floor were the tell-tale crumbs of the caraway jumbal biscuits, and a broken plate. 'Not quite to ourselves, I fear.'

The little dog made himself comfortable by the fire, turned to face Alpiew, bared his teeth and emitted a low continuous growl.

'They picked up a fellow for that actress murder,' said Mrs Cue, wiping her ink-black hands down her heavily stained apron as she scanned their piece, standing in the printers' yard in Shoe Lane. 'Mr Cue is setting the piece at the moment. Quite a story it is. Very juicy. It will go down well with this one of yours. People like scandals about players. They enjoy thinking all famous people lead weird lives. Makes them feel compensated for their own boring existence, I should imagine.' She flicked the paper. 'Yes. This is good.' She handed the Countess their fee. 'We're printing now, so it should be on the streets this afternoon.'

'Who did they pick up for the murder?' The Countess pocketed the money.

'Some fellow who lurks down there by the river a lot. Splendid name of Valentine Vernish. He's safely banged up in the Fleet now.'

'Not a vagrant, then?'

From the dark cavern of the printing room came an anguished call.

'Oh dear, Mr Cue is in a muddle with the presses again.' Mrs Cue beamed. 'No, he's an itinerant: the Punch and Judy man in Covent Garden. Moonlights by selling gingerbread anywhere a night crowd might appear. He was down by the river that night, hawking his sweetmeats. Couldn't be a better story.' She glanced into the print room. 'My husband wanted to run the headline "Watergate Scandal", but I told him that was plain silly. Who'd buy a paper with that headline? Must run.' She vanished into the print room.

The Countess and Alpiew strolled silently down Shoe Lane and into Fleet Street.

'So, that's that then . . .' Alpiew kicked a stone along, almost striking a dog busy sniffing a mound of rubbish. 'End of story.'

'I do not think so.' The Countess pondered for a moment. 'This arrest makes me feel sure we must keep on the trail.'

'But how?'

'I do not have a notion.' The Countess stopped to let a flock of geese, driven by a country farmer in a white smock, pass her. Hawkers all around were screaming their wares as she pushed on, 'Lambs to sell, young lambs to sell' running in a strangely haunting harmony with another vendor across the road crying 'Knives to grind, sharpen your blades.'

Alpiew made a pathway through the crush of people squeezing through Temple Bar, where the hawking sellers of pamphlets were crying out their goods. 'The vulgar and decimal arithmetic, delivered as to qualify for His Majesty's Revenues of Excise, Customs etcetera, but also for the recreation of gentlemen, merchants, goldsmiths . . .'

The Countess stopped in her tracks. 'We must find Anne Lucas's goldsmith. It is usual to provide mourning rings for your friends, sure, 'tis the first item in most people's wills. We saw those rings. Therefore either Anne Lucas left enough money to buy them, or someone else provided the funds.'

'Another thing: how did the goldsmith know who was to have a ring and who not?'

'How slow I am . . .' The Countess knocked her forehead with the palm of her hand. 'The goldsmith is the key. He must know about her will and . . .' She turned to face Alpiew. 'Where do people keep their savings?'

'Down their cleavage?' Alpiew shrugged. 'Under the floorboards?'

'No, girl, think. If you have savings you don't keep them in your house to be robbed and pilfered. And no sensible person would trust that new banking establishment.' She grabbed Alpiew's hand. 'People with money keep it in a safe at the goldsmith.' She marched along with great purpose.

'But, Countess, Mrs Leigh indicated there were no funds.'

'Ay, but there *were* funds to buy the rings. Anne Lucas would have forgone the expense of rings, and left the money for the care of her child and husband, unless . . .'

'I see what you mean.' Alpiew bit her lip. 'Unless there is more money.'

'Perhaps enough money to kill for. We will go to Paradise Row and see if Mrs Leigh knows the name of the Lucas's goldsmith. But frankly, Alpiew, I am not willing to walk up that beastly verminous Tottenham Court Road again, so I will treat us to a hackney.'

'But, Countess, a man has been apprehended for the murder.'

'Alpiew! I know him.' The Countess side-stepped a mound of horse manure. 'That gingerbread man is *no killer*. Tell me, would a man covered in the blood of a lady he had just killed stop to help another lady in distress by obliging her with his hat? And would he then run to fetch the watch to help him rescue her wig?' She ducked out of the way of a great spurt of water spewing from a burst pipe. 'The bailiff's wife and her friend did as they said they would. And now a poor decent man will swing for a crime he did not commit. We must find the true killer of Anne Lucas. If it turns out to be Rebecca herself we will be sorely out of pocket, but we will have saved a man's life. And to that end, first we will search out Lucas's goldsmith, then we must track down the abominable Mrs Rebecca Montagu, now Lady Rakewell. For I feel that her secret is the key to this whole business.'

'And apart from that, she owes us – we mentioned her name over and over today in the *Trumpet*.'

'Don't think about money, Alpiew, for remember: I am also indebted to *her*. But our income is not the issue here any more. It is a man's life.'

A shabby-looking carriage stood in the path outside the Lucas's home.

From inside they could hear screaming. Alpiew leapt down from their hackney and ran into the cottage through the front door, which hung open.

In the front room a woman was fighting off two parish men. In the corner behind her cowered a young boy.

'I tell you,' cried the woman. 'If you will only give the child a day's grace, I will have the money to keep him.'

'But you said the same yesterday, Mrs Leigh.'

'Ay, but something must have happened. The agent should

be here any minute. They must have been delayed. Please, sir, leave the boy to me another day.'

'What's going on?' The Countess stood in the doorway. Mrs Leigh put out her hands imploring.

'We have not the money for the rent, and the child does not want to be taken to the workhouse.'

'But you told me . . .'

'Yes.' Mrs Leigh panted from her exertions. 'But since then it has been made clear that Anne Lucas left enough money to provide for both her son and husband to go on living here, and to keep my services.' Alpiew and the Countess exchanged a look. 'The executor sent a message that the money would come today.'

The Countess stepped forward. 'Then may I ask you to unhand the lady, sirrah. Mrs Leigh, who sent the message promising funds to keep Mr Lucas and the boy? Perhaps we can go to them and find out what has held things up.'

Not releasing his grasp on Mrs Leigh's arm, the parish man turned to face the Countess and Alpiew. 'We cannot go unless you come with enough money to satisfy the rents, and more to supply the wants for this woman and the brat.'

'The Bedlam cart has already carried off poor frenzied Mr Lucas. And my fear is that if they take Jack, I may never find the child again. You know the London workhouses . . .'

'Alpiew, call back the hackney if 'tis not too late.' The Countess gave the parish men a withering look. 'Mrs Leigh will prepare you a little bite to eat, gentlemen, while Mrs Alpiew and I go to the goldsmith and bring you the proof that the child can be supported.'

'Would you do that for us, Countess? It's Mr Orchard, in Leadenhall Street, between Black Raven and Angel Alleys, at the sign of the Parrot and Pearl.'

'Give us an hour, gentlemen.'

The parish men shrugged and sat, ready to wait, especially now they were to be fed.

'I believe there may be a slight misunderstanding.' Mr Obadiah Orchard was a small hairy man. He sat at a large desk behind mounds of paper, picking at his nails with a grey quill. 'I have no client going by the name of Lucas. Neither a Mr nor a Mrs.'

'But Mrs Leigh, in Paradise Row on the road to Tottenham Court, told us that you were her executor . . .'

'I am a goldsmith, madam.' The man pulled open a drawer inside which lay a sleeping cat. 'I keep people's money and valuables in my safe, under my protection. But I have nothing for anyone named Lucas.'

'And you know of no person going by that name?'

'I know of a Lucas family.' Orchard pulled a small sardine from a paper packet and dangled it before the cat, who drowsily sniffed at it. 'Another of my clients has a relationship with them, which I am not in a position to disclose.'

'Can you tell us the name of this client, then?' Alpiew wanted to shake the little man and strangle his cat. 'People's lives depend on this matter.'

The cat tugged the fish from Orchard's hairy hand with an equally hairy paw.

'Absolutely not. But I can tell you that they were due to appear here today to deposit certain funds and make allowances for others. However, they have sent no word, and until they do so I cannot act to release the promised monies to relieve the Lucas's plight.'

The cat smacked its lips and settled down again to sleep.

'You didn't provide the rings for Anne Lucas's funeral?'

'No. As I said, another client of mine wished to make a charitable donation to a family called Lucas. That is all I know.' The man shook his head. 'I'm sorry if this has caused any upset. I am simply an engine of others.'

'It's not us that needs an apology,' said the Countess. 'That poor family is being split asunder, without hope, waiting upon a word from you. The least you can do is let them know you are *not* going to save them.'

'All right. I will send a messenger.' He slid the cat's drawer back in, and got up to show the Countess out. 'So sorry to have wasted your time.'

And our money, thought Alpiew, calculating the enormous amount they had spent on the hackney to Paradise Row and back, which had risen shilling after shilling in the city getting stuck behind carts loading up outside Leadenhall Street's herb market, fish market, flesh market and finally skin market.

Disconsolate, they wandered back on to the street. 'So now what?'

'Let's see what they know at the playhouse.'

A sour-faced band of protesters stood on the playhouse's steps reciting their anti-theatre slogans.

'Keep the streets safe,' chanted a dismal-looking woman in drab clothes. 'Keep violence off the stage.'

'She should make up her mind where she wants it,' snapped the Countess. 'Out or in, for surely it will pop up somewhere eventually.'

They jostled through the mob and entered the back door. A group of actors sat in the green room, sipping beer.

'So, ladies!' said Cibber, rising and tossing his copy of that day's *Trumpet* on to the bench behind him. 'Rebecca has been erept the stage.'

'Erept?' said Alpiew.

'Stolen from us, lured away by the temptation of a title.'

'We did manage to get a little mention in for you . . .' The Countess left the sentence hanging, hoping he would dig in his pocket and give them the puff money that he now owed them.

'We have a performance at four, and no Roxana. What are we to do?' Cibber glanced into the corner where the buxom blonde from the previous performance was going through her lines with a leery-looking George. 'We've only just trained Statira into her role and she speaks verse about as well as a Mesopotamian monkey. Now we have lost Roxana too. Rich has sent to the Lincoln's Inn company to see if they have a promising junior who could read. But it's bad news all round. You see, without Rebecca, we're one step nearer to Rich getting his way and turning this place into a medley house of performing monkeys, squawking castrati and tumbling rope-dancers. I hear he's trying to negotiate with the Palace to hire the royal lions from the Tower for a performance of *The Empress of Morocco*.'

'Aren't you at all worried about Rebecca?'

'Why should I be? She'll always land on her feet. And it's not as it was for Anne, is it?' He started riffling through his script. 'At least they've apprehended the villain that killed her.'

'A lady will join us for this afternoon only.' Rich loomed in the doorway. 'She will be here shortly. If you'd care to make yourselves ready while we wait, I shall talk to you all in a moment.' His face erupted into a smile. 'Mistress Alpiew, just the person I have been wishing to see! Could I have a word in private?' He shook the Countess by the hand, surreptitiously pressing two guinea coins into her palm. 'I will be but a moment . . .'

He led Alpiew into the dark scenery wings. 'I have a prop-osition for you. I would like you to join the acting company full-time.'

Alpiew gulped.

'No, don't interrupt me. You see, I have a plan. I will provide you with any role you wish in any play, and together with the tire-woman we will create a little trick of engineering upon your stays. She will provide some sort of drawstring, which you can pull at a given moment each night, so that your delightful snowy bubbies may be let loose from their captivity, to the general delight of the paying public. They went down so well with the audience. So very well last time!'

Alpiew's jaw hung open.

'No, no, Mistress Alpiew. Let me go on. You see, the response to your last manifestation upon our stage has been overwhelming. All these little poseurs of players have no idea what the public really want. Certain types of play-goer may follow a hard-bitten female like Rebecca, but they're mostly dried-up harridans. Their presence in my audience is neither here nor there. And those clever-clever actresses will never put rumps on banquettes. Whereas, if the populace could be lured in with a glimpse of your – what shall I call them? – fore-buttocks . . . Why, then it could be house-full every day!'

Alpiew raised a knee and slammed it as hard as she could between Rich's legs. 'Pize on you, sir, and all your buttocks – back, fore or mid!'

Alpiew made for the door, grabbing the Countess as she passed.

Cibber stood in their path.

'Where is Rich? I need a word with him.'

'Mr Rich is behind the scenery.' Alpiew pushed through the door. 'Preparing himself for a new career as a soprano.'

Godfrey had the fire built up and was casually flicking through a book. The work was thinner than his usual fare. The Countess peered over his shoulder to see what it was. To her amazement it was a copy of a play.

'Godfrey! What a change has come over you. Has Mr Collier and his anti-stage diatribe been consigned to the fire?'

'She would have been excellent in this role.' Ignoring her comment, Godfrey looked up at the Countess. 'I'm sorry I missed it.'

'I am going to write down all the information we have gathered.' Alpiew sat at the table and started scratching away on scraps of paper. 'And all the names of those involved.'

'Start at Anne Lucas and spread out.' The Countess pulled up a chair.

'Anne Lucas.' Alpiew put the piece of paper to one side, and handed the Countess a second. 'Mr Lucas.'

'Incapacitated by reason of being a lunatic.' The Countess put his paper beside his wife's. 'Now in Bethlehem Hospital, god bless his poor frantic soul.'

'Master Lucas – a mere child, now put in the workhouse, due to his mother's death.' Alpiew put that on top. 'Do you think we should try to find the child, help him in some way?'

'Alpiew, do you know how many poor-houses and work-houses there are in London? We would easier find a grain of salt in the ocean.'

'Ah yes.' Alpiew scribbled the name on another scrap. 'Mrs Leigh, nurse-maid to Master Lucas. Now homeless and unemployed.'

'So that pile is without suspicion, for Anne Lucas's death has brought them no benefit. Contrarily, it has ruined their lives.'

'Cibber is so preoccupied with himself and his career I can't think that the subsequent tumult can be welcome to him.' Alpiew put him in the centre of the table. 'Whereas Mr Rich is delighted to lose professional actresses, so that he can replace them with . . .' She hesitated, not wanting to include herself in his predilections.

'What of that peculiar Italian? Where has he got to?'

Alpiew wrote down the name Lampone and placed the paper in the centre pile, then laid down her quill. 'What is the point, madam? We can go over it and over it. We get no nearer. In fact, each time we leave the house it seems more and more of a goose-chase.'

'We must find Rebecca to help us.'

'Godfrey, has Sarah been back here?'

'Yes.' Godfrey let out a low burp. 'Picked up her things. Left Red, though.'

The dog was curled up at Godfrey's feet.

'Where was she going?'

'And how should I know that?'

'I suppose she spent the whole time here in silence?' The Countess sighed. 'She must have said something.'

'I just let her in, helped dump her clothes into a trunk and showed her out.' Godfrey rubbed his eyes. 'She muttered about staying at Little Hart Street for a couple of nights while she made her preparations, and then she was going on to a better life, she said, now her mistress had gone.' His chin started to wobble and he thrust his book up in front of his face. 'I swear to you, milady, if I get my hands on that Rakewell character he won't live long.'

Alpiew and the Countess sneaked each other a look.

'There are three more things we can try,' said the Countess, glancing at the clock. 'The day is slipping by. Let us call at Mrs Montagu's lodgings, and try to squeeze something out of that nasty little maid. Then we must search out Rakewell. Finally we must to the Fleet to pay a visit to my friend the gingerbread man with the wonderful name.'

'Can you be so sure, madam, that this Valentine Vernish fellow is innocent? He was there, he was unaccounted for, and the watch may have good reason for picking him up.'

'Alpiew, as you well know, the watch have about as much chance of catching a real murderer as I do of winning the lottery. Besides which, I heard the bailiff's wife. An itinerant would be picked up – regardless of whether they were guilty or no.'

'Why would they want to do that?'

'How should I know? Something to do with being seen to do their job? Mayhap they wish to sell their miserable house (which, I may remind you, is only round the corner from the site of the murder) and don't want the price of property falling. Or he might be looking for promotion within the forces of law and order.' The Countess gathered up all the scraps of paper. 'What did Rich want with you, by the way?'

'He asked me to be a player.'

'A player, indeed!' A snort came from behind Godfrey's book. 'And you'd get lots of fellows following you around . . . I don't think.'

'I can't see why Alpiew wouldn't be very successful. She has charm, a good figure . . .'

'You're thinking of that harlot, Nell Gwyn. It's different these days. To be a player nowadays a female must have an open soul to receive the impressions of the Passions in to the brain, and then, making use of the appropriate cavities in the brain, the power to express them externally. It says so here –' he stabbed a finger at another book at his side.

'Thank you, Godfrey.' The Countess threw on her cloak. 'Come, Alpiew. Let us leave the fellow to his fantastical ruminations on the nature of the Drama in contemporary society.'

*   *   *

The door to Rebecca's rooms was opened within moments of their knock. Sarah took one look at them and her face fell.

'What do you want?'

'Is Mrs Montagu here?' The Countess held out Red, who she was holding in her arms like a baby. 'We would like to return her dog.'

'You know that she's not.' The girl blocked the doorway.

Alpiew shoved past her. 'Then you won't mind if we look around.' She went straight into the living room. It was clear that someone was at home in here. Candles were lit in the sconces and a pair of wine-goblets waited on the table.

Alpiew went through to the dining room. The tea chest was there. Alpiew flicked up the lid. It was still full of tea. She pulled open the closet. It was stocked as before with brandy.

'Mrs Montagu has not been back here, then?' She turned to the girl who stood insolently in the doorway.

'I haven't seen her.'

The Countess put the dog on the floor and he scampered off along the hall, pushed open a door with his muzzle and went in. The Countess followed and found herself in Rebecca's bedroom. The bed was made up, and more candles burned in the wall brackets. The dog was jumping up, making an effort to get on to the high-sided four-poster bed. 'Who has been sleeping in there?' The girl ran up and tried to shut the door on her.

'No one.'

'To burn best beeswax candles in an empty bedroom seems a wild extravagance.'

'All right then,' said the girl. 'I admit it. It's me. So what? If she's away, I'll sleep where I like.'

'At this time of day?' The Countess shot her eyebrows up. 'But if Mrs Montagu should discover you?'

'I don't give a pize what Mrs Montagu thinks. I hope I never see her sneering face again.'

'You can't go on living in her rooms with an attitude like that. Believe me, she will be back.'

'Let her then. I will be gone.'

'Gone?'

'The day after tomorrow I shall be leaving this country forever.'

'Forever!' The Countess raised her eyebrows and a shower of dust sprinkled her décolletage. 'Indeed!'

'That's right. I am going to the Brave New World, to America. And I will live like a great lady, with slaves and acres and acres of sugar and tobacco and potatoes: every kind of potatoes, sweet ones, sour ones, mashed ones and even maniacs. And they'll all flourish outside the door of my little house on the prairie in New York.'

'Come, Alpiew!' The Countess realised she would get nothing but ridiculous fantasy from this surly girl and she marched to the door. 'If your mistress contacts you before you leave for your new life as a member of the affluent society, will you please tell her that I need to talk to her.'

'I'm not joining no Effluent Society,' spat the girl. 'I'm getting married.'

The Countess reached the exit and stopped in her tracks. Before her, hanging from a hook on the back of the door, was a green velvet cloak. With nimble fingers the Countess felt the front fastening. She turned the fabric round to get a look at the buttons. 'Identical!' she muttered. And at the top, near the collar, there was a tuft of ragged fabric, where once another button had been. She turned and in a wall mirror caught the girl's face watching her.

'What are you doing with that?' Sarah tried to grab at it. 'Are you trying to pick the pockets?'

'Whose is it?'

'Whose do you think?' The girl uttered a guttural sigh. 'My mistress's, of course.'

'Who are you expecting?' Alpiew was behind her, pointing in at the living-room table. 'I assume someone is joining you for a bumper of wine? It's her, isn't it?'

'No, it isn't . . .' The girl spun round as she realised she had almost been tricked. 'It's no one.'

'You always drink from two glasses at once, do you?'

'If you don't get out . . .' Sarah grabbed the door handle and pulled the door shut. 'I shall call a constable and have you removed.'

As they descended the stairs the Countess put a finger to her lips. In the street they looked up. Sarah was peeking out from the window. 'Keep walking,' said the Countess.

They turned the corner into a small court, waited a moment, then doubled back.

They arrived just in time to see the dark figure of a tall man striding up the stairs two by two.

They looked at each other. 'Who'd believe it?' Alpiew gazed after him. 'Signior Lampone!'

'Serving maids don't look to his taste at all,' said the Countess. 'I always imagine Italians to have rather sophisticated taste. After all, their country produced Dante and Leonardo da Vinci.'

'Ay,' said Alpiew. 'And Lucrezia Borgia.'

At Rakewell's mansion they were shown straight in to see him. He sat staring into the fire, nursing a brimmer of brandy.

'You two she-devils! Where is my wife?'

'I would have thought you were rather young to be married, you are a mere boy.' The Countess held out her hands to warm at the fire. 'Most fellows of your age want first to sow their wild oats.'

'Besides which, my lord,' said Alpiew, 'we have done you a signal piece of service.'

'And how do you conceive that?' Rakewell swung round to face Alpiew. 'You helped her escape from me.'

'We have reason to believe that your "wife" is a killer, my lord.'

Rakewell glared at them from lowered eyelids. 'A killer?'

They nodded.

'A killer, you say?' He leapt from his chair and grabbed them both. 'Tell me news! We *all* think Rebecca killed Anne Lucas. Me most of all. And that is why I made her mine. Because women have no business making mayhem. When she

163

began to misbehave I felt quite entitled to avail myself of her fortune.' He pulled them up close to his face so that they could feel the moist heat of his breath, smell the brandy. 'If you know where she is, you had better tell me at once. I believe she would think nothing of cutting you both down if you got in her way, just as Mrs Lucas had to be got rid of, lest she disrupted her great financial plan.'

As Alpiew and the Countess stood blinking in the face of the onslaught, he let them go. 'I see you know nothing, get out.'

As the door closed behind them, they heard the sound of his glass smashing against it.

It didn't take long to get Mr Vernish to the grille at the Fleet. The Countess instantly saw the panic deep in his eyes, reflected in the flickering light of a passing link.

'I didn't do it. Really, madam. I did not kill Anne Lucas.'

The grille was not at its most crowded, but the seething mass of prisoners trying to get a glimpse through to the free world writhed and murmured all around him.

'I know that. However, we need you to cast your mind back again.' The Countess pressed her face close to his. Darkness had fallen and the moon hid behind a cloud. 'Find a dark hole somewhere in the prison and go through that night in your mind, second by second. Memory by memory. Alpiew or I will return soon, and you can let us know what else you remember.'

'I will be hanged for this death.' He gripped the iron bars and pressed his face close so he could whisper. 'Hanged for a few illicit guineas!'

'Which guineas are those?' The Countess pondered. Selling gingerbread could hardly be called an illegal employment.

'How much?' Alpiew squeezed up close enough to feel the rancid stench of the prison oozing up to meet the cold night air of the street.

'Not enough to die for.'

A sudden movement of prisoners shifted the man along the grille, until his face was squeezed against the filthy black side wall.

'Get her here.'

'Who?' Alpiew knew what was coming.

'You know who . . .' Valentine Vernish thrust his hand through the bars, and grabbed the Countess by the hand. 'Becky! Dark Beck! She must confess. Bring her to me. Tell her of my plight. Only *she* can help me now . . .'

The heaving sprawl of faces and hands changed their pattern, and Vernish's desperate countenance vanished back into the crowd.

'To think we had a cold-blooded killer sleeping under our roof.'

'To tell true, we were always frightened of her though, milady.'

'Ay. Except Godfrey, who came round to her, I believe.'

They turned the corner into German Street and paid the link-boy they had hired to light them home.

'We must invest in a good stout lantern, Alpiew.' The Countess shivered as she strode up the hall. 'These link-boys will break us with their fees.'

'Trouble is, you have to carry the dusty thing everywhere you go in daylight,' said Alpiew, pushing open the kitchen door. 'I hope Godfrey has got us a steaming hot supper.'

Godfrey sat at the bare table grinning at them with his new teeth aglimmer.

'Godfrey?' said Alpiew, scanning for pots on the fire for signs of Rebecca's return.

'What is got into you now?' The Countess flopped down opposite him. 'The teeth must be in for a reason.'

Godfrey emitted a strange gurgling sound. He was gripping a piece of paper.

'Are you feeling quite well?' The Countess reached for the note, but Godfrey snatched his hand away. 'Spit it out, man,' said the Countess, hoping he didn't take her request literally.

Alpiew was at the fireplace, pulling the lids from all the empty pots.

Godfrey made another noise, this one like a watery groan.

Finally he reached for the teeth and hauled them out of his mouth, drizzling the table with strings of spittle.

'Pox o' these rum-gigged munchers.' He laid the false teeth gently on his lap. 'A fellow can't make no sense with 'em in place.'

'Well?' snapped the Countess. 'It vexes me to the pluck, Godfrey, when you don't tell us straight what is going on.'

'She wants to see me.'

'Who?'

'Rebecca.'

'*Rebecca!*' Alpiew dropped a pan-lid and it rolled across the kitchen floor, clattering to a standstill at the pantry door.

'Rebecca has been here?'

Godfrey nodded. 'She pushed a note under the door.'

'Let me see it.' The Countess thrust out her plump little hand. Godfrey handed over the drool-covered note. The Countess read aloud: 'Ten of the clock. Rosamund's Pond. R.'

Alpiew gasped. '*Rosamund*'s Pond.'

'Alpiew, you are beginning to sound like a cross between the new engine at the waterworks and a player repeating his lines. Do try to maintain a little dignity when under duress.' The Countess looked intently at Godfrey. 'There is no signature. How do you know it is from her?'

'There was another note.'

Alpiew's jaw dropped. '*Another note?*'

'Alpiew!' The Countess turned back to Godfrey and spoke softly, as though addressing a mentally bewildered infant. 'When did this other note arrive?'

'Oh –' he waved a weary hand – 'days ago. I picked it up and read it, but Sarah snatched it out of my hand and told me it was for her.'

'And what did it say?'

'Something about putting it off to the day after tomorrow.'

'Putting what off . . . ?'

'How am I to know? It was for Sarah, and she doesn't like to talk.'

'And how do you know it was Rebecca's writing?'

'Because Sarah told me it was.'

The Countess looked again at the note. The hand was elegant, clearly that of someone educated and literate. *Ten of the clock. Rosamund's Pond. R.* She leaned across the table. 'And finally, Godfrey, how do you know this one was meant for you?'

Godfrey shuffled in his seat and made a face. The Countess would have described it as the expression worn by one suffering intense indigestion, but Alpiew instantly recognised it as the Passion called Simple Love – the forehead smooth, the eyebrows slightly raised to one side, the eyes sparkling and elevated, and a warm pink glow in the cheeks. Godfrey's mouth was a little open, and his withered lips ever so slightly moist. 'It could only be for me,' he whispered.

'Very well and very good.' The Countess rose and handed the note back. 'But Godfrey, we cannot allow you to fulfil this assignation alone. We will accompany you.'

'But . . .'

'Don't trouble yourself, we will not interfere with any lover's tryst. We will merely lurk in the shadows in order to protect you.'

'But . . .'

'St James's Park at night is not the safest of places, would you not agree, Alpiew?'

'Yes, milady. 'Tis a well-known rendezvous for cutpurses . . .'

'The Tityre-tus . . .'

'Vagrants of the lowest order.'

'And all ladies and gentlemen of the night.' The Countess wrapped her cloak around her. 'If you understand my meaning.'

Alpiew was thrashing around in the pantry.

'What are you doing?'

'I know there is a very old horn lanthorn at the back of the top shelf in here. I am not venturing into the park without light. Voilà!' Alpiew emerged holding the filthy black lantern aloft.

The Countess pulled a thick candle from a sconce and lit it over the fire. She thrust it upon the rusty spike within the battered old lantern and shut the hatch. Through the darkened horn shutter it gave out only the faintest yellow glow.

'Well, Godfrey, better put those startling white gnashers back into position, and we'll be off. We have ten minutes till your romantic assignation.'

There were chandeliers and sconces glimmering through many windows at St James's Palace and Cleveland House as they passed. Alpiew noted that when they were in the park and heading home, those buildings would be a good landmark by which to steer a course, just as sailors made use of the stars.

Godfrey walked a few paces before them as they entered the park. Holding the lantern aloft, Alpiew went first, the Countess gripping on to her elbow.

In the distance an owl shrieked.

'We should chatter gaily,' said the Countess in a low voice. 'So that we seem unafraid.'

'Cold, isn't it?' said Alpiew.

'Yes,' the Countess replied as loudly as she could.

'Even for April.'

'Indeed.'

They trudged along in silence, passing under a small copse of elm trees.

'What if she is lurking here, ready to kill us all?'

'There are three of us, Alpiew, and only one of her.'

'And what if she has brought a gang of roughs?'

'Sssssh!' The Countess looked around her. 'Are you sure this is the right way? Godfrey! Where is the Pall Mall?'

Godfrey stopped and looked about him. He pulled out his teeth. '*The* Pall Mall or Pall Mall *Street*?'

'We are in the park, Godfrey,' hissed Alpiew. 'Why would we be looking for Pall Mall Street?' As Godfrey slid his teeth back in, Alpiew watched the Countess's face in the lantern's yellow glow. She could see Terror on her features. Alpiew felt it too. She reached out and squeezed her mistress's hand.

Alpiew's heart was already thundering when something hot and damp touched her neck. She slowly turned. The Countess was gripping her so tightly she knew she had felt it too. Someone was behind them. Standing very close, breathing into their ears. Alpiew slowly raised the lantern to the space between their shoulders.

The Countess let out a little squeal as she came eye to eye with a great hairy face.

'Oh lord, Alpiew, what kind of a filthy beast is that! It won't kill us, will it?'

'Criminy, madam' – Alpiew let out a long sigh of relief – ''tis only a milk cow.'

Godfrey was now some distance away.

Alpiew ran a hand through her hair. 'We should have alerted the watch before we came into the park.'

'And get turned in as a pair of wanton trollops, touting at the pond for night business?'

'Sure, milady, you are right. We could never have explained why we needed them here.'

'And who would believe that a famous actress was a murdering villainess who had made an assignation with an ugly old bugger like Godfrey?' She waved her hands. 'Look at him scampering onwards.' She raised her voice. 'Godfrey! For goodness' sake, slow down.'

He marched on as though he had not heard.

'Godfrey!' yelled Alpiew.

Godfrey stopped and turned, his teeth glowing in the dark like a strange hovering butterfly.

'Lord, Alpiew, that is a more terrifying sight than the beastly cow!' With renewed courage the Countess strode on. 'I feel well protected with our own bizarre white talisman as vanguard.'

The grass came to an end, and the three edged uneasily on to a path. 'At last, Alpiew. We are crossing the Pall Mall. I recognise the crunch of cockleshells underfoot. Rosamund's Pond is to the right now. We must take care not to fall into the Long Canal, the end of which we should shortly pass to our left.'

A fluttering ahead was followed by a high-pitched squeal.

'What was that?' Alpiew waved the lantern about, exposing a small herd of deer huddled under one of the lime trees that lined the walkway, and a swan nearby flapping its wings.

'Nature!' exclaimed the Countess. 'Phough, I abominate it. Nature should keep to its place, which is as far away from me as possible.'

A great splosh to their left caused them again to stop in their tracks and the Countess let out a little squeal.

'More swans, I think . . .' whispered Alpiew. 'Or a leaping fish.'

The thrashing wings of a mallard skimmed over their heads.

'March on,' said the Countess. 'As Francis Bacon said, "Nature cannot be ordered about." It is clearly here in bulk tonight to terrify innocent walkers like us.' She gripped on to Alpiew's arm and stepped back on to the grass. 'There is the Long Canal. I can see the water twinkling. Charles swam there, walked his dogs around it, fed the ducks . . . Oh, what a king he was!'

Godfrey turned, illuminating them with his teeth, and emitted a gurgle. He whipped the teeth out to speak. 'We are late. Please stop gossiping and come along.' He shoved the teeth back into place and strode ahead.

'Oops!' Alpiew giggled.

'Scrinkle-shanks on the path to true love!' The Countess rolled her eyes up. 'I think I prefer him uncouth. Come on.' She hoiked up her skirt and tripped nimbly in Godfrey's wake, with Alpiew scurrying along behind waving the lantern.

A cluster of trees ahead delineated the oval of Rosamund's Pond. They reached the edge of the pool and stood in silence. The only sound was the steady lapping of water on the shore.

'Should we wait here or venture around its circumference?' Alpiew peered into the gloom from left to right. 'Or should we divide and walk either side?'

'We stick together'; 'We divide.' The Countess and Godfrey spoke in unison.

'I am staying near the light,' said the Countess. 'If Godfrey wishes to go alone, that is his prerogative.'

Godfrey lurched off into the gloom.

'Come, Alpiew.' The Countess spoke in a firm tone, loud enough to be heard at some distance. 'We will take the anticlockwise direction.' She looked around her and whispered, 'I don't like it. It's too quiet. Listen! Even Nature seems suddenly to have been gagged.'

'Perhaps the lady is lurking in the dark, waiting for us.' The water rippled gently at their feet. 'I don't believe she is here at all, milady. It is some kind of trap.'

The Countess turned. 'Let us find an out-of-the-way seat and wait there for Godfrey to complete the perimeter of the pond.'

Alpiew stretched out her arm and lifted the lantern. The Countess grabbed her and jerked it back. 'Hide the light. It barely helps us find our way, but illuminates us as brilliantly as a piece of Dutch chiaroscuro. If someone is lurking here to do us harm, the light helps them find us.'

'Madam?'

'Shove the poxy lamp under your cloak. Now!'

Alpiew extinguished the light by hiding it within the folds of her clothing.

They both stood, gripping each other in total silence. 'I believe Rebecca would stop at nothing.' The Countess applied her lips to Alpiew's ear. 'Why are we here? Someone has lured us out of our home. Was it so they could ransack the place while we are out of it?'

'Lord, madam, I believe you have hit it.' Alpiew's stomach tightened. 'In this black we will never find the love-seats, placed so artfully around the pond. Let us rest here upon this grassy knoll, and when Godfrey returns we will all three run home as fast as we can.'

They settled down, and peered into the darkness across the rippling water of Rosamund's Pond.

'It's warm here.' The Countess shifted uneasily. 'Why is that?'

'That will be the lamp, madam. It is still burning under cover of my cloak.'

They both listened. The steady tramping of Godfrey, having circled the pond, grew nearer, coming towards them from the right. Indeed, as their eyes tried to penetrate the murky shadows, they could both pick out the jigging form of a white grin floating.

'Thank goodness for that.' Alpiew stood up. 'Now we can go home.'

They could hear the burble of Godfrey attempting to speak through his absurd teeth.

'Is he with someone?' The Countess squinted into the dark.

Alpiew stared ahead, trying to make out a more solid shape. 'No.'

'Good.' The Countess reached out for Alpiew. 'Rebecca may want us to be here, but I am certain she would have no more intention of making a nocturnal assignation with Godfrey at a notorious place like this than of strolling naked up Fleet Street. So help me up.'

As Alpiew stooped to haul the Countess to her feet, something crashed into her back, and she dived for cover, sending the Countess sprawling beneath her. Then some white thing flew past and landed on the grass. Godfrey's false teeth.

'Rebecca?' Godfrey groped around on his knees.

'No, you withered, senseless, quibbling, drivelling, fumbling nincompoop! 'Tis I, man. Countess Ashby de la . . .'

Grappling around on the grass, Alpiew's cloak fell open. She grabbed for the tumbling lamp but it rolled out of her grasp. 'The lantern, the lantern!' She sprawled out on the grass trying to reach the light, which was spinning away towards the water's edge. 'Grab it, Godfrey!'

There was a moment of silence as all three watched the flame go out, and heard the guttering of the candle-wick as it touched the water.

'Godfrey,' barked the Countess, stretching out her hand. 'Help me up.'

'I'm trying to, madam, but you have to help me.' Godfrey grunted, and tugged.

'Alpiew?' The Countess crawled about on the wet grass.

'I am here, madam. I have hold of your hand but, lord, madam, you are a weight.' Alpiew heaved.

'What are you both talking about? My hands are both down here, trying to locate your feet.' The Countess gave a little squawk as she located a foot. 'Ah Alpiew, is this your ankle? The shoe is dainty enough.'

'Madam?'

Alpiew let go the hand she was holding and stooped down. 'I am here, madam. Behind you.' She felt along the Countess's arm until she too was holding a foot. 'Oh lord, madam. This foot is neither yours nor mine, and is most certainly not Godfrey's.' She was filled with a cold terror. 'Do not move, either of you.' She scampered down to the water and retrieved the lantern. Fumbling frantically in her pocket she found her tinderbox and struck sparks, which ignited into the night air like tiny lightning flashes. Alpiew looked down. A heap of green and pink. A hand. A shoe.

'Godfrey, quickly. Help me dry the wick.'

'But . . .'

'This is urgent, man. Help me!'

While Godfrey wiped the candle with a greyish handkerchief, Alpiew with trembling hand flashed the tinderbox until the wick sputtered back to life. She held the lantern, gate open to increase the light, and waved it low over the ground.

The sight that greeted them was gruesome.

In a green velvet cloak lay a woman's body. The ornate jewelled peach satin mantua she wore was flooded with spreading patches of blood; her snow-white hands lay at her side; her skirt had ridden up, displaying her shapely legs, lifeless in their luxurious silk stockings, and her feet were shod in dainty satin slippers. Her pale shoulders were bare but smeared with blood.

The Countess gripped on to Alpiew, and Alpiew held Godfrey. Facing them in the eerie flickering of the candle's glow was the blood-smeared stump of a neck, a pearl necklace gleaming through the gore, life blood still sluggishly pumping on to the dark stained grass. The poor woman's head had been hacked quite off.

SEVEN

Despair

Absolute privation of hope is Despair.

*Consists of grinding teeth, biting lips, furrowing
the forehead. The eyebrows drawn down over
the eyes, tightened towards the nose.
The mouth open, and drawn back, the under lip
full and turned out.*

'It's her!' said Alpiew when she had got her breath
back.

'Rebecca?' The Countess edged forward.

'That's the dress she wore to play Roxana, milady. I spent
so long staring at it onstage, I'd recognise every bead, every
sequin.'

'And those are her pretty shoes,' sobbed Godfrey. 'Let me
lay my hands on the villain who did this . . .'

'I can't bear it.' The Countess snatched the lantern from
Alpiew. 'Let's not look any more.'

They turned away from the body.

'The killer is probably still in the park,' whispered Alpiew.
'Her body is still warm.'

'Had we arrived a few moments earlier' – the Countess
grasped Alpiew's hand – 'we would have seen the murder.'

'Oh, madam.' Alpiew's teeth were chattering. 'What shall
we do?'

'We should raise the hue and cry.' Godfrey's voice was weak
and shaky. 'Call for the watch.'

'Knowing the idiocy of the watch,' the Countess swallowed, 'if we stay here they will apprehend us for the crime.'

'We can't just leave her.' Godfrey fell to his knees.

'When we get on to the road again we will get a link-boy to raise the hue and cry.' The Countess stooped and gently helped Godfrey to his feet. 'It is better that way. Really, Godfrey. She wanted you to protect her, not to be hanged for her.'

'Rosamund! It has to be a coincidence.'

As dawn rose over German Street, while Godfrey slept fitfully in a brandy-induced torpor, the Countess and Alpiew sat at the table amid a stack of paper scraps.

The Countess doodled with her quill. Both she and Alpiew had been unable to sleep after the horror of finding the body in the park.

'Or could Rosamund's Pond be the secret "Rosamund" Rakewell talked of?'

Alpiew pondered. 'Maybe she made money by prostituting herself.'

'I cannot see that possibility, Alpiew. Neither her temperament nor her fame would allow it. You told me yourself of her horror at being seen passing through a whore house when running from the street battle between the Tityre-tus and the train-bands.' The Countess threw up her hands. 'Besides, if she wanted men, as an actress she could easily have looked higher than the common frequenters of a whore's rendezvous. Look at that floozy Nell Gwyn, and her orange-touting pal Moll Davies. They used the stage to snare a king. Peg Hughes caught Prince Rupert. Rebecca could have had anyone she pleased.'

'She got Rakewell!' Alpiew slid the two pieces of paper together. 'And didn't want him. Perhaps she wanted money from men, but needed anonymity? Remember, Countess, when a player catches a wealthy cove there are people like us who would make sure the world knows about it.'

'I believe, Alpiew, there is something here infinitely complex.' The Countess toyed with her quill. 'Explain to me why a woman of Rebecca's character, fame and wealth would go alone to a nasty, dangerous place like Rosamund's Pond in the mid of night? And why send us a note to meet her there? If she wanted to see us, she could easily have come here.'

'She was running from Rakewell?'

'Ay, ay, but he cannot keep a watch on our house day and night. If we could evade the bailiffs she could equally get past him. And she could enter the way she left, over the back wall.'

'Did Rakewell kill her, do you think?'

'It shocks me to say so, but we know the not-so-noble lord thinks nothing of cutting people down. Although their honoured lordships have thought to use the law to set him free, 'tis clear he has already murdered two men, and . . .'

'Of course!' Alpiew slammed her cup of chocolate down. 'If you were right and he somehow escaped the Tower that night and was at York Buildings, then he could easily have killed Anne Lucas too.'

'Or perhaps Rakewell had a month's mind for Anne Lucas. Maybe he is the mystery benefactor of her family. Perhaps Rebecca killed Anne, as we always thought. And Rakewell killed her in revenge.'

'But why would he renege on his promise to send the Lucas family the money to keep the child from the parish and the husband from Bedlam?'

The fire let out an almighty crack, causing the Countess to jump and bang her pen upon the table. A spatter of ink sprayed her face. She wiped her eye. 'He was busy that morning chasing after Rebecca. It is possible that her running away put the matter temporarily out of his mind.' The Countess put her fingers to her lips, thereby staining them black. 'And talking of running away, why did not Anne Lucas run from her killer, especially if they were running at her with an axe?'

Alpiew screwed up her mouth and thought in silence. Then she clicked her fingers. 'Remember in the shop at the New Exchange, Rebecca declined the belladonna – BUT she said that Anne Lucas used the drops on stage. Well, she had been on stage the night she was killed. Whoever it was that killed her, she would not have seen them, or at least she would not have been able to make them out properly. Belladonna drops blur the vision something terrible.'

There was a rap on the door. The bulky figure of a constable stood on the step, gripping his painted sceptre of office.

'I have been sent by the Justice to inquire of persons in this area whether they heard or saw anything untoward in the hours of darkness this evening last?'

Alpiew shook her head.

'Why, Constable?' asked the Countess, cocking her head to one side. 'What has happened?'

'A brutish and bloody murder, madam. Not three furlongs from here.' He nodded towards his scrawny assistant. 'And the only clue we have as to the identity of the assailant is this pair of painted wooden teeth.'

The assistant held up Godfrey's teeth.

'Teeth!' Alpiew grinned. 'Neither my lady nor I have the need for false teeth, Constable.'

The Countess bared her decayed row of yellow incisors.

'What about that old boy who looks after you?'

'On what I pay him? Where would he get the money to buy such trumpery stuff?' The Countess let out a little laugh, then leaned forward and whispered, 'Who is the victim? Do you know?'

Alpiew shifted uneasily. She could hear Godfrey tumbling about in the kitchen.

The constable also lowered his voice. 'Some fireship.'

'Fireship?'

'Punk, trull . . . in short, madam, a whore. Fancy clothes fit for a queen, but . . .' He wrinkled up his nose. 'I don't like to say in front of a lady, milady.'

'Say what, Constable? I am not squeamish.'

Godfrey lurched groggily into the hallway. Alpiew rushed to grab hold of him and steer him back into the kitchen.

'He had a night on the bottle, I'm afraid, Constable. You were saying?'

'Why would any woman go to Rosamund's Pond on a cold night, if she was not a whore?'

'A whore?'

'I'm sorry to use such language, but that's about the size of it.' He leaned forward and lowered his voice. 'No head. He must have kept it as a souvenir. Once we find the head, I feel sure, milady, we will find the trull's killer.'

'It is good for us, Alpiew, that only *we* know the identity of the body. The watch are still foxed, and will be until they discover the poor woman's head.'

'You are right milady.' Alpiew grabbed hold of the Countess, who had almost stepped into the path of a hay wagon, which had somehow become unhitched from its horse and was rolling backwards down Drury Lane. 'We can presume the only other person who knows the identity of the body will be the person responsible for hacking the life out of it.'

The players were in a busy huddle in the green room.

'Had an all-nighter.' George, who stood alone near the door, rolled his eyes in their direction and stumbled over to them. 'Trying to put on plays like this with two buffle-headed women who barely understand the structure of a three-word sentence is a tricky business.'

Although it was still very early in the morning, George was fumy from beer.

'What do you mean?' Alpiew glanced round the room and recognised, from her days working as a dresser, all the para-phernalia of an all-night rehearsal. The dirty plates got in from the tavern next door, the empty bottles, cloaks and loose bits of baize rumpled up on the benches where players had tried to grab a moment's sleep during any scenes they weren't in.

'You were all here all night?' The Countess glanced round the room at all the heavy-eyed actors.

'And it's still plaguey long and dull,' growled George. 'The performance isn't till four this afternoon, but we have to get it right. Rich has warned us.'

'Warned you?'

'We make a success of this play or he's closing the acting company down altogether and replacing us with dancing dogs, singing monkeys and prancers on the slack wire.' George threw his hands in the air. 'Bartholomew Fair curiosities. No thinking necessary.'

The Countess noticed that Cibber was not present. 'No Colley?'

'Oh, he's here all right.' George indicated the men's tiring room. 'When he wasn't onstage trying to assist the silly girls in their roles, he was in there scratching away at the new play.'

The Countess wandered off to take a peek, leaving Alpiew with George.

'No news of Rebecca?' Alpiew carefully watched his face.

'Wild Beck! No. Even though I don't enjoy her company, I would welcome her back with open arms.'

'You don't enjoy Rebecca's company?' said Alpiew. 'Why is that, George?'

'She's a very good actress, don't misunderstand me. But I'm terrified of her. She has me by the tallywags all too often.'

Alpiew smiled blandly.

'Not literally, you understand. A woman like that wouldn't touch me with a ten-foot pole. She's a mighty cold and haughty madam.' He took a noisy slurp of beer. 'And also too noble. And too kind.' He put his arm on Alpiew's shoulder. 'I prefer my women warm and buxom and loose, like yourself.'

Alpiew shifted herself, and George's arm flopped back down against his side.

'Rebecca, too noble? Come, come, George, you are speaking in your cups.' They sat on a bench near the open door and watched the street come to life as shops pulled open their shutters, and wandering hawkers made the first stroll along their daily beat.

'She gave us a chance, but we proved too mean for her. She showed us up, did Becky. Proved herself an angel.'

'Rebecca, an angel? What do you mean by that?'

'The business with the rings.'

'What rings?'

'You saw it. I know you did. Before the funeral. I felt awful afterwards. Anne Lucas died without enough money to pay for mourning rings. But it would have looked appalling if we'd not had them for her. The world would have thought she hated us, or was too mean to have left us the money. Rebecca decided we must have them. She asked us all to contribute.'

'And you turned your backs?'

'I gave her the coins in my pocket,' George mumbled into his tankard. 'But she jeered me, and told me 'twould be only enough for St Audrey goods. She flung my money to the ground. And she was right. I was being mean.'

'So where did those rings come from? I heard the boy say . . .'

'Rebecca had rehearsed him. It's why she was late for the funeral herself. She always wants everything to look right, even if she herself comes out of it looking badly. She bought the rings herself. She paid for them.' He started to sob.

'Mrs Lucas did not have enough money to leave for her own mourning rings?'

'That's right. Every penny she earned she spent trying to care for her husband and son.'

George wiped away a tear. 'Poor Anne. Such troubles, but always kept so cheerful. She didn't have an enemy in the world.'

'Except Rebecca.'

'Rebecca!' George leaned back as though trying to focus on Alpiew's face. 'You jest! No, no. Of all of us, Rebecca was closest to Anne. She adored her. They were always in the corner together giggling and plotting japes. Becky was her slave. She would have done *anything* for her.'

The Countess peeked round the curtain to the men's tiring room. Cibber sat at a table with reams of paper in stacks before him. Beside him on the bench sat the Reverend Farquhar, the Tower chaplain.

'Countess!' Cibber rose. 'We have all had a heavy night!

And now I am grabbing a few moments while Reverend Farquhar runs through my new scenes.' He held up a piece of foolscap. 'It is amazing to me how many opportunities that hack Shakespeare missed with his Tragedy of Richard. Take the last act, for instance. After that tiresome catalogue of ghosts . . . I have Catesby say:

> '*"Were it but known a dream had frighted you,*
> *How wou'd your animated foes presume on't."*

'And Richard realises at that moment that he must seize the day, forget the night that went before, so:

> '*"Perish that thought"* he says.
> '*"No, never be it said,*
> *That Fate itself could awe the Soul of Richard.*
> *Hence, babbling dreams, you threaten here in vain."*

'Then I have him turn to the audience with a cocky smile:

> '*"Conscience Avaunt – Richard's himself again."* '

' 'Tis excellent,' said the priest, slamming his hand down on the papers. 'A great improvement. More to the character of a villain.'

'In the manner of my Lord Rakewell . . .' The Countess left the sentence dangling, hoping for a response.

'Yes. And, er, and then' – Cibber grabbed another sheet of script – 'when Richard addresses the murderers in Act Four I have him shout: "*Off with his head . . .*" Then I hope to sneak a little wink at the audience: "*. . . So much for Buckingham!*" That'll get a clap, I'm certain. Especially as the head in question will be George's!' Cibber flopped back and laughed. 'You see, Countess, there are only two sure signs of success for an actor. And they are the laugh and the clap.'

'You've heard nothing from Rebecca?' said the Countess, inspecting for his reaction.

'She always was impetuous.' His face betrayed nothing. 'She'll have gone off to do what she wants to do with that fellow. But she'll come back, tail between her legs, wanting all her parts back when the allure wears off. That sort of woman always does.'

'And Rakewell will suit her for a while?'

'If he throws his money around like he did on that frolic at the *Folly*, I can't think why not.'

'Reverend Farquhar, you must have brushed against the noble lord.'

The priest looked up at her. 'Why is that?'

'When we met last he was imprisoned in the Beauchamp Tower.'

'Oh, him! That Tityre-tus fellow. No. I've heard tales about him, of course, from the Gentlemen Warders.'

'Do you know of any way he could have escaped from the Tower on the night of Lampone's lecture on the Passions?'

'Escape!' The priest blushed. 'With guards, and portcullises, and moats and lions to get past? I don't think so.' He screwed up his face in thought. 'And if the fellow escaped, why go *back* to the Tower? With his money he could have been on the night packet to France and safe away by dawn.' The priest picked up another page of Cibber's play. 'I love this line,' he said with a chortle: ' "*Princes farewell, To me there's Music in your Passing-Bell.*" Now there's a conceit for you.'

'I flatter myself, that I have a way with a new-turned phrase, Reverend Farquhar.' Cibber picked up his pen and dipped it into an inkwell. 'I must get back to work, Countess. We authors! You know how it is. Especially in my case, with all the additional burden of being a player in a company that has had to replace two of our leading players in one week, and is under threat of closure from a profit-hungry philistine.'

The Countess moved back into the green room. The players had been here all night. On top of that it was obvious no one here even knew that Rebecca was dead. But if she was not wrong, Cibber certainly had some connection with the unpleasant Lord Rakewell.

The Countess and Alpiew decided to speak to the bookseller downstairs before investigating Rebecca's rooms. After all, that sullen Sarah would probably be there poking her nose about.

Above the shop door the sign of the Brazen Serpent swung fitfully in the breeze.

Inside, the place was dark and dusty, books lined the walls and were piled in squat stacks on the floor.

'Can I help you?' The bookseller looked up from his newspaper.

'We are looking for Rebecca Montagu.'

'Ah, that would be upstairs.'

'No. She's gone missing from the playhouse . . .'

'Ah yes, read about that in the paper.' He rifled about on his desk and snatched up a copy of the *Trumpet*. 'Ran off with some fellow.' He glanced up at them. 'Pardon me. I don't always get this rag, but sometimes it's quite fun to have a little scandal with my breakfast, you know. And if you want scandal the Strumpet's the place to get it.'

The Countess winced when she heard the name. Why had the Cues not thought how easy it was to ridicule when they'd named the wretched paper.

'Professionally speaking, I often think I've made a bad decision.' He put the paper down. 'These books don't move like they used to. *The Maxims of De La Rochefoucauld* and *The Memoirs of Madam D'Aulnoy* used to sell like hot cakes, and even poetry and plays: Mr Lee and Mr Dryden moved off the shelves faster than whippets. But now I'm reduced to stocking up on the old self-improvement books and quackery pamphlets like: *The Housewife's Closet Unlocked, containing receipts for feeding a happy family and decorating a pretty home*; *Magic Ways with your Garden*; *The Mysteries of the Secret Disease* . . .' They are the only things that sell, and they sell like the devil. Them and newspapers.' He patted the *Trumpet*. 'Yes, newspapers. Like it or not, books are dead and newspapers are the future.'

'So Rebecca Montagu? You've not seen anything going on at her rooms?'

'Saw a fellow come out last night. Strange looking. Long black moustachios like a Turk. It was dark, so I didn't get much of a look. He was carrying a big bag. But it seemed empty. Not long afterwards, I believe I saw her . . .'

'Rebecca?'

'I couldn't be sure. But it was a woman, and she was wearing a green cloak, with the hood up.'

'What time was that?'

'Very late.'

'You didn't see anyone else go in or out?'

'Are you here to buy' – the bookseller folded his arms and glared at the Countess – 'or just to nose about?'

'How much is this one?' Without looking, the Countess picked up a book from a pile at her side and handed it to the bookseller.

'Two shillings.'

'I'll have it.' The Countess smiled at him as he started to wrap it. 'You were saying . . .'

'Heard some footsteps nipping up and down a little later. But that could have been anyone. Light tread though, might have been a child. More like it was that slattern of a maid.'

The bookseller handed the Countess the wrapped book.

'It takes all kinds . . .' The bookseller gave the Countess a sideways glance as she walked out of the shop and shouted after her: 'But it goes to show – it's sex and scandal that sell. If I stuck to them I could be a rich man.'

'Lampone!' hissed the Countess as they tiptoed up the stairs. 'We saw him go in. He saw him go out. Perhaps he was looking for Rebecca and, not finding her, went to meet her in the park.'

'But he says Rebecca came out after Lampone. Was she hiding there all along, while we argued with Sarah?' The Countess pushed open the front door and peered along the hall. All was quiet. She looked behind the door. The green cloak was gone.

'Where could she have hidden when we were here?'

'Under the bed. Anywhere. In a closet or garde robe.'

They opened the living-room door. Someone had definitely

been here since yesterday. Someone with no good intention.

The room had been ransacked. Papers were scattered across the floor, books tumbled from the shelves and chairs and tables were overturned. The dining room was the same but for one thing: the tea chest was gone. Alpiew rushed over to the closet and pulled it open. It was bare.

'Who has taken these things? Was it Sarah?'

The Countess was pulling open drawers. They seemed undisturbed. 'Strange, not to have had a go at these.'

'Perhaps it was Sarah's mystery lover?'

'Or maybe an altogether more sinister person?' The Countess glanced into one of the many looking glasses. 'Let's see the bedchamber.'

Alpiew pushed open the door. The room was white, dredged with an explosion of feathers. Ripped bolsters were tossed amid mountains of down. The blue figured-velvet bed curtains were pulled shut. The mattress was hauled off the bed and slewed drunkenly on to the floor.

Alpiew and the Countess looked at one another. What if someone was hiding on the bed, waiting to leap down at them with an axe?

Alpiew grabbed a walking cane from the box by the door, and stepped gingerly forward, holding the stick out before her like a fencer with his rapier. She stood to the side and hooked the drapery, lifting it so they could get a look in.

They waited for a moment.

Nothing moved. No mad axeman leapt out. Alpiew and the Countess edged forward from each corner until they could get a clear view in through the curtains.

Bolster covers, blankcts and velvet curtains were piled high in the centre of the bed. And staring wildly, her face contorted in horror, on top of the mound of drapery was Rebecca's head.

'Oh fie! Fie! Fie! Fie!' The Countess whipped out her fan and fluttered for air.

Alpiew dropped the cane and grabbed hold of a bedpost to steady herself. 'Oh lor', milady. What a shock!'

They both backed away from the bed.

'What shall we do?'

'I would say,' said the Countess, making for the door, 'that we should get out of here fast. We might have been able to explain being beside the corpse when it was found, but then to be first on the scene where the head is discovered puts a very strong finger of suspicion in our direction.'

Within half an hour they were back at German Street huddled up in the kitchen. Godfrey was outside, sitting in the privy.

'What a day! Should we let the watch know we have found the head?'

'If we do, that silly bookseller will tell them he saw us go up there, and the world will assume it was us brought the wretched thing in.'

The outer door slammed and Godfrey slouched in. 'It wasn't a nightmare, was it? It really happened. She's dead.' His eyes were red, and his face hung in an expression of misery, exacerbated by his renewed lack of teeth.

'I'm afraid, Godfrey, that is so.'

'Who'd do that to a lovely woman like her? Let me at 'em, I say. I'd show 'em.' He slumped over to the fire and adjusted the kettle. 'Anyone like a cup of tea?'

'Yes please.' The Countess was running through the further horrific discovery in her head.

Godfrey put the kettle to a pot he had already prepared and stood it on the table.

'Sugar?' He placed three cups round the pot.

'I will, thank you.' Alpiew went to fetch the sugar-loaf from the pantry.

'Godfrey, you must try to keep a brave face. Remember, no one but us (and her killer) knows that Rebecca is dead. And the constable is looking for the owner of your false teeth.'

Godfrey let out a grunt and turned away. 'That fellow's been out there again,' he said in a voice indicating he wished to change the subject.

'Fellow?' The Countess pulled her chair up to the table. 'Not Lord Rakewell?'

'No, no. This is an old fellah. Appeared the day Rebecca first came here.' Godfrey carefully stirred the pot. 'He stands out there all hours of the day and night, looking up at her window.'

'Mmm!' The Countess noticed her hands were still shaking. 'How strange.'

Alpiew put the sugar-loaf on the table, hacked a block off, and smashed it into small enough pieces to sweeten a cup of tea. She prayed it was not the bum-bailiffs with another shock for the Countess.

'I sat up in her room, afore, trying to contemplate, and there he was. I thought he must be the poor-rate collector or some official, checking the houses for the by-laws, or perhaps making a survey of the buildings in St James's. But when he saw me looking down at him he turned and walked away.' Godfrey held up the pot and poured. 'It's not a tally-man, is it, after 'is payment?'

'Godfrey, I would thank you to remember that I do not buy my clothing upon tick. It is all bespoke.'

'That's one word for it,' said Godfrey, glancing across at the frayed cuffs and worn elbows of the Countess's mantua. 'But whoever 'e is, 'e ain't up to no good. That's for sure.'

The Countess and Alpiew picked up their cups and stirred in unison.

All three raised their cups to their lips and took a sip.

'Mmm,' said Alpiew, wondering whether the mysterious man might not be an agent of the Justice sent to watch the house after the death of Anne Lucas. 'Delicious.'

'I love tea,' said Godfrey.

'I have to confess, I love it too,' said the Countess.

'Yes,' said Alpiew. 'There's nothing like a cup of tea.'

All three gave a contented sigh.

The Countess stared down into her cup and gasped. 'Tea!' she yelled, banging her cup on to the table so that the liquid splashed. 'Where did we get the money to afford tea? Godfrey, I hope you haven't wasted all our housekeeping on tea!

Luxuries like this we can do without. We could get a barrel of oysters for the price of few cups of the stuff.'

'Calm yourself.' Godfrey rose and went to the door. 'There's no expense. Come and see.'

The Countess and Alpiew followed him into the front room. Alpiew glanced surreptitiously out of the window. No one was there. She shuddered. Perhaps the strange watching man had seen them go out last night, followed them to the park, and come to the conclusion that they had killed Rebecca.

'Here!' Godfrey whipped away a beautiful damask cloth, which the Countess had never seen before, from a large wooden chest tucked under a table behind the door. He lifted the lid. 'See!'

The Countess inched forward. The chest was full of tea. She picked up a few leaves and ran them between her fingers before sniffing them. 'Gunpowder!'

Alpiew leapt away from the window, ready to shoot out through the front door.

'No, madam, truly.' Godfrey picked up a handful. 'It's not gunpowder. It's tea.'

'Yes, yes, clod. It's a very expensive tea called Gunpowder. Either that or Twanky. Both of them are served only at the best tables. Lords, ladies, royalty . . . It must be worth a fortune.' She closed the lid, placed the cloth back in position and turned to Godfrey. 'So, sirrah, how did it get here?'

'I brought it in,' said Godfrey.

'You!' Alpiew stared. 'How could you . . .'

'When?' snapped the Countess. 'How long has it been there?'

'After the wake. It was on Jemmy's coach and Rebecca asked us to bring it in for her. So we did, and stashed it in here. Out of the way.'

'And who told you that you could help yourself?'

'Rebecca did, milady.'

'Rebecca did!' The Countess pondered for a moment then remembered the brewed tea on the table and marched back into the kitchen. 'Then let us not allow that most precious tea to go to waste.' She slurped from her cup. 'I only hope no one else knows we have something of such value in our front room.'

'It was dark when I brought it in.' Godfrey's chin started to wobble. 'Poor lady.'

'Now, Godfrey, it is your job to keep an eye out for that mad fellow who watched the house.' The Countess could see that Godfrey was on the verge of tears and decided keeping him active would be good for him. 'If he comes again, see if you can corner him. Find out who he is. Follow him home if necessary. See what he wants.' The Countess tried and failed to suppress a yawn. 'My eyes draw straws. I'm for the land of Nod, if only for an hour.'

After a short snooze by the fire, Alpiew and the Countess walked out into St James's Park and sat on a love-seat under a tree near Rosamund's Pond, in clear sight of where they had found the body the night before.

The water twinkled in the sunshine. Lovers walked past, gazing into each other's eyes. Children ran about playing catch-me. A dog stood at the edge of the pond, barking at the ducks. Geese nibbled at the grass, and under the trees the deer sought shade. A row of milkmaids sat milking the cows near the Pall Mall, and selling cups of the warm white stuff.

A mallard was preening itself at Alpiew's feet. It shook itself and waddled back into the water.

'It all seems so different by day.'

'Two actresses,' said the Countess, 'both beheaded at night. Is that all they had in common? Why would anyone want to kill them? Either of them.'

'If the players were rehearsing all night, I suppose that clears them of suspicion.' Alpiew lay back and gazed up into the budding leaves of the tree. 'Though they're a scurvy bunch.'

'Perhaps they are all in it together.'

'Impossible, madam. Players hate each other and cannot hold their jabber.'

'You are right, Alpiew. In truth, I think Rakewell is guilty of both murders.'

'Because he hates players or women?'

'Perhaps he had a month's mind for Rebecca from the start. If Rebecca and Anne were so close, as George swears they were, then could not Lord Rakewell have disposed of Anne, thus weakening Rebecca's resolve? And when Rebecca refused him, he married her anyway in that trick ceremony. Perhaps it was his constant importuning that drove her to want to live in my house. Maybe he sent the note . . .'

'One moment, madam. Why would Rakewell want to marry Rebecca? For her money?'

'Of course.'

'But despite all this talk of money, she lived in rented rooms. She worked as a player in the inferior company. She was not the daughter of any famous or titled person . . .'

'As we discussed, her father was a barrister. Lawyers are always rich. Through fire, famine and pestilence they are the only ones always in profit. So let us ask at the law court or Doctors' Commons. They must have a record of those quali-fied to practise law. And the court of probate must have a copy of his will. And his name must be Montagu.'

'Not necessarily, madam. What if she were married already?'

'No. If she were married she could have got out of that marriage with Rakewell on grounds of bigamy.'

'She may have been a widow.'

'Oh pish, Alpiew. You are right. This trail is too convoluted. We need to find that wretched girl Sarah. She surely knows the answer.'

'But we do not have much time, if she is leaving tomorrow for the New World.' Alpiew rose. 'We must go to the girl's lover, Signior Lampone.'

The Italian's lodgings were in a large set of rooms in Cock in Hole Court, looking out over the lower walks of Moor Fields.

Alpiew rattled the knocker.

They waited.

She rattled the knocker again.

'I wonder, madam, that we are not too late. Perhaps he is

on his way to the docks already, embarking for America with his miss. Settling into his cabin . . .'

Footsteps echoed within and the door was flung open by a figure, white from head to toe.

'*Che orrore! 'O cinquecento cosi di fare! Avanti!*'

'What's he rattling on about?' Alpiew looked to the Countess.

Putting on her best accent, remembered from the voice of one of Charles's hussies, Hortense Mancini, the Countess addressed the Italian in his own language. 'Signior Lampone, *per favour?*'

'*Si! Si! Mi chiamo* Lampone.'

'Yes, yes.' The Countess was getting impatient. 'Where is Signior Lampone?'

'*Sono* Lampone,' the white apparition shouted at the top of his voice.

'*Ah Sicilia! Veleni mia!*' cried the Countess, imitating as best she could remember the things Mancini always shouted when annoyed. '*Banditti mia! Assassini mia!*'

'*Al diavolo!* What are you talking about?' Lampone yelled for no other reason than to shut her up. 'I am Ruggiero Lampone. Who the devil are you?'

The Countess peered at him. The features were indeed familiar.

'Why have you turned white?' said Alpiew, reaching out to touch his crackly skin.

'Avanti. Come. Come.' He turned and ran back inside, the Countess and Alpiew at his heels.

His studio was white too. Empty casts lay on the floor and weird forms draped with great sheets filled every corner.

'Gesso! Gesso!' he cried, thrusting a stick into a large pot and stirring the white contents. He felt the side of the pot. '*Mama mia!*' He picked up the pot and poured the creamy contents into a row of prepared casts.

The Countess looked at the water buckets and sacks of plaster of Paris lined up beside them. 'You are very busy, Signior Lampone?'

'Very, very busy. I am making an exhibition.'

Alpiew was perambulating the room inspecting the drawings, detailed studies of the Passions: Weeping, Acute Pain, Scorn, Hatred, Horror, Terror, Despair, Wonder, Love . . .

'Signior Lampone –' The Countess puffed herself up. 'Where is your paramour? Your inamorata?'

Lampone stiffened. 'Why you ask?'

'It is important. We need speak with your lover.'

Lampone threw his arms into the air and let forth a string of Italian invective. He stood at the bottom of a dusty paint-stained staircase in the corner of the studio and hollered up. '*Gioiello!* My jewel!' Lampone marched back to his casts and started banging them wildly on the wooden floor. 'My lusty-guts will come to you. Now I must work.'

The Countess moved to join Alpiew at the foot of the stairs.

'What?' A figure draped in snatched bedding stood at the top of the steps and slowly padded down towards them, head hung low, wiping the sleep away.

'Two women for you, *tesoro*.' Lampone was still bashing at the casts. He turned to the Countess to explain. 'We have been in bed. Art makes love, you know.'

'Sorry to disturb you, miss!' the Countess shouted up the stairs. 'But before you leave the country to set up your love nest with Mr Lampone, we need to know some information.'

The figure threw the sheet down and stood before them totally naked. 'What sort of information?' But the naked person before them was not Sarah. Lampone's lover was a tousled young man.

Unabashed, the Countess turned back to Lampone. 'But what of Sarah? You are supposed to be eloping with Sarah?'

'Sarah?'

The sleepy youth stood on the stairs smouldering in Lampone's direction.

'Sarah – Rebecca's maid.'

'Lampone! Play at buttock-flap with a mere maid! Me?' Lampone's eyes grew large and his moustachios twitched. 'The great Lampone, to cavault with a runt of a servant-girl. 'Ow

193

dare you!' He picked up the large stirring stick still dripping with plaster and ran at the Countess.

Alpiew was already at the door. The last thing the Countess heard as she joined Alpiew bolting out of the studio was the boy screaming, 'You faithless Italian mutton monger. Who the devil is Sarah?'

'Oh, whoops!' gasped Alpiew as they reached the street.

'Artists!' said the Countess. 'Always the same. We should have thought. A man of culture wouldn't waste his time with that slammakin dowdy of a girl.'

'But perhaps a violent and rough bully would . . .' Alpiew gripped the Countess's arm. 'Sarah was there the night Anne Lucas died – perhaps she disobeyed her mistress when she told her to go home, and did not leave the scene. And she could have lured Rebecca to St James's Park too. Perhaps the great man she hopes to elope with is Lord Rakewell.'

The Countess stopped in her tracks. 'So Rakewell would extort the money from Rebecca, and then leave for the plantations with Sarah. Of course! He is the type to have interests in the New World.'

'One thing keeps worrying me, though, Countess.' Alpiew leaned on a tethering post. 'Has not Rakewell money of his own?'

The Countess seemed to be getting shorter and shorter as she walked. 'God damn these marshy fields,' she cried. 'Let us head for the central avenue before I quite sink beneath the sod.'

Alpiew took her hand and guided her towards the lime walk.

The Countess's shoe made a great sucking sound as she pulled it free from the mire. 'In my experience, Alpiew dear, there is no single member of the aristocracy who does not claim to be destitute. The cost of the houses, the overheads, the lands they lost to Cromwell . . . They all believe themselves to be poorer than church mice. Pox on this mud! This place used to be a skating rink in winter, you know, Alpiew. They have drained it since. Not very successfully, it seems.'

'What is that noise?' Alpiew turned and glanced across the

fields to the far end of the path. A huge cloud of dust obscured the view of two horses, the riders racing each other along the path behind them, and heading speedily towards them. 'Hold, milady!' She caught the Countess's arm and pulled her back on to the soggy grass out of their way.

Dirt swirled up and showered them both as the racing horses thundered past. The Countess spat out a gritty mouthful. 'Phough! The Tityre-tus again, no doubt.'

Alpiew rubbed her eyes. 'They wear the pink ribbon.'

'See there! What a noble pile, Alpiew.' She walked briskly along the path towards a beautiful palace. 'Which great man lives in that magnificent edifice?' They stopped at the steps leading up to the gates. 'Is it the home of the Lord Mayor of London?'

On top of each of the piers, which supported the great iron gates, sprawled a stone statue of a recumbent but anguished man. 'Lord!' The Countess gave a little laugh. 'Those fellows don't look too happy. Where are we?'

'No doubt but they are miserable indeed, madam,' said Alpiew, lowering her voice, 'for this beautiful place is Bethlehem Hospital.'

'Bedlam!' exclaimed the Countess. 'This palace is a house for mad folk? In truth I think they must be mad that built so costly a residence for the housing of lunatics. It looks like the Louvre Palace in Paris – the home of a king.'

Alpiew nudged the Countess. The two horses that had almost knocked them down were tethered to a post at the foot of the steps, steaming as they drank from a trough.

'Where are those dreadful boys and their pink ribbons?' The Countess peered about her. 'Not waiting to ambush and rob us, I hope.'

'Gone in to entertain themselves inspecting the poor mad souls within, I suspect. Indeed, we live in a mad age, madam. So!' Alpiew dug into her pocket. 'As we are here, shall we pay our tuppence, and go in?'

The Countess toyed with the idea. 'Perhaps we may get a glimpse of Mr Lucas . . .' She grabbed hold of Alpiew and they marched up the great steps and entered through the elegant door. Alpiew dropped their entrance fee into the pretty money boxes that were part of two painted statues of begging gypsies. Behind the figures stood a large man dressed in blue and gripping a large staff. 'West gallery for female patients; east for male,' he barked. 'We have some very entertaining sights today in both galleries, ladies, if you'd care to make your choice.'

They veered off to the left, passing through an iron barricade into the male wing of the hospital.

The noise that greeted them was overwhelming. The rattling of chains, drumming of doors, ranting, singing and screaming, were louder than anything either woman had ever heard, even while incarcerated during the worst riots at Newgate and the Fleet.

'I wonder where we might find Mr Lucas?' screamed Alpiew, adding her vocal contribution to the cacophony.

Some of the patients were behind bars, others, considered harmless, wandered free. Alpiew peered through the wickets, one by one. 'Sure, madam, it smells worse than hartshorn or sal ammoniac. What a frowzy place. It's as bad as the menagerie.'

A man within was muttering about bread and cheese as he munched. 'Cheese is good with bread, and bread is fine with cheese, and bread is bread and cheese is good, and bread and cheese . . .' Another next to him marched on the spot.

'What is your business,' asked Alpiew, 'that you tread and tread so?'

'I am trampling down conscience under my feet, lest he should rise up and fly in my face.' He leapt forward and rattled the bars. 'Take care! Take care! He is as fierce as a lion when roused, he roars thus and thus.' He let out an almighty roar, causing Alpiew to leap back, and the bread-and-cheese man to shoot his chewed mouthful out through the bars, showering the Countess.

At the next section an old man was squeezed up against the bars yelling, 'I am old enough to have hair where you have none.' He patted his breeches. 'Come take a look, ladies.'

Alpiew averted her eye and marched briskly on.

'Oh, Alpiew,' cried the Countess in alarm. 'What frantic humours possess these creatures to make them thus?'

A pretty boy near them was jigging up and down, muttering intensely.

'What does he say?'

'Help, help, help, help, madam.'

'How can we help you, boy?' asked the Countess, hoping to give him a sweetmeat or money to alleviate his evident suffering.

'No one can help me now. Take care, old dame, for I am trying to hold back my piss, but when it comes forth you will surely be drowned along with all the souls in here.'

The Countess stepped swiftly away. 'What a bubble is life, Alpiew. A mere puff!' She raised her 'kerchief to her nose to mitigate the stench.

'These poor, poor wretches.' Alpiew gazed into the next row of frenzied inmates. 'Alas, alack, madam . . .' A man near to the Countess leaned towards her and shook his head. 'These are sad souls indeed.'

'A pitiful spectacle, sir,' replied the Countess, through the filter of her bunched 'kerchief. 'We are here seeking out a friend. Mr Lucas?'

'Lucas? No. I know him not.' The man fell into step with her. 'I am a stock-jobber in the City. I like to wander the galleries here. For my sanity's sake. Money is my business. And a fine one it is, to be sure. Money rules the world these days.' He touched the Countess's elbow. 'Could you take a tip from me. Invest, madam! Invest your gold. You can double it, treble it!'

Although she didn't have much gold, and certainly none to spare for investing, the proposition sounded intriguing. 'Which stock, or commodity, or company would you suggest, sir?'

The man looked around to check he was not overheard. 'Air, ma'am. That's the thing. Air. It will go higher and higher.'

The Countess flinched. What was the man waffling about?

'Believe me, ma'am. I know my business. I had the tip from the man himself.'

'Which man is that, sirrah?'

'Why the man in the moon, of course.' The man shrugged and nodded knowingly. 'And if he doesn't know, madam, who does? Tell me that?'

'Remember, milady, some of the patients have the liberty of the gallery.' Alpiew grabbed hold of the Countess and steered her safely on. 'In this, the men's wing of the place, we cannot be sure who is a patient and who not, unless they are, like us, female.'

A tumultuous hallooing burst out behind them. Alpiew turned back to the Countess and raised her voice. 'It's hopeless, madam. There are so many here. And what can we gain from it? Of all people, surely Mr Lucas cannot tell us anything new, can he?'

'Who knows? Sometimes there is a speck of something which the mad can see, but which we do not.'

Then they heard it: in the distance, a soaring song floating above the clamour: 'Oh bonny Anne, I'm your man. Bonny, bonny Anne, catch me if you can.'

The Countess crammed her 'kerchief back into her pocket, hiked up her skirts, turned and rushed towards the singing. Alpiew followed.

They could see him at the far end of the gallery, near the entrance.

'He seems terribly tall, Alpiew. What has happened?' gasped the Countess, as they shoved through the throng of bystanders. 'Is he walking on stilts?'

Alpiew jumped up to get a better view. 'No, madam. He seems to be riding on someone's shoulders.'

The crowd was thick. They pushed past bunches of people gawping through the bars.

The singing stopped.

'Alpiew, can you see him still?'

Alpiew bounced up to take another look. 'I see him, madam. He is heading for the way out.' She jumped again. 'Oh, no.' She increased her pace.

'What is it, Alpiew?' The Countess's waddle turned into a canter. 'What is happening?'

'He is being carried by those two boys, madam – the pink ribbons who passed us in Moor Fields.'

'Tityre-tus!' The Countess tried leaping up, but only succeeded in knocking her wig askew. She grabbed it and propelled herself forwards. 'Come, Alpiew, we must save him. The Tityre-tus are wretched heartless villains. They would think nothing of dispatching the poor fellow for a jest.'

They left the patients' gallery and veered across the central hall, leaping down the marble steps two at a time. Alpiew was some way ahead, despite colliding with a gang of giggling girls coming up. She pushed through the huge doors and across the courtyard. As she made it through the piers of the great gate she watched the two boys gallop away with Mr Lucas riding pillion.

'Well, I don't know,' gasped the Countess as she limped up to Alpiew. 'What is going on?'

'I don't know.' Alpiew put her arm round the Countess. 'But it is very ominous. I fear for the safety of the poor bewildered gentleman.'

'Ay.' The Countess stared at the cloud of dust disappearing into the distance. 'The poor man may be cracked, but there's already been enough misfortune in that pitiable family. And Rakewell is quite the most unscrupulous operator I have ever encountered in my life.' She turned and looked about her. 'Which way is quickest to Lincoln's Inn Fields? I believe there is only one course left us.'

'Oh, madam –' Alpiew bit her lip – 'what would that be?'

'We must go to the Justice and tell him everything.'

EIGHT

Astonishment

*Excess of Wonder, when we know not whether
an object is good for us or not.*

*The eyebrows raised, more in the centre than the
ends. The mouth open, the lips dry.*

Aparade of elegant houses called Newman's Row made
up the northern side of Lincoln's Inn Fields. The Justice
lived on the western corner.

Alpiew saw the Countess to the front door then marched
on alone to German Street.

The Countess knocked. A footman answered and showed
her inside.

Within minutes she was ushered in to the great man. He
sat in an elegantly turned chair, smoking a long pipe. As the
Countess entered, he rose and offered her a chair on the other
side of the fireplace.

'So, Countess! I have not had the pleasure previously, I
believe. How can I be of service?'

'I am here about a murder. Or rather a brace of murders,
an illicit marriage ceremony, an escape of a prisoner from the
Tower, bribery and corruption at the highest level, a burglary
and an abduction.'

'My word!' The Justice blew out a great cloud of bluish
smoke. 'Now there's a catalogue of crime for you. Are you
trying to keep me out of retirement?'

'I knew one of the murdered women. And am horrified not

only by the crimes themselves, but also by the trail of mayhem that the perpetrator of these heinous acts has left in his wake.'

The Justice rang a small hand-bell and a servant bobbed in. 'Bring us a pot of tea, and some biscuits please, Tom.' He looked to the Countess. 'Or would you prefer a glass of Nantes?'

'Brandy! Mid-afternoon?' The Countess shifted uneasily in her chair. Did he take her for a mad old soak? 'No thank you, my lord, tea will be lovely.'

When the servant had gone the Justice leaned across the small table that separated them. 'Name him!'

'Name whom?'

'I presume you suspect someone. So who is this villain who has left this trail of mayhem behind him?'

'A certain titled gentleman, sir. A fellow with the arrogance and confidence of someone who believes himself to be above the law, my lord.'

'Above the law, indeed!' The door opened and Tom reappeared with the tea tray. He laid out the cups in silence and left. 'I cannot say I approve of having such a desperado within the Town. So spit it out, Countess. Let us apprehend this scoundrel and restore some sanity to a troubled world.'

'The man is the leader of the Tityre-tus,' said the Countess, raising her cup to her lips. 'Lord Rakewell.'

'Giles Rakewell!' The Justice drained his cup, then picked up his pipe again and stuffed it with a wad of tobacco. He leaned towards the fire, lit a spill, applied it to the bowl and puffed until the blue smoke rose in a curling ribbon. 'Thank you for bringing me that information. It has been most useful.'

'Don't you want to hear the details?' The Countess could not believe that the Justice seemed so at ease with this information. 'I know of times, places . . .'

'That won't be necessary, Countess. We are all familiar with the misdemeanours of Rakewell and his midnight boys.' He rose and held the door open for her. 'I shall look into the matter. It's most kind of you to come here. Londoners will sleep easier while people like you show such compassion.'

Before she knew it, she was out on the street again.

A lamplighter was up a ladder, replacing the candle in one of the hanging lanterns in the square. How strange, thought the Countess, that the streets which are so elegant and crime-free are the ones with the greatest protection. Perhaps it was the same for people as places: the most powerful had the most protection. For in her bones she knew that her visit had been pointless. The man was going to do absolutely nothing about her information and Lord Rakewell need have no fear of being apprehended by Lord Justice Ingram.

'He was here again,' snarled Godfrey as Alpiew came in. 'The snoop. Stood out there a good hour. When I opened the front door to call him over, he rushed away.'

'What does he look like, this fellow?'

'Ordinary,' said Godfrey, sticking a poker into the fire and shaking the coals about until the glow started to warm the room. 'Greyish hair. Medium height. Shabby clothes. Bit younger than me.'

Alpiew put the Countess's newly purchased book down on her bed. She was tempted to open the wrapper and see what she had bought, hoping it might be some challenging work of philosophy, but decided she had better wait for the Countess to return first. She had noted that writings scribbled across Lampone's sketches of the Passions frequently quoted from Descartes as well as Hobbes and hoped to lay her hands on something by him too, now that she had finished *Leviathan* and returned it to its normal position under Godfrey's bed.

Just then she noticed that a deep gurgling sound was coming from beneath the Countess's bed.

'What is that?' Alpiew had no sooner bent down to investigate than Rebecca's dog sprang out at her and took the hem of her dress between his teeth, shaking it like a rat. 'How the devil?'

'Oh, he was waiting on the step this afternoon.' Godfrey bent down and pulled the dog away from Alpiew and placed him on his lap, where he was immediately docile as Godfrey scratched his head. 'Looking for *her*, I shouldn't wonder. Don't worry, boy, I'll take you back to her place later, and make sure that girl feeds you.' He stroked the dog for a few moments, and Alpiew noticed tears building up in his eyes. She looked away and busied herself.

'I keep thinking on her,' said Godfrey. 'And the monster that could do such a thing.'

Godfrey's face was set in its usual grouchy expression, but Alpiew did not miss the quiver in his voice and his trembling chin. What was the Passion for that, Alpiew wondered. Was he covering up sorrow for want of seeming soft?

She put her hand on Godfrey's shoulder and joined him staring into the fire.

It was growing dark when the Countess arrived home, flustered and wet. 'The heavens have opened.' She shook her clothing and beckoned. 'Quickly, Alpiew. I need to go to the constable's home before he is called out by the usual night-time delinquencies.'

'What about the Justice, madam?' Alpiew grabbed cloaks for them both. 'Did he send you to the constable?'

'No. The Justice has no more intention of investigating Rakewell than I do of becoming a member of parliament. So we are going to the constable, and we are going to identify the corpse for him. Perhaps once the forces of law know who it is they will speed things along a little.'

'Countess, what a pleasure.' The constable showed them into his hall. 'So what has happened? Has there been a burglary? Footpads stalking about the well-ordered streets of St James's?'

'No, Constable,' said the Countess. 'We are here about the body of the woman you found last night in the park. We believe we may know the identity of the murdered woman.'

'Ah yes, the lady in the green cloak.' He lowered his voice. 'I wouldn't worry too much on her account. 'Tis true, milady, she died of murder all right, but . . .'

'But what?'

'I wouldn't involve yourself with the likes of her. These night-walkers bring these things upon themselves. You can't go round touting for men in lonely places and not expect trouble.'

'But . . .'

'Anyhow, in my opinion, she was better off dead. It may have been a merciful release.'

'I'm sorry, Constable, I fail to understand you.'

'She'd had it anyway!' The Countess was almost bowled off her feet by the rancid smell of his breath as he whispered into her face. 'A matter of weeks, I'm told, and she'd have been as dead as she is now.'

'Constable, I have no idea what you are talking about. Why would she be dead?'

'Because she could no longer go on living.'

'You mean she was being shadowed?' Alpiew thought about the man Godfrey said was watching their house. 'Her killer would have found her in due time?'

'In a manner of speaking, yes.'

'Well, Constable, will you kindly discover this villain to us? I hope you have arranged for him to be held under lock and key.'

'I've lost you again, madam. I say she would have been dead, 'tis true, but her killer was no man . . .'

'A woman?' Alpiew gasped.

'She was ravaged, milady.' The constable screwed his eyebrows together and applied his lips to the Countess's ear. 'Ravaged with the Scotch fiddle, madam. Frenchified with a Naples canker.' He pulled himself up to his full height. 'In plain English, Countess: she was Scabbadoed!'

'I fail to comprehend you, sirrah.' The Countess drew away and gave her ear a wipe to remove the spittle that had adhered to it. 'When you promise us plain English, you might oblige by delivering it.'

'Sorry, milady, yes, indeed. Plain English. Well, you see, the dead woman may have been murdered, but according to the chirurgeon who attended her corpse, murdering wasn't necessary.'

The Countess shot him a look of total bafflement.

'The unfortunate woman,' he continued, 'would have died soon without the aid of an assassin, for she was in the final stages of the Spanish Pox!'

'Spanish Pox!' said Alpiew in a low voice. 'You mean she had syphilis?'

'Riddled with it, ladies.' The constable screwed up his face in distaste. 'We saw the moment we took the clothes off her. Never seen a body in such a bad state. Sores, cankers . . . Eeeeuch!' He shuddered.

Rebecca riddled with syphilis! The Countess couldn't believe it. How could a girl so intelligent and beautiful let something so avoidable happen to herself? And the news would destroy her memory. The Countess bustled Alpiew towards the door. 'I have made a mistake, Constable. The lady we are missing cannot be the one you refer to. Come, Alpiew. I am so sorry to have taken up your time, sirrah.'

It was raining still and dark. The Countess and Alpiew pulled up their hoods and huddled close to each other.

'That was a queer turn, Countess. Why did you not tell him?'

'Rebecca is dead. But she was well known. I don't think informing the constable that the body was hers, and that therefore she was infected with the pox, would serve any purpose but to give the citizens of London something unnecessary to drool over.'

Alpiew, while seeing the irony of this decision (for after all, she and the Countess were in the business of spreading such tales) agreed. She wondered whether the Countess might be saving it up for the benefit of the *Trumpet* readers at a later date.

'I worry about Godfrey.' The Countess lurched forward into the rain. 'We must protect him of all people from this awful news. At least until he seems to be his old self.'

They trooped along in silence. When they reached German Street, they found Godfrey huddled in a doorway some way along the street from their own house. He jumped out and blocked their way. 'He's here again! The house-watcher.' He cocked his head backwards.

The Countess screwed up her eyes and peered ahead. A man, wrapped up in a great cloak and rough felt hat stood in the torrential rain, staring up at the first-floor window of the Countess's house.

'Oh lord, madam –' Alpiew gripped the Countess's arm – 'I know him. It's that mad fellow from the playhouse. He was in the ladies' tiring room . . . Name of Nickum.'

'You're sure, Alpiew? Godfrey, you are certain it is the same man *you* have seen loitering here before?'

'Oh, that's him all right.'

'So he is one and the same.' The Countess huddled in a doorway while peering up the street. 'I thought they had passed a law against men going backstage?'

'They have, but he sneaked in. It was in the middle of the play, madam. I recall that Rebecca was frightened of him. I got him out. But he was a right queer cove. He follows her about. He openly admitted it to her.'

'Come, my friends, we had better talk to this fellow, and find out why he is spending his days admiring our dirty sash windows. Alpiew, run round through the church, and come up upon him from the other direction.'

Alpiew bolted off at once.

'Now, Godfrey, it is very important that we get him into the house quietly. We don't want the Charlies coming and picking us up for causing an affray.'

A minute or two later they pounced, dragging the damp and bewildered man into the front room and sitting him down, while the Countess turned the key in the lock and pocketed it. Godfrey lit a candle.

'Well?' Alpiew stood before him, hands on hips. 'Why are you watching my lady's house. Are you a burglar? We could turn you in and have you locked up, if it took our fancy. So if you don't want to spend tonight on a sack on the floor of the Bridewell, you'd better tell us what it is you're after.'

'I know you.' He stared up at Alpiew. 'You're an actress, ain't you? I met you with *her*.'

'Her?' The Countess rounded on him. 'And who is "her"? The Sultana of Mesopotamia?'

'Did she play that?' The man pondered. 'The Sultana of Mesopotamia? What play was that in? I don't remember it.'

'So you are referring to a player, Mr . . . ?' The Countess smiled. 'I'm sorry – what *is* your name?'

'Roper, madam. Nickum Roper.'

'So now, Nickum – you don't mind me addressing you as Nickum, I hope?'

'No.' The man wiggled in his chair. 'Where have you hidden her?'

'I cannot see how we can answer that question unless you can tell us to whom you are referring.'

'You know who . . .' The man let out a sigh that was more vocal than a grunt. 'Becky. The great Becky Montagu.'

'It was *you*, wasn't it?' Godfrey lurched forward and grabbed the man by his cravat. 'Why oh why did you do it?'

The man grabbed Godfrey's elbows and started wrestling with him. Alpiew jumped across the room but the Countess held her back, putting a finger to her lips, while the two men struggled in the flickering light.

'I didn't do nothing . . .'

'So what are you a-playing at, you scurvy rat, loitering outside my mistress's house day and night?'

'And it come to that, what were you doing with *her*? I knows she was alone in this house with you several times. What claim have you on her? She's mine.'

'Mine!' growled Godfrey.

'Mine!' shrieked Nickum Roper.

'You finished her off, didn't you?' Godfrey's face was dark. 'You went to the park and . . .'

The Countess gave a yelp. It was vital that she stopped Godfrey before he let Nickum know that Rebecca was murdered. Both men momentarily turned to face her.

'All I know is, since she came here I've lost sight of her.'

Nickum Roper started to sob. 'I always knew where she was, day or night, whether it was Lincoln's Inn or Limehouse, but now, unless you have her locked up in an attic, or dead and under the floorboards, she has clean vanished off the planet.'

Godfrey gave him a good shaking.

'Put him down, Godfrey. I think Mr Roper is already upset enough.' She indicated the tea chest. 'Alpiew. A brew for our guest. Godfrey, please help Alpiew with the tea-kettle, you know how heavy it is.'

Alpiew steered Godfrey out of the room and carefully closed the door.

'Even that sullen girl of hers is nowhere to be found.' Nickum Roper tumbled back into the chair. 'I've been to her rooms. But no one's there.'

The Countess perched on a stool beside him. 'So how long have you been following Becky, Nickum?'

'I don't follow her.' He shot her an indignant look. 'I keeps her company. Sometimes she ventures off into dark and dangerous places on her own, and I likes to think I am there as a voluntary personal watch service.'

'Very commendable, Nickum.'

'Until she becomes mine, that is.'

'Yours?'

'I told her. I wrote to her. If she'll have me, I'll get rid of my wife and marry her.'

'Get rid? Will you kill her, or merely go to the Lords and procure a divorce?'

'There's no point talking to you.' Nickum took a step towards the door. 'You don't understand.'

The Countess most certainly didn't understand. She edged forward. 'You mentioned going from Lincoln's Inn to Lime-house, Nickum. Was that a figure of speech?'

'Ain't you never heard of them? The first is a theatre near where the lawyers work, the other is a place full of sailors, out past Wapping Wall.'

'Indeed and indeed.'

'She *was* going to marry me, you know. I could offer her a

nice home. I live in the City. One of the alleys off Paternoster Row.'

'How lovely!' The Countess knew the area. Any alley round there would be a dark dismal passage. Paternoster Row itself was a shopping street lined with haberdashers, booksellers and some rough taverns. There were also houses of ill-repute: fortune-tellers, apothecaries who specialised in poisons and love-philtres, and procuresses who were quite willing to perform abortions when their alliances led to unwanted offspring.

'Do you work in the locality?'

'I am retired now.' The man hung his head. 'Since my wife died. We had a little shop together. We were fishmongers.'

'Fish! How wonderful.' The Countess beamed. 'I adore fish.' What was the fellow talking about? A few moments before he had talked of disposing of his wife.

'Oh yes, we sold all sorts: bream, cod, tunny, turbot, haddock, carp, trout, eel . . .'

'That must have been so fascinating.' Making a mental note of some more fish names for when she next encountered Mr Cibber, the Countess brought him to a stop before he gave her the entire catalogue of marine and river life. 'I am almost salivating at the thought of your lovely fish. But back to your wife . . . ?'

'I am not going to discuss my dear wife with the likes of you.' Nickum's face darkened. 'You could never understand . . .'

'Then let us talk of Becky. *We* have lost her too, Nickum, and were wondering when you last saw her?'

'That would have been . . .' Nickum knotted his eyebrows together and held the bridge of his nose between thumb and forefinger. ' 'Twas yesterday. Night before, she had been at a party on board The *Folly*. I saw her get off and jump on top of a coach with that fellow she often has drive her about.'

'Jemmy?'

'That's the one. Nice enough chap. I believe him to be a relative of some kind.'

The Countess nodded. 'Cousin.'

'No, no. More like her brother, I would say.'

'Not, perhaps, a lover?'

'Take that back, madam!' Nickum leapt from his seat. 'You are an indecent smut-monger. I will not suffer such stuff.'

'Sorry!' The Countess held up her hands. 'It's only that with her recent marriage to Lord Rakewell . . .'

'That marriage, madam, is a fiction.' Nickum stood in the fireplace and gazed coldly down at her. 'I knows for a sure and absolute certainty that my Beck would never, ever marry a scoundrel like him.'

'Mr Roper!' The Countess raised her painted-on eyebrows. 'I was the witness. I beheld the ceremony with my own eyes.'

'No, no, no, no, no and no again.' Nickum Roper pursed his lips and stood resolutely shaking his head. 'I knows for a certainty that Becky would never have married that man, even if she had been held at the end of a pistol.'

'Love is a strange thing, Mr Roper. It throws together the most unlikely people.'

'I have heard her telling that poor unfortunate Mrs Lucas how much she despised him. They had a plot underfoot.'

'A plot?' The Countess edged closer. 'Rebecca and Anne?'

'Oh, I see! You don't know about that.' He sat down and relaxed in his chair. 'There I have a power over you. Now you're listening to me, all right.'

'What kind of a plot?'

'Something to do with Mrs Lucas's benefit, I gathered.'

'Her benefit performance?'

'I presume so.' Nickum Roper shrugged. 'I heard the word "benefit".'

'Where was this conversation?'

'They were sitting down in the piazza taking a glass of buttered ale one evening a few months ago. That blackguard had whipped through the place a while earlier with his boys, knocking down stalls and the usual scurvy things. I sat near them and heard them laughing about how they would use him to their own ends. They would make him a number one fool and booby in front of his friends.'

Godfrey and Alpiew came in with a tray of tea.

'Mr Roper was telling me about his fish-shop, Alpiew.'

Godfrey laid out the cups and poured, while Alpiew dropped in lumps of sugar.

'He seems to have led a delightful life in a lovely little house near Paternoster Row with his lovely late wife.'

'Prudence. She was indeed a lovely woman.' Nickum reached out and took his cup. 'This is a real treat. To be with fellow admirers of the great Becky. Did you see her in *The Plain Dealer*? She took an excellent part in that: Fidelia, who teases her lover beyond vexing.'

'You saw it,' said Godfrey. 'I have only read it. I know she would have been a marvel.'

'Oh ay.' Nickum slurped at his tea. 'It was her best role. I enjoyed her carousing with the sailors. She made a very realistic tarpaulin. But of course Becky was the expert on that. She knew all about the nautical life.'

Alpiew and the Countess spluttered into their cups.

'What had Rebecca Montagu to do with matters maritime?'

'Surely you'd worked that out.' Nickum looked up at them, puzzled. 'Her parents are sea-folk.'

'Sea-folk . . . ?'

'Her father was a barrister . . .'

'No. Sailors, both. He used to be a boatswain, and she was a marine-victualler.'

The Countess and Alpiew spoke together: 'Boatswain!' 'Marine-victualler!'

'Yes. Out at Limehouse. They're so proud of her.'

The Countess rose and looked firmly at him. 'How did you come by this information?'

'She went out there most Sundays. She'd ride out with Jemmy and take lunch with her parents. Sometimes I'd take a beer or two in the tavern next door to their humble house and talk to the local characters. They all know Beck.'

Next morning Alpiew knocked on the mews cottage that housed the Duchesse de Pigalle's coachman, and, after bribing him with a packet of tea and a promise of more to follow, the Countess, Godfrey, Alpiew and Nickum piled into the Duchesse's grand coach and started on the long journey out of Town to Limehouse.

'Are we near Scotland yet?' cried the Countess when they were half a mile past the Tower. She took to reading the milestones aloud. 'Radcliff Highway, Execution Dock, Wapping Wall . . . I have never heard of these places. Does the driver know where we are going?'

'Don't worry, Countess.' Nickum glanced out. 'This is the way Becky always comes.'

At Shadwell Market they could hear stallholders screaming their wares: 'Sprats, mussels, trotters, grey peas and baked sheep's head.'

'At least we're not eating here, thank the gods.' said the Countess, taking out her fan and flapping as she gazed out of the window. 'We are heading into the wilds of the countryside, Alpiew. I can feel it.'

'No, madam. I assure you Limehouse is on the easternmost edge of the metropolis.'

'What was that?' shrieked the Countess, gripping on to the leather hand strap as the coach passed over a large lump in the road. 'A dog?'

'No, madam. These are very poor roads.'

'Harrumph!' The Countess collapsed back into her seat. 'I thought you said we weren't going into the country?'

As they bumped along Gravel Lane, Alpiew herself feared for the coach. She certainly didn't want to have to deal with the Countess should the coach overturn or lose a wheel in these rough parts. Nor would she fancy finding the money to retrieve and repair the coach to its pristine condition. A paint job on a carriage like this would cost a fortune, what with repainting the coats of arms on the doors.

The coach swerved and leaned precariously to one side before finding its equilibrium. The driver swore. Alpiew popped her head out. 'Is everything all right?'

He indicated a coach that had passed them. 'Women

drivers!' he grumbled. 'Took the centre of the road. And going too fast.'

Alpiew watched the battered old coach speed away towards the City and resumed her place inside.

The houses lining the road seemed poorer and poorer the further east they travelled. Women holding babies stared up at the elegant coach as it rattled by. 'Look at the wonder on their faces, Alpiew,' the Countess marvelled. 'You'd think they'd never seen a duchesse's coach before. It is as though we were a blazing star just appeared in the east.'

The coach clattered to a stop, then took a sharp left turn as they came up to the riverside wharves.

'Are we almost there?' The Countess seemed to be holding her breath.

'Only a little further,' said Nickum.

The Countess let out a grunt and shot a dirty look in Godfrey's direction. 'I don't know that I can stand another moment of this stink,' she cried, unfurling her fan.

'Don't look at me,' said Godfrey, kicking Alpiew.

The Countess started frantically flapping. 'What in heaven's name can be causing it?'

'That could be many things,' said Nickum. 'The tanneries, the breweries of Shadwell, or the lime oasts and kilns of Limehouse . . .'

'Phogh!' spluttered the Countess. 'Pox on the place. It stinks like an old whore's undergarment.'

'Not to mention the foundries for anchors, nails and chains. The sheds where they spin the ropes, cordage and sails . . . there's a slaughter house and salting facility for dried meat for the voyages, a mill for gunpowder . . .'

'Ah, gunpowder!' Godfrey lurched into action. 'We have a chest of it. Very tasty.'

Nickum looked at him as though he was demented.

On their right now were stretches of docks, stacked up with all kinds of ships: from brigs, barquentines, frigates and men-of-war to the lowliest barges, yaughs and excise cutters.

'I always wanted to go to sea!' Godfrey whooped. 'Look at

'em fellows hanging from the stays, yard-arms and fo'c'sles. That's the life for a man.'

Alpiew shuddered, remembering her own voyages to America and back.

'Can't take you any further.' The coach lurched to a stop and the driver yelled down into the cab. 'It's the end of the road.'

Nickum opened the door and leapt down. 'Here we are.'

The Countess gazed out. The lumpy road ended abruptly and ahead lay only miles of marsh.

'That's the Isle of Dogs.'

'Mmm,' said the Countess, pursing her lips as she gingerly lowered herself on to the boggy grass verge. 'And, from their absence, I assume even dogs don't fancy it.' She turned her back on the wharves and quays of the riverside and faced the line of houses on the other side of the road. She shot a look at Nickum. 'And you are trying to tell us that the great actress and fashionable London celebrity, Rebecca Montagu, hails from this dismal shanty town crawling with amphibian tarpaulins?'

Nickum nodded gaily, pointing towards the last house in the row.

The Countess looked it up and down. A few doors away was a tavern.

'Godfrey!' She dug into her pocket for some pennies. 'Would you take Mr Roper to the tavern and treat him to a tankard of ale, while Alpiew and I make some inquiries at this house, which fortunately seems genteel enough' – she looked about her at the desolate dockside landscape – 'considering . . .'

The house was two storeys high, with new sash windows, unlike its neighbours which had only peeling casements. From the roof flew a red flag with a yellow anchor and an arm wielding a cutlass. The panelled door was furnished with a shiny brass knocker, which Alpiew applied herself to with some vigour.

The door was opened by a great swarthy bear of a man in a blue jacket and trousers made of sailcloth.

'I hope I am not mistaken in this address,' said Alpiew. 'For I have brought my mistress, the Countess Ashby de la Zouche, from London to visit you on business concerning Mrs Rebecca Montagu, the player.'

'Becks!' he said with a huge grin. 'Hey day, Sal, here's friends of Becks come to visit.'

He ushered them into a dark parlour decorated with beautiful Indian silks and carved furniture; instantly a large rosy-faced woman sailed in to join them. 'Gentlefolks,' said Sal, 'you are as welcome as if you had been here a hundred times, and pray, Jake, get us something that is wetting for Beck's two lady-friends.' She indicated two large polished barrels that had been upholstered and fitted with carved backs. 'Be pleased to sit. Sure, whether you be Christian, heathen or renegado, 'tis strange to see two rum-gigged ladies like yourselves so many leagues out of the smoke to visit our humble pinnace.'

The Countess inspected the bizarre clothing sported by these two marine creatures and wondered, if they were dropped in the civilisation of St James's, who might be considered the more rum-gigged, she or them.

A few moments later Jake re-entered carrying a bowl of rum punch so big the Countess wondered if he designed they should bathe in it. He plonked it down on a circular table decorated with compass points. Sal gave it a twirl and ladled out two glassfuls.

'Would either of you like a pipe of tobacco?' said Jake. 'I have the best Virginia.'

Wanly the Countess and Alpiew shook their heads.

'I prefer a sneaker of punch or a can of good flip to your t'other-end-of-town Green tea, don't you?' said Sal, swallowing a mouthful of the evil-smelling brew. 'Tea, in my opinion, is nothing but hot water and sugar, and your poisonable bohea I find always makes me bring up my dinner.' She sat back cradling her cup. 'It's a rough journey getting out here in a coach. A lot of luffing and lurching. You were better to take a lighterman. Not enough stowage in the hold of a coach, and badly weighted ballast for the land-straights in these parts.'

Jake puffed out a cloud of blue smoke. 'Your guts must be a-wobbling after such a journey. Can we offer you a dish of burgoo?'

'Burgoo?'

'Ay, 'tis a pleasant sea-dish made up of boiled oatmeal with salt, butter and sugar.'

Alpiew briskly declined.

'Or some salmagundi? My mate, Sal here, makes the best salmagundi in any latitude north of Biscay.'

'All the best ingredients.' Sal grinned and rubbed her hands together. 'Pigeon, herring, salt meat, pickled cabbage, mango, anchovies, olives and hard-boiled egg.'

'No thank you. We have only just eaten.' The Countess felt a wave of nausea sweep over her at the mere thought of a bowl of salmagundi. 'Now, about Rebecca . . .'

'Aargh, pretty Beck, that's our gal!'

'She has . . .' The Countess paused. She could not possibly break to them the terrible news without some preamble. '. . . gone missing.'

Jake and Sal exchanged a look. 'Missing?'

'Yes. She had a difficult run-in with a notorious scoundrel called Rakewell and since then has not been seen.'

Alarm shot across Sal's face. 'When would that have been?'

'Two mornings ago.'

'She'll be all right.' Sal sighed and relaxed. 'She's very good at looking after herself. She came into this world in a Barbary Coast tempest, and after a childhood spent before the mast I reckon she can weather the likes of that miscreant.'

'I think it may be more serious than you suspect . . .'

'Oh, you land-lubbers! Our Becky will find a way to keelhaul the likes of him.' Jake tapped the side of his nose. 'No cure, no pay, if you know what I mean.'

'I don't think you can realise,' ventured Alpiew, 'how dangerous a man this Rakewell is.'

'Oh, our Beck'd have him spliced and strung to the topgallant yard sooner than get beat by the likes o' him, truly.'

'But . . .'

'I'll warrant she's pooped, all right, but she'll pass through the Doldrums soon enough, and a fair wind will fill her shrouds again afore long.'

'Talking of shrouds . . .' Having made a number of tries, the Countess seized the moment. 'I'm sorry, but I fear I have some very bad news for you.'

'I suppose that wretched grommet of hers has upped sails and left port,' said Jake with a grunt. 'She always had the surly look of a mutineer.'

'I'm sorry?'

'Sarah. That sullen female who looks after Beck's London quarters.'

'It's worse than that, I am afraid.' The Countess spoke quietly but firmly. 'The night before last, Alpiew and I had the terrible misfortune to find a body in St James's Park. And I fear that body belonged to Rebecca, and she was unmistakably dead, on account of her head was no longer about her person.'

Jake and Sal sat in silence looking at the floor.

'Perhaps you are confused, Countess,' said Sal.

'I'd venture that the body must belong to someone else,' added Jake. 'And they've forgot where they left it.'

'Perhaps,' said the Countess. How could you make yourself understood by people who talked this incomprehensible argot? She grasped at a straw. 'Mayhap it is you who are confused, Mr Montagu. I was hoping you might tell me that your Beck is not one and the same person as Rebecca Montagu, the famous player.'

'Our daughter *is* the player, your ladyship. "Roxana", the Town folk call her, after the part in the play. I know it might seem as though humble sea-folk could not create such a beautiful and talented child, but Rebecca Montagu is our Beck, indeed.' He puffed another blue cloud of smoke into the room. 'And, for your interest, I am not Mr Montagu. I go under the tag of Jake Zuñiga.'

'A Spanish name?'

'My great-great-grandfather sailed over with the Armada,

got wrecked and settled in Cornwall. It's where our Beck gets her dark smouldering looks from. She changed her name for the playhouse, to sound more London-ey, if you know what I mean.' He pulled out another wad of tobacco and rolled it on his knee.

'I can assure you, Countess, Jake is right, our Beck is alive,' said Sal rising. 'You can count upon it.'

'But,' insisted the Countess, 'we have seen her body. With no head.'

'Poor you!' Jake sighed. 'I've known strong men think they'd seen mermaids and syrens and basilisks and all sort of creatures when they were half-seas over.'

'Have another sip of punch,' said Sal, holding up the ladle. 'A hair of the dog generally works wonders.'

'I don't think you understand what we're trying to tell you, Mrs Zuñiga. Rebecca Montagu is dead. She has been murdered.'

'Beck's springing a luff, Countess, it's true. But, as Sal says, that body of yours can't be hers, I vow to ye.'

A sudden banging erupted upstairs. All eyes looked to the ceiling.

'Ah, the old monkey on the poop is calling for Sal's attention.' Mr Zuñiga rose and held the door open. 'We've got a paying guest in the crow's nest. He'll be wanting another bowl of salmagundi, i'gad. Now, you'd better be a-taking your journey home, for Boreas may blow sweetly today, but, mark my words, the wind is veering on a south-westerly tack and bodes ill. Thank you for your concern. We'll tell Beck as how you were asking after her when next she blows into harbour.'

'One last thing, Mr Zuñiga.' At the door Alpiew turned. 'Would you know if a ship has left for the New World today?'

'The New World? No. Hasn't been one for weeks. And no Cap'n's going to set sail today, nor tomorrow, I doubt. I reckons as there'll soon be a storm fit to blow the devil's head off. So if you were hoping to venture forth to the Americas, you'll have a bit of a wait on.'

*   *   *

'They are mad. Stark mad.' The Countess jolted on the coach seat, flapping her fan at an alarming rate.

'How can you be sure they are Rebecca's parents?' Alpiew asked Nickum as the coach tore along the roads leading back into the City. 'It seems an unlikely prospect.'

'I know. I told you she visits them every week. More in the summer when the theatre breaks.'

'That tavern was full o' mad folk too,' said Godfrey. 'All talking some kind o' nonsense language. I think they may have been Muscovites.'

'They're just tarpaulins with their own ship-shape jargon,' said Alpiew. 'It's a weird kind of English they speak round the docks.'

'English!' growled Godfrey. 'The only English word I could make out was "Mad". But I wonder they had the nerve to call other folk mad when they're all barking themselves.'

'Oh, Godfrey!' The Countess gave a little chortle. 'They thought *you* were mad?'

'No, not me. They said the chap living next door was a Bedlamite.'

'Well,' said the Countess. 'In that they were not wrong, if they were referring to Mr Zuñiga.'

'Madam –' Nickum tensed – 'I would fight with you if you are implying that Rebecca's parents are anything but wonderful. As are all things connected with her.'

'Now, sirrah.' The Countess pursed her lips and turned to Nickum. 'You live in the City, I believe, so we can drop you at your home.'

'It's preferable to me to walk.' Nickum's mouth was drawn tight, and he gripped hard upon the leather door strap. 'I am as well served if you take me to your house . . .'

'I insist.'

'It would not be appropriate . . .' Nickum squirmed in his seat and seemed to become quite agitated. 'My wife . . .'

'But you are a widower?'

'It's difficult to explain . . .' Nickum tightened his lips and stared out of the coach.

'I'm sure it is. Your wife no doubt knows nothing of your intentions to marry Mrs Montagu?'

'My wife is dead. And I needs must find darling Beck.' Nickum glared at the Countess as though daring her to contradict him. 'You would not understand, but I feel some great misfortune has befallen her.'

'Oh, I see!' Godfrey was lowering in his direction. 'It was *you*, wasn't it . . . ?' Suddenly he leapt from his seat and took Nickum by the collar again. 'You did it.' The Countess pulled at Godfrey, while Alpiew shouted at the top of her voice for the driver.

The coach ground to a halt, the coachman jumped down and pulled open the door.

'Do you need some assistance, ladies?'

The Countess shoved Godfrey towards the open door. 'My steward has elected to ride the rest of the journey on top with you.'

'I ain't done no such thing,' snarled Godfrey. 'Let *him* go up.'

'That's all right, Godfrey,' said the Countess. 'You keep your seat inside. I see where we are. I will get out, and Nickum will come with me.' She held out her hand for the coachman to help her out on to the cobbled street.

'Alpiew,' she called over Nickum's shoulder, 'get the coach safely back to the Duchesse's stable and then wait for me at home.' She slammed the door shut as the driver climbed back into his seat.

'But madam . . .' Alpiew stuck her head out of the window. 'What am I to do there?'

The Countess cupped her hands together and shouted after the coach as it sped away up Little Tower Hill. 'You must wait for me.'

'So, Nickum –' the Countess linked arms with the man and waddled towards the Lion Gate – 'who is it that you suspect?'

'Of causing ill to come to Becky?' Nickum's hand was quivering. 'Lord Rakewell, madam.'

The Countess nodded and fished inside her pocket for the

entrance money to the Tower. 'And of what particularly do you suspect him?'

'I think he has done Rebecca a mischief.'

'A mischief?'

A Yeoman stepped forward and asked for their weapons. They passed on.

'Where are you taking me, Countess. Is she in here?'

'Say nothing . . .' The Countess nodded and stepped forward to be frisked. 'Tell me, Yeoman, where might I find your fellow Warder who goes by the name of Jones.'

Nickum tugged away. 'This is some sort of trick, is it not?'

'Come along, Nickum. Trust me.'

Nickum reluctantly presented his body to the Yeoman for inspection.

'If you want Jones, you'll have to wait there.' He pointed at a large mounted gun slightly up the hill towards Tower Green.

Just beyond the Wakefield Tower they waited, speaking in low voices. 'I thought this would be a good place to talk, Nickum, because in here, strangely, we are free. Within these antiquated walls no one can arrest you; so you are free to tell me everything, however incriminating, and I can do nothing about it.'

In silence Nickum perched on the gun.

'I swear to you, Nickum, if you say you have murdered her and thrown her body in the Thames, they cannot apprehend you whilst you are in the Tower.'

Nickum looked at his feet. The Countess realised he was clearly not going to help her.

'Then answer me a simple question: Why do you follow her about?'

'Because she is wonderful.'

'And where is she now?'

'Where should she be? She's in her skin.'

'Then, where is her head?'

'Atop her body, I shouldn't wonder.'

'And where is her body?'

'Countess, if I knew that I wouldn't have spent the last day wandering from pillar to post searching for her.'

'Which pillars and posts?'

'Your house, where I knew she stayed the two nights previously. Rakewell's house, after I read the *Trumpet*. The playhouse. Her lodgings in Little Hart Street.'

'And what did you see in any of those places?'

He looked to the ground again and started grinding a stone into the grass with his toe.

'What did you see?'

He pursed his lips and shrugged.

The Countess pressed on. 'Something suspicious, by your demeanour.'

'I'd rather not say.'

'I remind you, Nickum, within these stately walls no one can be arrested. So whatever you say it is safe.'

'If you insist. But I am surprised you have so much trust – who is to say what might happen once we are outside the walls again?'

'You can trust me, Nickum.'

'Then explain this to me.' Nickum looked the Countess square in the eye. 'What were you and Alpiew doing in Mrs Montagu's lodgings yesterday that made you both tear out of the place like bats from hell?'

'Simple,' said the Countess. 'Alpiew has a particular fear of Mrs Montagu's dog, and he leapt out of the curtained bed and frighted her out of her seven senses.'

'Red?' Nickum screwed up his face. 'Red is still at her rooms, and not with her? That is strange indeed, for Beck never is seen anywhere without the creature, except it be upon the stage.'

She could see Yeoman Jones striding down the hill and wanted to move Nickum on his way before she made her other inquiries with the Gentleman Warder. 'Nickum, thank you for your time. I see you are as genuine as we are in your desire to find Mrs Montagu.'

Nickum nodded, rubbing his chin. 'So I can go?'

'As long as you promise to keep us informed of anything you may find out.' The Countess grasped his hand like a merchant making a deal. 'And by this handsel we make a pact. We need to find out as much as we can about her woman, Sarah. We must find that wench to help us find her mistress. And soon. I know you will help.'

Yeoman Jones was upon them.

'So, Nickum, here is a shilling for your pains. And I will be looking forward to your report. You will call on me at my home in German Street?'

Nickum took the money and scampered away. 'And, Nickum,' called the Countess, 'if we find out anything, we will come to you.'

'No need to bother yourself.' Nickum stopped in his tracks. 'I will call on you daily, on my rounds.'

Alpiew and Godfrey jumped down from the coach outside the Countess's house. Having thanked the driver, Alpiew turned to enter.

Sitting on the doorstep, glaring up at her, was Rebecca's dog, Red. He was filthy and mud-spattered, and bared his teeth in a threatening manner when she tried to get near the door.

'How did you get out here?' Godfrey gave the dog a rub behind the ears.

'Deal with the beast, for goodness' sake and let us go inside.'

Godfrey pushed open the door and the dog waddled along the hall ahead of him into the kitchen.

'Ickle Red feeling hungry-wungry, then?' said Godfrey in a strange gurgle, pulling open the pantry door. The dog sauntered into the pantry, reared on to his back legs and waved his paws in the air. 'This what you want?' asked Godfrey, pointing at the end of a loaf of bread. The dog stopped paddling his paws. 'This?' Godfrey held up a jar full of biscuits – cinnamon knots that Rebecca had made. The dog yelped, and waved his paws while leaping in the air. ''E's almost human,' said Godfrey, tossing a biscuit down for the dog to catch.

Alpiew wondered where Godfrey had ever seen humans who behaved like this, unless it was the tumblers at last year's Bartholomew Fair, though they'd have expected more encouragement than a biscuit.

'I'm going to try and teach him some tricks,' said Godfrey, scratching his chin. 'I could take him up to Covent Garden Piazza and make a fortune if I could get him to do card tricks, or jump through hoops.' He clapped his hands. 'Come on, boy. Godfrey'll look after you.'

The dog ambled back into the kitchen, took one look at Alpiew and snarled, then leapt forward barking and baring his teeth till Alpiew left the room, slamming the door behind her.

Alpiew went upstairs to the room that Rebecca had made her own.

The furniture she had hired in was still there. Alpiew wondered where she had got it all from and how soon someone would come banging on the door expecting payment. Sarah's small bed was arranged to form a T at the end of Rebecca's more stately post-less one. Alpiew poked about, hoping she would find something telling, a letter, anything that might give them a clue.

Rebecca's fine linen underwear and a couple of mantuas hung from a nail driven into the peeling wall. A pair of her dainty satin shoes sprawled on the dusty wooden boards, and her pattens stood together by the door. There was nothing on the small table but the Countess's own candlestick. No letter-writing equipment, no pots of complexion, no books.

Sarah had obviously taken away the small personal items when she had run off.

Alpiew closed the door and came downstairs. How strange it felt to go poking about in the effects of a dead person. She shivered and entered the kitchen.

Godfrey was busily sticking pieces of bread on to the large set of prongs the Countess had stolen a few years ago from the park-keeper, who used it to pick up leaves. 'Like some toast?'

Alpiew sat on her bed and sighed. 'No thank you. I'm going to lie down and think. Maybe I'll work on the Passions.' She lay back and opened the book. 'What's that smell?' She sniffed and rolled over. 'Phough! Is it you, Godfrey?' She wrinkled up her face and breathed in, turning over to face the wall. 'Lord, Godfrey, where is it coming from?' She lowered her head on to the pillow and leapt up again. 'It's my bed.' She jumped off and stood up peering down at the bedding. 'It's urine!' She turned and glowered at Red who, leg cocked, was energetically licking his nether regions. 'It's that ballocky dog! He's made a piss on my pillow!'

''E didn't mean no harm. Poor little thing.' Godfrey rose and lowered at Alpiew. ''E's lost 'is mistress, who was a fine woman. So leave 'im alone.'

The dog stopped licking and snarled in Alpiew's direction.

'I've had enough.' She grabbed the copy of Hobbes from the bed. 'I'm going upstairs.'

'Rakewell!' Yeoman Jones led the Countess up the spiral stone staircase to his room in the Beauchamp Tower. 'Of course, no one would forget him. He is a terrible fellow, but had a strange charm about him.'

'In what way strange?'

'Let us say that I never fell under the spell, Countess. And for some inexplicable reason I seem to have been the only one. But as for his last night, I do remember that. I was on guard here. His room is directly above mine. He went, with some of the other prisoners, to a service at the chapel. He was out of his rooms for about half an hour, then came back.'

'Why would you remember that so well?'

'I thought it strange, that the boy should suddenly take to religion when he had not done so theretofore. But my fellow Yeoman, Partridge, explained that he had a superstitious belief that night that if he attended the service his trial would go swimmingly. And as it turns out he was right. I would have sworn he was going to go down for murder. But no. Like the time before, their lordships thought fit to acquit him.'

'Why do you think that happened?'

'Who could tell? He seems to have a very good lawyer.'

'What makes you think he is so good?'

'Oh, he worked all hours to serve his lordship. He came here just after midnight the night before the trial with papers and boxes.'

'What was that about?'

'Last-minute pleas, I believe. Mitigating circumstances. I remember hearing the bolt slip downstairs as my fellow Warder let him in, and he passed up those stairs.'

'Did he stay long?'

'Only a few minutes. I remember feeling quite sorry for the fellow, thinking of him trudging around in dead of night for that ne'er-do-well, Rakewell. Especially it being so cold and the poor fellow so swaddled up in a great cloak and scarf and hat pulled down low over his eyes. I heard raised voices, too. Rakewell shouting at him that it wasn't good enough and such stuff. I'd have told him where he could shove it.'

'Would you escort me to the chapel?'

St Peter ad Vincula lay just past the old scaffold. 'Some famous heads fell here,' said Yeoman Jones, back into his usual speech. 'Lady Jane Grey, Essex, Ann Boleyn, Catherine Howard. There were only seven executions within the walls. All rather sensitive ones for whichever monarch that ordered them.'

'Who were the others, then?'

'Margaret Pole, an old lady of seventy, feared by Henry VIII, Catherine Howard's lady in waiting, and Lord Hastings for plotting against Richard III. The roll call of names buried within these walls is most impressive: Thomas More, Bishop Fisher . . .' Though the chapel was empty, the Yeoman lowered his voice as they entered the porch. 'The Duke of Monmouth, and the overseer of the bloody assize against him and his followers, Judge Jeffreys (though his family claimed his body a few years back).' He pushed open the heavy door into the chapel itself.

'It was only after the Duke of Monmouth had lost his

head that people realised he had never sat for his portrait, so the head was hastily sewn back on and a portrait painter brought in. And that is why his face is so pale in the picture.'

The Countess looked along the chapel towards the altar. It was as she expected. A heavy wooden reredo blocked out the light behind the altar, and either side of the aisle cumbersome box pews, some six foot high, and other lower ones with red curtains dangling from brass rails.

'As you can see, the chapel has been brought into the present style, with up-to-date fixtures.' The Yeoman was still stuck in his official guided-tour patter.

The Countess could see for herself that, like most new churches in Town, the chapel could accommodate private parties who did not wish to mix with the hoi-polloi, in the same way that ordinaries had private dining rooms. She peered round inside a couple of them. 'So where would the prisoners have been placed? I imagine it would be a very complicated piece of security.'

'They go into the stalls, like the others . . .'

'Others?'

'Yeomen, the Governor, Lieutenant and other officials of His Majesty.'

'And if a prisoner went wandering . . . ?'

'Ah, no problem there, Countess, for they are counted in and out. We would soon know if someone had strayed.'

But the Countess had found out all she needed to know about Rakewell, and now knew for certain he had been the man who had whipped off her wig at York Buildings on the night Anne Lucas was murdered.

Alpiew stared at Rebecca's bed. It looked comfortable enough. She could lie there and read. As she perched on the blanket and started to unlace her boots, she remembered what the constable had said and leapt to her feet. Her body was riddled with pox. Suddenly the expensive feather mattress and soft woollen blankets lost their charm. She glanced at Sarah's small box-bed. The sheets on that one did not look too clean.

Looking at the whole scene brought her to a decision. All the sheets must be laundered as soon as possible.

Gingerly she set about pulling the linen from the bed and dumping it into piles which she and Godfrey could tackle later.

As she pulled the bottom sheet from Sarah's bed a piece of paper wrapped in a green ribbon tumbled to the floor. Alpiew inspected it. Nothing but a few letters upon it: W.G. G.V.D.O.B. VIII. R XX. She crammed the note into her pocket.

She went to sit on Sarah's mattress, but as she lowered herself she noticed that the box frame had ornate hinges in its middle. She tugged at one end of the wooden bed and it moved upwards. The whole thing folded upon itself into a square the size of a gentleman's travelling trunk. Alpiew had never seen anything like it and hoped no one would come to reclaim it as she fancied it for herself. She folded it closed and perched herself on top. She started to read her book just as the front door slammed. The Countess was back.

Alpiew rushed down the stairs.

The Countess, still in her cloak, stood at the back door staring at Godfrey, who was in the yard scrubbing with an enormous besom.

'Godfrey? What on earth is going on?'

Giving his toothless grin, Godfrey looked up from his task, applying the whisk broom to the paving with one final twitch.

'Getting it over and done,' he growled.

'Getting what over and done?' The Countess sniffed the air and threw her arms up. 'Do we have to live with this filthy smell now till the sun comes out and dries it all off?'

'I was only following orders.' Godfrey emptied the pail into the mud of the privy.

'Godfrey, have you quite lost your senses? I gave you no orders to wash down the yard.'

Rebecca's dog leapt up and paddled his paws on the Countess's skirt, leaving muddy streaks down the fabric. 'Oh fie! That does it! Is this animal still here?'

'I'm looking after him. He's clever, and he was hers.' Godfrey threw down the broom, grabbed the dog in his arms and strode past the Countess into the kitchen. 'I've done all this work to please you.' He kicked the bucket over. 'Red needs a walk. I'm off to the park.'

Alpiew stood by the bucket Godfrey had prepared and stared at the printed page beside it. '"To Wash your Yard: half a pound of sarsaparilla, five ounces of senna stalks and leaves, handful of agrimony, horsetail and sow-thistle, eleven cloves, one nutmeg, some hartshorn burnt, one and a half drachms of mercury precipitate, a pint of malmsey and three quarts of water . . ."'

The Countess picked it up and peered at it. 'This seems an unlikely concoction with which to scour a paved yard.'

'Godfrey?' Alpiew waved the paper after him. 'Who gave you this?'

Godfrey shifted uneasily. 'It fell out of the book.'

'Which book?' Books were strewn all over the kitchen, sat in stacks against the wall, propping up every piece of furniture. Alpiew followed Godfrey's gaze to the Countess's bed. A book lay there, the pages of the *Trumpet*, which had been used to wrap it, undone and lying on top of the Countess's pillow.

'I had to open it because the dog was pawing at it, and I didn't want it damaged before her ladyship got home. I was trying to put the book up on the mantelpiece, but little Red was so playful about my ankles that I dropped it and that page fell out, and I saw what it said so I thought her ladyship must have brought it home for me to start on, and I'd have ignored it, except I feared you'd make such a fuss about the dog, and I wouldn't be able to keep him. I thought I'd do something good, so's she at least would be pleased with me.' Godfrey strode out into the hall with the dog.

Alpiew snatched up the book and opened it at the title page. It was the pamphlet the Countess had absent-mindedly bought to humour the bookseller in the shop beneath Rebecca's rooms. 'The Secret Disease, plainly describing each degree and symptom. Wholly new in method and practice, wherein both sexes may, with privacy and small charge, without any other medicine or being exposed to quacks, cure themselves of that distemper which, if neglected, are dangerous as well as ignominious.'

She glanced back on the receipt Godfrey had used to make up the cleaning concoction.

In tiny letters at the foot of the page were the words 'erratum: page 49'. She flipped the book to page 49. It was blank. Alpiew started to laugh.

The Countess was still brushing paw-marks from her skirt. She looked up. 'Would you perhaps like to share the jest, Alpiew?'

Alpiew handed the book to her mistress.

'The Secret Disease . . .' The Countess flicked through the pages in disgust. 'Why does Godfrey have this book?' She read. '"Syphilis is caught by copulations, sucking or giving suck, immoderate kissing, dalliance, by sweat, by exhalation or lying in bed close to an infected person." Oh lord, Alpiew! Phough! Godfrey debauched and diseased! I never took Godfrey for a gallant.' She read on. '"The infection presents itself first by soreness of the privities, gleets and a running itch." Oh, what nasty stuff! "With time this progresses to a swimming of the brain, tinning noise, hardness of hearing, pocky skin, hoarseness, red eyelids, and eventually, if not stopped, flies to head . . ."' She gasped and lay the book down. 'The affliction must have spread to Godfrey's brain. Why else did he clean the yard with that syrupy stuff?'

'His action proves his purity, milady. The book is yours, and he failed to understand what little he read of it.'

'Alpiew, speak to me clearly, not in riddles, please.'

'He mistook one word for another.' Alpiew picked up the book and flicked through a few pages. 'Listen! "Syphilis is also gotten through sodomy, and kissing if either party have an ulcer in the throat or mouth from which a slimy juice proceeding . . ."'

'Hurry along there, Alpiew' – the Countess was fanning like a mad thing – 'before I disgorge.'

Alpiew read on '"... but the principal site of infection is inflammation of the *yard*."'

'The yard?' The Countess looked down, then wafted her fan through the air and indicated her pubic area. 'You mean Godfrey thought . . . ?'

'Poor Godfrey!' Alpiew shook her head and gazed out on to the glistening, sticky paving stones. 'Godfrey mistook his pillicock for a back-yard.'

NINE

Disgust

*Aversion towards an object which arouses
contempt.*

*The eyebrows drawn together, the pupils bright
and staring.
The nose drawn back, the nostrils open. The
mouth pulled down and tight shut.*

'Do you think we might light a candle?' Alpiew paused on the stairs before opening the door to Rebecca's rooms. 'I confess, milady, I am mighty scared of being alone in a dark place with a dead head for company.'

The Countess shushed, and they tiptoed across the threshold. It was only evening, but as dark as though it was midnight. 'If Sarah sees a light, I doubt strongly if she will come in, and we needs must speak with her.'

They had decided to come to this place as it was the only possible starting point from which to track Sarah down. Alpiew pointed out that, in her position as Rebecca's maid, Sarah would know all the comings and goings in Rebecca's bed, and, because of her intimate relationship with her mistress's laundry, a whole lot besides. It was imperative they find the wench, and where better to start the search but her mistress's rooms.

Alpiew froze and let out a little shriek when she saw her own reflection passing in one of the looking glasses in the hall. She gripped the Countess's arm and pointed ahead. A long glowing line marked the bottom of the far door, which as Alpiew remembered was a small kitchen, pantry and washroom.

'She's here,' mouthed the Countess, teetering on the spot for fear of creaking floorboards giving them away. 'What shall we do?'

'I'm not afeared of the likes of her, milady.' Alpiew pulled up her sleeves and walked towards the glowing doorframe. At the same moment the light went out.

Alpiew ran towards the door and hurled it open. In the black a cloaked figure lurched from the room, one arm raised and holding aloft a large knife that glimmered in the mirrors.

'Save yourself, Countess,' screamed Alpiew. 'I will deal with this.'

The knife tumbled to the floor as the figure struggled to escape Alpiew's grip. Alpiew lifted her arm, and smashed her fist into the interloper's face. The victim staggered forward a few steps, then, wrapping the heavy black riding cloak tight, lurched along the hall and loped down the stairs, taking them three at a time. Alpiew leaped forward, stumbling down the steps in pursuit.

The Countess listened as their footsteps echoed along the cobbled street. They were heading towards the piazza, where the crowds would surely provide an excellent opportunity for the mystery intruder to vanish.

When all was quiet she tiptoed to the kitchen door and pushed it open. The room was warm. A small fire burned in the grate. The Countess groped around on the table. She found the candle so recently extinguished and applied it to a glowing log.

On the floor was a china basin full of warm soapy water. A damp towel was draped over a nearby chair.

She inspected a pot hanging over the fire. It held a bubbling stew, which smelled delicious. The scene could not be more domestic.

Only one thing seemed out of place, for on the table, beside an empty bowl (no doubt attending the stew), lay a pistol and a pink ribbon, the famous symbol of the Tityre-tus.

Alpiew had less trouble than she expected keeping pace with the fugitive. No doubt her firm doust to the villain's chops had slowed him down. But the usual evening parade of revellers in the piazza came between them. She could see the fellow's short black hair bobbing ahead between the flaming links carried aloft, and all the hats and hoods of people out for an evening's fun, but as she passed the central pillar suddenly the runaway was gone. She stopped at the Punch and Judy booth and looked about her. The rascal had vanished into the crowd. A bunch of drunks were shouting obscenities at the puppets as they shrieked the opening song of Punch's morbid little show.

Alpiew turned and took a few steps, then something dawned on her. This was Valentine Vernish's booth and he was banged up in the Fleet. How was it the show was still operating? She stood for a moment and watched. Punch was singing, as usual, in his high nasal tone.

> *'Right foll de riddle loll*
> *I'm the boy to do 'em all*
> *Here's the stick*
> *To thump old Nick,*
> *If he by chance upon me call.'*

Alpiew strolled away. Of course the whole point about actors is that, whatever they might like to think, they are all replaceable. And where easier to find a stand-in than in a puppet show?

'Oh dear, oh lord,' squawked Punch as, still scanning the crowd for the tall dark boy, Alpiew spied a knot of Tityre-tus the other side of the pillar, leaping and hollering. 'Talk of the devil and up pop his horns . . .'

Mr Punch started bashing Old Nick, and Alpiew increased her pace. The Tityre-tus had someone in their grasp and were bouncing them up and down.

She tried to push her way to the front of the crowd, but a fat swarthy fellow shoved her away. 'This is not women's business, lass. Keep your nose out.'

Alpiew elbowed her way further into the throng.

The youths had hold of Cibber's friend, the Tower chaplain, Reverend Farquhar, and were tossing him this way and that. His hat was off and one of the boys grabbed his wig.

'Murder!' the priest shrieked. 'Help me! Help me!'

'I have it,' called a red-haired boy. 'Someone pick up his clerical hat, 'twill fly like a bird!'

As soon as one of the boys had hold of the hat they dropped the priest with little ceremony and dashed away. They had what they wanted of him.

Alpiew bent down and tried to help the man to his feet. Behind her the boys were throwing his peruke and cap in the air, aiming them to land on the globe atop the column.

'Not showing any of your upper anatomy to the gentlemen of the pit this evening, Mistress Alpiew?' As though from nowhere, Cibber was at her side, also lending his arm to the priest.

'Thank you for that, mistress.' Reverend Farquhar brushed himself down, looking about him. 'Most people are too frightened of those bullies to help anyone.' He felt his bald head. 'I shall look more like a monk in my wigless state. I hope I am not lynched now by some other fanatical mob, mistaking me for a Catholic!'

'Oh no, Reverend,' gasped Cibber. 'Your bag, your bag. What have they done with it?'

'My books!' The priest gaped at the ground. 'The devils have run off with my bag of books.'

'And it was a new one,' said Cibber. 'The absent-minded fellow only lost another last week!'

Alpiew looked all around them. There was no bag.

'I think with the ruckus some cove's made off with it, your worship. Probably not even the Tityre-tus, just some pilferer.'

'Well,' the priest continued, brushing down his breeches, 'he shall have little fortune from it.' He considered for a moment, then shrugged. 'The thing is full of history books, and much good it may do whoever stole off with it.' He smiled. 'I hope one day I can thank you, madam.'

'Still no sight of Rebecca?' said Cibber.

'No,' said Alpiew. 'Nor of her morose maid, Sarah. They seem both to be missing. Have you seen either of them?'

'We've a lot of work to do, Colley,' said the priest, stepping forward, grasping Alpiew by the arm and giving her a hearty hand-shake. 'I'm sure Mrs Alpiew has plenty to do, also, without our standing here gossiping about errant actresses.' He linked arms with Cibber, and the two men strode off in the direction of the theatre.

Alpiew realised that she had left the Countess for a long time in a dark and dismal room only a few steps away from a severed head. She picked up her skirts and ran, climbing the stairs two by two. She threw open the door to find her mistress seated at Rebecca's kitchen table. On her lap was a drawer, and she was going through the papers in it while sipping from a bowl of warm soup.

'Did you catch him, Alpiew dear?' She fumbled further into the drawer, pulling out a wad of papers. 'Not much here. Receipts for those lovely dishes she cooked for us, mostly. I'm quite tempted to copy them out. Help yourself to some soup. It's delicious.' She slurped another spoonful.

'You can't eat that,' said Alpiew, gaping in amazement.

'Why not? It's here, it's hot and whoever cooked it shouldn't have been here at all. At least we were friends with the poor, dead woman.' She blew on the spoonful hovering at her lips before slurping it up. 'That boy must have been Tityre-tus. Look –' She held up the pink ribbon. 'All dressed in black too.'

'They're at their usual japes in the piazza,' said Alpiew, ladling soup into a bowl. 'Didn't see him with them though. He gave me the slip.'

Alpiew started rifling through the side of the drawer nearest her. 'Bills and invoices; washing lists and receipts. I see what you mean.' She looked round the room. 'Is there any bread?'

'Do you think, Alpiew' – the Countess puckered her lips

and frowned – 'that if there was it wouldn't be on my plate? Hey day, what's this?' She pulled a note from the drawer. 'Fan me ye winds! Look, Alpiew.' She laid the piece of paper flat on the table-top. 'That is in her writing – or rather the same writing that Godfrey told us was hers, is it not?'

'But, madam –' Alpiew gazed at her – 'what is so strange about that? These are her rooms, after all.'

The Countess smoothed the paper over and read: 'Tonight. G.V., Duke of Buckingham.'

Alpiew cocked her head. 'Did he write it?'

'Who?'

'The Duke of Buckingham.'

'Don't be silly, Alpiew, it is writ in the same hand as the note we have asking Godfrey to go to the park, i.e. it is Rebecca's.'

'Rebecca's hand? So why is Rebecca pretending to be the Duke of Buckingham?'

'I know not, Alpiew, but we shall both think on it overnight.' She wiped her mouth with her sleeve and rose. 'Come . . .'

Alpiew tried to shovel a few spoonfuls of soup into her mouth while gathering up the drawer to return it to its hole in the dresser, but as she turned she lost her balance and spilled the contents of the drawer on to the floor.

'Alpiew, pshaw, you clumsy child!' The Countess got on her hands and knees and helped pile everything back. She swept her hand under the dresser to catch anything that may have slid below, pulled out a wodge of items, and was about to drop them into the drawer when she said: 'What on earth are these?' She held up a small packet tied in a green ribbon.

'Oh lor', madam. They are not to be seen in polite society.'

The Countess teased one of the be-ribboned items from the packet of eight. She unfurled a long cone of thin sheep gut. Inspecting it carefully inside and out, she puzzled as the thing dangled from her chubby hand. 'Is it a one-finger glove? For counting money, perhaps. Or a thing in which to steam carrots? I can't imagine what it could be.'

Alpiew tried to snatch it from her hand. 'Truly, madam, it is not to be discussed.'

'Well, if you know, spit it out!' The Countess whipped it away and turned to inspect it more closely in the firelight. 'What is it?'

'It is called a salvator, madam.' Alpiew put the packet on to the table.

'A salvator? What can this flimsy thing save anyone from?'

'It is a French sheath, madam. A condom.'

'Phough!' The Countess dropped it and it landed on the coals and frizzled to ash in a moment. 'Fancy Rebecca keeping a nasty thing like that in her kitchen.'

'Ladies seldom keep the things, madam. Excepting certain types of women who ply their trade hereabouts. I think we should go down to Old Mother Blackham's at the shop next to the hummums in the piazza, to see if she may have sold it.'

Alpiew pocketed the packet, then pulled out the other note and the green ribbon she had found wrapped round the note in Rebecca's room at Anglesey House. 'I knew it was familiar!'

'The ribbon or the hand?' The Countess perused it. 'Almost the same message: see, set in the middle of the letters are "D.O.B.": Duke of Buckingham.'

'I found it amid the linen in their room at your house.'

The Countess flipped the note over. ' "Anglesey House." ' She turned it back again. ' "W.G. G.V.D.O.B. VIII. R. XX." ' The Countess held out the note and gazed at it. 'And most definitely in the same hand again! "R. XX." So whoever wrote it endorses themselves with an R.'

'R XX . . .' said Alpiew. 'Would that be like kings are: Roger the twentieth?'

'Silly!' The Countess giggled. 'The letter is endorsed with an initial and two kisses, Alpiew, dear. Have you never had a love letter?'

Alpiew blushed. She could not believe she had not seen it. 'So it is a love letter to someone from Rebecca. But why would Rebecca send a love letter to herself? Or, for that matter, to her maid?'

'Think of the possible Rs present in this conundrum, Alpiew. There's Lord Rakewell, Mr Rich, Nickum Roper . . .' The

Countess read the note aloud again. 'That VIII! There you are most probably right. I believe that must be a numeral.'

'Eight. Eight what?' Alpiew gazed down at the notes. 'How about eight o'clock?'

'That must be it.' The Countess laid the two notes side by side on the table. 'So one at least is a love note which came to Anglesey House, inviting Rebecca to an assignation at eight. The other came here, we may presume. Perhaps they allude to the same rendezvous, perhaps they are similar trysts, but on separate occasions.'

Alpiew was busy comparing the ribbon that had tied it with the ribbon from the packet. The two ribbons were identical. 'Why would Rebecca want salvators at Anglesey House?' Alpiew grabbed the Countess by the elbow. 'You don't think she was at it with Godfrey?'

'Decorum, please, Alpiew,' gasped the Countess. 'Or I shall exgurgitate that soup.'

Naturally, though it was late, the sex shop was open for business. Night was their busiest time.

'Alpiew, dear, I think you and your friend should come through to the back.' Mother Blackham pushed through a curtain into a small dark room. 'Pardon me while I light up.'

She lit the candles one by one as the Countess looked about in amazement.

The walls were lined with display cases that were crammed with objects the like of which the Countess had never seen in her life. 'What is this thing, pray?' she said, picking up a long black leather item with linen straps.

'That, madam, is a dildo.'

'A dildo? How quaint, a falder-iddle-dildo kind of thing?'

'It is a substitute penis, madam, for men who can't or who want one.'

'I'm sorry' – the Countess squinted down at the huge thing in her hand – 'I don't follow.'

'Men who *can't* get it up apply it thus . . .' Mother Blackham grabbed the item and held it against her pubic region. 'Men who *want* to be assaulted with such a weapon tie it to a chair, thus . . .' She sat the thing on a chair. 'Then they bounce up and down upon it until –' she made an expansive gesture – 'voilà!'

However calm the Countess tried to appear, her face writhed in distaste. 'Of course,' she spluttered, making a mental note not to ask any more random questions.

'These are what we have found,' said Alpiew, proffering the packet.

Mother Blackham glanced down. 'Ah yes, the Fallopius Salvator. A superior make.'

'Superior to what?' asked the Countess.

'To the Hercules Saxonia, or the Capote Anglaise, of course,' cried Mother Blackham. 'These are of the finest sheep gut, the others mere linen soaked in brine. All need must be washed out between uses, as you can imagine, but the linen ones lose much efficacy with each wash.' She peered at Alpiew's packet. 'Medium size.'

'Medium?'

'Ay. There is a great deal of call for large, much for medium. Few buy the small size, though in my experience most men have need of 'em, and I believe the large ones would be better used as hats by those vain fools who purchase 'em.'

'And these men, they use these things to prevent pregnancy?'

'To avoid unwanted brats, yes . . .' She pointed up to the upper shelves, which were stacked with strange metal implements. 'Otherwise I find *I* have to deal with the consequences. Women come to me, and I abort 'em. More often than not the men pay for the operation, for they are usually married, and needless to say not to the women they have impregnated. However, these days condoms are as frequently used to protect the gentleman from venereal disease.'

The Countess clucked.

'Syphilis and gonorrhoea flourish today and, if you are unlucky enough to become infected, they are a death sentence. Few men desire to renounce carnal copulation entirely, and in the face of this danger pursue their concupiscent appetites in places and with women who are easy . . .'

'Do you sell many Fallopius Salvators?'

'Depends what you mean by "many". Most folk buy the cheaper ones.'

'Did Rebecca Montagu ever buy a packet from you?'

'Mrs Montagu, the player? Roxana? I should say not.'

'Nor her woman, Sarah?'

'I wouldn't know her, so I can't tell you. But it is extremely rare for women to purchase the things.'

'Lord Rakewell?' ventured the Countess.

'Oh, him! His amours are as public as Charing Cross. And yes, he does purchase the Fallopius. Though, if my memory fails me not, he took the large size . . .'

'Naturally.' The Countess was staring at a strange lump of something that looked like meat. 'What is this?'

'Ah, lady, that is a gentleman's yard infected with the pox.'

The Countess peered into the dark box. 'How did you get it? Did you cut it off the fellow?'

'It's made of wax.' Mother Blackham laughed. 'I was left it by a local chirurgeon who was studying the dread disease, and had many such specimens of both the external and internal signs of the pox. Naturally he died of it himself.'

'Perhaps he did his research a little too thoroughly,' said the Countess, squinting again at the horrid object.

'He left me all his papers as well as this display.'

'Oh lord protect us!' The Countess looked closer at the other boxes; some held models of babies covered in scabs, others various parts of adult anatomy bursting with weeping sores. 'What a foul thing it is, this pox.'

'Ay, madam, it is an insidious visitor, sent by the Almighty to restrain our too wanton lusts, caught so easily by an impure touch, especially in copulation and sodomy.'

'I am lucky,' said the Countess. 'I only ever slept with two men in my whole life. A king and my husband.'

Mother Blackham gave a smirk. 'Many women, unknown to themselves, have been infected by their husbands. And the husbands keep up the pretence. Those poor wifely creatures believe they are suffering from the measles or the smallpox, and never suspect the truth, even on their deathbeds.'

'What filthy lying creatures men can be.' The Countess moved slowly along the hideous display. 'If the wives knew, surely they would rush at those who had infected them with a knife or gun and take their revenge, for, to be sure, by making love to them, their husbands have as good as murdered them.'

'Is inspecting a fellow's yard the only way of discovering who has it from who is safe?' said Alpiew, frantically galloping back in her mind to all the lovers she had had.

'Ah, if only life were that easy,' sighed Mother Blackham. 'Many infected people look as though they are in the first bloom of health, no outward signs at all, but for a greenish gleet. Yet they are then at their most contagious. As death looms nearer, the give-away signs begin to show. The facial sores, a body covered in tetters, boils, buboes and shankers, then comes the dissolved palate . . .'

'The what?' The Countess had her fan out again.

'The palate is eaten away from within, starting at the uvula until the nose collapses. Sometimes a poxy person might drink at the mouth and dribble it all out at the nose. Next the nose itself goes.'

'Milady!' Alpiew gripped the Countess by the arm. 'Are you thinking what I'm thinking?'

'Signior Ruggiero Lampone! Another R.' The Countess grimaced and snapped her fan shut. 'He has no nose at all.'

TEN

Anger

The appetite or desire of overcoming present opposition.

Red, inflamed eyes, the pupils restless and shining. The forehead furrowed, with wrinkles between the eyes. The nostrils flared, the lips full and turned out, with the under-lip raised over the upper, with the sides of the mouth slightly open in a disdainful grin.

They had no trouble finding a link-boy in the piazza to light them the way to Moor Fields and Lampone's studio. Carousing men and women lurched from post to post, swinging tankards of ale and singing bawdy songs. It was a long walk, passing many dark shadow-filled alleys. Grunts and groans of carnal copulation echoed along the route.

'Is everybody at it, Alpiew, all of the time, like this? Is vice lurking in every entry? Is London become Sodom?'

The link-boy snorted with laughter.

They walked on in silence. As they passed through Moorgate the boy turned. 'I'll wait on you here, if you wish. But I'll not light you across the fields at night. 'Tis a vile place for footpads and all kinds of human vermin.'

'But you said you would take us all the way.' Alpiew glared at him.

'I value my life,' said the boy. 'After all, I'm young. It is all right for a pair of broilers like you to get set upon, but I have my life before me.'

'You impudent rapscallion.' Alpiew grabbed his flaming torch. 'Await us here, then. And if we are not back by the time the clock strikes one, then you must raise the hue and cry. This lady is a very important person. Her name is the Countess Ashby de la Zouche, and she is a personal friend of the King.'

'Oh yes?' The boy looked the Countess up and down with a scornful expression. 'And if pigs had wings what lovely birds they'd make.'

As Alpiew turned to give the boy a belt across the ear, the Countess tugged her by the elbow. 'Come, Alpiew. Soonest done, soonest home and safe in our nice warm beds.'

Alpiew held the link aloft and the two women marched on to the boggy green of Moor Fields.

The only sounds were of owls shrieking and the squelch of their feet. They reached the central lime walk and looked back. The huge sprawling edifice of Bethlehem Hospital loomed behind them.

'Let us stick to the path while we head north,' said Alpiew. 'I am mightily frighted that we will lose our shoes in this mud. We can nip across at the top of the walk.'

The crisp crunch of gravel was vaguely reassuring, but the link gave the trees ghostly shadows that danced wildly on the ground around them.

'Children today seem to be full of self-assurance, don't you find?' the Countess started in a loud voice, then continued in a whisper: 'Someone is behind us. Don't you hear their tread?'

'Indeed, madam,' Alpiew replied, taking the Countess's arm and increasing her stride. ''Tis shocking.' She lowered her voice. 'This wretched link illuminates us to the world.'

'Ah, look,' cried the Countess gaily. 'There is my husband waiting for us.'

Instinctively Alpiew flinched – she loathed the Countess's husband – but then realised that her mistress was trying to warn off the pursuer.

'Quickly,' said Alpiew under her breath. 'We are in sight

of the entry to Cock in Hole Yard, let us run across the grass.'

Both women gathered up their skirts and dashed across the top of the field. They arrived at Lampone's door panting and with very wet feet. Alpiew lay the link in an iron holder on the wall and looked about her. 'Perhaps the villain took one look at us and realised we were not worth robbing,' said Alpiew, banging Lampone's knocker. 'There are advantages to wearing old worn clothing.'

The Countess bristled. Her clothes were of the first quality even if they were twenty years out of fashion.

Alpiew knocked again. Suddenly the door opened. Lampone stood there in a long white night-gown waving a rapier at them.

'*Assassino!*' he cried. '*Ladra!* What is it that you want in this night of blackness?'

Alpiew raised the link. It reflected beautifully in his silver nose.

'Signior Lampone,' cried the Countess. ''Tis I, Lady Ashby de la Zouche, Countess of Clapham, Baroness . . .'

'We need to ask you some questions of the greatest importance, sirrah,' said Alpiew boldly, 'concerning your friend Rebecca Montagu.'

Lampone lowered his sword. 'What of her?'

'She is in trouble,' said Alpiew.

'I should think she is,' said Lampone. 'Marrying a no-good scoundrel like Giles Rakewell.' He stood back and let them enter.

His studio was messier than before; great plaster casts covered the floor, and pots of powdered pigment stood in rainbow-like rows. Streaks of colour covered the floor and walls.

'It is the middle of the night, ladies. And I have important work this night, with a friend from the playhouse.'

'In your night-gown?' said Alpiew.

'Indeed, for it is the work of Venus. Tonight we make love.'

Alpiew glanced up the staircase. At the top stood the well-endowed young lady who had been brought in to replace Anne Lucas in *The Rival Queens*. She was stark naked.

'Hello!' she cried. 'Is there some trouble?'

'Go back to bed.' Lampone waved a hand. 'I will deal with them.'

'Aren't you the ladies from the *Trumpet*,' said the girl with a wiggle of the hips. 'My name is Elizabeth Lloyd. I have been acting only a short time, but have been very well received in my parts at Drury Lane. Mr Rich wishes me to go on in the company in the next plays too. When you mention me, the name has two "l"s.'

Lord what vain things these playhouse creatures were, thought Alpiew. Only ever thinking of increasing their fame.

After a puff, and not even offering to pay for it, thought the Countess.

'Signior Lampone,' cried the Countess, turning to Lampone. 'We are come here upon the matter of your nose.'

'My nose?' said Lampone, going cross-eyed looking down on it. 'What of it? It was cast out of first-rate silver, based on a clay model of the dear departed thing which I made from memory.'

'But why,' the Countess smiled primly, 'do you not have a nose of flesh and bone like the rest of us?'

'Because I lost it.'

'How careless,' said the Countess. 'And can you explain how you lost it?'

'I was a mere boy at the time. It fell nobly at the battle of Nish.'

'Nish?' all three women exclaimed in unison.

'Ay, Nish. It is some godforsaken place in Serbia, south-east of Belgrade. I fought under the Margrave of Baden-Baden.'

'Pardon?'

'Baden-Baden. Our adversary was the Grand Vizier Koprulu Fasl Mustafa Pasa. For many years he was protector of the Great Sultana.'

'You lost your nose for a raisin?' said Elizabeth Lloyd.

'A *great* reason,' said Lampone. 'I skirmished with the Ottoman.'

'You fought with a box?' Elizabeth screwed up her eyebrows and descended the stairs.

'No, a sword, naturally. The mighty Musselman overwhelmed us.'

'I've seen him perform at Bartholomew Fair,' said the actress, at last clinging to a concept she could grasp. 'He's called the Strong Man of Kent.'

'As the Serbian sun set, my nose fell to a scimitar.'

'I'm lost again,' said Elizabeth.

'At Nish.' Lampone put his arm around the naked girl. 'I was a hero.'

'Pish to Nish!' said the Countess. 'Are you certain, Signior Lampone, that this is not so much piffle to put us all in a maze?'

'The mighty Margrave rewarded me, and I returned to my home in the country of Sicily.'

'I fear you are lying, Signior.' The Countess gave a wry smirk. 'For I have reason to believe your nose was eaten away by the pox.'

'Pox!' Lampone raised his rapier and gave it a wild swish through the air, removing a few strands of hair from the Countess's already thin wig. 'Pox upon you and your pox!'

'Pig!' Elizabeth shrank away, looking down at her body in horror. 'No wonder you always make love in the dark, without so much as a candle to light us.'

'*Cara!* I love you,' cried Lampone, reaching out for her. 'You are a *ragazza stupenda!*'

'You scurvy Italian brute, I don't care if I never see you again.' The actress pulled a dust sheet from a large armature and wrapped herself in it. 'God bless my eyesight.'

'See! Witch! Look at what I have down there!' Lampone bent down and fumbled about with the hem of his night-gown then stood abruptly exposing his genitalia to the room. 'I am pure!'

The Countess reached out and covered Alpiew's eyes.

'My nose was not all I lost at Nish!'

The Countess squinted, taking a closer look. Lampone's penis was a mere stump. 'Lord, Alpiew,' she cried, dropping her protective hand. 'See. What a fascinating specimen! Like an acorn.'

'But you tumble me like a stallion.' Elizabeth Lloyd looked on, clearly startled by the revelation. 'How do you do it?'

Limply, Lampone reached inside his pocket and pulled out a strap-on dildo. The Countess's hand shot up again to protect Alpiew from the sight.

'Pardon me, signior,' said the Countess as she backed towards the door. 'We have been plagued with worry about Rebecca since she has disappeared. I am truly sorry we disturbed you.'

As they moved out of the room Alpiew noted Elizabeth's hand reach out and take the dildo from Lampone. She could have sworn she heard the woman asking if she could have a go.

As they left Lampone's house, Alpiew grabbed the still flaming link. She froze and raised a finger to her lips. The flame threw a shadow to the pavement. Pressed hard against a nearby wall there was the silhouette of a man.

'Talk to me,' she whispered to the Countess, handing her the link.

'How nice of Signior Lampone to offer us a lift home in his chaise.' The Countess spoke in a light voice. 'I hope the night will not be too cold for the pony.'

Alpiew tiptoed nearer to the man, flattening herself against the wall as she moved. With a swift movement she stretched out and grabbed the fellow by his coat, pulling him into the light. 'Show yourself, you dastardly son of a whore.'

Blinking in the torchlight stood Nickum. He threw his hands up to protect himself. 'Don't hurt me. 'Tis only I, mistress: Nickum Roper.'

'You peevish dog,' cried the Countess. 'What do you think you are at, following us about like a tantivy pig?'

Nickum Roper stood gaping.

248

'Come along, man,' said Alpiew, pulling him along the street towards the Countess.

'Well,' she said, when he stood before her. 'Don't just stand there, staring like a choked throstle. Explain yourself.'

'I meant no harm, Countess.' He shrank back as though expecting to be hit. 'I hoped you might lead me to Beck.'

'Nickum,' said Alpiew, ''tis past midnight. Should you not be at home with your wife?'

'She won't notice.' Nickum had a surly edge to his voice. 'Anyhow, 'tis no concern of hers.'

'Now, Nickum –' the Countess took him by the arm – 'you can hold the link and walk us across Moor Fields and then we will lead you home.'

Nickum hesitated, then took the link. 'The boy is still there. I will leave you at Moor Gate.'

'Why Nickum, you may walk with us. Surely you live on our way?'

Nickum marched on into the field.

'I have no need of a nanny, thank you. I will see you across this marshy place, then I will see myself home, if 'tis all right with you.'

The Countess and Alpiew arrived home after midnight. Godfrey was nowhere to be found, and the fire was out.

'How mysterious! I have never known him to leave this place at night.'

There was a note on the Countess's bed. She flipped it open. 'Mr Pepys has invited me to join him for a bumper of Rhenish tomorrow evening. How charming.'

Alpiew assisted the Countess as she struggled out of her mantua and corset and into a night-gown.

They both settled down in their beds and Alpiew blew out the candle.

'The wind is getting up, milady. Listen.'

'So those mad seafarers were not so crazed as we thought.'

The windows were rattling in their casements, and a great wailing came from the gap under the door.

'Light the candle again, Alpiew, I fear with this howling I will not sleep.'

'Indeed, madam, my mind is all a-race with the things we have discovered.'

'Let us stoke up the fire and have a hot drink while we ponder.'

Wrapped in blankets, they sat together on easy chairs and watched kindling crackle under the damp coal.

'What a day, Alpiew. We have visited the strange mad folk of Limehouse Reach who claim to be Rebecca's parents, yet show no fear even at the news she is dead; we were accompanied thence by a lunatic who devotes his life to shadowing a player, believing she would marry him (despite, I suspect, a wife, hidden away at his lodgings, whom he claims is dead).'

'Did you get anything out of him on your little walk at the Tower, madam?' Alpiew stoked the coal and pulled out an iron hook ready to suspend the kettle.

'Only that he seems to suspect us even more than we suspect him.' The Countess lifted her feet to warm them at the flame. 'But I talked to a Yeoman, and am certain now that Rakewell was there the night of Mrs Lucas's cruel death. 'Twas he who pulled off my wig.'

'How so?'

'On the night before his trial, he went to chapel. I believe that one of his cronies, posing as a lawyer, like the priest he brought on to the *Folly*, was there to attend the ceremony, and under cover of the box pews they exchanged cloaks. The crony went to Rakewell's cell for a few hours, then Rakewell himself returned after midnight in the guise of his lawyer when the crony left again, re-assuming his own identity.'

'At his trial there was certainly much talk of changing cloaks when he stabbed the poor man in Leicester Fields. Perhaps it is a common trick with him.' Alpiew mused as she poured water from a large ewer into the kettle. 'But, come to think on it, how did no one recognise the impostor?'

'It was dark.'

'Dark, maybe. But surely the Yeoman would have lit the

way with a lanthorn . . .' Alpiew placed the kettle on the hook and swung it over the fire. The wind was howling down the chimney by now, flattening the flame. 'And back in the cell, surely there would have been a candle burning . . . ?'

The Countess shuffled. She had not thought about that part of it. And indeed it did seem unlikely that the Warder, having shown a man back to his cell and locked the door after him, then later the same night let in his lawyer at midnight, would not have noticed either of their faces.

'So where are we left?'

'With the possibility that a man killed first Anne Lucas, then her colleague Rebecca Montagu. And that Rebecca had the pox.'

'What has that to do with the death of Anne?'

'How should I know?' The Countess flung up her hands. 'Is that drink ready yet?'

'What shall we have? A sack posset? A caudle cup? A dish of chocolate?'

'Let's spoil ourselves.' The Countess gave a wry smile. 'Let's have some tea.'

Alpiew took the candle and a dish to collect the leaves from the front room. The Countess picked up a piece of paper from the floor. She glanced at it. Clearly Godfrey had been doing some puzzle, for it consisted of letters cut out from a newspaper and glued on to a sheet of paper. She rolled it up and applied it to the coals, then lit another candle with it, before tossing it into the glowing fire.

The echoing of an almighty crash came from the yard.

'That'll be the back wall come down,' the Countess called to Alpiew. 'It never looked awfully safe.' She stooped down and picked up the bellows to give the fire a good blow. 'Of course, the killer could be one of those Antis. A madman who thinks all actresses are whores and believes that God has put him on Earth to murder lewd women.' She pumped the ancient leather bellows. 'Godfrey has changed so of late, hasn't he? I note he has taken to doing puzzles, Alpiew. I just found one cut out from pieces of newspaper.'

Alpiew came in with the tea. 'Where is it?'

'What?'

'The piece of paper?'

The Countess grabbed a poker and poked at the fire. 'I used it to light the kindling.'

'It is important, madam.' Alpiew poured the tea leaves into the pot. 'What did the note say?'

'It said "Keep away or else." What can that mean, do you think?'

'It means . . .' Alpiew gulped and kicked the hall door shut. Simultaneously a screaming draught swept down the chimney, dislodging a lump of soot, which flopped down into the grate, and all over the Countess's head and shoulders.

The Countess wiped her eyes and gaped at Alpiew, spitting black gobs into the fireplace.

A loud groaning sound was coming from the yard, even louder now than the wind outside.

Alpiew grabbed a poker. 'What's that?'

The two women stared at each other in silence for a second. Then with a gigantic crash the garden door blew open. Papers swirled around the room and the candle guttered and went out. The fire, severely damped with soot already, provided only the dimmest possible glow.

'You are a pair of wanton whores!' It was a man's voice, his heavy tread tramping towards them. 'And God will punish you for your debauchery.'

As Alpiew's sight adjusted she could see that the man was draped in white cloth, obscuring his face. His arm was raised and he wielded a long wooden pole. She gasped. Please God let it not be the handle of an axe.

The Countess was fumbling around with the candle trying to get some light into the room. Roaring, the figure advanced on Alpiew.

Suddenly, yapping at Alpiew's feet, the dog Red appeared, lunging at her ankles and nipping them.

'God will come upon you in an almighty fire, to cleanse your impurities.'

The Countess threw herself under the table.

In trying to kick the dog out of the way Alpiew dropped the poker. The man raised the wooden pole, aiming at Alpiew, just as the Countess tugged at the hem of his white garment, whipping it off him.

Before them, soaked through, waving a broom in the air, stood Godfrey. 'You bitches!' He burst into tears and stooped, taking Red into his arms. 'Don't touch my dog.'

'Godfrey!' The Countess dragged herself to her feet. 'What on earth has got into you?'

He thrust out his gnarled hand and pointed at the book on the table.

'I've been reading the filth you brought home. So which of you is it?'

'Godfrey, why have you been hiding in the yard dressed in a sheet?' The Countess tried frantically to make sense of it all, as Godfrey stood swaying, mad-eyed, before her. 'Are you quite out of your senses?'

'How could I sleep in this room with you, you drabs, you doxies, you trulls!' The dog started licking Godfrey's face. 'No one loves me but this dog. We went out and made a tent out of some sheets, but the wind fair blew the lot away, along with the privy.'

'Alpiew, puff up the fire.' The Countess sat. 'Godfrey, please to sit and tell me what on earth you are talking about.'

'I don't think as how it could be you, milady, but some-one has brought the pox into the house. Otherwise why are you a-reading of such books, and why is there a bottle of Dr Cockburn's Lenitive elixir, together with a packet of Diaphoretic extract and corroborative mercurial drops in the pantry?'

'For the book,' sighed the Countess, 'I bought it by mistake. As for the medicines, I cannot tell you. Alpiew, do you know about these things?'

'Certainly not, madam.'

'Then please close the door, the cold is going to give me chilblains and I shall be reduced to rubbing myself down each night with Mr Alcrace's Strengthening Balsamic Electuary. And you will both have to put up with the stink of it.'

'It's this changeling of yours, Countess.' Godfrey backed away from Alpiew as she crossed the room. 'This trollop, Alpiew. She's the one. You're trying to protect her.'

The Countess sighed. 'I assure you, Godfrey, I am doing no such thing.'

Godfrey strode over to Alpiew's bed and started throwing the bedclothes and pillows in the air.

'Godfrey! Will you control yourself.' The Countess rose and faced him. 'I was trying to protect you from this information, but you have gone too far in accusing Alpiew. The only infected person in this house was Rebecca. The constables told us the body was badly afflicted with the later symptoms of the pox. No doubt her woman Sarah kept the medicines in the pantry to be out of the way of prying eyes.'

'Rebecca was not a foul pockie person. How dare you!' Godfrey now turned, put the dog down, and advanced on the Countess. 'You . . . you . . . filth-monger!'

'Godfrey, I will not suffer such nonsense.' The Countess spoke firmly. 'Either you pull yourself together or you go and live elsewhere.' The dog leapt up on to her lap and started licking her hand. 'Now I suggest you hang your sheet in front of the fire till it dries out, and then we should all get some sleep. For tomorrow, Godfrey, I have an important job for you.'

Godfrey threw her a surly look.

'I want you to follow Nickum, and find out where it is *exactly* that he lives. All we know is that it is an alley off Paternoster Row. I believe there is something most suspicious about his home-life. He is covering something up. Perhaps he knows where Sarah is. Perhaps he was the last person to see Rebecca alive. For all we know, he was the person who killed her. Paternoster Row,' said the Countess. 'Strange name for a street, I always thought, and the others roundabout.'

' 'Tis where the Popish priests in the old days used to walk, chanting their beads. The Hail Mary's up and down Ave Maria

Lane, the Our Father down Paternoster Row, and they came to a full stop . . .'

'At Amen Corner, I suppose?' She tousled the ears of the little dog. 'Silly name for a road, isn't it, Red? Silly, silly name.'

Godfrey left before dawn, muffled up against the wind that still howled through the streets of London, to loiter outside the house until Nickum was in sight. His orders were then to track the man down to his home and bring the news of his address straight back to the Countess.

Alpiew and the Countess also threw on cloaks and left shortly afterwards.

The Hay Market was a mess. The stall coverings were flapping. Hay, straw and all kinds of provender swirled around in small tornadoes, while stallkeepers chased hither and thither trying to catch terrified animals that had broken out of their tousled pens.

'There are so many puzzles,' said the Countess, leaping out of the way of a goose that rose up before her flapping its wings. 'Who was that strange creature in Rebecca's rooms last night, and what did he want?'

'Ay.' Alpiew guided the Countess away from a bucket of eels that was on the verge of toppling, having been kicked by a nervous donkey. 'And where is that pesky girl Sarah, and it come to that.'

'Not gone to the New World, that much we know, the malkin trash!' The Countess hoiked up her skirts and stepped over a pile of horse dung. 'I cannot imagine what a woman like Rebecca was doing with such a sullen slattern for a maid. What did she ever do but mope?'

'Mayhap, milady, it is something to do with those strange seadogs out at Limehouse.'

'I cannot comment on them at all, Alpiew. I barely understood a single word they said. If we needs must visit them again, I suggest we bring along an interpreter. What language was it that they spoke?'

'I believe it was simple English, madam, but peppered with seafarers' jargon.'

'Well, a pox on their seafarers' cant, which in my opinion is so much gibberish.'

'Perhaps we might find someone who could unlock the cipher for us?'

'I suppose, Alpiew, you are now going to tell me you have friends who go upon the account, pirates and the like?'

'No, madam, but you know such a person.'

'I? What do you take me for? I'd have you know, wench, I have no picaroons, sea-robbers and corsairs in my acquaintance.'

'I was referring to Mr Pepys, madam, and fortuitously you are meeting him tonight for a glass of wine . . .'

'Alpiew!' The Countess stopped in her tracks. 'You have hit upon it! Old Pepys certainly knows about ships. It is *all* he knows about, admittedly, but perhaps he could give us a little advice.'

A hackney carriage hurtled towards them. The Countess threw herself into a doorway to avoid being splashed by its wheels as it surged through a great puddle. 'Maybe we should take him a present of a packet of tea.'

They walked on in silence for a minute or two. Alpiew stopped as they passed through the blue posts into Leicester Fields. 'So there is the fence that last time saved Lord Rakewell from dancing at the end of a hempen necklace.'

The trees on the Fields were swaying precariously. There were already torn-off branches littering the grass. The Countess and Alpiew stopped and looked at the miserable acre of grass where a man had died because he was in the wrong ward to be assisted.

'Rakewell is a man so brutishly wicked, so base and perfidious, so insolent and barbarous, I cannot but think that he is somehow at the bottom of all this mischief.'

'And what is the hold he has over those men in high places that they will not accuse him, even when the evidence flies in the face of their verdict?'

The Countess and Alpiew staggered into the gale that howled along from Dirty Lane. 'Fie upon this blustery wind! I doubt we will arrive at the Fleet in one piece.'

'I wonder if Godfrey will have any luck locating Nickum on a day like this. Perhaps the man will have a bit of sense and stay at home hugging a warm fire.'

The Countess laughed. 'He is probably a few hundred yards behind, tailing us, hoping we will lead him to Mistress Montagu.' She crossed herself. 'God rest her poor soul.'

'Is that what he really wants?' Alpiew helped the Countess gather her cloak, which was flapping in the air like devilish wings. 'I suspect the man is disturbed in his head.'

'Of course he is. But Rakewell is the more serious foe. What was the purpose, do you think, of the Tityre-tus taking poor demented Mr Lucas from the safety of Bedlam?'

'That is certainly a puzzle. Perhaps they wish to hold him for a ransom.'

'And who would pay it? His wife is dead, and his son in the poor house.'

'And I suspect that keeping a raving, frantic, moonsick fellow like him captive would be trouble beyond belief.'

A tree had fallen blocking the Strand near the Maypole and traffic in both directions had ground to a standstill. Drivers stood on top of their cabs yelling, hackneys and carriages lined up, while the horses, already frightened at the whistling wind, neighed and whinnied, some rearing, causing even more turmoil and damage to the cabs.

'For once I am glad we are going afoot and not by hackney,' cried the Countess over the cacophony. 'Plus, we save the fare.'

'Traffic in London is ridiculous,' said Alpiew. ''Twas not thus when I was a child.'

'The problem is that too many people have horse-drawn carriages today.' The Countess grabbed at her cloak which was whipping angrily. 'I'm told that in three hundred years, if we continue this way, the streets of London will be impassable, as they will be under five foot of horse-dung.'

Street signs battered and clattered against each other, smashing back and forth in the squall. 'We shall certainly get there faster afoot.' Alpiew ducked as the sign of the Naked Boy and Three Herrings snapped from its bracket and flew over her head.

'If we survive the journey,' said the Countess.

The grille at the Fleet was for once deserted, both inside and out. The bitter wind had deterred visitors and prisoners alike.

Alpiew applied her face to the bars and yelled for Valentine Vernish.

He arrived a few minutes later, whey-faced and dejected.

'I thought you had deserted me.' He had a cut on his cheek and bruises on his neck.

'What has happened to you, sirrah? What has somebody done to you?'

'Anne Lucas was a well-loved woman. There are folk in here who desire to punish me as the Justices have found me guilty without so much as an appeal to their clemency. The knife they found upon me they saw as proof positive.'

'Was it planted on your person by those who apprehended you?'

Vernish gave a hopeless shrug. 'It was my own. For the cutting and flipping of the gingerbread.'

The Countess remembered seeing it, a long sharp dagger-like thing. 'Think positively,' the Countess cooed. 'For by being held within these grim grey walls you have an unimpeachable alibi.'

'Against what?' Vernish seemed quite uninterested.

'A second murder. Done in the same style as the first.'

Vernish shrugged, causing the chains that linked his hands to rattle.

'Ay,' said Alpiew. 'But one which proves that your suspicions about Rebecca were unfounded.'

Vernish gave her a quizzical glance.

'Indeed,' the Countess added. 'For last time you told us that Rebecca Montagu –'

'Dark Beck,' Alpiew interjected.

'That Dark Beck "must confess". Well now, Mr Vernish, that will not be necessary. Indeed, 'twill not be possible.'

'And why is that?' Vernish spoke in an insolent and brash tone. 'What pretty excuse has she come up with this time?'

'She did not need . . .'

The Countess held up her hand to silence Alpiew before she let the cat out of the bag.

'Mr Vernish, as you know, I perceive you to be a man of integrity and manners. Rare commodities in these days of mass delinquency. So many young men are mere rogues, rascals, vermin and duns. I speak, naturally, of a parcel of the wickedest spirits in all hell's dominions – the Tityre-tus.'

Vernish made no response, so the Countess ploughed on. 'The leader of these odious swaggering ruffians is one . . .'

'Rakewell,' said Vernish with a snort. 'He and Rebecca have come to some understanding, I believe.'

'You know about the wedding?' said Alpiew. 'Who told you?'

'She did.'

'Rebecca?'

Vernish nodded.

'When did she come here?'

'She came several times.'

'And what did you talk about?'

'I would like to know what business that is of yours?' Vernish gave them a surly look. 'I told her to give herself up to the Justice and save my life.' He laughed. 'I may as well have told the devil to stop tempting sinners. She laughed in my face and told me she would do it, but in her own time. As you see, still I languish here, and tomorrow morning I am due to be hanged upon Tower Hill.'

Alpiew put her face in her hands and groaned.

'Rebecca cannot come, Mr Vernish. Nor can she appear before the Justice.' The Countess gripped hard at the iron bars. 'For, I am sorry to be the one to tell you, she was the second victim of the madman who killed Anne Lucas.'

Vernish blanched, then bent double, retching and gasping for air.

'Oh, Beck, Beck!' he cried. 'God have mercy on your soul. And mine.' When he looked up, his cheeks were wet with tears. 'Whom do they suspect?'

'The authorities have not yet realised the two deaths are connected. They were in different wards, and the body has not been identified. For the villain had cut off her head.'

'Then how . . . ?' Vernish grabbed the grille, a sparkle of hope returning to his eyes.

'We saw the body. I knew the dress, the jewels . . .'

Vernish sank down on to the ground sobbing. The interior of the prison was dark. And they could no longer see his face, only hear his wails, and the clink of his murderer's chains scraping along the stone floor.

'Mr Vernish,' said the Countess softly, 'we want to help you. What can we do? Tell us, how we can save you?'

'There is nothing left to do.' He wiped his face with a hand grimy from the filthy flagstones. 'When did it happen?'

'Three nights ago.'

He looked up. 'Three?'

The Countess and Alpiew nodded.

Alpiew felt so sorry for the poor forlorn man she tried to inject a positive note into a hopeless moment. 'Your puppet show is still playing, sir. Perhaps there may be some money we can bring you.'

'My Punch and Judy booth?' said Vernish, rising to his feet. 'In Covent Garden?'

'In the piazza, yes, sir.' Alpiew smiled. 'Perhaps the money could provide you with some small pleasure . . .'

A peculiar smile flickered upon Vernish's face. 'I want for one thing only.' He gripped the bar and pushed his face through to whisper. 'Rebecca's head. Find her head and bring it to me. Once you have that you will know everything.'

Hope

Appetite with an opinion of attaining is called hope.

The movements are internal, keeping all the parts of the body suspended between Fear and Assurance.

'We've come the wrong way,' said the Countess.

'Depends where we're heading,' said Alpiew, stepping into a shop doorway to avoid a startled galloping pig, run amok with fear at the wind.

Valentine Vernish's despair had infected them both with a kind of melancholy panic.

Alpiew stared into the shop-window, which was full of strange metal implements: drills, saws, cups on the end of long handles. 'What is this place?' She glanced up at the sign which flapped wildly on its bracket. The Head of Tycho Brahe and Quadrant. 'What kind of a fellow was this Tycho Brahe, madam, for look –' she pointed up at the clanking sign – 'the fellow has a silver nose, just like our Italian!'

The Countess surveyed the display of instruments and pushed open the door.

'Excuse me, sirrah,' she called to the little white-bearded man behind the counter. 'Do you mind if we shelter for a moment?'

'Delighted to have some company.'

The shelves were lined with pieces of curious equipment

made mainly of brass and leather. In the corner of the top shelf sat a ginger cat, fixing them with a glassy stare, and on the counter lay a stuffed alligator with a label round its jaw: 17/-.

'My woman, Alpiew, and I were most curious as to the exact purpose of all your lovely shiny gadgets.'

'Many folk wonder about that, madam. I am a purveyor of surgical and scientific equipment. Everything from saws to cut off your gangrened limbs to azimuth quadrants for sea-folk. And of course they have frequent need of both those two.'

'Knives too?' said Alpiew, gazing at the sharp-looking sets on the counter.

'Ay, knives are a popular line. More popular than the azimuth quadrant, but I have a particular fondness for the latter.'

The Countess bent over the display and slowly ran her eyes along the shiny blades.

'And what has this Tycho Brahe cove got to do with everything?' said Alpiew, waving out towards the sign. 'And where's his nose?'

'Herr, or is it signior – how does one address a Dane born in Sweden, for the fellow came from Knudstrup – Brahe was an astronomer. He measured the position of seven hundred and seventy-seven stars, and all without the aid of a reflecting telescope.' The man looked round the shop. 'Perhaps I ought not to refer to that fact, for they are one of my principal lines, both for the experimental philosophers of the City and the tarpaulins out at Wapping Wall.' He leaned forward to Alpiew. 'He was a bit of a hot-head, I'm afraid. Lost the nose in a duel. But the silver replacement gave him a certain charm, I think. And makes for a lovely sign for me.'

'And these Azimuth things – what are they exactly?'

'Fascinating tools, really. The arc of the horizon, if intercepted, or should I say the angular distance from any such meridian when interrupted by the magnetic meridian and the observed heavenly body . . .'

'Can anyone buy these knives?' said the Countess, cutting him off before he went into the whole catalogue of meridians.

'Do you keep a record in case they are misused in any way?'

'I cannot imagine, madam, to what you are referring.' The man looked stern. 'Are you implying that my tools are used by abortionists and suchlike?'

'No.' The Countess stepped towards him. 'But I suspect that, in the hands of a maniac, a knife like that one for instance' – she indicated the one which nearest resembled Vernish's gingerbread cutter – 'could be quite dangerous. Could even be used to hack a person's head off, like the poor unfortunate actress, Anne Lucas.'

'How little you know of human anatomy, you women!' The man threw his arms up in despair. 'You could no more take off a human head with one of those than with a toasting-fork. You would need a heavy sword or an axe.'

'Even in the frenzied hands of a maniac . . . ?'

'I serve no maniacs here, madam, either for knives, axes or Azimuth quadrants. The minutely balanced works, the gnomon fitted to the perpendicular plane, would be far beyond their grasp. Maniacs don't last long at sea, believe you me.'

Alpiew saw what the Countess was trying to get out of the man and drew him back.

'Would you need to be strong to behead a person with an axe, or could someone old or even female do it?'

'Are you planning a crime, miss?' The man stepped out from behind the counter. 'For if you are, I will raise the hue and cry, and have you brought before the Justice.'

'What is this?' said the Countess, picking up a large glass vial with a plunger at one end.

'You will have no need of that, madam. 'Tis a syringe.' The man pulled it from her and placed it in a drawer. 'Gentlemen make use of them when they are suffering from certain amatory diseases . . .'

The Countess looked vacantly at him.

'. . . for applying medicine to the . . . yard.'

'Oh, look!' said the Countess, rushing for the door. 'The wind seems to have calmed down now.' She stepped out just as Tycho Brahe's head flew off its bracket and sailed through the window of the shop across the road.

'He has simply further demonstrated Valentine Vernish's innocence,' said Alpiew, ducking out of the way of a flying piece of newspaper. 'It does not narrow our search in the slightest.'

'Except we know now that the murderer used an axe or broadsword.' The Countess pulled up her hood. 'Strange mangy cat he had, did you notice? Didn't move once. Even when we slammed the door.'

Though there were few pedestrians about, carriages, carts and chairs were jamming the thoroughfare so that the two had to squeeze themselves against the wall to pass.

'Another tree down, I suppose,' cried the Countess against the wind.

'No, madam,' shouted the driver of a hackney carriage. 'The Fleet has burst her banks. New Canal is exactly that, and the horses don't like the water!'

'Right,' said Alpiew, gathering up her skirts and heading for New Gate. 'Come on, milady, let us head for the protection of the City.'

'We must keep an eye out for poor Godfrey. That Nickum fellow lives not so far from here.'

'We will, madam, with all my heart. But after the strange events of this morning I want nothing more than a cup of chocolate to take the chill off my bones. There are many warm cheap places we could try at Newgate Market. And while we are there we could make some inquiries after Mrs Leigh. Did she not tell us she was moving to relatives in Newgate Market?'

They steered along Newgate Street, where the traffic was at a standstill in both directions. Market-men drove their live-stock through the melee, leaving the markets early for lack of custom.

'If we want to do something, we must decide where to aim our darts.' The Countess blinked as a handful of straw from a nearby cart blew into her face. 'Whom do we suspect?'

'Rakewell, who seems unassailable; mad Nickum, who is

incomprehensible; Sarah, who is vanished; Lampone, who is . . .'

'Incorrigible. And as for the weapon – why, even Godfrey has an axe!'

A large woman coming out of a side alley slammed into Alpiew, causing her to lose her balance and stumble into the path of a passing horse. She grabbed the reins to steady herself and turned to scream at the woman. Their eyes locked for a moment.

The Countess wheezed and pointed. 'It's . . . It's . . .'

'Mrs Leigh!' cried Alpiew. 'How have things worked out for you?'

Mrs Leigh huffed.

'Did you hear that poor Mr Lucas was abducted?'

But Mrs Leigh had turned on her heels and was running away from them. A boy came out of the alleyway. He was well muffled in a dark cloak. He saw Mrs Leigh take off and darted after her.

'What was that about?' cried the Countess. 'I am in a maze. What have we done to offend the woman?'

'I haven't a notion,' said Alpiew, striding forward. 'But I am going to catch her and find out. Wait for me at the Indian Queen in the market.'

The Countess watched Alpiew disappear down an alleyway in a flurry of petticoat, then staggered into the teeth of the gale – a hot dish of chocolate was now her holy grail. Under his cloak, she noticed, the boy was wearing heeled shoes and yellow stockings. Yellow stockings! She mused. Yellow stockings! As far as she remembered, these were uniformly worn by the orphan boys of Christ's Hospital to keep the rats from their ankles.

Alpiew followed the woman and child as they ducked through a few dirty courts. They still had a decent lead, but Alpiew knew that as long as she could keep them in her sight she would catch them up. She was certainly both younger and fitter than Mrs Leigh.

Because of the weather, Newgate Market was in even worse chaos than usual. The stalls flapped and blustered and the ground was littered with crushed cabbage leaves, sausages and anything else that could be swept away. Fluttering chickens scurried around her feet, and sheep scuttled about with madness in their eyes. But the weather had also deterred most of the market customers, so Alpiew managed to close the distance considerably. At Ivy Lane Mrs Leigh bustled back on to Newgate Street. That did it. Now Alpiew knew she was avoiding her. The only reason she could have taken such a crazy winding path was to shake her off. What was the woman trying to hide?

As she entered Blow Bladder Street, Alpiew saw Mrs Leigh turn into St Martins Le Grand and cross to the other side of that road. There was little more than the width of the street between them now. At that moment a substantial carriage drawn by eight horses rolled into her path. Just her luck! She darted back to nip round behind it, and squinted up the street after the fugitives.

Mrs Leigh and the boy had disappeared. She turned frantically and looked in each direction. How had they vanished in a moment?

She kicked a stone in fury and walked briskly up the road, searching for an alleyway or shop where the woman and boy could have taken cover.

There were premises belonging to calico printers and carpenters, oilmen and night-soil men. A large swinging door to her right announced in bold colours: MRS SALMON'S WAXWORKS – ALL NEW!

Eureka! This would be a perfect place for anyone to hide – among the tableaux.

'Did a woman and a boy come through?'

The doorwoman nodded.

Alpiew hurriedly dug into her pocket and plonked down the entrance fee. 'How many ways out are there?'

'Only the one,' drawled the doorwoman. 'At the end of the exhibition. No refunds, no . . .'

Alpiew pushed through into the dark. Only mirrored sconces lit the scenes. The first tableau was the execution of King Charles. The bearded monarch was poised over the block, and the masked executioner held a sword aloft. The door exit was swinging on its hinge. Alpiew moved swiftly on. In the next flickering display a woman lay in a bed surrounded by naked babies. 'Margaret Countess of Heningberg with her 365 children, all born at one birth' said the sign. A likely story, thought Alpiew, heading for the door.

She heard a rustle of clothing ahead. On tiptoe she moved briskly through to 'Hermonia, a Roman maiden, who saved her father's life, when sentenced to starvation by the Emperor, by letting him suckle at her breast.' A wizened old man knelt, sucking at his young daughter's naked breast. Alpiew resisted the desire to spew and moved briskly into the next room.

As she was so near, the Countess decided to make a little investigation before going to the Indian Queen for her chocolate.

Christ's Hospital, new-built by Sir Christopher Wren after the fire, stood on the site of the old Greyfriars monastery. The Countess approached the main entrance, strolling through the delightful garden. As she passed through the first portal she was stopped by a man in an academic gown.

'Could I help you, madam?' He had a sneering tone.

'I wish to make an inquiry.' The Countess shot him an imperious glance. 'Could I see the list of your recently enrolled pupils?'

'Impossible,' snapped the master. 'We have almost four hundred pupils, most of them taken from the dunghill, and it is our job to protect them from the brutish world and train them to rejoin society at a higher level . . .'

'I have a specific boy in mind . . .'

'You are looking for a boy to hire as a funeral mute, I presume?' The master gave a sigh. 'We do hire out the boys for this service, but I am afraid you must go through the proper channels and we cannot promise you any specific child.'

'Maybe I should point out to you, sirrah, that I am Lady Anastasia Ashby de la Zouche, Baroness Penge, Countess of Clapham . . .'

'You wish to make a donation towards the education of a specific boy?' The master struggled to put on a smile.

'I was thinking of doing just that.' The Countess gave a coy smile, and fluttered her eyelashes. 'But first I need to see whether the boy I want to help is here or no.'

A satin-clad Sultan sat on a sparkling couch, smoking a large hookah. Curls of smoke rose from his mouth. All around him sprawled the women of his seraglio in various poses and states of dress. Alpiew stood stock-still. She could hear breathing. It seemed to be coming from the floor behind the wax statues. She leapt into the display, peeping round the waxworks, looking for Mrs Leigh and the Lucas boy. Then she looked down and saw a clockwork mechanism at her feet. It was connected to a pair of bellows, they in turn were feeding a long tube. Damn. It was not the sound of breathing at all. It was the machine that produced the Sultan's smoke.

Then, through the door, she heard a cough. She crept into the next room.

No one but Old Father Time, head slowly shaking from left to right and back again, holding up his huge hour-glass, watching sand drizzle through. Alpiew bound through the swinging last door and out into the street.

She blinked against the light. The little court seemed peculiarly bright. The road surface itself was almost white, and the hunched-up buildings were sprayed with white blotches.

'Did you see a woman and boy come this way?' Alpiew grabbed hold of a passing man, carrying a large white sack. He shook his head.

'What is this place, that it is all white?' yelled Alpiew as she ran on in the only possible direction.

'Moldmaker Row,' the man shouted after her, his voice almost swallowed by the howling wind. 'We make casts in plaster of Paris. For the waxworks.'

Alpiew darted down alleys, nipping back and forth until she found herself back on Blow Bladder Street. She looked both ways, but there was no sign of either Mrs Leigh or Jack Lucas. They had got away.

Alpiew stamped her foot and cursed. 'Pox upon the wax-works.' She took a few lethargic steps then stopped and clapped her hands. 'Criminy!' she cried, gathering up her skirts and running back to find the Countess. 'At last I have hit it!'

TWELVE

Desire

*An agitation of the soul when one is disposed to
wish for something which seems agreeable.*

*The eyebrows pressed forward over the eyes,
they more than usually open and full of fire. The
nostrils pinched. The mouth open, with the
tongue perhaps appearing at the edge of the lips.
The complexion inflamed.*

ebecca's lodgings were quiet, and dark. The curtains
were still drawn. Alpiew grabbed the Countess's hand
and dragged her into Rebecca's bedchamber.

'Alpiew! In God's name . . . What pox has come upon you,
girl? Let us not go into this chamber of horrors.'

Alpiew stepped forward and ripped back the blue figured-
velvet bed hangings.

'Keep back,' whimpered the Countess, raising her hands to
cover her eyes.

Alpiew put up her hand to silence the Countess and
advanced gingerly towards Rebecca's tortured head, still
silently screaming at them from the mound of pillows.

Alpiew bent down and peered closely, looking deep into the
startled eyes. Then she puffed at the head, sending a whirl of
feathers round the chamber.

'As I thought,' she cried, picking up Rebecca's head and
tossing it towards the Countess, who screamed and ducked.
''Tis artificial.'

The head landed on the wooden floor with a crunch. The wig that had adorned it flopped casually to one side.

Still crouching with her head down, the Countess squinted towards it through parted fingers.

'Wax!' said Alpiew, picking it up again, and tucking it under her arm. 'And artfully executed, in my opinion. Look.' She thrust the head towards the Countess again, turning it upside down to expose the neck. 'It's made of wax! An artist isn't going to waste good paint colouring in the bottom part because the thing will always be resting on a stand.'

'Who would have done such a thing?' The Countess dusted herself down. 'Who were they hoping to frighten?'

'I don't know who placed it here on her bed. But surely the thing itself was executed by Signior Lampone, as part of his display on the Passions. He must have carried it here in that bag, which we saw full, but was empty by the time the bookseller saw him leave. It explains the whole conversation I overheard between Lampone and Rebecca.' She gazed down again at the contorted face. 'Horror or Terror, do you think? 'Tis only a fine line between them.'

'Alpiew, you have given me an idea. I think we should carry it about, like Mrs Walter Raleigh, in a bag. Then when we come face to face with any person we suspect of killing the poor woman, we can whip it out and watch their reaction. Come.' She stuffed the head under her cloak. 'Don't forget the wig. I don't know that she will have such an effect as the bald prima donna.'

'One moment, Countess. This revelation has made me think again on what we saw there in the park. What do you remember of Rebecca? Can you imagine for one second that she was the type to whore herself to anybody? I think not. She was fastidious in everything. Also there is the undeniable fact of her beautiful smooth skin. She didn't have a blemish on her face. She never patched. She had no pits or scars.'

'Skilful use of paint,' snorted the Countess, whipping out the wax head and inspecting it closely. 'Remember she bought only the finest, most expensive pots of addition.'

'But let us suppose that this woman, Mistress Rebecca Montagu' – Alpiew gazed down at the wax head – 'did go into St James's Park that fateful night, yet walked away alive . . .'

'We saw the body, Alpiew!' The Countess let out a guffaw. 'No one could have got up and walked away *without their head*.'

'But who is to say it was Rebecca's body we found? I only knew it by the clothing.'

'Then who – ?'

'Her maid, Sarah, is missing, is she not? What maid, given a chance, has not borrowed her mistress's finery to parade herself for a new beau?' Alpiew took the head from the Countess and placed it carefully on a nearby table-top. 'We know Sarah did have a beau . . .'

'Indeed, Alpiew, a beau who was going to take her to America . . .' The Countess gave her own wig a good scratch, thereby tilting it awkwardly over one ear. 'And, come to think on't, Sarah did have problems with her skin, and patched.' The Countess looked anxiously towards the door. 'Perhaps the Tityre-tus fellow we disturbed last night was Sarah's beau. Maybe he was waiting for her, and thought we were Rebecca coming home unexpectedly.'

'Ay . . .' Alpiew gazed down at the wax head. 'But I suspect that Sarah is never coming home. Rebecca surely lured her to the park and then . . .'

'Why? Why would Rebecca want to kill her maid? It doesn't make sense. Even when I thought you had eloped with my abysmal husband, I only wanted to give you a good hiding. I would no more have thought on killing you than . . .'

'But Rebecca is a different kettle of fish from you, madam. If she did kill Anne Lucas, for some reason, it is possible that Sarah knew about it. Perhaps she found the weapon . . . Maybe she simply guessed, and threatened her mistress with exposure.'

'I don't know, Alpiew. It doesn't seem quite right.' The Countess shuddered and made for the door. 'And one thing is certain. If Rebecca *is* still alive it is very dangerous for us to be here. Let us move on.'

They shut up and marched down the stairs.

'It may be that you are right and that the body was Sarah's.' The Countess threw up her hood. It was raining and the wind seemed even wilder than it had been before. 'But whichever it was, only one fact is incontrovertible, and that is that there is, loose on the streets of London, a murderous axe-wielding lunatic.'

'Gotcha!' A heavy hand landed on the Countess's shoulder as she stepped out into Little Hart Street.

The Countess leapt in the air, emitting a high-pitched squawk.

She spun round to face Godfrey, soaked through, and lurching from side to side, fighting the blustery wind.

'I found him.'

'Godfrey!' The Countess held her heart and wheezed. 'You have quite frighted me out of my seven senses.'

The little dog Red, on the end of a red leather lead, leapt up and down, although it was uncertain if he was greeting them or in a frenzy.

'Found who?' shrieked Alpiew. 'The ballocking dog?' As if on cue, the animal drew back his lips and snarled in Alpiew's direction.

'No, milady, the lurking lunatic, Nickum Roper. He lives in Mermaid Alley. At the house with the green door.'

The entry to Mermaid Alley nestled tightly between a stay-makers at the sign of the Wheatsheaf and Bodice, and a slop-sellers at the sign of the Jolly Sailor.

'Apropos,' hissed the Countess. 'To have a slop-seller near Mermaid Alley.'

'Nickum Roper ain't no sailor, milady,' grunted Godfrey. 'Why would he need slop-clothing, that's only for seafarers and fishermen and the like.'

'Do you know where the man is now, Godfrey?'

'Well, I've followed him about a bit. I only left him because I had seen you two coming up the street towards Rebecca's rooms. He was heading west. I presume his intention was to stand outside Anglesey House for an hour. He did an hour at the playhouse, after I first came upon him, then on to her place for another hour, then 'twould seem likely back to yours, then back to the playhouse and the rounds again.'

The Countess looked up and down the dingy alleyway then at the dismal front door and dusty windows of Nickum's house. 'How can you be sure that this is his house?'

'Well,' said Godfrey, 'after his first round I followed him back along Paternoster Row. I saw him nip into this court, but knew he'd see me if I followed him up here. So I waited at the corner of Ave Maria Lane and Amen Corner, until I saw him a-comin' out of the entry again. Then I darted back and asked a few questions. Made out I had a letter for him. Three people all pointed to the same door, so I suppose it would be the one.' He threw his shoulders back and rubbed his gnarled hands together. 'Then I ran after him. And caught him at the playhouse, asking his questions. There's always a crowd outside, tattlin'.'

'You first, minx.' The Countess pushed Alpiew forward. 'Maybe he really does have a wife.'

Alpiew stepped up to the door and rapped at the knocker. She waited a moment then knocked again. She turned and the Countess gave her the nod. Slowly she turned the handle. The door creaked open and she went in, the Countess behind her. As Godfrey stepped on to the threshold the Countess held up her hand. 'You must lurk in a doorway and keep watch.'

'And then?'

'If anyone comes . . .'

'Nickum, you mean?'

'Well, yes. If Nickum comes you warn us.'

The dog sat, lifted his leg and started energetically licking his rear end.

'How?'

The Countess pursed her lips. She saw his point. If Godfrey could see Nickum in this dead-end alley, their only way out was straight into his arms, and Nickum could not fail to miss Godfrey in this small cul de sac. 'Detain him. Take him for a cup of chocolate . . . Tell him you have found Rebecca. Anything!'

Reluctantly, Godfrey let the door close in front of him.

Alpiew stood at the end of the hall.

The Countess poked about on a small table. There was a pile of clippings cut from newspapers. On top was their own article from the *Trumpet*: 'The Wake at the *Folly*, together with . . .' Heavy underlinings and a liberal smattering of exclamation marks all over the page in a cheap brown ink were clearly the work of Nickum. 'Alpiew, come see . . .'

'Odso, madam!' Alpiew grabbed a handwritten scrap of paper from the pile. 'What is this?'

'Why, 'tis a note you wrote.' The Countess glanced at the creased paper. 'One of your famous lists, I believe.'

'Yes, madam, that is exactly what it is.'

'"Cibber, Rakewell, Lampone . . ."' The Countess looked again at the list. 'Why 'tis a list you made early on of the suspects for the Lucas murder.'

'Indeed, and indeed,' Alpiew sighed. 'But how came it here, into the lodging of Nickum Roper, madam?'

'Do you mean . . . ?' The Countess looked at Alpiew, aghast. 'Don't tell me the fellow has been poking about in our house?' She shuffled slightly on the spot, suddenly aware that she was in fact poking about in his house.

'Either that, madam' – Alpiew handed the note to the Countess – 'or the cove has made a deal with the night-soil men and taken it from our rubbish.'

'Oh, phough!' The Countess spat, and dropped the note as though it was a burning coal. 'What nasty things did he have to scour through before finding that?'

Alpiew walked away from the table and headed up the hall. She stopped outside the first of two rooms, gripped the door handle and turned it softly. Slowly she poked her head inside, then with a gasp jumped back. She started making shooing movements to the Countess.

'What is it, Alpiew?'

'Sssh!' Alpiew grimaced and put her finger to her mouth.

'We are not alone,' Alpiew hissed into the Countess's ear. 'Someone is in there.'

The Countess peeked over Alpiew's shoulder and whispered back. 'So why did they not answer the door when we knocked?'

'I can only see their back, in a chair. Perhaps they are asleep.' Alpiew was already at the front door and on her way out. 'Let's hope we have not woken them.'

'Piffle!' said the Countess, marching towards the room. 'They will be pleased we have come to visit on such a dreary day.'

Alpiew scampered up to join her as the Countess strode into the room.

'Good morning!' The Countess stood in the doorway, addressing the rear of a head, the brown-headed crown of which peeped over the top of an easy chair.

The head did not move.

The Countess looked about her. Though the room was dark and dismal, everything was neat and tidy. Two seats faced each other either side of a fireplace. The fire was out.

'Hello?' Alpiew quietly edged into the room. 'We were looking for Nickum . . .'

'Awake! Awake!' The Countess clapped her hands rhythmically and waddled forward, a pleasant grin on her face.

> '"*Awake my soul and with the sun*
> *The daily stage of duty run.*
> *Shake off dull sloth and joyful rise*
> *To pay thy morning sacrifice.*" Good day to you!'

As she faced the chair the Countess stopped, the smile frozen on her face, then staggered backward and toppled awkwardly into the other chair. 'Alpiew!' She only mouthed this, as her voice seemed to have left her. Slowly an expression of horror spread across her face. She pointed at the chair and tried calling Alpiew again. This time a feeble squeaking sound came from her lips.

Alpiew ran to the Countess's side. In the chair facing them sat a woman. She was clothed in a pretty mantua and her face was set in a gentle tranquil smile. Her eyes stared ahead. Her skin was a dark ochre. It was evident that she was not breathing.

'Who is it?' whispered the Countess.

'I don't know,' hissed Alpiew, tiptoeing forward and reaching out to touch the woman's face. 'But she is most definitely dead.'

'What has happened to her skin?' The Countess was fanning herself, averting her eyes.

'It feels like parchment.' Alpiew bent to get a closer look. 'I think she must have been stuffed.'

'Let's not get vulgar at a time like this,' said the Countess, craning round to look out of the window and avoid the sight of the smirking female corpse. 'Who has killed her? Or did she die of natural causes?'

'Whatever it was, milady,' Alpiew put her hand behind the woman's back, 'I imagine she died a long time ago. From the lack of smell, I think she has been embalmed and then a very good craftsman has had a go at her.'

'A go? What can you mean?'

'She is a mummy.'

'A mummy? You can tell she had children just by looking at her face?'

'Not a mother, madam, a mummy. As in a mummy of Great Cairo, a Memphis mummy, or a mummy of the pyramids of Thebes.'

'She is an Egyptian?' said the Countess, stealing another glimpse. 'That would account for the dark crispy skin, I suppose. All that sun!'

Alpiew peered directly into the dead woman's face. 'These eyes are glass.' She touched one with her finger, while the Countess squirmed around in her chair, grimacing in distaste. 'Yes, definitely glass.'

'So are you now telling me that this is Nickum's Egyptian mother!' screeched the Countess. 'And that she sports two glass eyes?' She thought for a moment. 'Poor woman. How the devil does she see?'

Alpiew lifted the mummified woman from her seat. 'Light

as a feather,' she said, peering down the back of her corset. 'It is as I thought. It is quite obvious from the back. She has had her innards stripped and then she has been cured.'

'Not a very good cure if it killed her.' The Countess was making little puffing noises and her fan was flapping wildly. She sat up. 'Or do you mean cured like a gammon of bacon?'

'I mean,' said Alpiew, propping the embalmed body back on to her easy chair, 'that something very odd is going on here. And in my opinion we should get out of this place forthwith.'

When they reached the street there was no sign of Godfrey. A small steaming dog-turd was the only evidence that he and Red had been there at all.

Alpiew grabbed the Countess's hand and they ran hell for leather till they reached the crowd milling into Newgate Market from the Paternoster Row entrance.

The Countess screwed up her eyes and scanned the street in both directions. 'Whatever has become of poor Godfrey? Has that terrible man Nickum abducted him, do you think?' The Countess grasped Alpiew's elbow. 'I wouldn't like poor Godfrey ending up stuffed.'

'Nickum must have appeared, and Godfrey will have led him away for a dish of chocolate hereabouts.' Alpiew glanced through the windows of the ordinaries, taverns and India houses as she passed. 'Either that or he got the hump and went home with that horrid dog.'

'Do you think the dog horrid?' said the Countess. 'I think he's rather sweet.'

'As for the wife business,' said Alpiew, ignoring the compliment to the vicious little dog. 'Did he kill her?'

'Well, we know he has a wife, and that his wife is dead, and that she has been stuffed. And hence we have an explanation for his suggestion that he might "get rid of her".' The Countess giggled. 'Though what the night-soil men would think about carting away a mummy with the rubbish, I can't imagine.'

'But as to whether she was alive or dead before he began

his project of stuffing her, who is to know? I suppose there is no law against stuffing your wife.'

'I wouldn't take to it myself, I am sure,' said the Countess. 'Even if I was dead.'

'The local priest would know.' Alpiew clapped her hands. 'For when she died he would have been obliged to mention it in the parish register.'

'No. They record burials. And unless he dug her up . . .'

'A Justice then, for she would feature in the bills of mortality. Though Mr Roper would not have been obliged to add that he was embalming her. She could have died of a tympany, a spotted fever . . .'

'Not that,' snapped the Countess. 'You would still see the marks on her skin.'

'Dropsy, imposthume, consumption, the stone, griping in the guts,' Alpiew listed the possibilities.

'Rising of the lights, an ague . . .' added the Countess.

'And now she is sitting by the parlour fireplace, dressed in her Sunday best, and crisp as a dried kipper.'

The Countess let out a little cry. 'Cibber! Don't even mention him, or you will conjure him up.' She stepped aside as a crocodile of boys from Christ's Hospital in their long blue gowns and yellow stockings filed silently past. 'I made some inquiries about that Lucas boy, Jack, earlier, while you were chasing through the waxworks. I just asked at the gate. It seems that he is a pupil at that school.'

'At Christ's Hospital? Odso, your ladyship, are you certain? The institution is for deprived children, but I thought there had to be some pressure from above, financial or . . .'

'And so it seems there is,' said the Countess. 'The Leigh woman would appear to have taken him out on an irregular exeat, they said. She has rooms in Newgate Market. They wouldn't enlarge upon the subject but assured me the boy would be back in his classes tomorrow morning. He has a wealthy sponsor.'

'Now we are here, let us have that dish of chocolate at the Indian Queen, while we consider what to do next.' Alpiew pushed open the door of the bustling establishment, and followed the Countess to a small table. 'Mayhap Godfrey will pass by.'

'Or Mrs Leigh and the child.'

The place was a-babble with chattering people exchanging news of floods and storm damage over the whole of London from Hide Park to Tower Hamlets.

'It seems much better now.' Alpiew indicated the sky, which had brightened considerably. The wind too had died down to a breeze.

'Merely the eye of the storm,' said the serving wench with a glum expression. 'I had some sailors in earlier. They're all marooned here till the storm blows through. Tonight will be worse than yesterday, they say.' She sighed. 'Chocolate, tea, buttered ale or coffee?'

'For your tea . . .'

'I wouldn't bother,' sneered the waitress. 'All corrupted with jasmine petals, and orange peel and cloves and the like. We charge the same as the real thing, but you don't get the full value for your money.'

'Buttered ale for me, please,' said Alpiew.

The Countess opted for the same. 'What is that commotion at t'other side of the room?'

A small bunch of market traders and ladies were crowding around a corner table.

'Oh, that.' The serving wench turned. 'It's that player, Sir Novelty Fashion. Never thought that much of him, myself. I prefer the rope-dancers.'

'Oh, lord save us, Alpiew! I told you we should not conjure him.' The Countess ducked down. 'Shall we leave?'

'Perhaps Godfrey got sight of him, preening himself as he strutted up Paternoster Row, and that's what drove him away.'

The waitress lay down two cups of steaming buttered ale and a plate of buns.

The Countess was nodding strangely in Alpiew's direction and glancing down with wide eyes indicating her lower parts.

'What is wrong, madam?' Alpiew whispered.

'Someone is on the floor, feeling about in my skirts,' hissed the Countess. 'It must be one of those child pick-pockets we read about so much these days in the newspapers.'

Alpiew slithered down under the table. After a short scuffle she yelped and then clambered back to her seat. 'It's the bal-locking dog.'

'Red!' The Countess bent down, lifted her skirts and scooped up the dog, who started frantically licking her face. 'Hello, little sweetheart.'

Alpiew winced at the thought of where the dog's tongue had been earlier that morning, and bit into her bun.

'Alpiew, this is not good.' The Countess rose. 'If the dog is here, then something must have happened to Godfrey. A man who is capable of stuffing his own wife is surely capable of anything. Come, we must go.'

A shadow loomed over them.

'Good morning, fair ladies.' Cibber stooped to take the Countess's hand and kiss it. 'I saw you come in and could not resist paying my devoirs.'

'Mr Turbot!' The Countess beamed.

'Cibber.' He flicked his lace cuff and pouted. 'I thought, mesdames, you would be interested in the latest news from the playhouse. Mr Rich, in his wisdom, has brought the place about as low as it can go. He is not only proposing to shorten the stage in order to cram in more seats, but guess whom he has booked to perform next week?'

Alpiew and the Countess shook their heads. If it was Attila the Hun singing castrati in a tutu, they couldn't be less interested.

'Eunice!' snapped Cibber.

Still they looked blank.

'Eunice, the Calculating Pig, together with her owner, the Incombustible Incognito, a man who devours burning coals.'

'I see what you mean,' said the Countess. ''Twould be hard for you to squeeze them into Richard the Third's blustering chronicle. Unless at the battle of Bosworth Field you rewrite it so: "A pig! A pig, my kingdom for a . . ."'

'And during yesterday's performance of *The City Heiress* a gang of those filthy Tityre-tus rushed the stage and started shouting obscene remarks about Beck Montagu (who, I gather, has gone to ground since that monstrous Rakewell duped her at the *Folly*). I was in the middle of a particularly hilarious piece of business with a bottle and a fan. Sir Timothy is a good role for me . . .'

'Unfortunately, Mr Sturgeon, you caught us just as we were leaving. You see, my man Godfrey has gone missing and we are at a loss . . .'

'Do you have any news on Beck?' said Cibber, peering over his spectacles. 'The playhouse is a sorry place without her. I say! Where can she be while her "husband" tears through the streets wreaking havoc?'

'Perhaps my Lord Rakewell will be tamed by the love of a good woman.'

Cibber snorted. 'He's come through here this morning, but the market was too quiet to effect any real damage. He's probably raising a riot in Covent Garden at this moment.'

He stooped forward and looked at Red. 'That's her dog, isn't it? Why then you MUST know where she is.'

The Countess tapped the side of her nose and rose. Cibber held open the door. As she swept past him he kept step with her, leaving the door to swing shut in Alpiew's face. 'I lent some trifle to her woman, Sarah. And the truth is she owes me money. Profits are low at Drury Lane these days, so I need every penny I can get. Could you put me in touch with her?'

'You lent money to that nasty wench?' The Countess shot him a look, and decided to venture a piece of information. She whispered into his ear. 'Betwixt you, me, and the bed-post, I have reason to believe that Sarah has been got rid of.' Cibber looked horrified. 'But no matter,' she added in a sinister tone. 'I know the fellow who did it. I am hoping to have him apprehended forthwith. How much was it that you lent her? If I could threaten the fellow, mayhap I could get it back for you . . .'

'A mere bagatelle . . .' Cibber was shilly-shallying. ''Twould be hard to pin the figure . . .'

'Help, ho!' Cries were coming from the far side of the market. 'For the lord's sake, raise the hue and cry!'

Men were standing on parked carriages, trying to see what was going on. Women were throwing up their arms and screaming. A band of Tityre-tus hurried through the crowd, shoving people to the floor to make a path.

'They said they would be back!' A man was sweeping all the fresh produce from his stall into boxes, to save what he could before the wild boys reached him. 'I wish someone would stand up to them.'

'Take on Rakewell and you take on the lot,' cried a woman clambering under a stall for protection. 'They're all cowards at heart.'

'There's two old codgers trying to take him on even now.' A man standing on a carriage was peering over the heads of the crowd. 'One's fighting him with a broom, the other with a rusty old sword!'

'Are you thinking what I'm thinking?' The Countess was on tiptoe, trying to get a glimpse. Red started leaping up too, yelping.

'Godfrey and Nickum!' Alpiew clambered up the side of the carriage. 'They've both sworn to finish Rakewell.'

'I think Rakewell has been hit.' The man on the carriage clapped his hands. 'He's holding his cheek and cursing. No, wait. Oh. He's run one of the old boys through! And now he's taken to his heels.'

'What of the two old men?' The Countess was leaping up and down. 'Alpiew, can you see?'

'Only the crowd, madam.' She leapt down. 'But Rakewell comes this way.'

People around them parted in a great wave as, running hell for leather in their direction, came Lord Rakewell, his hands crimson with gore. He was trying to throw his hood up over his head and cursing. He pushed Cibber out of his way as he hurried along, heading north towards Newgate Street.

'Stop that man!' screeched a woman in pursuit.

Alpiew darted back into the Indian Queen.

Two large market traders leapt over their stalls and blocked Rakewell's way out of the square. Rakewell drew his sword and cursed them, still advancing. 'Out of my way, you filthy curs.'

Alpiew emerged, grasping a large steaming cup of tea, which she flung in Rakewell's face. Instantaneously the Countess stuck out a foot and tripped him. Once he was down, his sword clattering to the ground, then Red leapt on the prostrate man, snarling and snapping at his periwig. The two stallholders advanced and pinned him down with pitchforks, while three large fish-wives flopped upon his legs. Lord Rakewell was caught.

'I'll be avenged on you for this, you superannuated fornicators!' He squirmed and writhed, but as he struggled more and more women piled on top of him. 'Pox on you, you monumental hell-cats.'

'A chair here!' A fellow was shouting at the other side of the square. 'The old fellow is oozing blood where that haughty devil has run him through. Make haste ho!'

Two chairmen hoisted the chair upon their shoulders and carried it through the crowd.

'Oh, ye gods!' The Countess staggered back towards Alpiew. 'What if it is Godfrey?' She gathered her skirts and followed the chair.

'Lord Rakewell . . .' Alpiew bent down so he could see her face, and she his. 'While we wait for the constables to be sent for to apprehend you, perhaps you might tell us something about the whereabouts of your wife?'

'That whore!' Rakewell spat. 'I suppose she lent her helping buttock among you to shove on my ruin. If ever I catch the strumpet, I'll sear up the filthy bung-hole of her firkin. I'll reward her for her bitching, cheating ways. Along with all of you nauseating vermin.'

'Pize on you, Lord Rakewell, for an insolent, arrogant crackfart!' Alpiew stood and looked to the north side of the square.

'Look you, here come the watch to carry you off to the Tower.'

Rakewell writhed about, snarling.

'I know you think you won't be imprisoned for long, but I assure you, sirrah, I am very nearly at a conclusion regarding the hold you have over people in high places. Be sure of one thing: I will discover it before you come up in front of his lordships a third time.'

In the meanwhile, the Countess shoved through the crowd towards the fallen man. There was a lot of blood in the gutter. A woman was tearing her petticoat and handing it to another on the ground for a tourniquet.

The Countess could only see a leg, bloodied and hanging limp in the crook of a woman's arm. She bent low and crawled across the straw-littered cobbles. She could see that the injured man was wearing Godfrey's hat. She gasped and reached out to pull the hat back from his face. But the white, agonised countenance that lay before her was not Godfrey's. The wounded man was Nickum Roper.

He stared glassily towards the Countess. His mouth was moving, but no sound was coming out.

'Tell me, Nickum.' She edged nearer and put her face close to his. 'What is it you are trying to say?'

'Godfrey,' he croaked into her ear. 'Godfrey, Duke of Buckingham. Tonight.'

Two leather merchants took Nickum by the shoulders and lifted him into the chair.

Nickum was pointing at the ground.

'He wants his sword.'

'It weighs a ton!' A woman picked up the rusty thing and handed it into the chair. 'Looks as though it's been around since the battle of Hastings!'

The Countess glanced at the sword and then at Nickum as the two men lifted the chair and set off at a brisk pace.

The woman shouted ahead. 'Make way there, ho! The wounded man goes forth . . .'

'Do you know that fellow?' The Countess faced the woman who had made the tourniquet.

'We all know him. Nickum Roper. Mad as a March wind, but harmless enough.'

'Did he really challenge Rakewell?'

'He came here about an hour ago with another old cuff who had a little dog that was yelping and leaping up and down. They seemed to be making some sort of pact together, for they shook hands over and over and swapped hats. Old Nickum asked me if anyone had seen Rakewell today. He told me they were going to finish him off, the pair of them. To avenge that actress.' The woman shook her head. 'Well, we all laughed. Two old dodderers like that against Rakewell and his gang.' She shook her head. 'I hope he survives. Poor old fellow.'

'And his friend? Is this his dog?' She indicated Red, who was sniffing at the puddle of blood at the Countess's feet.

'Yes. The dog ran off when the trouble started.' The woman gazed off to the south entrance of the market. 'And the old fellow ran off that way, chased by a handful of those hell-boys, all roaring and laughing like devils.'

Alpiew had heard all this and darted off in the direction the woman said Godfrey had gone.

'Run, Alpiew!' The Countess puffed after her. 'I am worried out of my wits for his safety.' She stood on the corner of Paternoster Row. Alpiew was some yards ahead, climbing on top of a hay wagon to get a better view.

'The gang seem to have split up, madam,' she yelled back. 'I see them all on horseback, heading in several directions.'

'No sign of Godfrey?'

'No, madam. But that is good. For he is certainly with none of them. Perhaps they have let him go.' She leapt down and marched back to the Countess. 'What we need now is a way to get to Rakewell in the Tower.'

'Nickum was burbling about the Duke of Buckingham.' The Countess scratched her cheek with one finger, inadvertently drawing a red line from the rouge on her cheekbone down to her chin. 'What has he to do with this affair that his name keeps popping up?'

'Perhaps he is a friend of Rakewell's?'

'But he said: "Godfrey, Duke of Buckingham. Tonight."'

'He thinks Godfrey is the Duke of Buckingham? The man is crazed, God help him. Perhaps he wants Godfrey to go to see the Duke of Buckingham tonight. What a mess!'

'Not only that, Alpiew. Nickum has a broadsword. Old and heavy.'

'But at least if he is our murderer he is out of action for today, if not forever . . .'

'Ay, and Mr Vernish is going to swing unless we find Rebecca.'

'And now we have to save Godfrey, too. I wonder what hold Rebecca has on Rakewell? We could go and ask him . . .'

'Alpiew! You think he would blab things like that to us?'

They walked on in silence.

'One moment, Countess, there is one person in all this wretched business that we have forgotten about. And I'm sure *she* could wheedle it out of him.'

'Who on earth is that?'

'Phoebe Gymcrack.'

'Gymcrack! The former fiancée.'

Alpiew waited round at the Gymcracks' back door, while the Countess approached at the front. These jumped-up City Aldermen had strange new ways, and odd formalities like gentry through the front door, servants through the back. With military precision, Alpiew and the Countess staged a two-pronged attack on the Gymcrack household.

The Countess planned (if she ever got that far) to apologise over the *Trumpet* article, claiming it had been a mistake, a confusion over identities. She was shown into the great hall. A heavy grandfather clock ticked.

Eventually the alderman himself, a short fat man with a ruddy face, came into the room.

'Ah, Alderman Gymcrack. I'd like a word with Phoebe, please.' The Countess smiled wanly.

'She is not here . . .'

'I need to speak to her.' The Countess braced herself

for the paternal explosion. 'I have a message from my Lord Rakewell.'

Alpiew was greeted by a footman. 'I've a message for Phoebe.' She looked about and spoke in a low voice. 'From Rakewell.'

'Oh yes?' The footman smiled. He seemed eager. 'You'd better come in.'

This was strange. Not at all what she had expected. 'Is she here?'

'No,' said the footman. 'But you can tell me. I'm in on it.'

'Oh good,' said Alpiew, panicking as she walked into the kitchen. What on earth could be a realistic message? 'I don't want to be overheard,' she whispered, padding for time.

'Odd fellow,' said Mr Gymcrack. 'Rather wild, but . . . well, I suppose that all goes with the rest of it.' He laughed.

The Countess, shocked at his nonchalance, hovered inside the front door. 'As a member of the nobility myself . . .'

'Yes, yes, of course.' Gymcrack rubbed his hands together. 'I suppose, like my daughter, you must have been enjoying Lord Rakewell's services for a long time.'

The Countess gaped. What could the man possibly mean?

'Phoebe has done us all a great service introducing him to the household. We all benefit from his . . . favours.'

Appalled, Alpiew sat.

'Cup of tea?' said the footman with a wink. 'That man, Rakewell, clearly knows how to tickle a girl's fancy. Mine too!'

Alpiew pulled the table closer. She knew Rakewell was a dissolute roué, but this revelation was far beyond anything she was expecting to hear.

'He's not been round for a few days now.' The footman brought the pot to the table and sat. 'The house is throbbing with frustration.'

Alpiew could not believe her ears. It was neither Rebecca nor Sarah who was the whore – but Lord Rakewell!

'Sorry, it's a bit weak. No more than water bewitched!'

The footman gave a gay little laugh and nudged Alpiew in a suggestive manner. 'Now that Rakewell has us all on rations, we're having to eke the stuff out. You know how it is.'

'Stuff?' said Alpiew.

'The tea, of course!'

Alpiew gulped.

'I presume,' said Gymcrack in a conspiratorial tone, 'you are here about the increased price of his lordship's tea?'

'Tea?' The Countess's mind raced. 'Tea!' How had she not thought of it before? Tea! One of the most highly taxed commodities in England. Rakewell must head a gang of tea smugglers, and peddle the stuff to the nobility and rich citizens of London. 'Yes, yes, Alderman Gymcrack. Delicious stuff. Which do you favour: Twanky or Gunpowder?' How best to pump him for information?

'I must say, I have always found, sir, that Rakewell presents a good bargain.' The Countess toyed with the door handle. 'So have you had your promised delivery?'

'The fellow has let me down.' Gymcrack grimaced. 'I'm down to my last few spoonsful.'

'Same for me,' said the Countess. 'I imagined others were in a similar position. Have you paid in advance?'

'Oh yes,' said Gymcrack.

'So there we are!' The Countess made for the front door. Red, though, stayed beside the chair and started scratching his left ear.

The alderman looked to her and then to the dog. 'Your companion looks to have a visit from the fleas.' He bent down and tousled Red's head. 'Poor boy, are your friends become your backbiters?' He looked up at the Countess. 'So are you come to offer me a competitive bargain?'

The Countess shrugged. Perhaps she could sell him the contents of the box in her front room. 'I could be . . .'

Alderman Gymcrack was suddenly tense. He looked hard at her. 'Is the dog not a symbol?'

'I believe he is a French Butterfly dog. A papillon.' She saw the man's face cloud over and realised she had somehow made a mistake. 'I was simply trying to establish, Alderman, how many others find themselves in the same position as myself.'

'Most of their noble lordships, I should think.' Gymcrack relaxed again. 'He had many "friends" in the House of Lords, the Judiciary, Society . . .'

'And you and I come pretty low on that list, I imagine.'

'Yes.' Gymcrack held open the front door. 'Despite my daughter's efforts! Lucky he married that actress, though, for there was a time I was worried the villain would actually fall for her!' He gave the Countess a wink. 'And though I'm happy to buy a bargain or two off the fellow, I wouldn't want my daughter hitching up with such a dissolute scoundrel. So what was your message?'

'I'm sorry.' The Countess smiled serenely. 'I must deliver it in person. For you see, Lord Rakewell has just stabbed a man, and is being carried at this very moment to the Tower of London.'

In a babble of revelations about tea, Alpiew and the Countess met round the corner.

'So, if any of the Gentlemen Warders have a fancy for the brew of China weed,' said the Countess, 'we can presume that they conspired with Lord Rakewell, and assisted him in his short period of freedom.'

'During which nocturnal sojourn, I suppose, he brought in another shipment of contraband tea and had it distributed throughout the Town.'

'Exactly. And then returned to his cell in time to be taken to the House of Lords for his trial. At which all present were either customers or beneficiaries in some way of this tea racket.' The Countess looked about her. 'The wench in the Indian Queen was right. The wind is rising again.' She pulled Red away from a rotting pile of meat that someone had dumped upon the roadway.

'And if Rakewell was overseeing the landing of a boat-load

of contraband that night, and Anne Lucas stumbled across his cache, it would be in his interest to kill her before she reported him to the excise men.'

'Maybe he felt sorry afterwards and promised money to her family.'

'Ay, and then forgot about it till it was almost too late. Then he arranged for the boy to be educated.'

'But, knowing about his trade in contraband tea, we may be able to put some pressure on him.' The Countess smiled.

'Perhaps the tea Anne Lucas stumbled upon is the very box that Rebecca left in my house. Yes, Alpiew. It is beginning to fit together. And my Lord Rakewell seems more guilty by the second.'

The clock chimed four. The dog barked at the sound.

'And do you know, Alpiew, I wonder whether Rebecca may not have been lying when she pretended not to want Rakewell. What if they were in this tea business together?'

'The woman was a player, after all,' scoffed Alpiew. 'And players can dissimulate at the drop of a hat. It is their paid employment so to do. Look how the haughty madam could assume the physiognomy of all the Passions.'

'We have been taken for a parcel of fools. You, me and poor, poor Godfrey. We have not much time. Evening draws on. And tomorrow poor Mr Vernish will die unless we work to save him. We must find Rebecca. Incomprehensible they may be, but I believe, if mad Nickum was right, the Zuñigas must know something.' She crossed herself. 'Poor lonely malcontent, I pray his wound is not mortal. While we are so near we should make some inquiries at St Bartholomew's.'

'But what of Nickum's poor, stuffed wife?'

'You can get stuffed alligators to sit upon your desk for seventeen shillings. If Nickum loved his wife, why not have the same service performed for her? Like the fellow in the shop at Tycho Brahe's Head.'

Alpiew stopped in her tracks. '*He* too has a stuffed wife?'

'No.' The Countess tutted. 'The immovable cat, remember, on the top shelf, with the glassy stare. Obviously stuffed.

There's no law against it, is there? And now that I think on't, I think it's rather a sweet thing to do.'

Alpiew gulped. The very thought of having embalmed corpses round the house filled her with horror.

An Augustinian nun in a brown-and-cream habit peered from the small hatch at the entrance. 'Can I help you?'

'I wish to inquire about Mr Nickum Roper. Brought in a while ago with stab wounds.'

The nun looked down at a great open ledger.

'Are you a relative?'

'Yes,' said Alpiew. 'I am his niece.'

'We tended his wounds, which luckily were superficial. A slash to the leg, another to the arm.' The nun smiled enigmatically. 'Mr Roper stayed for a bowl of milk pottage and sugar sops, downed a pint of ale, then some toothless friend of his arrived, none the better for drink, and off they went, without even a thank-you, let alone any contribution towards the apothecary's charges.' The nun thrust a piece of paper in Alpiew's direction. 'As a relative, you are responsible for his bill.'

Alpiew turned, but the Countess was already half-way across the adjoining churchyard of St Bartholomew the Less. Alpiew gathered up her skirts and dashed after her.

When they reached Newgate Street the Countess stuck out her hand to wave down a hackney carriage. 'Ghastly little man. Stuffing his wife! I've never heard of such an abomination.'

A hackney stopped and they climbed aboard, the Countess holding Red in her arms.

'You go on ahead to Mr Pepys.' The Countess brushed down her skirts, and tickled Red's neck. 'I wish to go home and mend my countenance after so much City smut. Tell Pepys I will wait upon him in an hour. Ask him if he will travel out with us to Limehouse and interpret the impenetrable sea-slang of the Zuñigas.'

'But how will we get to Limehouse, madam? I doubt that the Duchesse's man will lend us the coach again for such a journey.'

'Of course not, Alpiew. When in Rome . . .'

'We're travelling by litter?'

'No girl, by water!'

Alpiew banged firmly on Pepys' front door in Villiers Street. A sour-faced woman answered.

'Mr Pepys is very tired.' She looked down at Red, who was sitting at Alpiew's skirts, snarling. 'I'll show you in. But I doubt he will have time to sit and talk.'

Alpiew refrained from pulling a face at the woman, and followed her meekly up the stairs. She had no intention of staying long anyhow.

'Mr Pepys, Countess Ashby de la Zouche's woman to speak to you.' She heard Pepys groan, and the woman gave her a snide look before gliding down the stairs again.

'Come in, come in!' He had his back to her and was sitting in the window, gazing out at the river through a telescope. 'What can I do for you?'

'My mistress desires you to accompany her on a trip to Limehouse.'

He grunted.

'Tonight. To interpret some sea-talk.'

'Mmmm,' said Pepys, spinning the telescope round at another part of the river. 'Good.'

Alpiew sensed that she would get nothing out of this old fool, and turned to go. 'She will come here in about an hour.'

'There are interesting happenings upon the water this evening.' He took his eye from the telescope and rubbed it. 'Thank you so much, mistress . . . ?' He shot a look at Alpiew.

'Alpiew, sir.'

Still gazing at her, he slowly rose and tiptoed across the room. 'Lovely little dog, you have with you. I think we'll ask my housekeeper to take him for a walky!' He pulled open the door and shouted down the stairs. 'Mary! Be pleased to take the dog for a trot along the Strand. He needs a good half-hour, I should say.'

He slipped the lead from Alpiew's hand and led the dog on to the landing.

Alpiew stood in the centre of the room admiring the view from the large window.

Pepys returned, shut the door and leaned upon it. 'So, you saucy baggage, what do you have for me?'

The sudden change was quite alarming to Alpiew. She composed herself and gave a business-like smile.

'A message from my . . .'

'Ssssshhhh!' Downstairs, the front door slammed shut. Pepys grinned and tiptoed up to Alpiew, his eyes fixed upon her ample cleavage. 'Alpiew, is it? Well, aren't you a pretty dark-eyed tit!'

Alpiew stepped back and scowled.

'Ah, to be sure, you're a shy one. As my noble friend the Countess's servant, I feel a salute is due.' He teetered forward, his lips pursed. 'Come, come, child, buss, buss!'

'I reiterate, sirrah . . .' Alpiew had no desire for a kiss from Mr Pepys. 'My mistress will be here shortly and she wishes you to translate some sea-talk. A man's life depends upon it.'

'Ay, ay,' he giggled and fumbled at his breeches buttons. 'And a man's life depends on this too, I promise ye. What an impressive pair you have! Not since the days of . . .'

'I implore you, Mr Pepys' – Alpiew pulled up the front of her dress – 'to pull yourself together.'

'Saucy! Just a little feel. We need not go so far as *ce que je voudrais* if you don't want.' He gave her a wink. 'But if I may just finger your gargantuan bubbies . . .'

'Enough!' Alpiew gave Pepys a hearty slap across the chops. Pepys reeled back and landed in his easy chair. He winced, adjusting his breeches in the crotch area.

Alpiew took a deep breath. 'Now if we might return to the subject in hand.'

'You are a bold, merry slut and no mistake.' Pepys looked down at the bulge in his breeches. 'To be sure, you could make a man run mad.' He heaved himself out of his chair.

'When you have quite calmed yourself, sir, I will take my leave.'

'I've been a bad boy, haven't I?' Pepys hung his head. 'For

that I am heartily sorry. Now allow me please to make my peace with you. Would you join me in a glass of wine? I have of the finest Ho Bryan.' He indicated a chair near the window. 'Or a cup of humpty-dumpty, if you prefer. I know that lusty wenches like yourself enjoy something long and hot.'

'Thank you, sir, but I am not thirsty.' Alpiew perched demurely on the edge of the seat and peered out of the window at the dark flowing river. 'You have a lovely view.'

'I certainly have.' Pepys had not taken his eyes from her chest. 'York Buildings is a most pleasant place to live. We have the concert hall, the Watergate is most convenient if I need to take a trip by river, and the waterworks just along the way. There's New Exchange just up the way and Parliament the other direction. Theatres aren't so far either. Or the piazza, if I was after a lusty hour in a bagnio.'

Alpiew shot him a black look and he flinched.

'Why is this area called York Buildings, when all the streets have their own names?'

'Centuries ago the whole place was the Archbishop of York's palace. But the Duke of Buckingham bought it all up.'

'The Duke of Buckingham?' Alpiew leapt to her feet. 'Does he live near here?'

'No.' Pepys laughed. 'Vain old fellow's as dead as mutton.'

Alpiew sank down into the chair again.

'You seem disappointed?'

'I am trying to solve a riddle and his name pops up too often to be a coincidence.'

'I love a riddle,' said Pepys, eager to please. 'What is it?'

Alpiew dug into her pocket and pulled out the pieces of paper she had gathered over the last few days: 'Tonight. G.V., Duke of Buckingham' and 'W.G. G.V.D.O.B. VIII. R. XX'.

'Interesting!' Pepys scrutinised them carefully, nodding his head rhythmically as he repeated the letters under his breath. '"D.O.B. R. XX . . ." Yes, yes. Duke of Buckingham, mmmm.'

Alpiew leaned forward. 'So what does it mean?'

'I'd say, Mistress Alpiew,' Pepys pouted, 'if I'm to help you, then you should give me something in return.'

'Like what?' said Alpiew, eyeing him with some suspicion.

'Just a little tiny peck on the lips.' Pepys thrust the papers back, laying them upon her lap with a hand that he did not remove. 'A nice juicy smack for a lonely old fellow . . .'

THIRTEEN

Hate

An emotion of the soul caused by spirits which incite the desire to be parted from objects which appear harmful to it. Aversion with the presence of the object.

Wrinkled brow, eyebrow down and frowning, the eye restless and full of fire. Nostrils drawn back, open. The teeth clenched. The lower lip may be thrust out over the upper. The muscles of the jaw seem hollow.

'Godfrey? Godfrey?' The Countess stood in the hallway and hollered. The fire was lit, but there was no sign of him. The Countess had already checked the yard, and the privy, which was in a dangerous state of collapse, with one wall down and the roof off.

She pushed open the front-room door. The good furniture was pushed over, and drawers pulled out, the papers that had been within them were scattered over the floor. Why had she sent Alpiew on to Pepys? She did not feel safe alone. Perhaps someone was in the house now.

She tiptoed up the stairs, gingerly pushing open the doors on the landing and peeping inside. Godfrey was lying on top of Rebecca's bed, snoring.

'Godfrey?' The Countess edged into the chamber.

'Ssshh!' A tiny child leaped in front of her, fingers to his lips. 'You'll wake him.'

'Who are you?' The Countess inspected the ragged urchin. 'And what are you doing in my house?'

'I think 'e must be tired,' said the child. 'Between you, me and the bedpost, I'd say he was completely befuzzled.'

'Yes, yes . . .' The Countess tugged the boy on to the landing. 'But, I repeat, who are you, and what are you doing in my house?'

'The old buffle seemed a trifle wobbly on 'is legs, see, so I 'elped 'im up the stairs and put 'im to bed. Then I went down and stoked up the fire, and made a sort of posset, without the aqua-mirabilis, obviously. 'E drunk it straight up and then went to sleep.'

The Countess took the child by the hand and marched him down into the ransacked front room. 'Did you do this too?'

'No,' yelped the boy. 'Truly. I just helped the old fool inside.'

'Go on . . .'

'He was slumped on the doorstep. There was some queer cull with him, but he nipped off smartish when I approached.'

'Describe him.'

'Shabby, had bandages on his arms and legs.'

'All right.' The Countess dragged the child through to the kitchen. 'So now you can tell me what you are doing in my house at all.'

'Fie, sir!' Alpiew pulled away from Pepys' exploring lips. 'If you beslobber me at such a rate . . .'

'A mere exosculation!' cried Pepys, reapplying his lips to hers, and letting his hand wander up past the top of her corset and on to her breast.

'Enough, Mr Pepys!' Alpiew pulled his hand away and stood up, leaving him to lose his balance and tumble into the chair where she had been sitting. 'Please let us keep our decorum. My lady will be here in an instant, and your friend will be returning with the bastardly dog.'

Grasping his legs and wheezing, Pepys sat back into his chair. 'There it goes again!' He grabbed the telescope and directed it at the river. 'Do you see?'

Alpiew put her hands up against the glass and looked out. 'I see nothing, sir, but a black old river.'

'Look harder. Right over on the Lambeth side. On the bank, near the timber yards. There it goes!'

Alpiew pressed her face harder against the glass. She saw a dull flickering, then nothing. ''Tis a reflection only, sir.'

'I came upon this a lot in my Navy days,' said Pepys. 'You are right when you say 'tis a reflection. Someone over there on that desolate shore is holding a looking glass. And they are making signals to someone over here.'

'That's all very interesting, sir. Now, you have had your kiss, so will you give me your opinion as to the meaning of those letters?'

Unenthusiastically, Pepys picked up the note from the floor. ''Twas only a small kiss.'

'Ay, sir,' said Alpiew, looming over him. 'And you only asked for a "little tiny kiss", so you have had what you asked for and more. And 'tis only a few letters.'

'Duke of Buckingham.' Pepys pouted. 'He was mortal enemy to my Lady Castlemaine, an old rival of your mistress. Of course, Castlemaine was a sexual engine, a genius of the genitals. It was said she could perform every one of Aretino's postures . . .'

'So D.O.B. is Duke of Buckingham, sir. And the rest?'

'Oh yes.' Pepys squinted down at the paper again. 'G.V. will be George Villiers.'

'And who's he, when he's in his breeches?'

'The Duke of Buckingham.'

'I know, the Duke of Buckingham bit, but who is George Villiers?'

'A writer, like you. But you see, George Villiers and the Duke of Buckingham are one and the same.'

'And where would I find this George Villiers cove?'

'In his tomb. I told you, the poor fellow has been dead these thirteen years.'

'So when I was upstairs with the old spigot-sucker, I heard this noise downstairs and then the door slammed. So it was lucky we'd come in when we did. Someone must have been in here. But I believe we must have frighted him away, whoever it was.'

The Countess, busily applying addition to her cheeks, peered over the looking glass at the child, huddled close to the fire, clutching a mug of caudle cup.

'And why should I believe you?' The Countess licked a blue crayon and started applying veins to her bosom. 'When I don't know who you are and why you are here.'

Ignoring her, he dug into the pocket of his smock. 'Then this came.' He handed the Countess a note.

'Who is it from?' The Countess, seeing what a mess she had made of the veins, was busily trying to smudge the blue. The whole of her décolletage now looked as though it was covered in bruises.

'How should I know?' The boy frowned. 'I didn't open it, and even if I did, I don't know my letters, so I couldn't understand it. My name is Tim. Short for Timothy.'

The Countess glanced at him as she picked up a wodge of Spanish wool and started applying it to her cheeks.

'If you use so much red, missus, you'll look as though you're having an apoplexy. Here –'

He took the wool from her and gently rubbed the rouge into her cheeks. 'Needs to be higher up to lift the bones.'

'And how do you know so much about lady's paint, pray, Tim?'

'Got a sister, ain't I?' With the black crayon he started work round her eyes.

The Countess tore open the letter. The writing was familiar:

Help me. Rakewell has me locked in the Tower.

Rebecca

Yeoman Partridge has got this note to you. He has done all he can.

The Countess's mind raced. What kind of thing was this? So Alpiew was right and Rebecca *was* alive. But surely . . . Her mind darted this way and that. Everything about the woman seemed so dangerous . . . But what if this letter was genuine, and she really was in trouble? Rakewell certainly had a way of terrorising everyone. Who was to say the letter wasn't absolutely true? And if it was, and she ignored it and then something dreadful happened to Rebecca, could she abide with the guilt?

The Countess laid the note upon the table and took hold of the boy's shoulders.

'Who gave you this note?'

'A man.'

'Was he wearing a red suit with yellow ribbons?'

'It's the wrong end of the year for Bartholomew Fair, missus.' The boy started gently to smooth down the wild bush of the Countess's wig. 'It was just an ordinary man. In ordinary clothes.'

'Tall, short, fat, whiskers?'

'Just ordinary. Not a rich gentleman from the court, but not a market trader neither. Just a man.'

'Do you remember, Tim, did he have a strange manner of speech?'

'And you come to mention it, missus, he did have a way of goin' uh at the end of everything 'e said.'

Yeoman Partridge! The Countess stood. 'Quickly! I must leave.'

'Hey!' The boy threw down his crayon. 'I ain't done your lips yet.'

'Anon, anon.' She stooped and spoke firmly to him. 'I want you to do something for me. You're to go and deliver a note to my woman, Alpiew. Then I want you to come back here, and make sure Godfrey, that's the old bugger upstairs, is all right. Do you understand?'

The boy nodded. The Countess reached out and tousled his hair. 'Here's a penny for you. And if you do as I ask, there'll be a shilling more when I get back.'

The boy took the coin, bit it and thrust it down his sock. 'You write that note, while I get you a hackney, missus.'

'But . . .'

'Don't go all havy-cavy on me, now. After I've done your face-paint, you're to go in a hackney. A lovely-looking old bird like you shouldn't walk on a stormy night like this.'

'Of course buggery is now as common amongst our gallants as it is in Italy.' Pepys sipped from his wine glass. 'The very pages of the Town complain against their masters. But for me, damn the fashion, I still prefer the wenches.'

'Your housekeeper is giving the dog a very long walk . . .'

'Yes, and talking of dogs, I hear that on long voyages even the chickens are not safe from the amorous advances of the crew.'

Alpiew sighed, wishing there was any hope of steering the conversation away from sex.

The front door slammed. Alpiew leaped up. 'That will be the dog back, I hope.'

Pepys shook his head. 'From the loping tread upon the stairs I would say it is Will Hewer back from work.'

A head popped round the door. 'Everything all right, old chap?'

'Like to join us for a bumper of wine, Will?'

'Can't, I'm afraid. Been a hell of a ding-dong this afternoon. Another *Rosamund*, I'm afraid. A great shipment of brandy this time, and some silks, and a couple of cases of tea.'

Rosamund! Alpiew opened her mouth to speak, but Hewer was gone as quickly as he had come. 'What's he blithering about?'

Pepys put his finger to his lips and whispered. 'He's a big-wig at the East India Company. *Rosamund* was one of theirs. She got done a few weeks ago. Right in front of Custom House, too.'

'Was she badly hurt?' Alpiew was frantically making sense of it all.

'Well, if you mean damaged, no, not much. Stays got ripped, few scratches on her waist and one of her arms was snapped off.'

'I'd think I was pretty badly injured if someone ripped one of my arms off, I can tell you!' Alpiew exclaimed.

'Lost her shroud, too. But that's only to be expected.'

'She's dead and buried?'

'She's a fifth-rater.'

'Mr Pepys!'

'Twenty-six gun, 350 tons. Crew of seventy. Nobody saw a thing.'

'Crew? What are you talking about?' The light slowly dawned. 'Is *Rosamund* a ship?'

'Of course. All the East India ships have women's names. Turning to come into the Custom House at London Bridge, got caught in the tidal currents, banged against the bridge, and while all the crew were trying to pull her about, a few boxes of tea went overboard. Back at East India House, Hewer and his comrades jumped up and down. They never like this sort of pilfering at the John Company. After all, they've got the monopoly on tea.'

'The John Company – is that the same thing as the East India Company?'

'Yes, yes,' said Pepys, as though he was addressing an imbecile. 'But with the tax the way it is, they simply have to expect it. They make much more profit on tea than the Holland and German companies. I know that for a fact.' He leaned forward and lowered his voice. 'Like most people in London, I benefit from these, shall we say, under-cover brokers, and their nocturnal pilferings. My dealer, I believe, had something to do with the *Rosamund* hoist . . .'

'So this hoist . . .' Alpiew's brain was racing, trying to piece it all together. Here she had Rakewell, John and *Rosamund* all somehow in the same business. 'This *Rosamund* job – did it happen a few nights after the lecture on the Passions?'

'When little Lucas was killed? Yes. It would have been about three nights after that. There must have been a smuggler's boat waiting the other side of London Bridge, Hewer said. They got clean away.' Pepys winked. 'But next day, about lunch-time (once Hewer was gone to work), my dealer popped round with a box of tea, some brandy and a lovely cushion of China silk.' He pointed down to the chair where Alpiew had been sitting. 'That's it. Most pretty. I get all the latest Indies and Chinese curiosities. Some above board, via Hewer, and otherwise . . .' He tapped the side of his nose.

'And your dealer . . .'

'Aha! I see you are tempted.' Pepys patted the cushion for Alpiew to sit again. 'I suppose you'd like to get a supply of these cheap contraband goods, too?'

Alpiew could see what had happened. The East India Ship, *Rosamund*, had been off-loaded at London Bridge, and Rakewell had brought the stuff on to the *Folly*. The mock wedding ceremony was a cover-up so no one else would notice the thudding and banging on the decks as the stuff was off-loaded. Then next morning the scene at Anglesey House was all a blind, so that Rebecca could get away to gad about the town selling the contraband tea. 'Your dealer is . . . a woman?'

'A woman!' Pepys screwed up his face. 'Oh no. A boy. Tall, dark and handsome, but definitely a boy.'

The Countess grasped hard on the leather strap as the coach rattled down the cobbled streets leading to the Tower. She prayed to God that the cheeky ragamuffin made sure to get the message to Alpiew. She was frightened, but so long as Alpiew knew where she was things would be all right. Even if this was a trap, and Rebecca was somehow luring her to the Tower for some evil purpose, she was only a woman and a player at that.

But what if Rebecca and Rakewell were acting together? What if she was being lured here so that together they could . . . They could what? Kill her? Why would they want to do that?

Unless it was because they had killed Anne Lucas and thought she had worked it out. She took a deep breath and crossed herself. But no. The Tower of London was full of Yeoman Warders who had all served in the army and could defend her.

A strong gust of wind sent the carriage tilting on to two wheels. The Countess heard the driver curse and crack his whip to get the horses to restore an equilibrium.

Maybe it was Rakewell alone with his Tityre-tus who was luring her in. But then how had he forged Rebecca's handwriting? For she was certain the note was written in the same hand as the note Godfrey had received. Surely they must both have been written by Rebecca. After all, Sarah had shown Godfrey another note from Rebecca. The Countess whipped open her fan and flapped as she remembered that Godfrey's note had lured them into St James's Park in the dead of night to stumble upon a headless corpse.

Alpiew was starting to get worried. The Countess should be here by now.

'Mr Pepys, it has been lovely. Now I think I will step back to German Street to find my mistress.'

'But your dog?'

''Tis not my dog. My lady is taking care of it for someone.' She was already at the door. 'It has been a pleasure, sir. When I find my lady, I shall return for our river trip.'

She let herself out, but she had no sooner shut the front door than the air was pierced with a shriek. It was a woman's cry. She lifted her skirts and ran up Villiers Street. A few yards from the Strand she heard a woman sobbing in an alley.

'Hello! Are you hurt?'

'Yes, I most certainly am!' Alpiew immediately recognised the sharp tones of Pepys' housekeeper, Mary. 'I think I have broken my ankle. That ballocking dog!'

Alpiew was delighted that someone else felt the same as she did about the wretched animal. She ran forward to assist.

'Oh, it's you!' snapped Mary. 'Well, the dog has run off. He started barking like a mad thing, squealing and yapping as though the devil were in him, then he pulled me the length of George Street, Villiers Street, and Duke Street, and the minute we turned into Of Alley the verminous creature tripped me up . . .'

'Of Alley?'

'The dingy urinal in which I currently lie . . .' The woman waved her hand in the air. 'It's called Of Alley. Last thing I saw, the little bastard ran off down . . .'

'Don't tell me,' said Alpiew. 'Buckingham Street.'

'Of course Buckingham Street. So if you want him, he's headed for the Watergate.'

'Water Gate!' cried Alpiew. 'W.G.! G.V.D.O.B. I see! George Street, Villiers Street, Duke Street, Of Alley, Buckingham Street! It's just another way of saying York Buildings! York Buildings Watergate!'

'Are you going to help me up?' barked the woman. 'Or are you just going to stand there reciting street names at me?'

Quickly Alpiew helped the woman to her feet.

The coach sped down Tower Hill and stopped at the main gate to the Tower.

The driver, huddled up in a heavy hat and scarf, opened the door.

'How much?' The Countess prayed that the fellow would not charge the earth for a long journey like this on such a stormy night.

'Two pence,' he said.

Two pence! The man must be mad. The Countess looked up at him as he climbed back into the driver's seat, but he pulled his scarf further up, hiding his mouth. His hat was pulled so far down over his face that she could only see his nose.

Not wanting to provoke him in case he realised his mistake, the Countess blessed her good fortune and handed him the money, then tottered across the cobbles towards the entrance.

She did not turn, and therefore did not see the coachman jump down from his seat after she had passed through into the precincts of the Tower. Nor did she notice the shadow he threw as he followed her into the Lion Gate.

*　　*　　*

Alpiew ran down Buckingham Street. She could see the little dog in the distance as he stopped to sniff at a mud-scraper and then cock his leg against it. Some distance behind her, grumbling in a low voice, limped Mary.

Outside the concert hall Alpiew pushed out of her path a little boy who was stroking a huge black horse. When she was within a few feet of catching his trailing lead, the dog scampered away, turning into the riverside walkway.

It was dark. No lingering link-boys threw their light down the streets, and the black river seemed to suck away the last glimmer of lamp-light spilling from the windows.

Alpiew cursed as she stubbed her toe on a badly set cobble.

A few feet ahead of her now, the dog stopped, began yelping and reared on his hind legs. He leapt in the air a few times then started the peculiar paddling motion he performed when he was especially pleased. Alpiew tiptoed up behind him, then lurched forward, arms outstretched to catch him. But as her arms came together the dog darted off again, and scurried off into the Watergate.

Alpiew picked herself up and stumbled after. The darkness was impenetrable. She took a deep breath and plunged into the black gaping mouth of the gate.

She stood for a moment on the steps at the river's edge. The murky Thames waters lapped at her feet. The tide was high tonight. But there was no sign of the dog.

Alpiew groaned. The miserable animal had clearly decided to swim for it. Well, she had no intention of following. She turned back and re-entered the gate, just as a pair of black gloved hands reached out and covered her mouth. She struggled and writhed, but she was caught. In the gloom she could see nothing. But whoever was holding her was in black, and from the leather glove, which tightened round her mouth, dangled the infamous pink ribbon of the Tityre-tus.

The Yeoman who greeted her was perfectly civil, and showed the Countess straight into Rakewell's room. There was no way she could call it a cell, for it was better furnished and heated than any room in her own house. She felt tempted instantly to sign up as a member of Rakewell's gang in the hope that she would be apprehended for something and forced to spend a few months in such cosy comfort.

'Countess Ashby de la Nosey-parker Zouche, if I am not mistaken?' Rakewell sneered, holding out a glass of sack. 'Would you care to share my bottle with me? I am short of company this evening. Word has not got around yet, so my true friends know not where to find me.' He put his booted feet up on the table. 'I presume you are here to gather some more smut for the tittle-tattle column you write.'

The Countess perched on a well-upholstered chair by the roaring fire. 'I am here about Rebecca.' She watched his face for tell-tale signs.

'Dark Beck!' He raised an eyebrow. 'Has she sent you here to brow-beat me into submission?'

'Where is she? I know you have her under lock and key.'

'Lock and key?' Rakewell laughed. 'And how, precisely, do you think I, who am under lock and key myself, could perpetrate such an outrage?'

'I know you have Warders here under your evil control, bribing them with gifts of tea and Nantes brandy.' The Countess peered at his scornful face, inflamed with the heat of the flickering fire. 'I know you have ways of getting anything you want, my lord. And the Tower is a big place. There are lots of twisting passages, and small airless rooms. Where have you hid her?'

Rakewell shrugged and took a mouthful of sack.

'Lord Rakewell, what do you hope to gain by holding Rebecca?'

In silence he topped up his glass.

'Where did your boys put Mr Lucas? And why kill Sarah, or for that matter Anne?'

'Madam, what are you jabbering about?' With a leer, Rakewell turned slowly to face her. 'You, madam, are a sunt with a capital C. Now get out! Warder!' He leapt from his seat and strode over to the door. 'Yeoman Partridge – take this mad old harridan away and throw her into the moat! She is as mad as May-butter.'

The Yeoman hesitated.

'On second thoughts,' howled Rakewell, 'take her to the lady's cell, lock her up and throw the key into the moat!' He tossed the rest of his drink down his throat and laughed like a devil.

Alpiew struggled, but she was held tight. Her attacker had tied her wrists with rope and pushed her down into the stone seat.

She could hear footsteps all around her and see shadows of men filing past, carting dripping boxes up the steps from a small row-boat. A horse-drawn carriage pulled up in nearby Buckingham Street, and Alpiew understood that contraband goods were being loaded on to it.

As the cart rolled off, followed by the marching feet of the smugglers, the grip around her mouth loosened. Alpiew opened her mouth to scream but a voice hissed into her ear, 'Don't make a sound! For the sake of your lady.'

Her assailant turned and let out a piercing whistle. Instantly small feet scampered into the Watergate from the terrace.

'It's Tim. I'm here.' Alpiew's eyes were becoming accustomed to the light. She could make out the form of a small boy. The child held out a note. 'This came for her.'

'What's it say?'

Alpiew wished she could see the Tityre-tus fellow's face, for the cove had a strange soft voice, for sure.

'It calls her to the Tower,' said Tim.

'And did she go?'

The boy nodded. 'I arranged the coach myself.'

'Good.' Alpiew's assailant struck a light and applied it to a horn lanthorn. 'So she's still under our control.'

Alpiew turned to get a look.

Before her, in full Tityre-tus attire, her hair cropped short like a boy, her eyebrows darkened and a small moustache gracing her upper lip, stood the celebrated actress, Rebecca Montagu.

*   *   *

The dank cell was gloomy, with only a small slit opening in the wall. The Countess imagined this hole must have been used for the firing of arrows in the old days, when war was so primitive. She stood on tiptoe and tried to peek out, but she could not reach high enough. She listened. Through the gap she could hear nothing but the gush of water. So this was the river side of the Tower, and from the cataract-like roar she presumed she must be near to Traitors' Gate.

No point screaming out to a dark smelly river, she decided. In the day it would be a different matter, when so many boats of all sizes would be plying the water from Hampton Court and out to the sea. But on a stormy night, even if there were sailors out on deck of anchored ships, her voice would be drowned out by the howling, buffeting wind.

She explored the damp walls with her fingers, as her eyes slowly accustomed themselves to the black. She could feel indentations all over the place. Rows of letters, scratches marking off the days. Thus she realised many people had been imprisoned in this room before her, and been left here long enough to gouge their names and messages into the stone walls.

She found the door. It was a heavy one, with a great iron lock. She peered into the keyhole. She could see flickering light. This could be a nearby candle or a distant flambeau, who could tell.

'Hello?' she called out, in case some sympathetic soul might be nearby. 'Is there anyone else here?'

She held her breath and listened for a reply. The only sound was the rush of water through the nearby gates.

She slid down on to the stone floor and tried to gather her thoughts. She prayed that the strange child Tim had passed her message to Alpiew, for otherwise no one would know she was here. Who knew what hold Rakewell had over these Yeomen? Or maybe it was just the one, Warder Partridge. And as he was the only person excepting Rakewell who knew where she was, well, it didn't bear thinking about. She had read terrible tales of such prisoners, forgotten till they were emaciated and past all hope. If she was left here to die, then someone would know for her body would decay and the stench would alert them. But it would be rather too late by then. And anyhow, with the frequency of Tower Hill executions, and the mass burials of those whose bodies were not claimed, it wouldn't be too difficult to dispose of another old woman's body among the rest.

She was beginning to despair when there was a scratching upon the door.

'Countess?'

The Countess scrambled to her feet. 'Yes, I am here.'

'Are you alone?'

'Yes, yes. Rakewell had me thrown in here.'

'Please be silent. I am here to get you out, but it is important that we don't alert those responsible for putting you in here in the first place.'

A key rattled in the lock, and with a clank the bolt shot back.

The Countess stood back and the door opened. A man stood before her, his hat pulled down over his eyes, and a scarf wrapped round his mouth. He beckoned to her and she followed.

Rebecca cursed as she read the note Tim had brought her. She handed it to Alpiew. 'Do you recognise the writing?'

'Why do you ask, madam Roxana? Do you not know your own hand?'

'This is a fair hand, an educated hand.' Rebecca slapped the paper. 'My writing is appalling. This was not writ by me!'

'But you have an educated hand . . .'

'The only education I had was picked up on the orlop deck of a three-masted frigate.'

'But I have seen your writing before, madam. When you lured Godfrey to St James's Park to throw us off the scent of your new identity.'

'Alpiew, please tell me what you are talking about. I wrote no note to Godfrey.'

'You sent Godfrey a note asking to meet him at Rosamund's Pond in the middle of the night.'

'I did no such thing. I wouldn't be seen at Rosamund's Pond in the middle of the day, leave alone after dark. The place is a mere harlot's parade ground.'

'But a note from you arrived at our house.' Alpiew's mind raced back. It had not actually been addressed to anybody. 'We went, and as a result we stumbled upon a headless body dressed in your clothing.'

'Believe me, Alpiew, all this is news to me. I sent no note. Nothing would induce me into St James's Park at night, and I know not how my clothes came to be there upon a corpse.'

'They gave me the only clue to the body's identification,' said Alpiew, not convinced by Rebecca's protestations. After all, the woman was standing before her in full male attire, having just overseen a large run of contraband. 'I realised afterwards that the body belonged not to you but to your pox-riddled maid, Sarah. Did she know that you had killed Anne Lucas? Was that why you killed her?'

'You know about Sarah's disease?' Rebecca took Alpiew by the shoulders. 'Oh, God. You are sure she is dead?' She stamped her foot, and swore. 'This is serious, and time is against us. Your mistress's life depends upon it.' She turned to Tim. 'Matters are even worse than I thought. Is my horse still tethered by the concert hall?'

The child nodded.

'Take Red for me, Tim, and bring him to my lodgings. Stoke up the fire and wait for me there.' The dog crawled out from under the Watergate seat and obediently waddled off with the boy. Rebecca grabbed Alpiew by the hand. 'Can you ride pillion?'

'Rebecca!' Alpiew was starting to panic. 'You must explain what is going on. Where is the Countess? Is she in danger?'

'*He* wrote the note luring you to the park. Not me.'

'But who is *he*?' Alpiew rubbed her chin and bit her lip. 'That note had no name upon it,' said Alpiew. 'It could be that whoever wrote it, the note was really directed to Sarah, but Godfrey wanted it to be for himself.'

'This is terrible.' Rebecca marched off towards the concert hall, dragging Alpiew with her. 'I knew Sarah was in trouble. I felt sure she was dead when she disappeared without a word to me, leaving behind all of her clothing and possessions.'

'Why dead?'

'She was in love with a most nasty man. He bruised her once round the neck. When I warned her against him, she wouldn't have it, though I'd swear he had tried to strangle her. I told her to stop seeing him. And she told me she had stopped. But that is definitely his writing, I have seen it a dozen times.'

'She told Godfrey it was your writing . . .'

'Of course she did. She constantly lied about him. For some reason I gather it was important to him that their affair was kept secret. But that didn't stop her primping herself up for him. She constantly ransacked my wardrobe, and thought I wouldn't notice.' Rebecca untied the horse's bridle from the tether-post and put her boot into a stirrup. 'Get up behind me, woman, and hold on like grim death.' Rebecca vaulted into the saddle and helped Alpiew clamber up behind her. She steered the horse round and gave him a kick to spur him on. 'Luckily my stallion is sure-footed.'

The Countess followed the dark figure along a turreted walk-way and down a stone spiral staircase.

'Thank you for coming to my aid,' hissed the Countess. 'I thought I would be left there to starve.'

'Sssh!' The figure turned and put a finger to his lips. 'We must not alert the Yeoman Warders. Many of them are in his pay.'

They reached the bottom of the steps, and the figure stopped, pressed back against the wall. The rhythmic crunch of boots on stone heralded a small company of Warders on patrol.

When they had passed, the man beckoned. He stepped out

on to Water Lane and turned left past the roaring surge of the river flooding through Traitors' Gate.

The Countess held her breath and teetered along behind him. At least they were heading for the way out.

He reached the Byward Tower and waited for her to catch him up. The great gate was closed, but set within it was a small door. He pushed this open and held out his hand to help the Countess over the step. 'Quietly does it there. We only have a few minutes, for the Portcullis comes down at ten when they perform the Ceremony of the Keys.'

The Countess gathered up her skirts and tripped along the bridge over the moat. When she was half-way across, the dark figure put his arm round her waist and pulled her close.

'Hold off, sir,' she hissed. 'You need not to squeeze me so tight.'

'Why, so I do!' He pulled her around to face him, grabbing her by the elbows, and pressing his thumbs into the tender inner joint. 'For you are a whore and an adulterer!'

'Fie, sir!' The Countess struggled, wrestling with him as he pushed her further and further to the edge till he had her balancing with the small of her back on the top of the stone wall over the moat. 'Let me be!'

'No, you must die! You are a harlot and a two-penny punk, spreading your grincome scabs throughout the lives of honest folk.' He slid his hands round her throat and tightened them.

Alpiew wrapped her arms round Rebecca's waist and clung on as the woman skilfully raced her horse along the Strand. They had to slow down at the end of Fleet Street to let the horse paddle across the flooded road, where the river had burst its banks.

'I presume your emblem is fake?' said Alpiew, eyeing the pink ribbon that dangled from her glove. 'And that you are no more Tityre-tus than I am.'

Rebecca laughed. 'One way to make yourself safe from people who are so brutishly wicked is to seem to be them.'

Alpiew recalled the dark boy with the pink ribbon she had

chased across the piazza. 'The stew you had cooked that night we disturbed you at your rooms was delicious, by the way.'

'If I'd known it was you two, I'd have stayed in and enjoyed it. It was my first hour at home since Rakewell came for me at your place.' Rebecca pulled in the reins, and trotted down a side street. 'Damn! One spot of rain and the whole city comes to a standstill. He will have to take some stairs. Hold on.'

The horse slowly descended a flight of stone steps, and came out in Thames Street. Rebecca geed him up to a gallop. 'I pray to God, we are still in time.'

Alpiew closed her eyes and prayed too.

The Countess had managed to give the man a hearty knee in the groin and wriggle free. She stumbled blindly on, heading across the causeway and through the Middle Tower gateway.

The man was catching up with her, she could hear his footsteps. She ran to the nearest door and started banging as hard as she could. But there were no lights on in the building. She pushed herself into the shadowy alcove when a door she had not seen, which was shrouded in shadow, fell open behind her.

She stepped inside and, pressed against the wall behind the door, waited for the sound of feet running past. She held her breath and listened. In the distance she could hear marching feet. The Ceremony of the Keys! At any moment a whole brigade of Warders and guardsmen would be at the Middle Tower gate. If only she could get out of this wretched place and scream for their attention she would be saved.

But then the door slowly opened. The man had come in after her. He stood a foot away, on the other side of the open door. Above the pounding of her own heart she could hear him breathing.

Then, with a whoosh, he pulled the door away, and grabbed out for her. Stumbling blindly out of his reach, she ran away into the dark, stinking building.

*   *   *

Rebecca's steed galloped past the Custom House. Lights were showing in most of the windows. 'The hoard we took tonight has already been missed!' Rebecca yelled back at Alpiew. 'I fear we have given the clerks of His Majesty's Excise a sleepless night.'

They turned from Thames Street into the green of Tower Hill. Rebecca called the horse to a halt and jumped off, hastily tethering it. Alpiew clambered down after her.

Behind them the bells of All Hallows rang out the hour.

'Damn! That is ten o'clock. They will bring down the portcullis.'

Alpiew ran towards the Lion Gate, her heart torn with fear. The gate was open. With Rebecca close behind, she crossed the Lions' exercise yard and arrived at the Middle Tower just as the Chief Yeoman Warder gave the order for the portcullis to drop. 'An escort for the keys, there!'

An escort of armed soldiers stood next to the man in his long red cloak, holding aloft a tallow lantern.

'Please, mister!' Alpiew called out. 'There is a killer within your gates, and my lady's life is under threat.'

The Warder peered through the metal bars of the portcullis. 'Officer! There is some slut yelling. Please call her to attention.'

A guardsman stepped forward and shoved the muzzle of his musket through the grille.

'What do you want?'

Rebecca stepped forward. 'The woman speaks true. There is an ancient titled lady here in the Tower, and we have reason to believe she is in danger for her life.'

'And I should believe you!' the guardsman huffed. 'One of London's scum! The Tityre-tus!'

Rebecca looked down at her clothing. The pink ribbon still dangled from her glove.

'But she . . .' Alpiew knew any explanation could only make matters worse.

'Did you say Tityre-tus?' said the Lieutenant of the Tower, holding his lantern closer to the portcullis. 'Are you a friend of Rakewell?'

'No,' said Rebecca vehemently.

The Warder stepped back.

'Yes, of course we are!' said Alpiew, shoving her face close to the bars. 'We are both his lordship's valued and highly esteemed friends.'

The Warder gave a nod and the portcullis was raised.

'Any friend of Rakewell . . .' said the Warder with a smirk, as Alpiew and Rebecca darted past.

The walkway over the moat was empty, and the only sound above the rushing of water was the shouts of the Warder and his escort as he performed the Ceremony of the Keys.

As they reached Water Lane, Alpiew yelled to Rebecca, 'Let us split up, two sets of eyes are better than one. You take an anti-clockwise direction, I will start at the Bloody Tower.'

'Keep your eyes open for Jemmy, my other brother,' cried Rebecca, running towards the Lanthorn Tower. 'He is somewhere within these walls, muffled in a great cloak and scarf, with a hat down over his eyes.'

Alpiew turned left and scampered up the hill to Tower Green.

The Countess ran down a steep flight of steps and threw open another door. Ahead of her she could hear wild laughter, and a shrieking worse than any madman. It was almost as bad as Bedlam. But if she could only reach the fellow, she might get some help.

She stumbled along a humid corridor which stank worse than a hundred privies on an August afternoon, and threw herself through the door at the end. Before her, fur raised up all along its spine, stood a large animal something like a dog. It was the source of the strange demented laughing sound. On the front of his cage was writ in capitals: HYENA.

She was standing before one of the displays at the menagerie! The only way out of this strange room was back the way she came. But she could hear behind her the dreadful sound of running feet, closing upon her.

She spun round as the man, with a holler, burst through the door. And even in this murky light she could see that in his raised hands he was gripping a very large axe.

Alpiew darted this way and that, calling out the Countess's name. She was worried now that she had trusted Rebecca. After all, had she not talked about the Countess still being in her control. What could that mean? And now the woman had her here, trapped within the confines of the Tower.

She came up to the block and looked about her. Hands on hips, she threw her head back and yelled the Countess's name. As she looked up she saw some heads come to windows and peer out to see what all the row was about.

This place was huge and rambling with all its towers and lodging houses. What was she to do? Where could the Countess be?

She turned and ran, still calling out the Countess's name.

'Miss?' A Yeoman stood before her, holding a lantern. 'What is all the noise about?'

'I am looking for my lady. She is in grave danger.'

'There-uh has been-uh no lady-uh here tonight, I assure you.'

Alpiew watched his face in the flickering lamplight and knew he was lying.

'Do you take care of Lord Rakewell?'

He threw her an insolent stare.

'Alpiew?' Rebecca emerged from the gloom and stood at Alpiew's side.

Partridge instantly recognised the pink ribbon.

'Sir!' he addressed Rebecca. 'If the lady would like to wait here, I will show you something.' He gave her a wink, and walked off, throwing a sneering look in Alpiew's direction.

Rebecca followed him. Alpiew was undecided. Should she trail along after them or continue peeking in every corner hereabouts? She crept forward. A building lay directly in her path. There were no lights on within. It was the chapel. She stumbled towards the stairs leading down to the front door.

Why had she not thought about it before? The Reverend Farquhar could help!

She banged on the door.

No reply.

'Are you looking for the Countess?'

She looked behind her. A man stood at the top of the steps. He was dressed in a long black cloak. A hat was pulled down over his eyes and a scarf was wrapped round his chin, hiding his face.

Alpiew felt uneasy. She pushed at the door and it opened. She ran into the dark chapel.

The many stalls and box pews made the small room echo like a wood-lined cavern.

She darted along the aisle towards the altar.

The muffled man loped behind her.

Slamming the door to the front pew, she moved around it and nipped across towards the side of the stalls. A small gothic door stood ajar. She pushed through and slowly clicked the door shut. Then turned the key. She was safely locked in the vestry.

With shaking hands Alpiew pulled the tinderbox from her pocket and struck a light. She found a candle with ease and held it up. Another door lay ahead. Perhaps the chaplain's accommodation lay through it. She moved on.

'Reverend?' Alpiew stepped into the store room. In one corner was a small truckle bed. In another a writing desk. No one was here. She sat down to write the chaplain a note.

The Countess cowered on the ground against the hyena's cage as the man approached.

'How did you know about me?' He swiped the axe through the air. 'Nosing around in other people's business. Everyone has his own reasons for his actions. What business is it of yours?'

The Countess could see only the sparkle of his eyes, but even that much was enough to show that the man was in no mood for reason.

'Get up!'

The Countess did not move.

'Get up, I said!'

The Countess stared into his eyes as he raised the axe, using both hands. As he swung it down she threw herself to the side and scrabbled to her feet.

Damn! Her skirt was caught by the axe's blade and she could not move – she was fastened to the hyena's cage. She tugged at her skirt, until, with a rip, she tore the fabric.

The man meanwhile was tugging at the axe. Just as it flew free the Countess slipped out of the hyena's booth, and gathering up her tattered skirt ran like the devil along a horse-shoe shaped passageway, lined with great oak doors. At the end she came to a staircase, and she ran up, taking the steps two by two.

Panting, she found herself in a semi-circular stone gallery lined on one side with huge cages. On one side of each enclosure were thick iron bars, and on the other a waist-high stout wooden door.

She could hear the madman's steps hurrying towards her. She peered through into cage after cage. Each one was occupied by a lion, or tiger or other huge cat. At last she came upon one that was empty. She pulled open the wooden door and, kneeling, crawled inside.

She could hear that the man was not far behind her, prowling, tiger-like himself, and swinging his axe from side to side with a terrible swishing sound.

'I can't let you go now,' he howled. 'It's too late. Not now you know who I am. I know you're still here. There is no way out at this time of night. The portcullis is down on the Middle Tower, and the Lion Gate is barred. All the Yeomen are safely within the Tower. So it's just you and me.' He laughed. 'And the lions!'

As if on cue, the lion in the adjacent cage let out an almighty roar, which echoed round the stone walls. The Countess let out an involuntary whimper.

'Stay there, wherever you are.' The man laughed again. 'I

can wait. No one will disturb us till dawn. We have many long hours, during which you must not sneeze or snore or make any noise or you will discover yourself to me.'

The Countess lay still in the straw. The man gave a sigh of despair then stealthily moved away. She sat up silently. The only sound was the heavy breathing of lions in the next cage. She edged sideways to peek through the cage front.

Alpiew dropped the quill into a pot of ink while she rummaged about in a drawer for a scrap of paper. There were glue-pots and old newspapers, and boxes and boxes of pills. The priest certainly took a lot of medicine. There were packets of Wiseman's Prescription, (costing 7/6, Alpiew noted, enough to feed a couple for a week!), Lenitive Purge of cassia, tamarinds, manna, creme tartar and rhubarb, Lenitive Elixir, discutients and specific plaisters, Diaphoretic Extract, Balsamick Electuary, Vomiting Bolus of Antimony, consolidating injection (5/-) and a syringe with which to apply it.

At last Alpiew tugged out a piece of paper from the back of the drawer.

She pulled the pen from the ink and shook it. She looked down at the paper. It was a note written in a very poor hand.

Darlin Rev, my hart is woonded for not seing yu last nite during the lectoor. First sumwun tuk my cloke, then the dog run amuk, and I run hither and thither after hym, then the TTT run past and scered me owt of my witts. But when I come to mit yu at the WG you wos gon. RM nows nuthing of the pashuns cumpared to yu, my love, nor her frend the italyun. Rit to me agen at RMs rums. My hart brakes to see yu agen. Sarah xx.

Alpiew gasped. R! R for Reverend! W.G. G.V.D.O.B. = The York Watergate, VIII = eight o'clock – the time the lecture on the Passions began, R = reverend, xx = kiss kiss.

Another note was folded at the side of the drawer: '*We hav muvd to Germin streit. The blew door. Angulsea howse. S. XX.*'

On the desk before her she re-read a pill-box label: Electuary of mercury. What was mercury taken for but the pox? The priest was scabbadoed! And by Sarah!

She could not have believed it, but then she saw the final tell-tale sign. For wrapped around the ink-pot was a green ribbon. The very type and length of green ribbon invariably used to tie up a packet of Fallopius Salvators. Reverend Farquhar possessed the ribbon from such a packet, and one could deduce that he had once owned the packet itself, and was therefore in the practice of having sexual relations.

Alpiew moved quietly through to the vestry. There was a small slit in the wall, a peep-hole for the altar boys to see at what stage of the ceremony they were.

Alpiew applied her eye. She could see Rebecca, standing hands on hips looking the very model of a Tityre-tus rake. She was arguing with a man whose face Alpiew could not see, who was holding a torch and wearing a white night-gown and long tasselled night-cap.

At her side was the muffled-up man who had whispered from the top of the steps. He threw his arms up, ripped off his hat, and pulled his scarf from his chin. It was Jemmy.

'I *saw* that Yeoman lock the Countess in a cell. A short time later another man came and let her out. He was all wrapped up in scarves and a hat. I followed them as far as the Byward Tower, when that damned fellow stopped me, and marched me back.'

He pointed towards Yeoman Partridge, who stood a few steps away from them, head bowed.

'I managed to break from him and eventually discovered my sister . . .'

'Your sister!' Yeoman Jones looked the handsome dark-haired rake up and down.

'It's a long story,' snapped Rebecca. 'The important thing is the Countess!'

'You are right!' Alpiew pushed out into the chapel. 'The man has killed twice before. We have no time to stand and talk.'

'But who is it?' Rebecca turned to Alpiew.

'It's him,' she said, pointing back to the vestry. 'The Reverend. And he's certainly not in there.'

'I took a letter up to St James's for him earlier.' Yeoman Partridge stood forward. 'To some woman called Zela Douche at the blue door in German Street.'

'Oh God,' cried Alpiew, running towards the door. 'Make haste! He has her for sure.'

'Countess?' a gentle voice hissed. 'It's me – Reverend Farquhar. We met, with your colleague Mr Cibber.'

The Countess did not move.

'I saw that nasty fellow in the cloak slip off a minute ago. I have a pass key, you see, and I am coming in late from working on *Richard III* at the playhouse.'

Suddenly the straw behind her shifted, and something moved, rising from the ground and shaking itself. Dear gods! She was in a cage with a wild animal. Which choice to make? She turned slowly. Something was padding towards her in the gloom. She could hear the creature making a sort of deep purring sound, feel its warm damp breath against her back. A tongue darted out and licked her neck.

She edged swiftly to the side of the door, pulled it open and crawled briskly out.

'Oh, Countess, how dreadful for you.' The priest stood before her, smiling benignly. 'Did you have company in there? What a choice! But how were you to know that one of us was harmless, the other a wild killer?'

The Countess looked back at the cage. Leaning against the bars was an old tattered toothless lion. It was a pitiful sight. Standing on his front two legs, the creature looked mournfully through the bars, the rest of his body dragged behind him as his back legs were withered and deformed.

'Born like that, you see. A cripple.' The priest shrugged. 'But that's God for you, no sense of fair play.'

The Countess gasped. Now she knew for certain that she had made the wrong choice. For as her eyes became accustomed to the dark she saw, in a pile on the ground behind him, the cloak, hat and scarf that the priest had worn to chase her in, and swinging in one hand he still held an axe.

Yeoman Jones, in his white night-gown, carried a burning link and ran to the Chief Yeoman Warder's lodgings on Tower Green. He banged on the door.

'Help ho! Raise the portcullis and provide a guard for the lady.'

Alpiew ran ahead, with Rebecca and her brother close behind. They banged on the great gate of the Byward Tower. Shortly Jones appeared behind them, with the Lieutenant of the Tower who carried a huge set of keys.

The great gate was opened. The company ran across the causeway and banged on the portcullis of the Middle Tower. 'Who goes there?' called the Warder of that tower from an upper window.

'Open up, man,' screamed Alpiew.

'There, there, there, becalm yourself a little, wench!'

A great roar came from the menagerie.

'Just open the ballocking gate,' Alpiew cried, as Yeoman Jones ran up behind her and lifted his hand for the portcullis to be raised without delay.

'I'll need all hands to the wheel,' cried the Middle Tower Yeoman.

Alpiew and Rebecca rolled up their sleeves.

'Why should God choose me as a victim, and smite me down with syphilis?' wailed the priest. 'I am a friendly man. I tried to give that girl a bit of love. And all she gave me in return was the pox!'

'Surely priests are supposed to control such feelings. Lust, I believe, is one of the deadly sins.'

'There was a saint who tried to stop feeling aroused by dropping scalding bacon on his pudenda. I tried that. It only made me feel more excited. Afterwards the very thought of bacon became erotic.' He paced around the Countess, breathing heavily. 'The slut deserved to die. God knew that. He would have killed her himself in a month or two.'

'I understand that you killed Sarah because she infected you . . .' The Countess was trying to play for time as she edged nearer a pillar. 'But why Anne? Surely she was not your lover?'

'A player! Why would I involve myself with those haughty women who think themselves so far above ordinary mortals?'

'But you did kill Anne Lucas?'

'Yes, yes, yes!' The priest swung the axe in the air. 'It was a mistake. She was wearing the green cloak that Sarah usually wore, and waiting in the place we had appointed, on the terrace near the Watergate. The street was silent. Everyone was inside at the lecture. I came up quietly behind her and –' He slammed the blunt end of the axe down and it crashed against the paving stones. In one of the cages a lion roared into the night with a deep reverberating rumble.

'She crumpled like a puppet.' The priest hung his head. 'I dragged her limp body through to the waterworks. The stupid cloak caught on the fence and I ripped it off, leaving it upon the cobbles. I shut the gate behind me to finish my job. It was only when I used the axe a second time, to take off her head, that I saw I had killed the wrong woman. Her face lay there on the ground, glaring at me, accusing me. Averting my eye, I crammed her head in my bag. I heaved the body up into a butt near the gate. It was exhausting. When I had got my breath back I ran out on to the terrace. But suddenly the place was crawling with people. I dived into the Watergate, hoping to catch a waterman who would row me back here to the Tower, but there were no boats waiting. There were people everywhere. Then someone started ringing a handbell. I panicked. I thought the body was discovered and they were raising the hue and cry. My hands were covered in gore, so I thrust the bag under the seat and leapt down on to the strand, hiding on the beach under the shadow of the steps.

'Some burly fellow made me very nervous. He was going up and down the steps to the Watergate, bringing up boxes. Shortly you and your woman turned up, and some fat woman chatted with you. Then a row-boat came in to pick her up. I jumped on to the steps and asked if I could share. She was only going as far as Temple Stairs, but she said she would be charmed to share with God's own representative to protect her from the wicked tongues of the watermen. But in my rush to get into the boat I forgot to pick up the bag.'

Behind them a lion was growling. The Countess could hear other restless lions pacing up and down in their cages.

'The bag that contained Anne's head?' said the Countess.

'In the boat we passed others coming upstream. One man carried a flaming torch and I didn't want anyone to see my bloody hands. Frightened that the flabby great woman in my boat should notice, I flopped them into the water and let the fast-flowing Thames wash the filthy blood away.'

'Not Neptune's grandsire's grave with all his ocean folding flood . . .' Rebecca stood in the gateway '. . . could wash away that dunghill foul of stain.' She strode towards the priest, her dark eyes flashing like lightning in the radiance of Yeoman Jones' torch. 'That which you talk of with such disgust was the lifeblood of my dearest friend, you contemptible vermin.'

Farquhar swerved round to face her, the axe still swinging. As Alpiew lurched forward and pulled the Countess out of his reach, his arm swung upwards. Striding right into the path of the swaying axe, Rebecca ran at the priest and, thrusting both arms forward, gave him a mighty shove. He teetered for a minute, the impetus of the axe's swing throwing him off balance, then, taking two steps back, he stumbled and fell against one of the lions' cages.

Quick as a flash, a great paw shot out and grabbed the man by the arm. The lion roared as his teeth plunged into the priest's shoulder. As Reverend Farquhar squealed in pain, Yeoman Jones rushed towards the cage, thrusting his torch into the animal's face, but a lioness sprang up to the bars and joined the feeding frenzy. Within seconds the pair of lions pulled the priest's body through to their side of the bars and were busy tearing him to shreds.

*   *   *

326

Though it was midnight, the Lieutenant of the Tower and three Yeomen accompanied the Countess and her entourage to the home of Justice Moore in Cheapside. It was vital that legal papers be issued before dawn, when Valentine Vernish was due to start his long cart-ride to the gallows.

'I hope you are no member of the infamous Tityre-tus, young man,' said the Justice, pointing to Rebecca's ribbon. 'I hope to stamp down quite fiercely upon them. I hear there has been a lot of corruption in high places, and I am going to put an end to all this bribery with tea, and other contraband items. I have spoken to the King, the Lord Mayor, and the Lord Chief Justice. Giles Rakewell – and any of the vile ruffians who support him – will soon suffer the terrible wrath of the state. Believe me, shortly wearing the pink ribbon will no longer be a badge of indemnity from the penalties of the law.'

'I'm sorry, your worship. I am no Tityre-tus.' Rebecca reached up to her face and pulled off her moustache. 'I was merely rehearsing for a role.'

'I say!' The Justice gawped at Rebecca with open mouth. 'It's not . . . ? Are you . . . ? Not Roxana! My word, but you are my favourite actress.' He jumped up and down in excitement in his night-shirt. 'Oh, I am quite tempted to wake my wife! What an excitement, having Rebecca Montagu standing in my very chamber! I can't believe it.'

FOURTEEN

Laughter

*There is a passion which hath no name, but the
sign of it is that distortion of the countenance we
call LAUGHTER, which is always joy; whatsoever
it be that moveth laughter, it must be new and
unexpected.*

*The eyebrows arched over the eyes, with the
inner ends lowered. The eyes almost shut, the
mouth open and showing teeth. The corners of
the lips drawn back and raised, causing folds in
the cheeks. The face red, the eyes frequently
damp and weeping tears – but these are very
different from the tears of Sorrow.*

Waiting outside the Fleet for Vernish to be unchained
and freed, Rebecca told them Sarah's story. How
she had taken a girl from the gutter and tried to
save her from ruin, teaching her to read and write (though
her spelling was always appalling). Rebecca knew she had taken
to meeting a priest, she thought for moral counselling, but
had no idea that he was also her secret lover.

'It's hard. There will always be a desolation in my soul
because I have lost my best friend. All because she borrowed
my cloak to slip out. When Jemmy and Valentine said they
saw her in a green cloak, I realised that. And I thought that
whoever killed her must have mistaken her for *me*. No one
would ever want to kill Anne, she was too kind and sweet-

natured. But as for me . . . Then that note came: "It should have been you", so I felt sure.'

'But again,' said Alpiew, 'you were mistaken in thinking the note was for you.'

'It was delivered at my lodgings.'

'Yes, but the "you" intended was Sarah. The Countess got one too, after Sarah was dead – telling her to keep her nose out of it. She thought it was one of Godfrey's infernal puzzles and burned it. But,' said Alpiew, glancing at Rebecca's black leather gloves and male attire, 'what is the link between you and the Tityre-tus?'

'Obvious,' said the Countess, turning to Rebecca. 'You feel that it was your fault Anne was killed. And because her death left both her husband and son with neither attendance nor money, you took it upon yourself to get it.'

'That became what I was doing. But Anne and I hatched the plan together. It was last summer. We sat out on the piazza drinking buttered ale one evening. Anne was angry because Rakewell had just been acquitted for the murder of a young boy who was a trainee actor with our company. She wanted to avenge his death, as the law had failed. From what my parents told me about Rakewell's involvement with the illicit tea trade, it was easy to see how he had bribed his way to immunity with contraband goods. I suggested to Anne that we should take him on, outwit him. She was thrilled. And together we started plotting. With my knowledge and friends it was easy to pre-empt his every manoeuvre.' Rebecca shrugged. 'I knew every cargo, when it was due, how much it was worth, and I knew enough sailors to help me in the enterprise.

'I discovered Rakewell had some kind of landing planned during the lecture on the Passions, and another for the night of Anne's birthday. That was when she decided to book the *Folly* for her party.' Rebecca's lip was starting to quiver. She wiped away a tear.

'Tell us about the night of the lecture on the Passions. What was the plan?'

'We disrupted the delivery mid-stream.'

'How did you do that?' Alpiew leaned back against the tethering post and Rebecca's horse snorted in her ear.

'My father dressed as an excise man and followed them upstream in a small cutter. Panicked, Rakewell's men off-loaded their contraband tea and brandy into the river. The tide swept most of the boxes ashore along the beach near York Watergate. Mr Vernish's role was to keep checking to see whether the boxes were washing up and to haul them ashore, and then load them on to the coach.'

'But why did you need to disrupt the concert?'

'If the terrace was busy, we suspected that Rakewell's boys in the boat would not land on the north bank of the Thames, so anything washed up there was ours. Also, we thought that an itinerant vendor and a coachman loading up a hackney carriage in a crowded street, near a busy landing stage, would seem less suspicious than doing it at dead of night. So Anne went out to warn Jemmy to get ready to bring the coach round, but she also had to make sure Valentine had got all the boxes up from the beach and into the Watergate. With that her part of the business was finished. But then . . . she . . .' Rebecca let out a sob.

'Why was she wearing your cloak?'

'I don't know. I suppose because the day had been warm she had not prepared for the night to be so cold. Sarah brought the cloak to the concert hall. I remember seeing it hanging by the musicians' entrance.'

'Sarah wasn't expecting you to send her home,' said Alpiew, familiar with the ways of serving maids. 'I presume she ran up to your lodgings, threw something into the pot, then dashed back to York Buildings, arriving too late for her assignation.'

'She certainly returned that night,' said the Countess, 'for you had your dog with you in the musicians' green room.'

'And instead of the Reverend, she'd have found my cloak lying on the ground by the waterworks.' Rebecca had brought out a kerchief and was wiping her eyes.

'The night on the *Folly*,' said the Countess. 'Tell us about that.'

'Rakewell's raid was to take place just before the *Rosamund* docked at Custom House Quay. Our plan was to get at the ship minutes before he did.'

'Why did you go ahead with the raid, even after Anne died?'

'Her death was such a horror. Not only because I lost a friend, but by it her poor family would be ruined. We had always planned to split any profit, and use much of the money for the benefit of others. Once Anne was dead, I knew I *had* to go ahead with it, to get enough money to keep safe her distressed husband and child.'

'But how did Rakewell come to be on the *Folly*? Did he know what you were up to?'

'I imagine if I could find out what he was doing, he could do the same to me. He oiled his way round Rich to get an invitation. When I saw him on board, I panicked.'

'And that was why you went along with the silly wedding . . .' Alpiew remembered how she had swung in and out of the game. 'To keep him off the deck during the vital moments.'

'Yes. Jemmy and Valentine were loading the stuff. I realise now that he knew full well what we were up to and had a better plan. For by marrying me he thought to make all that I had his.'

'It will take some undoing – a knot like that.' The Countess gazed at Rebecca in the flickering flame of their link. 'Why did they pick on poor Mr Vernish?'

' 'Tis my belief Rakewell has all sorts working with him: constables, bailiffs, judges. They needed to find anybody who was on the scene, thus to close the murder case and prevent the honest and upright members of the forces of law snooping around their patch by the Watergate. The tea racket is a very lucrative business.'

'Leaving so many victims in its wake.' The Countess sighed. 'Mr Lucas is in the care of your family at Limehouse, I presume?'

'Of course! You were the boy at Bedlam . . . ?' Alpiew gazed at Rebecca, winding back to the day they had witnessed the abduction.

'Yes.' Rebecca tore the ribbon from her glove and threw it on to the ground. 'And I am sponsoring Jack to be educated at Christ's Hospital. And before you say it, I know that as his father is living the child is not an orphan. But I pointed out to the governors that poor Mr Lucas has more need of parenting than the boy. I believe little Jack is as good as orphaned, and after I made a large donation to the school they agreed with me!'

The great wicket gate rattled and opened. Rubbing his unshackled wrists, Valentine Vernish stumbled into the street.

Rebecca opened her arms and he fell into them.

'You left it a bit late, gal,' he said, kissing her passionately. 'When they told me you were dead . . .' He winced. 'I thought it was over for me. They could have hanged me if you were gone. What would have been the point of living without you?'

Alpiew and the Countess exchanged a look. What a turn-up this was! Rebecca and Valentine Vernish were clearly more than just friends.

'But then they talked about seeing the Punch and Judy playing. And I realised only you knew where I kept the puppets, so somehow you had to be alive.'

'I did two shows a day, as it happens. Put in some very racy lines about the players at Drury Lane, which got me better laughs than ever I did onstage. And it provided me with an excellent place to hide.' Rebecca turned to the Countess. 'He wanted me to confess to the smuggling. As though that would somehow exculpate him from murder!'

'The true killer has reaped his own desert.' The Countess shuddered. How close she had been to becoming his third victim. 'And thanks be to you and Alpiew, I survived to tell the tale.'

'I think we have a lot to rejoice about.' Rebecca grasped the Countess's hand. 'I know you've been through a lot, but would you come to my lodgings for a night-cap? My parents are there. They have been dispersing tonight's booty. Jemmy has gone ahead and will have told them about the latest revelations. I would bet you ten guineas my mother will have prepared a huge bowl of salmagundi.'

'Oh!' The Countess gulped and Alpiew grimaced. 'Why not?'

Jake Zuñiga grabbed the Countess by the elbows to welcome her into the room.

'What is it with you fellows that you do a hornpipe jig every time you shake a person's hand?'

'That, madam, is what is known at sea as the "sailors' handsel". We all do it out of habit. Not that I have any need in all these years, as I'm happy married to Sal and have no need of the charms of strange women.'

'And what has that to do with anything?'

'Look!' Jake demonstrated. 'As the hands grab the elbow, the thumb feels for swollen glands – the sign of infection. It's how sailors try to protect themselves when they're playing about in foreign ports.'

'What a clue!' said Alpiew. 'For didn't the Reverend Farquhar give us just such a maritime welcome when we were first introduced by Cibber that day at the Tower?'

'Ahoy there! It's the two nice ladies who sailed down our way.' Sal thrust a pair of steaming bowls of food in front of the Countess and Alpiew. 'Best salmagundi, made fresh tonight. And as you see I have adapted the receipt to suit a chill London night. It's hot. Grab yourself spoons and enjoy!'

They took the smelly stuff and exchanged a look.

'Of course' – Alpiew glanced round the room – 'when we need the ballocking dog, he's nowhere to be seen.'

The small room was buzzing with people: the Zuñigas, Signior Lampone, Mrs Leigh and Jake. Alpiew noticed that Godfrey was there too, sitting in a corner, chattering gaily. Beside him was Nickum, looking pale but happy, his arm wrapped in a great bandage.

'Everyone is here?'

'Yes,' said Jake. 'Once we heard, we sent our Jemmy around with the grommet, Tim, to round up all the folks who played their part. Eat up, eat up! Afore it gets cold.'

'Tim is your son too?' The Countess was playing for time.

'Oh yes,' said Jake proudly. 'Born on a passage from Zanzibar. 'Twas his surprise arrival decided me and Sal to settle down ashore for a bit.'

'And Mr Lucas was your "paying guest"?' she asked.

Jake nodded.

'He's here now, asleep in my chamber,' said Rebecca. 'When we've found some quiet rooms, Mrs Leigh is going to look after him again. Oh look, you have no spoons. I'll fetch you some.'

Mrs Leigh was standing nearby, tucking into a bowl of steaming salmagundi. She smiled at Alpiew. 'I'm sorry I gave you the slip yesterday morning, dear, but Rebecca gave me strict instructions that no one should see me bringing little Jack out to see his father at Limehouse.'

Rebecca handed them a spoon each.

'No Cibber?' said the Countess, plunging her spoon into the bowl and stirring.

'No players at all!' Rebecca glanced over at Valentine Vernish, who was deep in conversation with Lampone, the pair of them vigorously pulling various faces. 'Except Valentine.'

'Valentine is a player?' Alpiew was blowing on her bowl.

'He was at Drury Lane with me, but he left the company last year. We're bored with the theatre in London. It's as dull as a February afternoon. The old great actors are so busy impersonating themselves they've become a joke, and the new are up against the likes of the Kentish Strong Man. If Rich gets his way, any freak who can jump through a burning hoop or walk along a rope holding a monkey will be the next Betterton or Bracegirdle. Maybe the monkey itself will be the next Mrs Barry!'

Alpiew thought back to the day Rich had propositioned her

for a job and, glancing down, saw that Rebecca did not have the credentials for his company.

The Countess thrust her still untouched salmagundi down on to a table. 'You are retiring from the stage?'

'In England, at least. When such an infection has gained ground, who can tell where it will stop? So we're going to start afresh.'

'She's sailing out with us to the New World,' said Jake. 'She and Valentine.'

'We're going to start a theatre in America.' Rebecca looked about the room. 'We sail on the next ship out.'

Red appeared from beneath Godfrey's chair and waddled over towards Rebecca.

Alpiew sat and tried to edge her plate to the floor. The dog bared his teeth and snarled at her. 'Lovely dog,' she simpered.

'Watch out, Alpiew,' Rebecca laughed. 'He's after your salmagundi! Shoo, Red. Let the poor woman eat in peace.' She eyed their untouched bowls and grinned. 'You don't like it, do you? I have to say, it is an acquired taste.' She slipped both bowls under the table for Red to consume.

Rebecca smiled at the dog happily tucking in. 'Now come with me.' She grasped the Countess and Alpiew by the hand and whispered, 'I owe you both more than I can say. Nothing I could give you would ever be enough to repay my debt.'

Alpiew and the Countess followed Rebecca through to her chamber.

Mr Lucas was curled up in the big feather bed, fast asleep. Tim sat on the windowsill, swinging his legs, whispering to Jack, who sat on a bedside chair playing with the waxwork head. 'Give me a hand with this, Tim, then off you go.'

While Tim held up the hangings, Rebecca stooped and pulled out a chest from under the bed. She turned to the Countess. 'This is for you.'

'Not more tea?'

'All sold.' Rebecca laughed. 'Good old Tim came in late one night and cleared the place of all contraband. Rakewell raided the place next morning, while I was still staying out at

Limehouse, but he was too late. He slashed up my bed and left.'

'And frighted us out of our senses,' said the Countess, gazing down at the wax head.

'Whoever raided *your* house, Countess, it wasn't Rakewell's men,' said Tim, passing the head to Rebecca, 'for the tea was still there when they went. I checked.' The two children swung out of the chamber.

'It must have been the Reverend,' said Alpiew. 'Remember, milady, that you told Cibber we knew about Sarah. He must have told the priest, who was already worried that we were snooping about, and so sent the Yeoman to German Street with the note to lure you to the Tower.'

Rebecca placed the wax head on the mantelpiece. 'Why did you tell Cibber?' She pulled a key from her pocket.

'I suspected him,' said the Countess. 'He lied to me.'

'How did you know he was lying?'

'He said he'd lent Sarah some money,' said Alpiew. 'Every-one knows he is a tight-fisted hunks.'

'He didn't say money, Alpiew. He said it was a "trifle".'

'I'll bet it was he who got her the salvators,' said Alpiew.

'Sarah had salvators?' Rebecca grimaced. 'I do know that Cibber kept some in the men's tiring room. He was always offering them out – for a tidy profit.'

'So much for the new morality he's hoping to bring to the Drama,' snapped the Countess. 'I look forward to asking him about it when we claim the puff money.'

'Colley asked you to puff for him?' Rebecca smirked. 'He will never pay you, you know that?'

'Well, Mr Rich owes us too.'

'I would be even more astonished if *he* paid you.'

The Countess and Alpiew sighed. All that chasing about for nothing!

Rebecca unlocked the chest.

One half of it was filled with make-up: addition, crayons, powders and Spanish wool. The other was full of bottles of brandy. On the top lay a pouch. The Countess picked it up, spilling gold coins on to the floor at her feet. Alpiew fell to her knees. 'Why, madam, there must be fifty guineas.'

'And frankly it is not enough.' Rebecca nodded, wiping away a tear. 'I can never repay you for everything you have done for me. You and dear Scrinkle-shanks. He has been very good to my dog, you know. And has made friends with that strange phanatique who used to follow me about. They fought Rakewell together, they tell me. Now they are going to form an association of phanatiques. Nickum seems almost normal under Godfrey's tutelage.'

'A phanatique club?' said Alpiew, marvelling at the idea.

Rebecca fumbled about in the box. 'I have bought the old boy a new set of false teeth.'

'Please, I beg you,' hissed the Countess, seizing her by the arm, 'give them to someone else. It is too hideous a sight over one's breakfast. I will never be able to eat again!'

Joy

*An agreeable emotion of the soul consisting of the
enjoyment of a good which the impressions of the
brain signifies as its own causing a wonderful
delight of the mind.*

*The forehead is calm, the eyebrows motionless
and arched. The eyes open and smiling, with
bright shining pupils. The corners of the mouth a
little raised, the complexion bright, lips
and cheeks ruddy.*

The Countess and Alpiew sat on their beds rummaging through the box of goodies Rebecca had given them. It was almost dawn, but they had not slept.

Godfrey had gone home with Nickum, 'to meet the wife'.

'I'm glad Godfrey has found a friend,' said the Countess into a looking glass as she fiddled with a small pot and brush from the make-up chest.

'When I drew him aside to explain what he should expect to find when he got there,' said Alpiew, inspecting a small pot of eye-black, 'he just shrugged and told me that living with a stuffed woman had its advantages over living with two live ones.'

'I've been thinking about that Italian blade – do you know how his name translates into English?'

'Signior Ruggiero Lampone? I don't know, madam. I don't speak languages.'

'It means Mr Roger Raspberry.' The Countess flapped her hands to dry the base she had applied and hid her face behind the lid of the chest. 'Rather a good name, I think.'

'Please, milady,' Alpiew sighed, still eyeing the box of goodies, 'may I have another peep?'

'In a moment, dear. I just have to . . .' The Countess gave a little chortle and buried herself deeper in the box. Then she sat up. 'Eureka!'

Alpiew stared at her with some concern. 'Are you feeling quite well, madam?'

The Countess wore a startled expression.

'Your face is the very image of the Passion – it is pure Astonishment,' said Alpiew. 'Slightly open mouth, slightly wider eyes than usual, and as for your eyebrows . . .' She let the sentence dangle, for she suddenly saw that the eyebrows were in fact the problem. The Countess had applied a pair of new mouse-fur brows half-way up her forehead and as a result looked as though she had suffered a severe shock.

'You don't like them?' The Countess gave a winsome smile, exposing her yellowing teeth. 'I thought they gave me a girlish charm?'

'I'm sure,' said Alpiew, trying to be tactful, 'that if I fiddle about we could find something that would suit you better. Let me have another peep.'

'Alpiew, you and your peeps!' With no warning the Countess threw back the bed-covers and leapt to her feet, her arms flung into the air, her face the pure depiction of horror. 'Pepys!' she cried. 'Pepys! I have done it again! I have failed to turn up for an assignation.'

'Oh, well,' said Alpiew with a sigh. 'It'll give him something to write in his diary.'

'Are you quite mad, Alpiew?' howled the Countess. 'Samuel Pepys keep a diary! Phough, the man's life is one monotonous round of nothingness. What would he ever find to write in a diary? "Up in the morning. To the Admiralty. Talked about ships. To the theatre. Gave the eye to an actress. Home. Dined. And so to bed."'

'Milady, Pepys can wait,' sighed Alpiew, taking a sip of Nantes brandy and leaning back in the comfort of her bed. 'Let us talk of important matters.'

'Like?' The Countess slowly settled herself back into bed.

'Like what shall we do with all this money?'

'Oh, Alpiew' – the Countess pulled the bedcovers up to her chin – 'let's worry about that tomorrow.'